CONQUEST

"Come here," he said, very quietly.

Frances froze, her eyes widening. She didn't move a muscle.

"I dislike you intensely," she hissed between clenched teeth. "I'm going to bed!"

"My idea exactly," he said, walking slowly toward her. Frances tried to dart around him but he caught her arm and in one quick motion he hoisted her over his shoulder, carried her upstairs, and set her on his bed.

"Now, what will you give me, wife?"

There was no point in her protesting, for already his mouth was covering hers, his fingers dancing over her body in feverish exploration . . . and her traitorous heart racing so wildly with desire, she thought she would die. . . .

Midsummer ❧ *Magic* ❧

Midsummer  Magic

by
Catherine Coulter

AN ONYX BOOK

ONYX
Published by the Penguin Group
Penguin Books USA Inc., 375 Hudson Street,
New York, New York 10014, U.S.A.
Penguin Books Ltd, 27 Wrights Lane,
London W8 5TZ, England
Penguin Books Australia Ltd, Ringwood,
Victoria, Australia
Penguin Books Canada Ltd, 10 Alcorn Avenue,
Toronto, Ontario, Canada M4V 3B2
Penguin Books (N.Z.) Ltd, 182–190 Wairau Road,
Auckland 10, New Zealand

Penguin Books Ltd, Registered Offices:
Harmondsworth, Middlesex, England

Published by Onyx, an imprint of Dutton Signet,
a division of Penguin Books USA Inc.

First Printing, December, 1987
25 24 23 22 21 20 19

REGISTERED TRADEMARK—MARCA REGISTRADA

Printed in the United States of America

To Cynthia Wright,
as excellent a friend as a writer,
and that's about a ten!

*This story shall the good man
teach his son.*

—SHAKESPEARE

1

Wedding is destiny, and hanging likewise.
—JOHN HEYWOOD

England 1810

Philip Evelyn Desborough Hawksbury, Earl of Rothermere, handed his gloves and riding cloak to the marquess's butler, Shippe, glanced briefly toward the array of footmen who hovered nearby in the great entryway of Chandos Chase, and said quietly, "How does my father?"

Shippe, as tall as the young master, and blessed with a greater sense of his own worth, unbent slightly at the concern he saw in the earl's eyes and said, "His lordship is resting, my lord. I know that he wishes to see you the moment you arrive."

Hawk nodded, looking about him a moment at the vast house that was at the present moment quiet as a tomb. Even the liveried footmen looked like statues. It was as if there had already been a death. He resolutely dismissed that morbid thought and added over his shoulder to Shippe, "I've left my valises in the curricle."

"I shall see to it immediately, my lord."

"Please see that my valet, Grunyon, is fed, Shippe." A small smile flickered in his eyes. "He's testy after such an invigorating journey."

"Certainly, my lord."

9

Hawk turned and strode across the endless entryway, the heels of his Hessians clicking loudly on the
black Italian marble squares. He took the wide oak
staircase two steps at a time, remembering briefly how
as a young boy he'd dashed up and down these stairs,
falling once and breaking his right arm. His older
brother, Nevil, who'd been chasing him, had stood at
the top and laughed. Hawk shook his head at the
memory. There was no more Nevil to laugh or do
anything else. Nevil was dead. It is so quiet, he thought
again, his eyes going briefly toward the dozen or so
huge portraits of past Hawksburys that climbed the
wall beside the staircase, all of them inhabitants of
Chandos Chase, the seat of the Marquess of Chandos
for more than three hundred years. This was his first
visit in more than four months. And his father was ill,
possibly dying. He felt his heart rate quicken with
fear.

He turned at the top of the landing toward the east
wing and quickly made his way down the immense
carpeted corridor to the large double doors that opened
onto his father's bedchamber. He raised a gloved hand
to knock, shook his head at himself, and quietly let
himself in. His father's bedchamber was vast, very
warm, and in the early evening, it was filled with long,
dismal shadows.

Gold brocade curtains were drawn over the windows, and for a moment Hawk felt his breathing
quicken at the feeling of being closed in. His eyes
went to the grandly ornate bed on its three-foot dais.
He could make out his father's form, but the dim
candlelight shadowed his face.

"My lord, you are here," said Trevor Conyon in a
subdued voice, coming forward. Conyon was his father's longtime secretary, a man as rotound as his
father was lean, a man blessed with a kind heart and

an equally sharp mind. His bald head glittered like a beacon, shiny with sweat. Hawk had long before recognized Conyon's ceaseless loyalty to his father, had sensed his dislike of Nevil, and wondered what the man thought of him. He was, he thought briefly, still a dark horse of sorts, despite the fact that Nevil had been dead nearly fifteen months now and he, Hawk, was his father's heir.

"Yes," Hawk said. "My father?"

"Holding his own, my lord."

Hawk raised a black brow and Conyon merely nodded toward the bed, saying nothing more.

"Father," Hawk said, stepping onto the dais and leaning down to the quiet figure. "I'm here."

Charles Linley Beresford Hawksbury, the Marquess of Chandos, slipped a bony hand from beneath the brocade coverlet to clasp his son's strong fingers. "It's about time, boy," he said.

His father should have been called Hawk, the earl thought, staring down at his father's pale face, with that jutting nose of his. He met his father's intense hooded green eyes, eyes a shade darker than his own, and lightly touched his fingertips to the thick silver hair, smoothing it back from his broad forehead.

"Yes," he said, "I came as quickly as I could. I received Conyon's message last night. How are you feeling, Father?"

"Could be my last prayers," the marquess said, his voice sounding more frail than before, weaker. "Well, it doesn't matter, I've had a full life and a son to be proud of to carry on my line."

Hawk winced a bit at that, feeling guilt flood him. Some son—carrying on in London as if gaiety were to be outlawed soon and he had to have his fair share before it happened. "You're not going to die, Father. Where is your doctor?"

"In the kitchen, doubtless stuffing his mouth with Albert's ham." The marquess turned his head on the pillow and coughed.

The cough was dry and harsh. Hawk felt himself grow cold with fear, felt his throat choke with tears, and he clutched his father's hand tightly, wishing that he could give him strength. "What does Trengagel say?"

The marquess slowly eased his head back on the pillow, his eyes closing a moment. When he opened them on his son's face, Hawk felt seared by their intensity. "He gives me perhaps two or three more weeks. It's this congestion in my lungs. The fool wants to bleed my life away but I won't let him."

"No, Father, you are right. I saw men fade into death when the damned leeches bled them after battle."

The marquess heard the deep pain in his son's voice, and said softly, "You saw too much, my boy. But you're strong, you survived. The horror of it will grow less, you will see. Now, I must speak to you, Hawk."

"You're tired, Father," Hawk began.

"No," the marquess said firmly. "Listen to me. I will live to see your wife, see that you take that wife, as you promised to do."

Hawk felt himself stiffen at those words. That damnable oath! He'd forgotten; perhaps he'd wanted to forget about it.

Hawk slowly seated himself on the edge of his father's bed. The time had come and there was no way out of it, he knew. For nearly a year now he'd managed to escape the inevitable, throwing himself into the wildness and ceaseless gaiety of London—gambling, drinking, fighting. Not whoring. He didn't do that for the simple reason that he didn't want the French pox. He's seen too many soldiers rot with that. He thought of Amalie, his fun-loving and passionate mistress, and closed his eyes a moment. A wife. He didn't want a damned wife, not now. But there was no hope for it.

"Go to Scotland, son, and chose your wife, then bring her to me."

I don't want to marry some little savage from Scotland, tie myself to a female I've never even seen, all because of your damned honor, your ridiculous oath made when I was nine years old! Instead, he said, "Yes, Father, I will leave soon. I suppose it would be only fair to send a servant to the Earl of Ruthven and inform him of my coming."

"Conyon has already seen to it. He dispatched a servant two days ago. You may leave in the morning."

"I am well caught," Hawk said, more to himself than to his father. Honor, he thought, was sometimes a damnable thing. He'd said something of the sort a year before when his father had told him of the oath, told him it was his responsibility to make good on that oath. Indeed, he remembered yelling at his father that he should marry one of the girls himself. " 'Tis you who owe the Earl of Ruthven your life, not me. Why don't you elevate one of his sniveling daughters in the world? Make her *your* wife? Why leg-shackle me to some unknown girl? I did nothing, save be your damned son! Why didn't you force Nevil to do the dirty work for you?" And his father had said, very quietly, "I wouldn't have forced Nevil on a Soho trollop."

"It's not as if you're taking a pig in a poke, Hawk," the marquess said, eyeing the myriad expressions on his son's face from beneath his heavily lidded eyes. "You've the choice of three young ladies. One of them is certain to please you. Alexander Kilbracken is a fine-looking man. He wouldn't birth any trolls. You are fortunate that none of the daughters has yet married."

"So you've said, many times," Hawk said, and sighed deeply.

"You're nearly twenty-seven, son. Time to set up your nursery and ensure the succession." The old marquess allowed himself to cough again, his frail shoulders shaking.

"Yes, I promise, Father," Hawk said quickly, pain at his father's distress subduing his resentment. He thought of Lady Constance, daughter of the Earl of Lumley, well-dowered and beautiful, still hopeful of a proposal from him that would never come, that could have never come in any case. Damned honor, he thought again. He couldn't believe that he would marry a nobody with no property, no wealth, no connections, all because Alexander Kilbracken, Earl of Ruthven, impoverished laird, had saved his father's life in Scotland seventeen years before.

And I am the prize, he thought. For what that's worth to anyone. Damn Nevil for dying! If only he had married one of the Kilbracken daughters before he'd drowned. Hawk shook his head at the less-than-charitable thoughts. He knew that his father had chosen him to carry through on his vow, and not because he was the second son. What had Nevil done to earn their father's dislike? Hawk didn't know, not really. He hadn't seen Nevil for three years before his death. "Life is very unexpected," he said aloud.

"Indeed," said the marquess, his voice rumbling and deep. "You are tired, my boy, and you must rest before your journey. You will bid your farewells to me in the morning."

"Father," Hawk said, and the marquess knew his favored son was frightened that his father would be dead by morning.

"No, Hawk. I shall be fine—for several weeks yet. I will live to see your wife, 'tis a promise."

Hawk felt tears clog his throat and shook his head. "You have never broken a promise to me," he said. "Never."

"I do not intend to begin now. Go now, my boy. I wish you well with your courting."

It was dismissal and Hawk rose as quickly as he had when he was younger, heeding his father's orders. He looked toward Conyon, standing silently at the foot of the bed, lightly daubing a handkerchief over his bald head, but Conyon lowered his head.

"I will return with my bride as soon as is possible," Hawk said, turned, then paused a moment. "You will be all right, Father."

"I will be waiting," the marquess said. "Hawk . . ."

Hawk stared down at his father, trying to control the burning tears that threatened to overflow.

"You're a son to be proud of."

Hawk could only nod. He turned and strode from the bedchamber.

At seven o'clock the following morning, Hawk bid his father good-bye, relieved that he looked no weaker. He had a hard journey before him, five days to the northern end of Loch Lomond, where the Earl of Ruthven lived in Castle Kilbracken. Another week to select one of the daughters, he thought, as he tooled his matched grays down the long drive lined by naked-branched elm trees, then a couple of days to let her ready herself for her marriage, then five days to return. No, he silently amended to himself, with a lady, it would take him longer to return. Damned weak women. Damned miserable situation. He cursed softly under his breath.

"We're going to Scotland." Grunyon said the obvious after some twenty miles of silence.

"Yes," Hawk said between his teeth. "To get me married."

"Lucky girl," Grunyon said in a dry voice. He added, seeing the frustrated fury mingled with deep concern for the marquess in his master's green eyes, "His lordship is tougher than old Sergeant Hodges. He'll survive, my lord, you'll see."

"Old Sergeant Hodges died in his bed. I heard about it from Lord Saint Leven just last month."

A poor choice of examples, Grunyon thought, picturing the crusty one-legged old soldier who would follow Major Hawk to hell and beyond. Died in his bed. It wasn't to be thought of.

Grunyon sighed deeply. He sincerely doubted that life would be pleasant in the near future.

Frances Kilbracken stood at the northwestern edge of Loch Lomond, staring out over the calm, clear water. A cloud drifted across the sun, and the March air chilled suddenly. She wrapped her shawl about her shoulders, knotting it over her breasts. It was absolutely silent. Since the trees were still naked-branched from winter, there were no leaves to rustle. The birds were even muted today. Instead of the peace that usually filled her when she came here alone, away from her family, away from everyone, she felt as if her nerves were disordered, a condition her younger sister, Viola, indulged in quite often. When Frances would tell her to stop being a silly ninny, Viola would turn her languid eyes on her and say in a voice that brooked no argument, "But, Frances, I read that all ladies, real ladies that is, are highly sensitive."

Frances smiled and closed her eyes, finally hearing the soft lapping of the water against the craggy rocks near her feet. Slowly she sat down, wrapping her wool skirt about her legs, and hugged her arms about her knees. She stared toward the tall, rugged peaks of Ben Lomond and Ben Vorlich. Just beyond her, in the narrow upper reaches of the loch, she could picture the wild torrents, the rough crags, and the thick pine woods. A true Highland glen, she thought, untamed, uncivilized, and her favorite place in the whole world. She wouldn't leave here. Never. She felt a frisson of dread as she played again in her mind the incredible scene with her father just an hour before. One of her sisters would have to leave. She didn't want to think about it, but she couldn't help herself.

Frances, her older sister, Clare, and seventeen-year-old Viola were seated in the sparse and severe drawing room. Their father strode into the room, flanked by Sophia, their stepmother, and Adelaide, the daughter's governess and companion, now the unofficial tutor of little Alexander, the earl's only son.

Alexander Kilbracken, Earl of Ruthven, a handsome man, a formidable man, tall, barrel-chested, still possessed of a full head of auburn hair, paused before his array of daughters, looking at each of them in an assessing way.

"Papa, what is this?" Viola asked, fidgeting on the edge of her chair. "Kenard is to visit and I must see to my toilette."

"I think," Frances said, studying her father's face, noting the barely suppressed excitement in his gray eyes, eyes the same color as hers, "that we are about to see enacted a Family Drama."

A smile played about Ruthven's mouth at his daughter's tart voice and words. "Have you nothing to add, Clare?" he asked his eldest daughter, his voice bland.

"No, Papa," Clare said in her calm, well-modulated voice. "I will lose the morning light, however."

"You can dabble with your painting anytime," Sophia said, her voice a bit sharp.

Clare shrugged and fell silent. Frances was right, Clare thought, mildly interested. Something was going on.

Ruthven walked with his light step to the fireplace and leaned his shoulders against the mantelpiece. "I have three very lovely daughters," he announced. "You, my dear Clare, are all of twenty-one now, ready to be a wife and a mother. Despite your occasional lapses into the artistic realm, and your *vagueness*, you're a good soul." At this double-edged compliment, Clare started, staring at her father, but his attention was now fastened on Viola. "And you, child, are but seventeen, but a woman grown, nonetheless. You are bright, vivacious, vain, probably too pretty for your own good, and spoiled."

"Papa!"

"Aye, 'tis true, lass, and you know it. However, you too would make a passable wife, if your husband took the time to beat the foolishness out of you."

"I'm ready," Frances said, grinning and crossing her hands over her breast in a martyr's pose. "Bring out your finest artillery, Papa."

'You, Frances Regina," Ruthven said, unperturbed, "are a handful. Willful, too independent, a mouth that won't be silenced, and a damned excellent animal healer. You would be sorely missed by our people were you selected." He didn't add that he would be the one who would miss her the most; he didn't have to. She knew it.

"Selected for what?" asked Viola. "Papa, please! Kenard will be here shortly, and I must—"

"Marriage," Ruthven said, interrupting Viola. "One of you is shortly to be wed."

There was a moment of stunned silence, then a volley of exclamations.

"Whatever do you mean, Father?" Clare said, her voice at attention.

"Oh dear, what have I to wear?" Viola wailed, quickly reviewing her wardrobe.

"This is an altogether ridiculous display of drama!" Frances said, cutting to the core.

"The man who will make his selection is an English nobleman, the Earl of Rothermere, to be exact. He will arrive shortly."

There was another moment of shocked silence; then Frances said, laughing, "What a plummer, Papa! What would a proud Sassenach have to do with us? Come, I wish to go riding. Finish your jest and be done with us."

"Frances," Ruthven said with awful calm, "shut your mouth. Now, all of you will listen carefully. You all saw the servant that visited us, did you not?"

"I liked his livery," Clare said, lapsing into her artistic musings. "The gold and red—most impressive. I should like to paint him. His features were most interesting."

"The man was tired to death, not interesting!" Ruthven clamped down on his impatience. Frances was right, he thought, mocking himself silently. He did enjoy a bit of drama now and again, and here was Clare, taking all the fun out of his announcement. Paint a liveried servant, for God's sake! He cleared his throat, recalling all the wandering attention.

"He won't be here long enough for you to paint him," Sophia said, inadvertently taking the wind out of her husband's sails once more.

Ruthven cleared his throat again. "He is a servant of Lord Chandos, the Marquess of Chandos, to be more exact."

"We now have two very *exact* gentlemen," Frances remarked.

"Who is he, Papa?" Viola asked, cocking her head to one side. It was a pose she'd practiced before the mirror for many hours. She knew it made her thick hair tumble seductively over her right shoulder, showed off her slender neck. She would save her special pout for a more appropriate moment. "Is he a relation we didn't know of? How very odd."

"No, not really, but he soon will be," said her father, not noticing her feminine efforts.

Frances sat forward in her chair. "Tell us," she said, her voice suddenly tense, for she knew when her father was serious and when he was not. He meant what he said now, and she felt suddenly frightened.

Ruthven responded to the seriousness of Frances' voice, and said, "Listen well, all of you. It all began seventeen years ago, just after your mamma died in childbed. I was in the Lowlands, visiting a friend near Lockerbie—"

"More like you were raiding," Frances said, trying to break her awful uncertainty through jest.

"Not that time!" the earl roared. He mopped his brow, and continued more calmly. "I'd just left old Angus and was on my way home. It was late and a dark moonless night, and had started to rain. I sought shelter. Instead I found a villainous nest of bandits. They'd captured the Marquess of Chandos, planned to butcher him after they'd gotten some ransom money. In any case, I saved his skin. He was most grateful, as you can imagine. Couldn't believe that a Scot would save an Englishman, and all that. I told him I'd been educated at Oxford. The long and short of it was that he offered me anything—money most likely was on his mind." Ruthven halted a moment, shooting a look toward Sophia. He cleared his throat again, and plowed forward. "I'd just lost your mother, and was feeling like a miserable excuse for a man—indeed, that was why I risked my hide for the fellow. I simply didn't care. In any case, I never intended at that time to remarry. And I had three daughters whose futures were uncertain at best. I told Chandos that I wanted a husband for one of my daughters. He agreed. And that, my dears, is that."

"*That* was a long time ago," Frances said sharply, breaking the silence. "A very long time ago. I have difficulty believing that this Chandos would truly give up his son, particularly to a Scottish nobody. That is not the way marriages are made. Particularly not in England, as Adelaide and Sophia have told us many times."

"Lord Chandos is a man of honor," Ruthven said, his voice a bit cold and formidable. He looked toward plump, serene Adelaide. "Why do you think she's been here for the past sixteen years?"

For the first time Adelaide spoke. "Why, sir," she said, her placid eyes twinkling just a bit, "you didn't want your daughters to speak with a brogue as thick as the clouds at Ben Nevis."

Frances had a brief bout of insight. Was that also why he had remarried—an Englishwoman? Sophia was well-bred and educated, no matter that her father was an ironmonger in Newscastle. Was that the reason no soft brogue was allowed out of the mouths of any of the Kilbracken children? It was a chilling thought.

"True," said Ruthven. "Now, girls, have you any questions?"

"Questions!" Frances jumped to her feet. "You've never said a word about any of this! Questions, indeed! This is ridiculous! Marry a man none of us has ever seen? What could you be thinking about? What if he is a toad? A wastrel? What if we all hate him? I can't imagine that he could possibly have any fondness for us!"

"Fondness has nothing to do with this," said Sophia sharply. "He will be here shortly and . . . well, look each of you over, I expect. The advantages can't be lost, even on you, Frances. The earl is wealthy, he is heir to his father's estates and title. The one he selects will be able to help the others. A Season in London, new clothes, parties, eligible gentlemen, and all that."

"It's barbaric!" Frances shouted.

"Hush, Frances," Viola said, her green eyes narrowing in thought. "There are three of us. What makes you think the earl would select you?"

Because Frances is beautiful, intelligent, loving, and only occasionally willful. She is more like me than any of you. Ruthven said nothing aloud, merely looked from one daughter to the next.

"It's still conscienceless," Frances said. "Clare, you are appalled, aren't you?"

"Clare," Sophia interrupted, "just like you, Frances, and you, Viola, will wed the earl if he choses her. I needn't tell you that we are living in improverished splendor. Dear Alex will have little enough when he reaches his majority, not the way we are progressing, despite all your dear father's efforts. Indeed, it's true all over Scotland, as all of you well know."

Sophia was silenced at a look from her husband. *We aren't all that impoverished,* he was thinking. He would take care of his son, damn his mother's sharp tongue and her father's generous dowry. He said, "I have corresponded with Chandos over the years, as I told you. He has offered a settlement of ten thousand pounds—yes, that's right, ten thousand pounds—upon the marriage. And there's another advantage. The sister the earl selects will be able to help the other two." Sophia had already spoken volubly of this advantage, but he had seen the mulish set of Frances' mouth, and said it all again. "He is well-placed, needless to say. A Season in London would not be amiss, an opportunity for all of you to marry well."

"What does the earl look like, Papa?" Viola asked, cutting to the root of the matter.

"A fine-looking young man, so Chandos has told me," Ruthven said. "He was the second son, but after his brother died over a year ago, he became the marquess's heir. He was Lord Philip Hawksbury, but now is the Earl of Rothermere. He is about twenty-seven and was a military man until the death of his older brother." Actually, Ruthven thought suddenly, Chandos had thought to marry his elder son to one of the girls, until four or five years ago. Then he'd changed his mind, for whatever reason.

"Humm," said Viola. "Have you a likeness of him, Papa?"

"It's ridiculous," said Frances. "And I've heard all about likenesses. Adelaide told us about the supposed perfect portrait of Anne of Cleves sent to Henry VIII. She turned out to be a squat, myopic—"

"I wonder if he's interesting enough to paint," said Clare in a wistful voice, interrupting her sister's tirade.

"Do you know, Papa, what kind of lady he fancies?" Viola asked, trying another practiced ploy of running her fingers through a lazy curl of dark red hair on her shoulder.

Ruthven was quiet a moment, marveling at the different tracks his daughters' minds took. He remembered the words from Chandos' last letter. "Yes, a bit," he said. "He evidently fancies ladies who are charming, witty, very gay, in fact. And of course beautiful."

Viola laughed her gayest laugh. "Ah, how marvelous!"

"All of you are pretty enough to attract his attention," Sophia added, "so we needn't concern ourselves about that. I'm sure it will be a simple matter of personal taste, and none of you girls—I repeat, none of you—will be jealous of the one he picks."

The questions had flowed on and on until Frances was ready to scream. She'd escaped Castle Kilbracken as quickly as possible, tugged on old walking boots, and made her way to the loch. She was not, she thought now, shivering again, so conceited as to believe that it would be she the earl would pick to marry. Viola, although very young, was quite pretty and as charming and gay as any man could wish. As for Clare, at twenty-one, she still had the fresh innocence of youth and the softness of a compliant wife, despite her bouts of artistic endeavor. A compliant wife was certainly something a man wanted, no matter how witty she appeared before company.

"What a ghastly mess," she said aloud, and a bird chirped back at her from an overhead branch.

It came to Frances suddenly, and she leapt to her feet, staring over the still gray water of the loch. *I will ensure he doesn't want me. He wants a witty, charming, gay lady. Well, I shall be a mouse—boring, timid, diffident, a nonentity.*

You're being silly, she told herself. Such a ruse won't be necessary. He wouldn't want you. Still . . .

She touched her hand to her thick, untamed hair that tumbled down her back in a profusion of wild curls. Her father had once told her that her hair was the color of autumn in the highlands, an uncivilized blending of blond, red, and brown. Since his thick hair was the same combination of unlikely shades, she'd ignored his brief outpouring of parental compliments. A bun, I think. Yes, a very severe bun at the back of my neck. A high-necked gown—my old gray muslin, I think, should do it. It would make the earl bilious. And a sampler to stitch—there must be one somewhere, perhaps tucked away in the nursery. She wasn't really undermining her father's plans, she decided, turning away from the shore. The dear earl would be happier with either Clare or Viola as a wife. She was merely reducing the field, so to speak, saving the poor man time and effort.

Smiling, she strode from the loch, through the thick pines, back up the steep rise toward the castle. And, she thought, as a crowning touch, I will save the precious earl's groats. I should never want to go to London for one of their silly Seasons.

Never.

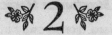

2

O, she is the antidote to desire.

—WILLIAM CONGREVE

"Reminds me a bit of the rough hills in Portugal," said Grunyon.

The earl cursed by way of reply as he gently eased his horses, beautiful matched bays, over the rutted stretch.

"See yon, Major Hawk, in the distance. That must be Loch Lomond, and there, on that rise, Castle Kilbracken."

"I'm enthralled," said Hawk, staring a moment in the distance at the stark gray-stone castle with its crenellated towers. "It looks to be crumbling." He closed his eyes a moment. "My father was senile seventeen years ago." He ignored Grunyon's use of his army name, used now by his valet only in moments of stress or excitement.

"His lordship never saw the castle," Grunyon said. "Poor country," he added.

Hawk would have said that it was a beautiful, wild, clean country, but he was tired, irritable, dirty, and so depressed that he could barely bring himself to be civil to anyone. They'd seen so few people, and the villages they'd passed through seemed out of the last century, not this one. It did remind him of Portugal, at least

26

the stark poverty did. He wished he was Major Hawk again. Even the poverty of Portugal was preferable to what lay ahead for him.

The sight of Loch Lomond, the largest freshwater lake in Britain, didn't move him. Nor did the striking three-thousand-foot peaks at its northern end.

Grunyon studied his master's profile silently, feeling right sorry for him, to be sure. He'd been the earl's batman in the army for five years, when he was Lord Philip Hawksbury, an officer Wellington could count on when the odds were rough, as they nearly always were. They'd been through battles together, seen more suffering and death than should be allowed, but now poor Hawk, as his friends still called him, all his military friends from the old days, that is, was ripe in the middle of a god-awful mess, a mess not of his making. And there was his father, perhaps in his last prayers.

"I feel like I did just after the Battle of Talavera de la Reina," said Hawk. "Well, dirty and tired, at least. I feel none of the elation."

"No, not likely," said Grunyon. "But young ladies are young ladies, my lord, and like you told me, the marquess said they were all pretty."

"Senile and probably blind," said Hawk. "They're in all likelihood as toothsome as Macbeth's hags. After all, my father was taking the word of Lord Ruthven for their collective beauty. Jesus, I don't damned believe this!"

Grunyon clucked in sympathy, then sniffed. Both he and his master were gamy as could be. "You could bathe in the loch, my lord. The water looks nice."

Hawk unconsciously scratched his ribs. "I think I will. That last inn we stayed in—if you could call that moldering pile an inn—had fleas, I'm sure of it."

"And other beasties as well, I imagine," said Grunyon.

Hawk's left eyebrow shot up a good inch. "Speaking like a Scot now, Grunyon? Beasties?"

"*Wee* beasties," said Grunyon.

"Your sense of humor will send you to the gallows. Oh, very well, I'll bathe. After all, I want to be sweet-smelling for my future wife."

"I brought soap, my lord."

"I need to shave as well. Might as well have me as presentable as possible for my execution."

Hawk guided his equipage through the undergrowth that bordered the loch. The day was warm for March, the sun bright. The water did look inviting, and he was tired of his own stench.

Frances had spent the past three hours delivering Cadmus' only cow of her calf. Thank God both had survived. Cadmus and Mary needed milk for their new baby. She was sweaty, the sleeve of her old gown rolled to nearly her shoulder, and there was still dried blood on her arm. She knelt beside the loch and bathed her arm. Sophia would have a fit were she to see her stepdaughter looking like a dirty peasant. Then too, Frances thought as she rolled down her sleeve, she was putting off her return to the castle. She sat back on her heels a moment, thinking about the changes in her sisters over the past four days. All through dinner the previous evening, Viola had carried on about her new gown, green velvet to match her eyes, hastily sewn over the past two days, and her eyes had sparkled with anticipation of the earl's male reaction. Even Clare was looking a bit smug, patting her lovely blond hair and speaking of the cucumber lotion she was using for her already perfect complexion. Thank God Clare no longer appeared to feel that Frances had betrayed her. It hadn't been Frances' fault that Ian Douglass had asked her to marry him, and not Clare.

Well, she'd sent him to the rightabout quickly enough, and now his younger brother was sniffing after Viola! Of course, since their father's announcement, Viola had ceased talking about Kenard.

Dinner had continued. Viola chattered and preened, Clare altered her vague look to one of wistful complacency. As for Frances, she'd kept her mouth shut, tightly shut, and stared back and forth between her sisters. Finally she set down her fork. The haggis suddenly seemed the most unappetizing concoction in the world.

"You really want to marry this man, this stranger? You want to leave Castle Kilbracken and Scotland?" she'd asked finally.

Viola tossed her head, but she grinned impishly at her sister. "Yes," she said, "I shall marry him, Frances, and yes, I shall leave Scotland."

"I shouldn't make all your plans now," said Sophia.

"I think perhaps the earl will like a more mature lady," said Clare, "one who exercises a bit more control over her tongue."

Not an ounce of vagueness in Clare now, thought Frances.

"But Papa said that the earl preferred ladies with wit and charm," said Viola. "And beauty, of course. Am I not blessed with all of those things, Clare?"

"I should allow others to make that observation before I did," said Adelaide, serenely taking another bite of her haggis.

Viola ignored this mild stricture and said in great seriousness to her sisters, "I shall marry him, but you needn't worry, Clare, or you, Frances. I shall find husbands for both of you, rich ones. There are so many rich Sassenachs, isn't that so, Papa?"

"A good deal more than are in Scotland," said

Ruthven, his eyes going toward Frances. She looked upset and he was sorry for it. As for himself, he was torn. If the earl chose her, he would lose the child who was closest to him in temperament, the child who rode beside him, free and easy as a boy, the child who hunted and swam with him, the child . . . He frowned, realizing that her attitude would most certainly put off any gentleman. He couldn't allow that. He supposed that he wanted the earl to choose Frances. He wanted the best for her, and he knew that in turn, she would care for her sisters. Hell, he thought, spearing a bite of boiled potato, he didn't know which would be worse, losing her or providing for her.

"I think, Viola," Clare said, her voice becoming a bit more strident, "that you shouldn't be so quick to announce your victory, just as Sophia said."

"Victory," Frances repeated blankly. "We don't know this man! He could be dreadful, mean and petty. He could be anything!"

"Frances!" said Ruthven, pinning his daughter with a fierce look. "That is enough."

Frances immediately lowered her eyes. She shouldn't have said anything, but her stupid, quick tongue . . . She wanted no discussions, no questions, about her own feelings toward this unknown earl. Now, she knew, she was in for a lecture from both her father and her stepmother. Stupid twit!

But neither of them had said a word to her. She sighed, looking out over the loch. She admitted now that she had been avoiding the lot of them. She laughed a bit, thinking that she was more conceited than Viola. All her machinations—she was in the way of believing that the earl would pick her! Goodness, she could probably appear a goddess and he wouldn't want her. Still, as old Marta was wont to say, " 'Tis better to wear a kilt than parade about bare-assed." Well, she was going to wear that kilt, in a manner of speaking. She would take no chances, none at all.

Frances suddenly became aware that the birds had grown loud and nervous. She looked up, studying her surroundings. Was it a tinker perhaps? No, it wasn't. Her eyes widened at the sight of a man—naked as a statue, but without the requisite fig leaf—climbing up some rocks that extended out over the loch. Dear God, he was going to dive in! She should tell him that the water, despite its inviting look, was cold enough to freeze off his . . . She swallowed that thought. Lord, Clare should see him, she thought vaguely. If she didn't faint from shock, she would be salivating to paint him. He was lovely, tall and muscular, his legs long and well-formed. Her eyes resolutely avoided the bush of thick hair at his groin and his male endowments. He was dark, his hair was as black as a raven's wing, his complexion olive. His chest was covered with tufts of equally black hair. Frances felt an odd warmth in her belly and rocked back on her heels. She was being a silly fool. She'd seen naked men before—well, actually, she amended, they'd been boys, swimming in the loch. He wasn't a boy. She saw him dive cleanly into the loch. He broke the surface quickly, and she heard his howl. However, instead of wading quickly out, he caught a bar of soap tossed to him by another man standing at the loch's edge.

He has more fortitude than I do, Frances thought, watching him vigorously lather his chest, then his thick dark hair. She shivered when he ducked under the water to rinse himself.

She felt gooseflesh rise on her arms in sympathy for him. He must be very dirty to stand that icy water.

She gulped when the hand holding the soap dipped

under the water. Who was he? she wondered. And
then she knew. He turned his back at that moment
and waded toward shore. She looked at the long,
clean back, the sculpted buttocks. She heard him say
something and saw a short, plump man standing on
the shore, holding a towel. She heard him laugh, a
rich, deep sound, filled with amusement at himself.

The Earl of Rothermere had finally come. Her only
thought as she sped back to the castle was that he
wasn't a troll.

Hawk and Grunyon arrived at Castle Kilbracken an
hour later. For the first time since he'd come out of
that god-awful loch, Hawk felt warm. That kind of
shock could kill a man, he thought, and again laughed
at himself.

Hawk pulled his tired horses to a halt in front of the
gray-stone castle and looked about for the stable. He
saw a long, narrow building off to the side whose slate
roof looked dark red in the bright sunlight. A dozen
or so chickens were squawking wildly at his intrusion.
The two cows regarded him with mild interest at best,
and the assortment of pigs snorted indignantly at the
whipped-up dirt from his carriage wheels.

As he climbed down from the carriage, he saw two
women dressed in coarse woolen gowns eyeing him
silently. Then one said something to the other behind
her hand, and the other giggled.

"See to the carriage, Grunyon," Hawk said. "There
doesn't appear to be a stablehand about that I can
see." Hell, he thought, there didn't appear to be anything civilized about. Suddenly a tall man who had
that indefinable aura of authority about him appeared
through the great front doors of the castle. He was
dressed roughly, in well-worn riding clothes, his black

boots dusty. They stared at each other a moment; then the man called out, "Rothermere?"

The Earl of Ruthven, Hawk thought, and managed to plant a smile on his lips.

"Yes," he said, and strode forward. Ruthven extended his hand and Hawk clasped it. A strong hand, Hawk thought.

"That your man?"

"Yes."

Ruthven raised his head and roared, "Ethelard!"

A scruffy boy appeared from behind the stables and raced forward. "See to the horses, boy. You, my lord, and your man come with me."

Hawk followed the earl through the great oak doors into an entrance hall that was in fact an old great hall, complete with blackened beams high overhead, and a cavernous fireplace that could roast an ox. There were ancient suits of armor lying about, and weapons fastened to the walls between huge flambeaux. The very air felt heavy and somehow old. Hawk felt as though he'd just stepped back in time.

He waved his hand about him and asked, "How old is Kilbracken?"

"Built back at the time of James IV, in the sixteenth century, you know. Tottle," he continued to a rheumy-eyed individual who had come up behind them in utter silence, "see to his lordship's man here. Feed him and show him his master's room."

"Aye," said Tottle.

"Been drinking again, curse him," Ruthven said under his breath. "Come my lord. The ladies are all in the drawing room. Used to be the armory long ago, you know, but things change. English wives and all that."

Hawk followed the earl silently across the huge expanse of hall toward another set of double doors. He flung them open and said grandly, "The Earl of Rothermere."

Hawk was aware of three sets of feminine eyes all trained on his person. One of the women rose and came forward, a smile on her face. "Hello, my lord, I am Lady Ruthven. Welcome to Castle Kilbracken and to Scotland." An English wife, Hawk thought, and hoped devoutly that all the daughters spoke with such clipped, clear English speech.

He kissed her offered hand and murmured something polite. She was much younger than Ruthven, in her mid-thirties, he guessed, and quite pretty. She had soft brown hair and large brown eyes, and, he saw with some appreciation, a very impressive bosom.

He was introduced to Clare and thought: She's lovely. As for Clare, she felt a moment of alarm. He was a large man, his jaw, her artist's eyes noted, was stubborn. Not an easy man. But handsome.

"My lord," Clare said, giving him her slender hand, whiter now from all the cucumber lotion. Hawk, dutifully, kissed the hand.

Hawk received a giggle when introduced to Viola, a little minx whose coloring was as lively as the gleam in her green eyes. "My lord," she said in a lilting voice, "I—we—have awaited your coming with great interest. I wish to hear all about the *ton*." There, Viola thought, seeing that he was a bit taken aback, I have shown him that I am not a provincial nobody. He will realize that I will fit perfectly into his life.

"I will tell you all that I can," said Hawk, grinning unwillingly at this charming confection of budding womanhood.

"And here is Frances," said Sophia, turning to greet her middle stepdaughter, who had just slipped into the room. Her eyes widened and she felt herself choke. She heard a snort from her husband, and felt for a moment an insane urge to laugh.

The Earl of Rothermere's thoughts didn't show on his face as he turned to study the third daughter. But he was thinking as he took the tanned, somewhat roughened hand, a strong hand, he added to himself, that at least two of the three daughters were worthy of a second look. Good Lord, this one should be locked in a closet, a water closet.

"Charmed," he said shortly.

Frances merely nodded, saying nothing. Nor did she raise her head to look at him.

How is that apparition possible, Hawk wondered as he watched her move away from him. Her hair was scraped tightly back into a fierce bun at the nape of her neck. Her eyes looked like little raisins behind the distorting glass of her ugly spectacles. And her gown—it was shapeless, the color a sickening puce. He could just hear Grunyon saying philosophically, "Well, my lord, all three of them pretty would have been heaven. Be thankful you've got two to choose between."

The moment he released her hand, Frances walked toward a chair she'd carefully placed in the corner early that morning. She sat down, picked up the stichery, only to find her eyes following the Earl of Rothermere. He was speaking to her father, and Viola and Clare were looking at him as if a Greek god had just come to earth. She heard swishing skirts and saw that Sophia was standing over her.

"This is not at all amusing, Frances."

Frances said nothing.

"You look like a . . . ." Words failed her. "What is the meaning of this, Frances?"

"Of what, Sophia?" Frances said, striving for bravado. She stuck up her chin. "Adelaide has always told us that the good Lord loves us for what we are, not what we look like."

Sophia snorted. "We're not talking theology, Frances! Your father will whip you for this, young lady, you may be certain of that!"

Sophia marched away from Frances, striving to regain her polite-hostess manners. She saw that Viola and Clare were staring at their sister, and she heard Viola giggle. She shot them a look that threatened retribution and they immediately quieted. She closed her eyes a moment, wondering where the devil Frances had found those immensely hideous glasses that perched on her nose. And her hair! Pulled back from her face so severely that it looked painful, and plaited into the ugliest bun Sophia had ever seen. She'd stolen the old lace cap from one of her mother's trunks, she imagined, and the gown as well, a muslin puce that had seen better days twenty years ago. She saw that Alex kept glancing over at his daughter, his gaze questioning, then somber, then narrow with anger.

English tea was served by Tottle, a relic, Hawk thought, that belonged firmly to the last century. He thought of Shippe, his father's noble butler, and shuddered. *I don't believe this is happening! My God, surrounded by a gaggle of females, one of whom will be my wife!*

He couldn't bring himself to look closely at any of the girls, save Viola. It was impossible not to notice her. She was young, as pretty as any young lady in London, and was staring at him with admiration and something akin to awe. Stiff, formal conversation floated about him, and he responded with all the breeding with which he'd been blessed, but very little of the charm for which he was noted. Somehow, he couldn't find it in himself—an animal on the block, smiling at his butcher?

Drinking his tea, he could fancy that he was in England. All the ladies spoke without a Scottish burr. The Earl of Ruthven spoke an odd mixture, interspersing his very English comments with Scottish idiom.

"I'm sorry, what did you say?" Hawk asked, suddenly aware that he'd been addressed by the Countess of Ruthven.

"Please, call me Sophia, my lord. I was just telling you that our Clare here is something of a painter."

That was at least something, Hawk thought, and forced himself to study Lady Clare again. She was leaning toward him, her face rendered more lovely by its intensity.

"What is it you paint?" he asked.

"Mostly people, my lord," said Clare.

"Ah," said Hawk.

Frances looked at him, but he was blurred by the wretched spectacles. She allowed them to slide down to the tip of her nose, and squinted. At that moment, his eyes slide toward her, and she saw him wince at the sight.

Good, you damned bounder, she thought, and squinted all the harder. She smiled to herself. Hawk thought: Poor little dowd, surrounded all her life by beauty. He had to admit to himself that Clare and Viola weren't at all difficult to look at. He felt sorry for Frances.

"Tell us about his lordship," said Alexander. "He does well?"

"No, sir," said Hawk, a glimmer of pain in his eyes. "He is quite ill at the moment."

"Damn," said Ruthven, running his fingers through his thick head of hair. His eyes settled on Hawk's face for a long moment, and he nodded silently, realizing why the young man was here. The Marquess of Chandos wanted his debt of honor paid before he died. He frowned. Something was odd here, very odd. He rose, and said to Sophia, "I shall show his lordship to his room now. And I promised Alex that he could meet him."

Hawk rose with alacrity, and after murmuring his thanks to his hostess and nodding to each of the daughters, followed the Earl of Ruthven from the drawing room.

Ruthven said without preamble as they climbed the stairs, "You're here to wed quickly?"

"Yes," said Hawk. "My father wishes to see my bride before he dies. The wedding must take place as soon as possible."

"Ah," said Ruthven. "It's sorry I am, my lord. I've a great fondness for your father." He frowned a moment, then said, "His illness came upon him quickly?"

"Very quickly. A congestion in his lungs."

Ruthven said nothing more for a moment. The Chandos servant who had been here but five days before had said nothing about any illness, and the marquess had merely written in his letter that his son would be in Scotland very soon. Yes, all of this was most odd.

"You are fortunate that none of my daughters has wed, my lord."

"Yes," said Hawk.

"There was a nice boy, Ian Douglass, who wanted Frances, but she would have none of him."

Hawk threw Ruthven an incredulous look. At his host's bland smile, he decided he'd said the wrong daughter's name.

"So," Ruthven continued, "since your father is ill, you are in something of a hurry?"

"I fear so," said Hawk. He drew a deep breath. "I have no intention to insult you or your family, my lord, but I must needs be quick to make my choice. I have promised my father that he will see his daughter-in-law before he . . ." Hawk broke off, fear, concern, frustration clogging his throat. He felt Ruthven's hand gently touch his shoulder.

" 'Tis all right, lad. You have something of a schedule, then?"

"Yes," Hawk said. "I've given myself three days to make my . . . oh hell, sir, my selection! Then another four to prepare for the wedding, and it's back to England."

"Your father is proud of you," Ruthven said unexpectedly. "He wrote to me of all your exploits. With Wellington on the Peninsula?"

"Yes. When I sold out, things still were in chaos. There are rumors flying about that Napoleon plans to invade Russia. One but prays that it will be ill-fated."

"Ah," said Ruthven, "here is my son, Alex."

The very image of his father, Hawk thought at the sight of the small boy standing in the open doorway of the nursery, his clear gray eyes fastened upon Hawk's face.

"Do your best, boy," Ruthven said, grinning down at his son.

"How do you do?" said Alex very formally, extending a small, somewhat grubby hand.

"I survive, Alex," said Hawk, and gravely shook the boy's hand.

Ruthven said, "I see that Adelaide hasn't cleaned you up, lad. Doubtless 'tis all the excitement with the girls."

"Viola's gown nearly made Adelaide blind," said Alex with some disgust. "You should have heard Vi-

ola simpering and carrying on in front of her mirror
. . . such a ninny!"

"That will be enough, I think," said Ruthven. "Now,
lad, off you go. Adelaide is most certainly ready for
your lessons. You can get to know his lordship better
after a while."

"Aye," said Alex.

Hawk watched the boy dash down the long, rather
barren corridor. "You are lucky, sir," he said. "A fine
boy."

"Yes, he is," said Ruthven. "Now, Rothermere,
here is your chamber. Marta cleaned it up quite nicely."

"Call me Hawk."

Ruthven raised an eyebrow.

"A name that has followed me from the army.
Rothermere was my brother's name for so long, I
can't accustom myself to it yet."

"Ah yes, Nevil. A pity." Ruthven strode into the
chamber, standing aside for Hawk.

It was a wonderful room, Hawk thought, staring
about him at the dark wood-paneled walls, the blackened fireplace, and the majestic bed that sat in isolated splendor in the middle of the room. There was
but an old armoire against one wall and a winged chair
in front of the fireplace. There was one red wool
carpet on the floor, small and faded.

"This is Frances' room," Ruthven said blandly, watching the earl's reaction at this announcement.

Hawk turned to look at his host in some amazement, a look that was not lost on Ruthven. There was
no evidence at all that a young lady spent her time
here. Of course, Hawk thought, Frances was such a
pitiful, homely little thing, she probably didn't want
any mirrors or dressing tables about to remind her of
her looks.

"I'll leave you and see that your man is sent up," said Ruthven. "Dinner is early here, six o'clock." He nodded and left the room.

I am going to kill Frances, Ruthven decided, striding back downstairs. I am going to wring her neck, shake her until her teeth rattle, then I'm going to thrash her until she can't sit!

Suddenly he laughed deeply. One never knew what to expect from Frances. At least she was never boring, curse her!

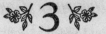

Was ever woman in this humor won?
—SHAKESPEARE

Frances was easing out of the kitchen door, freedom in sight, when she heard her father's roar.

"Frances!"

Her hand tightened on the doorframe, and one foot snaked past the step.

"Frances, if you take one more step, I'll murder you!"

Angus, the Ruthven woodsman, and Donald, a half-witted boy whose job it was to muck out the stables and run errands for the cook, Doris, stared between master and daughter, saying nothing. No one said anything when the earl flew into one of his occasional rages. Frances believed all their people were proud of her father's outbursts, and retold around peat fires in the winter how they had seen the earl do this or say that. Now, she thought, I will be the subject of a story. Angus spit in the corner, and shrugged, but Frances wasn't fooled, he was all attention.

"Yes, Papa?" Frances said at last, turning to face her father. "Did you wish something?"

"Did you wish something?" Ruthven mimicked her, and strode forward. "Come with me, my girl."

"Really, Papa, I—"

"Shut your trap, Frances!" He grasped her arm and pulled her through the door.

She took double steps to keep up with him. At least, she thought, there would be no scene this time in front of Angus, who was the most garrulous servant at Kilbracken. They walked past the stables, past Randall and Penelope, their two goats, toward the hill behind Kilbracken that was just beginning to burst with bright purple heather.

Ruthven released his daughter's arm and looked down at her in disgust. "What the hell do you think you're doing, you stupid girl?" He looked at her eyes through the disgusting spectacles, and shuddered.

Only the truth, Frances thought. She thrust her chin up and said, "I do not wish to marry this Sassenach, Papa. I will not marry him. I am merely ensuring that he won't give me another one of his arrogant looks."

"Arrogant? Rothermere? Why, the boy's fine, just fine. If he's a bit stiff, I can't say that I blame him. Like you, Frances, it was not his choice to come up here and take himself a wife. He's behaving quite properly. What's more, you stupid twit, the boy's father is gravely ill. How would you feel—warm and friendly and bursting with good spirits?"

Oh dear, Frances thought. She'd not known about Rothermere's father. Well, she was sorry, to be sure, but it had nothing to do with her. She raised her chin, and the spectacles slid down her nose. "Papa, I don't want to marry. I don't want to leave you or Kilbracken. I belong here. Please, Papa."

That brought him up short, but just for a moment. "Just what makes you believe that he'd give you a second look in any case? Talk about conceit, my girl! You're no better than Viola."

"I know," said Frances. She sat down in the midst

of a clump of heather. "But I simply don't want to take the chance."

Ruthven was silent for a moment. Frances, uncomfortable with his silence, much preferring his rages, waved her hand about her. "Would you want to leave this, Papa?"

"What I want," he said at last, "is what's best for you, Frances."

"That man," she said in budding anger, "is certainly not it. Oh, he's well-enough-looking, I grant you that, but he's English, Papa. English! He probably thinks we're all savages, you know he does."

"With our proper British speech? Not likely, my girl. Frances, you're getting me off-track. Now, I want you to appear as yourself at the dinner table."

"No," said Frances.

Ruthven, who had seldom heard any form of negative from his favorite daughter in all her nineteen years, merely stared at her. He said finally, "Do you have any idea how awful you look? How homely and dowdy?"

"Of course, I practiced in front of the mirror, before I removed it from my bedchamber." She tilted up her face. "The bedchamber Sophia so kindly gave to *him*."

"I can't see the man camped amongst pink frills, for God's sake, or breathing in Clare's oil paints."

"He could have slept in the tower."

"Stupid girl! And have the floor collapse beneath his feet?"

That was true enough, Frances thought, but now she had to sleep amongst Viola's pink frills.

"Where did you get those damned spectacles?"

"From a trunk in one of the attics. I rather thought they were a fine touch."

"I'm going to thrash you, Frances."

"If you do, I'll look even more awful."

The both of them knew it was an empty threat. Ruthven didn't know what to do. Damn her for being so much like him! "You refuse to obey me, Frances?"

"Please, Papa," Frances said, rising and grasping his hands in hers, "please don't make me. Besides, he won't want me anyway. Did you not see how he was gazing at Viola? She's young and malleable, and gentlemen want that. And she's pretty as Clare, and so vivacious. You said the earl preferred lively ladies. I would make him miserable, you know. Even Clare would please him more than I would. She could be quite an asset—she could paint portraits of all his friends. Think about the poor man, Papa."

Ruthven was thinking about the poor earl. He was fond of his other two daughters, but they weren't Frances. They wouldn't make the Earl of Rothermere remotely happy, and if he weren't happy, how could they be? Unlike Frances, Ruthven knew of Hawk's character, at least from his sire's undoubtedly biased perspective. He decided to think about this. Perhaps he could speak to Hawk, tell him of the deception, tell him what a fine girl Frances was, encourage him to be . . . He frowned. Hellfire, he could just see the look on the young man's face were he to tell him that his middle daughter couldn't abide the thought of being his wife and had made herself purposely ugly to avoid it. He cursed fluently. Frances could see the pulse pounding wildly in his throat.

"At least change out of that rag you were wearing," he said, his voice rough. "And rid yourself of those wretched spectacles."

"Very well, Papa."

"And you will not be rude."

"All right, Papa."

That stopped him cold. Frances was never so sub-

missive. Ruthven sighed, then winced at the sight of
her hair. Her beautiful hair looked like a hag's crop.
Even if he forced her to appear as she should, he
knew well enough that she would manage to make
herself exceptionable. He wouldn't put it past her to
spit in the earl's face if provoked. No, he amended,
she'd insult him down to his boots, and so cleverly that
he would in all likelihood look like a gape-mouthed
fish. And no one would be able to accuse her of being
precisely rude. It was too much.

"I will see you later, Frances," he said, and left her.
What was he to do? He finally decided after two
glasses of his finest sherry that he would study the Earl
of Rothermere's behavior very closely, then decide if
he was worthy of Frances. If he was, then he would
act.

Frances stared after her father, so relieved that she
wanted to shout. She already had selected a gown for
dinner. Its pale yellow color made her look so sallow
as to appear ill with the plague. "I'm sorry, Papa,"
Frances said to the spindly gorse bushes with their
budding yellow flowers, "but you don't really want me
to leave. Who would see to the sick animals? Who
would drink whiskey with you and listen to all your
stories? Who would trade jests with you? Who would
ride with you, spend long nights camping in the moun-
tains in the summers?"

Frances rose and stared about her. Why couldn't life
be simple again? She forced herself to shrug. The earl
would select either Viola or Clare. There would be
peace again at Kilbracken.

She *could* look worse, Ruthven thought as he settled himself into his high-backed chair at the head of
the long dining table. Still, she didn't hold a candle to

Viola or Clare, both of whom looked as delicious as treats from a confectioner's shop.

The Earl of Rothermere, even to Frances' jaundiced eye, was immensely handsome in his black evening clothes. She heard Viola suck in her breath at the sight of him, and Clare sat forward, thinking, in all likelihood, that it was in evening clothes that she wanted to paint him.

If I could paint, I'd paint him naked, striding out of the loch.

Stop it, you silly fool. No matter. He will leave soon and take either Clare or Viola with him. I'll remain here, safe and sound.

Hawk was polite. He seated himself on Ruthven's right, and regarded his dinner, silently served by Tottle. The butler's black sleeve, close to Hawk as he leaned over him, looked shiny and smelled musty. Did he normally wear a kilt? Was a man normally bare-assed under a kilt? Hawk wondered. Weren't kilts still outlawed?

" 'Tis partan bree, or crab soup," Sophia said brightly as Tottle served a goodly amount into the earl's bowl.

"It looks delicious," said Hawk, dubiously eyeing the anchovies that floated darkly in the light stock.

"It is not so tasty as your English dishes," Viola said. "Perhaps you can tell us some of the foods you enjoy."

Oh, shut up, Viola! From what Papa says of English cooking, it is unimaginative and boring! Frances toyed with her soup, not looking up, her lips a thin, flat line.

"I doubt it," said Hawk somewhat obliquely. He turned to Ruthven. "I find your coat of arms most fascinating." He smiled upward at the colorful Ruthven shield, and read slowly, " '*Vivit Post Funera Virtus.*' "

"Aye," said Ruthven. "A good motto—'Virtue outlives the grave.' Nonsense, of course, but our ancestors had noble causes and ideals. The fork-tongued lions guarding the crown—they look noble and strong enough, but there is our history to disprove it."

A sticky subject, thought Hawk, and merely nodded.

"What is your family's motto, my lord?" asked Clare.

" 'With a strong hand—*manu forti*.' "

"Just like the English," said Frances under her breath. "More accurate would be 'With a strong fist.' "

"What did you say, Frances?" asked Ruthven, tickled that his daughter had finally opened her mouth.

Frances didn't move a muscle, but continued to study her soup. "Nothing, Papa," she said in an emotionless voice.

Hawk spared a glance at the girl. At least her nose was naked of the spectacles, but her hair looked a bird's nest beneath the ghastly cap. He wondered if she could even see her soup. He noticed that Adelaide was looking at Frances, her expression bemused and, he thought, wondering a bit, somewhat amused as well.

He brought his attention back to his dinner as he was served kippers with rice balls, and something thankfully that he recognized—salmon.

He knew that he should be studying the girls. He had set a time limit on his delibrations, and he had to get on with it. Beginning in the morning, he would meet with each daughter individually. Oh hell, he thought, he might as well get started now. He asked Viola a question, something about her interests, and she regaled him with her domestic talents. Talk about outlandish stories for a winter's night, Frances thought.

Hawk, all polite attention, then turned to Clare, and she too seemed all too ready to say anything that would please him. "I should like to see your painting," he said, and she agreed readily.

I can't completely ignore her, Hawk thought, turned his eyes to Frances, and said politely, "What do you enjoy doing, Lady Frances?"

Frances quivered a bit with anger. The arrogant, conceited pig was pitting sister against sister. "Nothing," she said, not looking at him. That won't do, ninny!

She heard her father say quickly, "Frances plays and sings beautifully."

"Almost as well as a performing dog," she muttered, earning a glare from Sophia, who had heard her.

"I should like to hear you perform, perhaps after dinner," Hawk said, wondering how he would hide his bored yawns. Lord, this was worse than a London Season with all its terrified little debutantes trying to make good impressions on the eligible gentlemen.

"An excellent idea," said Sophia, sending Frances a dagger's glance.

The dinner drew to a close with a trifle. Poor Doris, in an excess of exuberance, had used too much sherry and the cake was soggy. Hawk thought he would be ill.

Ruthven saved him. "Tottle, remove the stuff if you please. If it is all right, Hawk, we will continue on to the drawing room with the ladies."

Hawk! However did he come by that nickname? Frances wondered.

Clare brought out several of her paintings.

They were quite good, and Hawk found he could praise her without deception. There was a charming rendition of Viola that must have been done recently. The girl was laughing, her lap filled with colorful flowers. There was no portrait of Frances, he realized, but added to himself that likely the oils would curdle if used for painting her.

Viola amused him with a practiced series of local jests.

Hawk laughed. The chit had wit and was droll.

"Play for us now, Frances," Ruthven said, his voice so stern that Hawk stared at him. He watched Frances walk to the pianoforte, her head lowered, and seat herself on the stool. She hunched her shoulders forward and he could see her shoulder blades. A most unappetizing female, he thought, then scolded himself. He had to be fair. In the next moment, he had stiffened. Her voice was as wooden as the piano stool, and when it reached for several high notes, he fancied that any glasses present would shatter. She missed many notes.

Ruthven glared at his daughter. He would thrash her, he thought. He met his wife's baleful eye and nodded toward her.

When Frances finished, Hawk dutifully applauded. There was no applause from either Ruthven or Sophia. He heard Viola giggle. Clare was looking at her sister in the oddest way. No one requested an encore.

Hawk rose, and said in an expressionless voice, "Thank you, Lady Frances. Ma'am," he continued to Sophia, "I thank you for a charming evening, and an excellent dinner. I fear I am rather fatigued from my long journey. I bid all of you good night."

Escape. He mopped his brow as he strode up the stairs and down the drafty corridor toward his bedchamber.

Grunyon was waiting for him, his round face alight with curiosity.

"An enjoyable evening, my lord?"

"God-awful," said Hawk, and walked to the narrow windows. He pulled back the brocade drapery and stared out. What bit of moon there was didn't lighten the black landscape.

He closed his eyes a moment. "I feel like a piece of meat on display at the butcher's shop. Worse than that, I am to charm my butcher!"

"I should say that the young ladies must feel the same way."

"Bosh," said Hawk, turning around. "Oh hell, ignore me, Grunyon." He raked his fingers through his thick hair.

"Two of them, I noted, are really quite lovely, and they speak English."

"Oh yes, indeed they do. They would likely fit quite well into London society." Hawk paused the moment the words were out of his mouth. He stared thoughtfully at Grunyon, but said no more.

Frances pretended sleep, but it didn't work. Viola lit the candles on her dressing table, then carried the branch to the bed and set it on the small night table.

"Come on, Frances. I know you're awake. Ah, here's Clare."

Frances gave up and pulled herself to a sitting position as Clare quietly closed the bedchamber door behind her.

"Papa is furious with you, Frances," said Clare.

"And so is Stepmama. As for Adelaide, she just sits there and smiles."

Both Viola and Clare arranged themselves on the bed, something they'd done as children, with cups of hot chocolate and Doris' broonies.

Now everything was different. Frances sighed.

"Why did you do it, Frances?" Viola asked.

Frances didn't immediately respond, and Viola said thoughtfully, "I don't understand you. The earl is very handsome—even with those wretched spectacles you could see that."

Frances drew her thick braid over her shoulder and

began pulling it loose out of habit. "Yes," she said finally, "He is. But that has nothing to do with anything, Viola."

Clare sat forward, drawing her dressing gown closer about her. "I know you were appalled when Papa told us about the debt of honor and all that. But I thought you would be reasonable about it."

"I am being reasonable," Frances said.

Viola continued in mid-thought, "And he's rich and titled, everything a girl could want in a husband."

"He wants nothing to do with us, Viola," Frances said. "He has to offer for one of us. How could you want to marry a man who didn't love you or even care about you?"

Viola shrugged. "Ian cared about you, yet you didn't want to marry him."

Frances shot a look toward Clare and saw her sister stiffen just a bit at Viola's thoughtless words. Clare had wanted Ian, but the damned man had been blind. Frances was in the mood to believe that Ian had wanted her simply because she would care for all his wretched animals.

"No," she said finally, "I didn't want to marry him. There simply has to be something more, something . . ." Her voice dropped off, for she didn't know what that something more was, she simply knew it had to exist, somewhere.

"You're being a silly romantic," Clare said. "Goodness, I am the only one who loves poetry, but I realize that marriage has nothing to do with all those high-flown, lovely sentiments."

"Papa loved our mother," said Frances.

"Frances, that has nothing to do with us! Now, I don't mind that you appear like a witch because it will make the earl's decision easier. He now has to choose only betweeen Clare and me."

"He's awfully large and dark," said Clare, and she shivered.

"If you would stop giggling long enough, Viola," Frances said, "you would see that he's also cold and arrogant."

"He doesn't like being here, that's all," said Viola, shrugging. "But once married, things would be different. Besides, what choice do we have? None, I tell you. I heard Papa telling Sophia that whichever of us the earl picks, he won't argue, and neither will we. There's the ten thousand pounds from the earl's father that will come to Papa upon the marriage."

"It's sordid," said Frances.

"Well," Viola said, "I for one don't wish to talk you out of your marvelous disguise. I want to marry a rich man. I want to be somebody. What else can a woman look forward to anyway?"

That was perfectly true, of course, Frances thought, suddenly depressed, but it wasn't fair. She repeated her thought aloud. "It's not fair. We should be able to do anything we wish to do."

Clare shook her head. "I fill my time with my painting and my poetry. Viola enjoys flirting and her stitchery. You, Frances, you fill your time with animals, and swimming, and wandering about the hills. But it's not enough. A woman must marry, or she becomes less and less every year. She becomes an object of pity, an embarrassment to her family. I agree with you, Frances, it isn't particularly fair, but there is nothing else."

"And the Earl of Rothermere is the grandest gentleman available," said Viola. "I know Papa doesn't have enough money to send us to Edinburgh, much less to London, to meet many different men." Viola giggled suddenly and tossed a pillow at Clare. "We shouldn't try to talk her out of this. Heavens, the poor man would have a very difficult time if he had three equally beautiful daughters to choose from!"

Frances looked closely at each of her sisters. "You, Clare, you would marry the earl gladly if he chose you?"

"Yes, yes, I would. I would even bear the . . . other. Titled gentlemen in particular must have an heir."

"And what else is a woman good for?" Frances said, her eyes darkening to a cold gray.

Viola said in a reminiscing voice, "I kissed Kenard, and I didn't mind it at all. With all the earl's experience, I'll wager he's even better at it than Kenard. That's another thing, you two. Gentlemen husbands are taught to be very sensitive to their wives' feelings about that sort of thing, at least that's what Adelaide said. They don't act like animals with their wives."

"You're not making sense, Viola," Frances said. "Do you want the earl to kiss you passionately or do you want him to be a gentleman husband?" Unbidden, Frances saw the earl striding out of the loch, his beautiful body glistening with water. Stop it, you fool!

"I don't know," Viola admitted. "He is awfully handsome. And just think of all the fun! Parties, routs, balls! Oh dear, I hope I'm not talking you out of your spectacles, Frances!"

"No, Viola, you're not." Frances smacked her fist into a feather pillow beside her. "This is awful, all of it! I wish . . ."

Both Viola and Clare looked at her patiently.

Frances drew a deep breath. "I wish I could meet a man I could respect and like . . . perhaps fall in love with."

Clare said in a soft, resigned voice, "But then again, maybe the man you wanted wouldn't feel the same about you."

"Oh Clare, I'm sorry. I didn't mean—"

"I know. I also know that if the earl selects Viola, I will still get to go to London. Maybe there, I will find a gentleman who will feel properly."

There was a soft tap at the door and the daughters swiveled about. Adelaide peeked in, took in the scene, and smiled. "How lovely you look, Frances," she said. "I can hear the earl pacing. This will prove most interesting. Yes, most interesting. Good night, girls. Come along, Clare."

Clare dutifully slipped off the bed and followed Adelaide from the bedchamber.

"Well," said Viola, not bothering to stifle her yawn, "I for one don't want smudges under my eyes. Let's go to sleep, Frances. And I'll thank you not to flail about during the night."

And like the woman-child she was, Viola was breathing evenly within five minutes of dousing the candles. Frances lay awake staring into the darkness. Something more, she thought. There must be something more.

Ruthven reined in his stallion, Sterling, and pointed toward the southern end of Loch Lomond. "A sight I never tire of," he said to Hawk. "All the small islands—quite uninhabited, you know. But Frances and I have always enjoyed rowing out to them and tromping about."

"Frances?"

"Yes," said Ruthven, "Frances." He eyed Hawk and saw that the younger man looked quite surprised; then he nodded, and Ruthven realized he was thinking that a homely little thing like Frances would like that sort of thing. He said no more.

"I bathed in the loch before I arrived. It was cold, but most invigorating."

It was on the tip of Ruthven's tongue to say that Frances loved to swim in the loch, but he didn't say it. Lord, what to say to him? What gentleman wanted a hoyden for a wife, and that would certainly add to the impression he'd already given the earl. How to describe his daughter? Warm and loving and pigheaded and honorable, and looks like a hag. "Damn," said Ruthven.

"Pardon?" said Hawk.

"Nothing, my boy. Ah, here comes Alex on his pony. A shaggy little beast, isn't it? It's from the Shetland Islands, you know."

"Papa! Adelaide told me you'd ridden out with his lordship. Good morning, sir," Alex added, staring up at the English earl.

"Good morning, Alex," said Hawk. "Are the ladies up and about yet?" He knew he should use all available time to study Viola and Clare.

"Just Frances," said Alex. "She went off to help Robert."

Ruthven lurched forward in his saddle at that bit of information. Surely Frances as an animal healer wouldn't appeal to an English nobleman. "Enough, Alex," he said sharply. "Hawk and I are riding back soon. You have lessons, do you not? You mustn't keep Adelaide waiting."

Alex carped and complained, but nonetheless, from the set expression on his father's face, knew it was no use. He click-clicked Dancer about and returned to the castle.

Frances wasn't at the breakfast table, Ruthven saw immediately, and determined to take a strip off her hide. Damned little fool! He'd give her an ultimatum, he'd . . .

"Alexander?"

"What m'dear?" Ruthven said to his wife.

"Viola and Clare are going to take his lordship

visiting this afternoon. The Campbells are visiting the Dugals, you know."

"Excellent," said Ruthven without much enthusiasm.

"Yes, indeed," said Hawk. He'd spoken briefly to Ruthven before they'd entered the castle. He would meet briefly with Clare, alone. It was only fair that he meet with the eldest daughter first.

Some thirty minutes later, Hawk was pacing the drawing room waiting for Clare to appear. A damned interview, he thought. It was humiliating for him and for the ladies. But a wife was an immense responsibility, a lifelong responsibility. That brought another shudder. Something deep within him rebelled, but just as quickly, he saw his father's pale face, heard that deep, hacking cough. He heard a swish of skirts and turned, planting a smile on his lips.

"Lady Clare," he said, bowing slightly.

"My lord," said Clare.

He took her proffered hand in his large one. She is lovely, he thought. He was partial to blond hair and fair-complexioned women, and she was endowed with both. He cleared his throat. "I realize that this situation is a bit difficult for the both of us."

"I understand, my lord. More so for you, of course."

"I doubt that sincerely, my lady."

Clare's hands fluttered a bit, and she forced down her nervousness. He was so very large. It was disconcerting. "Have you seen the Elgin Marbles, my lord?" she asked abruptly.

"Yes," Hawk said. He saw that she was leaning forward, her eyes wide with interest. Damned hunks of marble! Who cared? "They came from Greece," he said inadequately, then proceeded to listen to Clare explain everything about their origins and current condition. At least it passed the next fifteen minutes. He nearly collapsed with dread when she asked his opinion of George Gordon.

"He has become an overnight sensation," said Hawk of Lord Byron. "The ladies are most enthusiastic about his poetry, I understand."

"As am I, my lord," Clare assured him. "Have you read this passage, my lord?"

> Earth! render back from out thy breast
> A remnant of our Spartan dead!
> Of the three hundred grant but three,
> To make a new Thermopylae!

Hawk didn't know whether to applaud or bow his head. He was spared doing neither.

"I should like to paint him," Clare said. "Indeed, my lord, I should like to paint all your family and your friends."

"It would perhaps be a bit difficult."

"Why? Shouldn't we live in London? Shouldn't we meet everyone?"

He suddenly pictured himself introducing Clare: "This is my wife, she would like to paint you, after Lord Byron of course. You are not family, but you are a friend, or at least an acquaintance. She will sing Lord Byron's praises to you whilst you sit there not moving a muscle."

"I am not certain," he said finally.

Clare continued. "And all the museums! How I should love to meet Mr. Turner!"

"I do not like Mr. Turner's work," Hawk said, finally honest.

Clare skittered to a mental halt. "How odd," she said, "but of course, I am certain you are correct."

"Why would you think that?" he asked.

"You are a man, my lord, a gentleman of learning."

"I am more a soldier than a scholar, Clare," Hawk said.

"Still," Clare said, softly insistent, "Papa tells us that ladies should always be guided by their menfolk."

"I wonder," Hawk mused aloud, "what Sophia has to say to that?"

Clare blushed. Sophia would, of course, pay lip service to that sentiment, but nothing more.

"My stepmother is most wise," Clare finally managed.

Hawk stared at her. The last thing he wanted was to have a wife. The next-to-last thing was a wife who wanted to be guided by him. That meant dependence and propinquity. Would that mean then that he would be responsible for Clare's happiness? Would she fall in love with him?

He sent a surreptitious look toward the clock on the mantel. The thirty minutes were blessedly up. One down.

"Well, my lord?" Grunyon asked some minutes later in Hawk's bedchamber.

Hawk sighed. He wanted to say that she would suit him about as well as a six-fingered glove, but he knew he wasn't being fair. Then again, life had ceased being fair.

"She is lovely and talented. And excessively malleable, I would say."

"Oh dear," said Grunyon.

"She told me all about the Elgin Marbles."

"Gracious, no!"

"Hell and damnation," said Hawk. "Pour me a glass of something strong, Grunyon, I am due to see Lady Viola in ten minutes."

Like night and day, Hawk was thinking after five minutes in Viola's fluttering company.

She was so young and so anxious to please, and she chattered endlessly.

"Please tell me of Almack's, my lord," Viola said, her voice a blend of pleading and flirting. "I cannot wait to visit and meet all those marvelous people."

"It is a boring place," Hawk said, "and the refreshments are niggardly, to say the least."

He was not cooperating in the least, Viola thought. "A lady must mind her figure," she said. "There is dancing, is there not?"

"Oh yes," said Hawk. Some nasty imp made him add, "I do not like to dance."

"Even that new German dance I have heard about, my lord? The waltz?"

Hawk felt a stab of guilt at the wistful tone of her voice. He sighed. She was so eager. Lord, he would feel like a rapist taking her to wive. "I enjoy the waltz," he said finally, "but it is rarely danced in public. The patronesses of Almack's haven't approved of it yet, you see."

Viola beamed at him, and gave him one of her practiced smiles. It worked quite well on Kenard; indeed, it made him blush adorably and stammer.

Hawk arched a dark brow. The little minx was trying her feminine wiles. He wanted to laugh at her budding efforts, but of course he wasn't completely lost to good breeding. He thought suddenly that within a year, with practice, Viola could flirt with the best of them. It was a chilling thought. "Do you like poetry, Viola?" he asked, clutching at one of Clare's straws.

"Goodness, no!" Viola exclaimed, her voice so appallingly earnest that he was hard-pressed not to smile. "Well, of course, Adelaide forced all of us to read good works, sermons, and such things."

"Frances also?" he asked, wondering how she could manage to read with her bad eyesight.

Viola gave him a very fetching grin and a pretty

shrug. "Oh, Frances does what she pleases." *And you don't please her, my lord, but I shan't tell you that!*

"I see," said Hawk. He slid a look at the clock on the mantel and saw that the time was up. Two down.

After a quiet luncheon with Viola, Clare, and Lady Ruthven, Hawk dutifully arrayed himself in the togs Grunyon set out for him. Thirty minutes later, after Viola had found her missing glove, he found himself sitting between the two sisters in his own carriage.

Frances, seated upon a hill that gave a full view of the castle, watched them leave. She grinned, rose, and shook out her skirts. She kissed her fingers to her lips at the retreating carriage. She had a lot to do before they returned. She'd left Robert's croft after treating his one swaybacked horse for thrush. "Robert, ye mustn't let Sally stand about in her own muck," she said, adapting her speech to the farmer. "I've treated her as best I can, but ye must keep her hooves clean. Ye ken?"

Robert kenned, at least she trusted that he did. She returned to the castle, hoping to slip up to her temporary quarters in Viola's room. One thing Frances could be certain of—neither Viola nor Clare would say a word to the earl about the strange behavior and the equally ugly appearance of their sister.

"Frances!"

It was her father, of course, and he was livid. She felt a strange sort of calm wash over her, and turned to face him.

"Yes, Papa?"

"Don't you 'Yes, Papa' me, my girl! I have endured more than a parent should have to, and this is the end of it, Frances!" He strode toward her.

Frances stood her ground. "Then beat me, Papa," she said, "for I shall not change. I will not leave Kilbracken and that is that. Do as you wish."

"Damn you, Frances, he even applauded your miserable performance last night!"

"Yes, he did. What did you expect? That he would start laughing, howling, cover his ears with his aristocratic English hands?"

Ruthven was silent a long moment, and Frances didn't like that, not one bit. Please roar, Papa, she pleaded silently. Instead, Ruthven said finally, "Very well, Frances."

He turned on his heel and strode away.

What, she wondered, worrying her lower lip, was he up to?

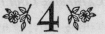

4

*Was this the face that launch'd a
thousand ships?*
—CHRISTOPHER MARLOWE

"Good Lord! Isn't that your sister?"

Hawk held back the curtain on the carriage window for Viola to look out. He felt her stiffen; then she gave a trilling laugh. "Oh no, that's not Frances. That's one of the crofter women."

He didn't see the quick glance that passed between the two sisters.

Hawk said nothing, but he did gaze out the window one more time. It was Frances, he thought, not a crofter woman. She looked a rumpled, filthy mess, and those were men's boots on her feet. The sleeves of the fading gray wool gown were rolled up beyond her elbows, and she was striding—yes, striding about like a damned man. He leaned back, a frown puckering his brow.

"Did you enjoy the Campbells, my lord?" Clare asked.

Hawk wondered at the nervousness in her voice. As for Viola, he could have sworn that she was snickering.

"Yes, of course," he said, lying fluently. He had been so bored he'd believed death by slow torture would have been preferable, then decided that he'd had the torture.

"We so enjoy visiting witty, charming people," said Viola. "And London, so many parties to attend! How thrilling it will . . . must certainly be."

Hawk was suddenly blessed with a very clear vision of his future. Either Viola or Clare as his countess, his hostess for an endless series of boring routs and soirees and balls and dinners. Giggling, gossiping, demanding his time, flirting with his friends. Or painting his friends and quoting Lord Byron. Life as he knew it would be over. It would die without a whimper. He wished at that moment that he'd never sold out, that he'd never left Wellington's command. Dammit, he wanted to be free, and that included freedom from a wife. He wanted his newly found life of the past fourteen months to continue intact. He wanted to continue keeping Amalie, wanted to see the sheen in her eyes when he came inside her, feel her fingers digging into his shoulders as she arched up against him. He remembered vividly Saint Leven's words to him, said in his slow, lazy drawl: "My boy, you've harangued me about this damned oath your father made. A wife won't be a bad thing, you know." Then he'd paused, and a wolfish grin had curved his lips. "Incidentally, I've always found Amalie very . . . endearing. Will you continue to keep her?"

"Yes," Hawk had said between gritted teeth. "Damn you, Saint Leven, yes I will." In his fourteen months in London, he'd realized that most gentlemen, married or not, kept mistresses.

But how could he, with a wife dangling on his sleeve in London? He couldn't, wouldn't embarrass a wife in that way. Neither little Viola nor well-meaning artistic Clare would understand it, of that he was certain. And he knew as clearly as he could see, that with a wife in London, discretion wouldn't be enough. There was a pronounced streak of maliciousness in the ladies of the *ton*. He cursed under his breath.

"Oh yes," he heard Clare say with great enthusiasm, drawing his thoughts away from a future that chilled him. "So much to see, so very much to do."

"Indeed," added Viola. "To meet all your friends, all the famous ladies in London—I cannot wait!"

Hawk wanted to cry and howl at the moon.

Frances was present at afternoon tea. She bore no resemblance at all to the frowsy woman he'd seen from the carriage window. She was neatly dressed, her hair in a severe knot at the back of her neck, and looked so homely that he felt a spurt of pity for her. She said absolutely nothing.

Viola regaled him with spicy gossip, and flirted outrageously.

Clare gave him wistful looks, but thankfully made no more mention of the Elgin Marbles.

Lady Ruthven refilled his teacup until he thought he would float away.

He was on the point of excusing himself when he saw Frances ease out of her chair and walk briskly toward the door.

He had to do it, he had no choice.

"Lady Frances," he said, rising quickly. "May I have a moment of your time?"

So, Frances, thought, her back still toward him, it was her turn to be interviewed for the post of wife. Well, she had to admit, at least he was fair.

"Very well," she said, turning slightly. "In the gun room?"

"Yes, that will be fine."

"I shall see you there, my lord, in ten minutes." She slipped out of the room and headed toward the gun room. She pulled the spectacles out of her pocket and onto her nose. A stray strand of hair had worked itself loose and she left it hanging along the side of her face.

She realized her heart was pounding. She couldn't be rude, not overtly. She had to be . . .

"Lady Frances?"

She started, whirling about to see him standing in the open doorway.

"Yes," she said, not moving an inch.

"I haven't had much chance to speak to you."

"No," she said.

Damned ungrateful wench, Hawk thought, then immediately felt guilty. She couldn't help her appearance, couldn't help that she looked a fright next to her lovely sisters.

"Clare showed me many of her paintings. Has she done one of you?"

Frances looked over at him for the first time. She squinted, and wanted to grin at the slight stiffening of his face. "Yes."

"I should like to see it."

He was trying to be pleasant, damn him. "I don't know where it is."

"Oh, a pity. Do you like to read?"

She heard the distaste in his voice, and realized that Clare must have gotten carried away with Lord Byron. She should have known that Clare wouldn't realize that English gentlemen had blocks in their heads for brains. Poor Clare, wasting her precious poetry on an oaf of a man.

Frances raised her chin, wishing she could see him more clearly through the murky lenses. She realized that she was a bit disappointed that this man in particular fit her image of English gentlemen in general—gentlemen who thought the printed word a pleasure only for fools. "Yes," she said, forcing her voice into a boring monotone. "I read the classics, of course. In

Greek and Latin, and I much enjoy reading Chaucer *aloud* on long winter nights." Did he look as if he'd just swallowed more of Doris' soggy trifle? Take that, you arrogant . . .

"Do you like to visit and go to balls and parties?"

He likes gaiety, wit, and charm.

"No," she said, with not so much as a creak of hesitation. "I much prefer being alone."

"With your Greek and Latin?"

"Yes."

"And you like to be outdoors, do you not?"

"Yes, alone."

"Ah."

There were several minutes of absolute silence. She felt no compunction to say anything. It was his bloody interview, after all. She kept her eyes on her toes.

Hawk cleared his throat. "Thank you, Lady Frances," he said, turned, and left the room.

His brow was furrowed as he strode to his bedchamber. By the time he opened the door, he was smiling with grim determination.

Grunyon wasn't there.

Hawk finally found him in the north tower, gazing out over the barren landscape.

"Tottle told me where you were. I think the bloody butler was drunk. I have reached a decision," he continued baldly.

Grunyon searched his master's face. He seemed calm, morbidly so.

"If I wed either Lady Viola or Lady Clare, my life will change. I will have a prattling wife hanging on my sleeve, demanding my time, quoting poetry, painting, giggling, flirting."

"I see," said Grunyon slowly. "There is, however, Major Hawk, the matter of the oath."

"I know. God, I know. I will wed Lady Frances."

Grunyon could only stare at his master. "Wh—what, my lord?"

Ruthven stood below, listening with unabashed interest. He'd planned to discuss things with Hawk this very evening, in his library, over a brandy. He leaned outward, his ears ready to be filled, a crooked smile on his face.

"Lady Frances," Hawk repeated. "Yes," he went on doggedly, as if convincing himself. "She is homely. That is her only failing. On the other hand, she dislikes people and parties, she doesn't carry on like a damned magpie. She would leave me alone. The servants would learn to put up with her wretched singing and playing."

"That appears to be true," said Grunyon, "but I do not believe I understand."

"For God's sake, Grunyon, I could take her to Desborough Hall, breed a child on her, then take myself to London. Everyone would be content, especially the lady. Lord knows, if I don't wed her, she'll end up a spinster."

"You pretend that you are doing her a favor?"

"Don't you try your damned sarcasm on me! It is the solution, I tell you."

Ruthven wanted to laugh at the poor earl's misguided impressions, and he had to press his hand over his mouth to keep himself quiet. *Ah, my smart little Frances, you've done it this time. Outsmarted and out-flanked. As for you, my boy, you don't know what you're in for.*

"It still doesn't seem very fair," said Grunyon, digging in. He felt sorry for the lady.

"Fair be damned! My father is responsible for this wretched debacle, not I. I am making the best of it. I wouldn't be a proper husband to either Viola or Clare, that is, I'd try to be, but it would be a misery. I would never be alone, I could no longer visit Amalie. Lord, I'd probably have to make intelligent conversation over the breakfast table. As for Frances, you'll see, Grunyon, she'll be happy as a lark in Yorkshire. The only thing missing is a loch and some heather. She can stride about the moors to her heart's content, read Chaucer *aloud* to the servants, and do in essence what she does here."

Ruthven very quietly left his post and wandered back into his bedchamber from the balcony. He was thoughtful, examining the consequences of the earl's decision. The decision was, after all, cold-blooded in the extreme. But Frances, his thinking continued, Frances wouldn't allow him to stay cold-blooded. She'd give him fits. His Frances wouldn't be able to keep her tongue quiet in her mouth for very long. "It will work out," Ruthven said to the empty bedchamber. "Ah yes, it certainly will. I must write to the marquess immediately."

If he could have justified it to himself, he would have arranged the marriage between the earl and Frances, but he'd realized he couldn't exclude Clare or Viola. Now the earl had fallen in with Ruthven's wishes, for all the wrong reasons. He shrugged, then grinned widely, picturing the look on his daughter's face. He wanted to dance a jig.

He saw Frances that evening before the family met in the drawing room. She looked as awful as possible, and he smiled at her. "Good evening, my dear," he said. "How are you feeling?"

Frances stared at her father. "What is wrong?"

"Wrong? Don't be a fool, my girl. Why should there be anything wrong?"

"You are not behaving as you should," Frances said slowly, studying his face. "Has the earl offered for Viola or Clare yet?"

"No, no yet," Ruthvan said. "But I suspect that he will speak to me soon enough now."

"Ah yes, he did allow himself three days, did he not?"

"You have a sarcastic mouth, Frances." On those less-than-loving words, he patted her shoulder, leaving her to flounder like a ship in a storm, sails flapping in the wind. What was he up to? she wondered, but there was no answer, none at all. She squared her shoulders, then immediately hunched them roundly, and went forward into dowdy battle. The mouse cometh, my lord earl, she thought, and laughed.

She was pleased with her performance of the afternoon. She was certain the earl was disgusted with her, and not just her face. Her answers, short and curt, had been inspired. She felt smug and safe.

She was unaware that during the interminable meal, the earl was gazing at her beneath half-closed lids. He was relieved that she ate like a lady. He was more than relieved that she said not a word, unlike her sisters, who seemed to be competing with each other for his attention. The time he would have to spend with Frances in the future stretched out before him in peaceful silence.

He could always have the pianoforte removed from Desborough Hall when he visited.

He determined to take an ax to the pianoforte himself after a half-hour of Frances' singing and playing. He'd known the servants at Desborough Hall since he was a boy. They were loyal. He didn't want them to run from the hall with their hands over their ears, and leave his employ. He forced himself to applaud when she finished. To his surprise, this time both Sophia and Ruthven applauded also.

He did notice the odd looks passing between Viola and Clare. It was as if they were restraining themselves from bursting out in laughter. It angered him. How could they treat their sister with such barely veiled contempt? It wasn't her fault, after all, that she lacked so much of everything that they had in abundance.

"Frances, my dear, a moment, please."

Frances halted her long stride at Adelaide's bedchamber door. Her long-time friend, clothed in a voluminous white nightgown, motioned Frances into her room. There was but a single candle burning. Everyone else was long abed. Frances had wanted to walk off her excess of energy before retiring.

"Yes, Adelaide?" Frances said, knowing what was to come.

"My dear child, you've been behaving outrageously. You know that, of course, there is no need for me to point it out. You're being dreadfully unfair to your papa, and that, perhaps, you haven't realized."

Frances couldn't quite meet Adelaide's concerned eyes. She said at last, "Not really, and I know what's best for Papa. He would miss me dreadfully, Adelaide, you know that."

"Frances, you know that every young lady must wed. It is a fact of life. The alternatives for ladies aren't to be considered, at least in your case."

Frances heard no bitterness in Adelaide's voice, and she'd never married. She tried to lighten things. "I plan to be the most indulgent aunt imaginable, Adelaide."

"Don't be a bore, Frances," Adelaide said sharply. "You've been overly protected, despite all the freedom your father gives you. You must realize that life is waiting outside the confines of Kilbracken. You cannot stay here forever."

"Perhaps," Frances said, her voice just above a

whisper. She hated to feel guilty, particularly when she deserved to. "But you would say the same things about Viola and Clare. At least one of them is assured of a grand marriage."

"Neither of them has your . . . strength, Frances."

"So, you're now telling me that you believe the earl a hard man, a man who will make them miserable?"

Adelaide sighed, realizing her words had come too late, far too late now. "It no longer matters," she said, wondering if her little sermon would have done any good before. She kissed Frances on her cheek. "Good night, dear. Sleep well."

"I wish you wouldn't be so nice," Frances said. "You make me feel like a selfish wretch."

"Don't. As I said, it no longer matters."

Adelaide stood in the open doorway of her bedchamber watching Frances stride down the corridor to Viola's room.

Frances was whistling as she made her way down the stairs and across the entrance hall with her long-legged stride. The three days were up today, she thought, grinning at a suit of armor that was sagging against the wall next to the fireplace. Lucky Clare. Or lucky Viola. She cringed just a moment at the memory of her conversation the night before with Adelaide.

"Frances!"

She turned about to see her father beckoning to her. "Yes, Papa?"

"Come here, child."

She walked toward him, her expression wary, her head cocked to one side in silent question. He looked down at her, a gentle smile curving up the corners of his mouth. Suddenly he drew her into his arms and hugged her to him.

"I am very pleased, Frances. Now, do me proud."

Confused, Frances said automatically, "Why, of course, Papa. Why ever shouldn't I do you proud?"

"Go into the gun room."

"You wish me to repair one of your guns?"

"No, no, I don't. Do not shame me, Frances. Go now." He gave her a gentle shove, and Frances, staring back at him, opened the door and slipped inside. Shame him? Why the devil would he say such a thing as that? She would kill for him, she would do anything for him.

"Good morning, Lady Frances."

Frances jumped at the sound of the earl's voice. This is most bizarre, she thought as she turned to face the Earl of Rothermere, her expression one of confusion.

"Does one of your guns need repair?" she asked. "Papa sent me in here. Is there some problem?"

"No," said Hawk. Get it over with, he told himself, before you lose your nerve. His eyes moved from the top of her head downward. The gown she was wearing was frumpy, too big, outmoded, and too short for her. But, he realized, her body wasn't all that bad. She was slender at least. He would be able to bring himself to bed her.

Frances stiffened at his ill-disguised scrutiny. She quickly fished in the pocket of her gown for her spectacles. She slipped them on and squinted at him. The lecherous man was looking at her. Her hands curled into fists at her sides.

She squinted all the harder. "What is it you want, my lord?"

"I have selected you, Lady Frances," Hawk said.

She understood immediately, but could only gape at him. Was he blind? Utterly without taste? And he was looking at her as if her very presence gave him pain.

She said without thinking, her voice clipped and as cold as the loch in January, "Then unselect."

Hawk blinked. He couldn't have heard her aright, could he? He repeated himself, trying to keep the awful fatalism from his voice. "Lady Frances, I am . . . choosing you as my wife."

"Are you mad?" Frances asked, looking him squarely in the eye now, no longer squinting over the spectacles hanging precarously on the tip of her nose. "Why?"

Her clipped voice, her words, startled him. He'd expected her to accept him immediately, in all likelihood with gushing pleasure. After all, how often did the ugly sister win out over the other two? Perhaps, he thought, she didn't believe he was truly serious. The poor girl probably couldn't believe her good fortune. He smiled at her and said, "I do not believe I am mad. I believe we shall suit admirably. Now, your father and I have worked out the details of the marriage settlement; I am leaving for Glasgow. I will return on Friday for our wedding. As you know, my father is quite ill. We will leave immediately after the ceremony for England. Here, this is for you."

He took three steps forward, clasped her hand, and shoved his grandmother's exquisite emerald ring upon her finger.

She's speechless, overcome with disbelief, he thought, but that was fine. If she never spoke, he would be pleased. He forced himself to lightly kiss her forehead and look down into her face. She'd shoved her spectacles back up and her eyes looked small and distorted behind the thick lenses. At least at night, in bed, he wouldn't have to see her. He'd allow no lamps to be lit, otherwise it was a strong possibility that he wouldn't be able to do his duty in the marriage bed.

"I shall see you on Friday, Lady Frances," he said, and strode from the room. It didn't occur to him that she should have said at least a brief yes to his approval, expressed some opinion after he'd given her his very clipped, detailed plans.

He closed the door of the gun room behind him and strode through the great hall to the drawing room, where Ruthven awaited him.

He thought he heard Frances say something, but the thick door muffled the sound. He kept going.

Frances stood still as a stone, her mind numb, disbelieving of what had just happened. Then she looked at the ring and shouted, "No! This is ridiculous! No!"

There had to be some mistake. Lord, all he had to do was but look at her. What about Viola? Clare? The man was mad, she was certain of it. Well, she would just have to put a stop to it now. She jerked the door open and marched into the great hall. Sophia was coming from the drawing room, an odd look on her face.

"Where is Papa?" Frances asked. "Where is that man?"

"Come with me, Frances," said Sophia. "You've been well caught, my girl. Come."

"No, I must speak to Papa," Frances said, her voice thin and shrill. "It's a mistake, Sophia. All a mistake."

"I think so too," said Sophia, "but the earl has made his decision and you, my girl, will abide by it." She caught Frances' arm as she tried to pass her.

"No, Sophia!" Panic rose to choke her. "No! This can't happen!"

"You listen to me, Frances Kilbracken," Sophia said in a fierce whisper, tightening her grip on her stepdaughter's arm. "You thought you were being so very clever, didn't you, appearing like a troll, a diffident little mouse? Well, for whatever reason, the earl has picked you, not Viola, not Clare. And you, you devious creature, will abide by it."

"It makes no sense," Frances said. "No sense at all." She tried to pull away. "I must see Papa. I won't do it, Sophia!"

"Oh yes you will! Look about you, you idiot. Yes, look at all the glory of Kilbracken! The castle is crumbling about us, Frances, and what will be left for your brother? Clumps of heather, that's what, and an empty title! You heard what your father said before the earl arrived—the old marquess is turning over ten thousand pounds upon this marriage. Ten thousand pounds, Frances! The earl cannot be turned down!"

"But what about Viola? Clare?" Frances felt herself sinking into deep waters, felt herself being dragged down, suffocating.

Sophia looked at her, her eyes stern and commanding. "I wanted him to pick Viola, I will admit it to you. She is a lovely girl, and she deserves to be rich. She needs flattery and parties, and masculine attention. As for Clare, well, the same holds true for her. But it is not to be. You will wed the earl, my girl; then you will see to providing for your sisters." She shook Frances' arm. "Do you understand me?"

Frances stared down at her stepmother, her mouth working, but no sounds emerging.

"Well, no matter. Once you are the Countess of Rothermere, you will do all that is proper for your sisters. You will not fail me in that, Frances. Now, if you dare throw a tantrum in front of the earl, your father will never speak to you again. Have I made myself clear?"

Frances stumbled from the castle. It took her several minutes to realize that it was raining, a thick, muzzling rain that was as cold against her skin as she was inside. She ripped the spectacles off her nose and stuffed them in a pocket. The cap was the next to go. She watched it sink under the weight of the rain into a mud puddle. She started to shiver, and began running toward the stable. Once inside, she climbed up into the loft and flung herself down upon the rotting hay. There was a leak in the roof, she thought vaguely, smelling the moldy, sodden hay.

Why?

The one word kept careening through her mind. It made no sense, none at all.

Why?

Suddenly Frances sat up and wrapped her arms about her knees. She forced herself to think slowly and clearly. Why would an admittedly handsome bachelor select a dowdy mouse to wed when two quite lovely and amiable non-mice were available? Even if her father had told him that it was a disguise, what man would want a wife who obviously didn't want him? Had he seen through her disguise himself? She shook her head, remembering his look when his eyes had roved over her. He'd been disgusted, yet he had still selected her.

It made no sense, none at all. How could it be true, particularly after he'd heard her sing and play?

She could think of nothing until an offhanded remark of Viola's flitted through her mind.

I daresay the earl is most popular with the ladies in London. He told Clare and me that he spends much of his time there. All the entertainments, I suppose. I'll wager he has a mistress. I wonder what I shall do about that? Certainly he will have to give her up, and then we will be very happy together. Oh yes.

The Earl of Rothermere was a handsome man, Frances thought objectively. And it was quite true that he must have ladies fawning all over him. And mistresses. *And the last thing a gentleman like that would want is a vivacious, charming, demanding wife.*

"My God," Frances said, expelling her breath in a long, disbelieving sigh. "He couldn't. It is too vile, too outrageous a thought." She heard a nicker from one of the horses in the stall below.

She refused to dismiss the idea. Could he have picked her because she wasn't any of those things? Had he chosen a dowdy mouse so that he could continue in his carefree, likely profligate ways?

Frances had to know. She rose to her feet and shook her skirts free of the moldy hay. She paused in the doorway of the stable. It had stopped raining. To her consternation, she saw the earl's man, Grunyon, climb into the carriage. The earl was driving, whipping up the horses now. She rushed out of the stable, waving and calling out.

But it was no use. Muddy water splashed up from the wheels. The horses snorted. The earl was paying no heed to anything except driving.

Frances watched the carriage disappear down the winding road. How long had she stayed in the stable loft? *Long enough so that the bastard could escape.*

She squared her shoulders and marched back to the castle.

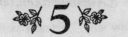

5

*Marriage has many pains, but celibacy
has no pleasures.*

—SAMUEL JOHNSON

"Put the ring back on, Frances."

The heavy ring bounced and slid across the table.
Frances made no move to retrieve it. Its weight was
unconscionable on her finger.

"No," she said. "I shan't, Papa."

Ruthven prepared to give her the full blast of his
temper, when Viola and Clare burst into the gun room,
Sophia trailing behind them, her face a study of con-
flicting emotions.

"I don't believe this!" Viola stamped her feet. Oh,
Viola, Frances wanted to yell at her sister, you are still
such a little girl. The earl would make you utterly
miserable.

"What did you do, Frances?" Clare demanded.
"What did you promise him? Stepmama told us that
the earl has offered for you, but that's impossible!
You look awful, you look—"

"That's enough!" Ruthven shouted over the female
din.

"I agree," said Frances, eyeing her two very furious
sisters. "Listen, you two, I don't wish to marry the
earl any more than he wishes to marry me."

"Then why?" Clare asked. "He could barely bring
himself to look at you, just as you planned."

"I think I know why," Frances said, keeping an eye firmly on her father's face. "The earl selected me because I am a dowd, a miserable excuse for a female. He selected me because he didn't think he would have to change his life. I imagine he plans to dump me somewhere, probably one of his moldering estates, and go about his business as if none of this had ever happened."

Ruthven couldn't help it. His eyes widened and his fingers clutched the table edge until the knuckles were white. How could she have guessed so quickly?

"So," Frances said, expelling a deep breath, "it is true, isn't it, Papa?"

Bluster and rage, thought Ruthven, but he said nothing.

"I don't understand," wailed Viola.

Frances turned to face her sister. "Then allow me to explain it," she said. "You, Viola, and you, Clare, are exactly what the precious earl likes in ladies. You are both very pretty, charming, gay. However, the earl doesn't want a wife. A wife, in his mind, would change everything, and he doesn't want anything to change. Now do you understand?"

"He is a bounder, a cad," said Clare.

"At the very least," agreed Frances.

"I still want him," said Viola. "I could change him, make him happy, content—"

"Don't be a fool, Viola," Frances interrupted. "He would eat you for breakfast and spit you out. The man is selfish, ruthless, and unworthy. But of course," she added, giving her father a furious look, "he will provide money. Rather, his father will."

"Frances, you will not condemn a man simply because he is endeavoring to . . ."

"To what, Papa?" Frances asked furiously when her father faltered. "I am the one to be sacrificed."

"Sacrificed, ha!" Viola yelled. "You will be a countess—rich, all the clothes you want—what does it matter if your husband goes his own way? You know nothing about how ladies and gentlemen conduct their marriages. It is a marriage of convenience, as is proper. You, Frances, should be shot, hanged— "

"That is quite enough," said Sophia briskly. "The die is cast, as it were. Now that all the drama is over and everyone has vented his spleen, you will come with me, Frances. We have but three days to do something about a trousseau. The earl returns early on the morning of your wedding. There is much to be done."

"You are sacrificing Frances," Clare said clearly.

"Sacrificing!" Sophia yelled. "You are a silly ninny! And you, Frances, you should be jumping for joy at your success."

"Papa . . ." Frances said very quietly.

"One day, you will thank me, my girl," Ruthven said.

"Both of us will be long dead before that day comes, Papa." Frances turned, defeated. She followed Sophia out of the gun room, promising to meet her in her bedchamber within the hour.

Frances then stalked to her own bedchamber. It smelled like him, she thought, and she viciously ripped the sheets off the bed. She was standing in the middle of the room, the sheets in a white pool at her feet, when Adelaide slipped through the open doorway.

"Goodness, my love," Adelaide said, "what an uproar you have caused."

"I know."

"This is for the best, Frances."

"Yes, I imagine that it is. At least I am saving Viola and Clare from unhappiness." It is difficult to be noble, she thought, so very difficult.

"A husband is a husband, my dear, and to my mind,

the earl shows more promise than most. He was placed in a most awkward position. If he selected you for all the wrong reasons, well, he will soon see the error of his ways."

Frances looked much struck. "I hadn't thought of that, Adelaide. What shall I do?"

Adelaide patted her arm. "You will gather up these sheets, love, then I imagine you will give quite a bit of thought to your alternatives."

Frances did give furious, endless thought to her very limited number of options. She spent many hours imagining the look on the earl's face were she to appear lovely, charming, and gay and demand that he take her to London. That made her smile, but she wondered if he would beat her for her earlier deception. Men were such unpredictable creatures—she'd observed enough of them to be certain of that.

She didn't come to her decision until the evening before her wedding. She was standing in front of her bedchamber window, staring out into the inpenetrable darkness.

"Frances?"

"Yes? Sophia, do come in."

Her stepmother was wearing a silk dressing gown and her lovely hair was long and loose down her back. She looked younger.

"Is there a problem?" Frances asked. "Has Doris broken out into spots? Has Reverend MacLeod had another argument with Papa?"

To her surprise, Sophia didn't meet her gaze directly, nor did she respond to Frances' attempt at humor.

"Papa!" Frances exclaimed. "He is all right, is he not?"

"Yes, yes," Sophia said. "Sit down, Frances. There are things I must speak to you about."

"Things?" Frances walked to her bed and climbed to the center to sit cross-legged.

"Your responsibility as a wife," said Sophia.

"I assure you, Sophia," Frances said, her voice a bit nasty, "that I shall be quite able to have the earl's meals on the table when he wishes them."

"No, Frances, I'm speaking of your intimate duties as a wife."

"Oh!" Frances stared at her blankly, then cursed herself silently for eight kinds of a fool. She hadn't realized, hadn't thought that the earl, that stranger, would touch her and ... She swallowed.

"Yes," said Sophia. "Do you understand what husbands and wives do together? In bed?"

Frances knew enough and she was horribly embarrassed. She kept her head lowered and merely nodded.

"Your father believes, as I do, that the earl will be sensitive to your feelings." That wasn't precisely the truth, but Sophia chose to severely edit her spouse's remarks on the subject. *Aye love, 'tis a lusty man Hawk is. He'll teach our Frances a thing or two!*

Sensitive to my ... "What does that mean, Sophia?"

"It means that he won't embarrass you, he'll treat you with the respect due a wife. Of course, when he sees what you really look like, he will doubtless be quite pleased and more ... attentive, despite his ... well, I'm not certain exactly ..." Her voice trailed off.

Frances gulped. "I see," she said.

Sophia felt a stab of concern for her stepdaughter despite all her husband's assurances. She said very gently, "He will, of course, want an heir, Frances. That is your primary duty as his wife."

"An heir," Frances repeated.

Sophia sought for some reassuring words, and was surprised when Frances raised her face and said quite

calmly, "Thank you for telling me, Sophia. I understand, I truly do. How stupid of me not to have
realized . . . Well, now I know."

After Sophia had left, Frances huddled under her
covers, drawing her knees to her chest. She pictured
him naked, striding out of the loch. She knew well
enough that that male appendage swelled to a horrible
size and was shoved between her legs. It was a ghastly
thought, repellent and embarrassing. So utterly sordid. But he could, would do it, because it was his
right. If she struggled, he would probably beat her.
That was his right too. She didn't seem to have any.
None at all.

Frances hadn't realized until that moment that she
was crying. Angry with herself, she dashed the silly
tears away with the back of her hand and sat up. She
remembered clearly how he had looked at her with
such distaste when he had proposed to her—no, she
added angrily to herself, when he informed her of his
decision. As for her decision, she'd made it. She would
be as dowdy, timid, and stupid as could be until he left
her, which she was certain he would do, as quickly as
he could honorably manage it. She wanted him to
leave her, preferably without laying a hand on her.
No, a hand she could manage; it was that other thing
she couldn't bear to think of.

It won't be bad, she told herself. I shall live in my
own house and do as I please. He can go to London
and enjoy all the charming, lively ladies he wishes to.

Hawk lay back, sated and sleepy. Georgina Mor-
gan, a delectable bit of womanhood, snuggled beside
him, her thigh thrown over his belly. She was a widow,
several years older than Hawk, and very affectionate.

"Ye're an excellent lover," Georgina said.

"So are you," Hawk said, and lightly kissed the top

of her head. "I must leave before dawn. I have to return to Loch Lomond and Castle Kilbracken."

"Ye have business with the Earl of Ruthven?"

Hawk should have told her it wasn't any of her business, but he wasn't in any mood to play the gentleman. He said, his voice cold and clipped, "Yes, indeed. I am to marry one of his daughters on the morrow."

Georgina sucked in her breath at this unexpected news. She'd rather hoped that the earl would stay in Glasglow for a while longer, and in her bed. "Pity," she said.

"I agree," said Hawk. He felt her knee slowly move over his manhood. "You'll wear me out, then?"

"Aye, 'tis no more than ye deserve."

Hawk glided his hand over her belly, his long fingers gently searching for her. "And what do *you* deserve, I wonder?"

"Frances, damn you, girl, I won't allow this!"

Ruthven reached for the offensive spectacles, but Frances ducked out of the way. "No, Papa, leave be. I am marrying your precious Hawk, and that is all you can ask of me."

"You look like a damned witch."

"No, my lord, not a witch," Adelaide said quietly, coming into the bedchamber, "more like a girl who is very frightened to be herself."

That drew Ruthven up. "Is this true, Frances?"

"Leave be, Papa," Frances said, sending Adelaide a wounded look. One tended to forget that Adelaide was so very perceptive. "The earl proposed to a mouse and that is what he will marry. I shan't disillusion him."

Ruthven gave her a long, searching look. "Very well, Frances. I shall say no more about it."

"And you won't say anything to the earl, Papa!"

"No, I won't."

When her father had left, Frances turned to Adelaide. "Is it time?"

"Yes, love. Frances, don't cheat yourself out of what can rightfully be yours."

Frances merely nodded, beyond words. "I shall be along in just a moment, Adelaide."

When she was finally alone, Frances walked to the window and gazed out. The day was gray, cold, and it had begun to drizzle.

If I were of a romantic disposition, she thought dispassionately, I should keep a journal. And I should write in it that I am beginning a new life and that I am deliriously happy.

She meant to giggle at her foolishness, but instead, it was a sob that broke from her throat.

The Reverend Mr. George MacLeod, a longtime friend of the Earl of Ruthven, presided over the ceremony. The two men had spent many satisfying hours arguing the merits of Presbyterianism versus the Church of England. MacLeod thought the English groom was polite, a well-bred young gentleman. When Frances finally entered the drawing room, he saw the earl's expression change. Now, MacLeod thought, he looked about as happy as a dead trout. His eyes went to Frances, and widened. Good gracious, he thought, stunned. She looked like a nightmare, and miserable to boot. What the devil was going on here? What had happened to his bright, laughing Frances? He knew this was an arranged marriage, but he'd had no idea that . . . He shot a questioning look at Ruthven, but Alexander was smiling benignly.

The words were spoken and he blessed the couple.

The wedding breakfast was less festive than a funeral.

The Reverend Mr. MacLeod, who had held Frances

on his knee when she was two years old, managed to catch her alone after she'd changed into traveling clothes. She looked sullen and pale. Where had she gotten those wretched spectacles? What was he to say to her?

"Good-bye, my dear," he said, and lightly kissed her forehead. "I will pray for you and your new husband."

"I should certainly appreciate that, sir," Frances said, squinting up at him. "In fact, a bolt of well-placed lightning at this moment would be most welcome."

"You marry against your will, Frances?"

"No," she said, seeing clearly that he was worried for her. She saw her father frowning at her from the corner of her eye. She saw her husband impatiently slapping his gloves against his thigh.

"Good-bye, sir," she said, and stepping to her tiptoes, kissed him on the cheek.

Frances was thankful for the spectacles. They hid her brimming eyes. Viola, Clare, Sophia, and Adelaide each hugged her. She reached her father.

"Frances," he said very quietly, "trust me, my girl. And trust yourself. You are strong."

"Yes, Papa." She took one last look around the hall. She wondered silently if she would ever see Kilbracken again. She followed her husband out of the castle. She eyed the closed carriage for a moment with dread. Then she turned and waved toward all the people she'd lived with for nineteen years. Doris, who had baked her wedding cake, was dabbing her eyes with the corner of her apron.

"Frances," Hawk said sharply, his hand on the open carriage door. "We must be on our way now."

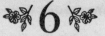

Claret is the liquor for boys;
port for men;
But he who aspires to be a hero must
drink brandy.
—SAMUEL JOHNSON

Hawk raised his silver flask of brandy and drank deep. Instant warmth hit his stomach and he didn't move for a long moment, savoring the feeling. He turned in the saddle and saw the lurching carriage coming nearer.

His wife was inside that carriage. His *wife*.

He closed his eyes a moment, still disbelieving that it was done. He didn't feel married, not even remotely. The Reverend Mr. MacLeod's words had floated about his head, not really part of him, even though his responses had affirmed that they were.

It was drizzling again. The sky was a moldering gray. The little foliage that clung for life among the barren rocks and crags looked sodden, limp, and ready to collapse from fatigue. The damned road was little more than a jagged path littered with rocks and deep mud puddles. There were occasional crofts to be seen, thready lines of smoke circling from chimneys, but no people. Only utter fools would show their faces on a dismal day like this. He accepted being an utter fool. Anything was preferable to sharing the carriage with her—*Frances Hawksbury, Countess of Rothermere.*

He thought of his father, as he did many times every hour, an automatic prayer on his lips that the old autocrat still clung to life. Suddenly it occurred to him that his father might just take one look at Frances and keel over from the shock. He resolved that before he took his wife into his father's bedchamber, he would make her rid herself of the spectacles, perhaps remove the bilious cap she would probably be wearing. It didn't matter if she couldn't see his father clearly. It did matter that his father didn't keel over at seeing a living nightmare that was his daughter-in-law.

He should have married Clare. No, he should have married Viola. Younger, more amenable, more pliable.

I must have been insane to attach myself to Frances.

He wasn't being fair, he knew it, but somehow it didn't make him feel more than a bit guilty. At least he'd spent the previous night burrowing himself into a lovely warm body. He didn't feel more than a bit guilty about that either. That brought his thinking to his wedding night. His hands tightened on Ebony's reins, and the stallion pranced to the side, his right-front hoof coming down in the middle of a mud puddle. Hawk cursed as the thick brown muck splashed his boots.

He heard Grunyon shout and wheeled Ebony about. When he reached the carriage, he turned his stallion to face Grunyon.

"What is it, Grunyon?"

Grunyon felt miserable, and so cold that he believed his very bones were frozen. "It will be dark soon," he said. "I looked at a map. We should be nearing a town called Airdrie. There should be a decent inn there."

Hawk vaguely remembered passing through Airdrie on his way to Kilbracken. It had seemed a quaint little town, but now he imagined it would look about as dismal as both he and Grunyon felt. Hawk looked at the darkening sky overhead. He didn't want to stop, not yet. He wanted to keep going until they reached

England. He wanted to keep going until he reached Greece.

"I also want to relieve myself," Grunyon said. He nodded back toward the carriage. "It seems likely, my lord, that your poor wife must be in a similar difficulty."

Hawk, who had taken care of his natural functions more than an hour before, felt a surge of guilt.

"Very well," he said finally. "Let us find a marvelous accommodation at Airdrie," he added, his voice filled with sarcasm.

Frances leaned back against the comfortable squabs, her lips drawn in a thin furious line. Miserable bastard! She was cold, hungry, and yes, she wanted to yell out the carriage window at her *husband*, she did need to relieve herself.

The carriage lurched forward once again.

Airdrie. She'd visited the small town the month before with her father to buy feed. There was an excellent inn there, the Devil's Lair. Fitting, she thought, very fitting.

She wished she had some little beasties, the biting kind, to place in his bed. *His bed*. Oh dear, he wouldn't, would he?

Frances squared her shoulders. No, he wouldn't. She wouldn't allow it. She found herself hoping her wretched husband caught a chill from his ride, then quickly reversed that thought. No, she wanted him to remain nauseatingly healthy. He would leave her all the sooner.

It occurred to her that her anger at her husband was keeping her from feeling utterly wretched about leaving Kilbracken.

The Devil's Lair looked about as inviting as an old abbey ruin in the dull rainy evening light. Hawk dismounted and shouted for an ostler. A man the size of a stout oak barrel emerged from the inn and shouted, "What wish ye?"

"Rooms, dinner, and a warm stable for my horses," Hawk called back in a tone of voice that would have brought all his men to startling attention in his army days.

"A Sassenach," old Harmon grunted. "See ye to the gentleman's horses, Enard," he told a gangly youth whose head was covered by an old tattered scarf.

The carriage door opened and Grunyon smiled into the dim interior. "My lady?"

Frances, stiff-legged, cold, and in a foul humor, gave Grunyon her gloved hand and descended the carriage steps.

Hawk walked slowly toward the cloaked and hooded figure.

"We will stay here for the night," he said.

Frances didn't look up. She'd forgotten to put her spectacles back on.

"Excellent," she said, her voice just as clipped and cool as his.

"I will see that your room is made ready for you."

"Most gracious," said Frances.

The tone was slightly acid, and Hawk frowned a bit. No, he thought, shaking his head as he strode into the inn, leaning over a bit to keep from hitting his head on the darkened oak beams, not acid. She was diffident and shy. Her voice was weary, that was it. She was probably very fatigued. He sighed, resolving to be more amiable over dinner.

There was no private parlor at the Devil's Lair, but the miserable weather had kept all the usual habitués away. There was only one snoring old man in the corner, curled up next to the fireplace, and old Harmon quickly rousted him out and into the taproom. Frances, having scraped her hair into a ferocious bun, adjusted her spectacles and marched into the parlor. She paused, sniffing delicious smells. Her stomach growled loudly.

Hawk looked up and caught himself smiling at the sound.

"My lady," he said, rose, and pulled back a chair for her.

Frances kept her head down and seated herself.

So much for a polite greeting, Hawk thought, and reseated himself. "A glass of wine, perhaps?"

"Yes, please."

"Look, I'm sorry if you're tired. It's just that I want to get to my father as soon as possible."

"I understand." *And I'm not tired; I'm bored from riding by myself in that awful carriage, and I don't like you.*

He poured wine into her goblet, and watched her wrap her fingers about the blunt stem. He found himself frowning a bit. Her hands were slender, the fingers long and graceful. The fingernails were buffed and short. Without thinking, Hawk reached out and took her hand in his. He turned her hand over. There were calluses and a few scratches. It was a strong hand, a capable hand.

Frances yanked her hand away and raised startled eyes to his face. For a moment she forgot to squint.

"You have lovely hands," Hawk said.

"Oh?"

There was a wealth of sarcasm in that one word, and Hawk found himself surprised at it. He repeated again to himself that she was tired, and kept an equally stinging comment to himself.

Old Harmon's wife, Nedda, entered carrying three huge covered trays.

Frances' stomach growled again, and Hawk laughed.

"Oh," she exclaimed as one tray was uncovered

beneath her nose. "Clootie dumplings! How marvelous. And forfar bridies."

What the devil were clooties and bridies? Hawk wondered, but the delicious smells dampened his revulsion at the bizarre names.

"Be that ye, Lady Frances?"

Frances, cursed herself, aware that Nedda was regarding her with something akin to horror. She managed to say calmly enough, "Aye, 'tis I, Mrs. Rapple."

"What do ye wi' this mon?"

Scots were known for their bluntness and their lack of class distinction, Frances thought, grinning to herself.

"He is my husband, Mrs. Rapple. I am leaving Scotland."

"But, what do ye wi' yerself, ye don't look—"

"Kippers with rice balls! I'm certain everything will be delicious, as usual."

She shot Mrs. Rapple a pleading look, and the good lady, confused but sensitive to that look, merely nodded and left the parlor.

"You are acquainted with our good hostess?" Hawk asked as he served Frances' plate.

"Yes, of course. We are not that far from Kilbracken. I should like a lot of everything, if you please, my lord."

Hawk obliged. He took a gingerly bite of the bridies and nodded. "Quite acceptable. What is it?"

"Steak pies."

"Ah."

"Where is Grunyon?"

"In the kitchen eating his dinner. Incidentally, perhaps you should call me Philip or Hawk, as you wish."

Frances' hand halted its progress to her mouth. "Where did you get the nickname Hawk?"

"During my army days—in Spain, to be exact."

She would have liked to know more, but was so

hungry she didn't want to interrupt herself. How kind of him, she thought acidly as she chewed on a rather tough piece of steak. His lordship giving the pitiful savage permission to call him by his given name, or the name of a stupid bird. She swallowed the bite, then drank more of her wine. The meal continued in silence.

"I prefer Philip, I think," she said sometime later.

"I shall try to answer to it," Hawk said. "It's been some time since anyone called me that. Do you prefer being called Frances?"

It's better than "ugly hag," which is what you're thinking.

"Frances is fine," she said.

Silence again.

Frances was licking her lips free of the thick sugar from the clooties when Hawk said suddenly, "After you have seen my father, we shall buy you some clothes."

Frances stiffened as straight as a board. She swallowed at least three thoroughly insulting retorts. So now she was the poor little mouse whose husband didn't want to be embarrassed if someone chanced to see her with him. She chose to say nothing.

Hawk found himself wondering aloud, "Both Clare and Viola dress beautifully. I find I am curious as to why—"

"I am very fatigued," Frances said, pushing back her plate. No, she thought quickly, that wasn't the way to proceed. She carefully schooled her features, her brain working furiously. Finally she said coldly, "I do not find lovely clothes at all desirable. 'Tis sinful to turn oneself out in a gawdy fashion. It goes against all my . . . religious beliefs."

My God, Hawk thought, astounded, staring at her. I've got a religious bigot on my hands! He felt ill, and was uncertain if it was from the clooties or the frightful realization of the real woman he had married.

Take that, you bounder! Frances rose slowly and said, "I am going to my room now. I assume that you will wish to leave early on the morrow, my lord?"

It was nearly painful to look at her, but he did. Odd, he thought during the visual passage up to her face, but her body was really quite acceptable. She was slender—indeed, his hands could span her waist—and her breasts looked full and well-formed.

Frances wasn't stupid, nor that ignorant. She understood that look, indeed had seen it on Ian's face, and sucked in her breath, backing away. "Good night, my lord!"

His eyes were on her face then and he saw the fear and panic.

"Frances," he said, his voice gentle now, "we are husband and wife. I know too that we are strangers. We will, however, consummate this marriage—"

His very calm orders made her forget herself. "Why? There is no reason I can think of for you to want to . . . Well, you understand what I mean."

"As I said, we are husband and wife."

"No! I will not allow it! I—"

"Frances, stop carrying on so. We will consummate this marriage, but not tonight. You are tired and so am I." He saw the utter relief make her shoulders sag and smiled ruefully to himself. Never in his life had a woman not wanted to share his bed when he wished it.

Frances turned without another word and bolted toward the door. She didn't stop bolting until she reached her small bedchamber on the third floor of the inn.

She was huddled in the soft bed within five minutes, the bedchamber door bolted securely from the inside.

Hawk toyed with his brandy. She was nervous about

sex, something to be expected from one's bride, he supposed. Well, he would be kind to her, get it over with quickly, not embarrass her more than was inherent in the act. He'd spoken to enough married gentlemen, and all of them agreed that wives, the wives who were true ladies, that is, were meant to be breached gently, not plowed with enthusiasm. They were to be treated with thoughtful decorum until they conceived, then left alone. He would give her another day to accustom herself to the idea. He would not embarrass her by speaking of it again. He would simply do it. He downed the rest of his brandy. He simply couldn't imagine making love to Frances in a lighted room. The thought of her squinting up at him made him shudder.

He did wonder, though, what she looked like naked, from the neck down.

Ruthven pulled Sophia closer and she felt the rumbling laughter in his deep chest.

"What is it?" she asked, tugging on the hair on his chest.

"I was just wondering how long it would take my Frances to show her true colors. Lord, to see the look on Hawk's face when she does. I find myself pitying the poor fellow."

"You believe her so impervious, so strong?"

Ruthven was silent for a moment, no longer laughing. Sophia always had the knack of cutting through his bravado. "Yes," he said finally. "She must be."

"But you are worried now, aren't you, Alex? All your plotting—oh yes, I know that you've written to the marquess about Frances and how you hoped she would be the one his son selected. But that young man doesn't care for her, not at all, Alex. Your Frances had made quite certain that he doesn't. It is possible that he will be cruel to her."

"No! Dammit, Sophie, he won't. The boy's a gentleman."

"Frances," Sophia said dryly, "is known to enrage you, my dear, and you are also a gentleman."

"I am her father. That is much different."

Sophia could practically hear him thinking, worrying, shoring up flaws in his logic. She hugged him. "Why don't you try to sleep now, Alex."

"You don't think that he will really hurt her, do you, Sophie?"

"No," she said truthfully, "I don't. If she maintains her pose, there would be no reason. Who would want to strike down a timid mouse?"

"Hmmm," said Ruthven. "Tonight is their wedding night."

"If I know Frances," said Sophia in a dry voice, "she will somehow have convinced him that lovemaking with his bride is the last thing he desires."

"I heard him say he wants to breed an heir quickly."

"Not tonight, he won't."

But Frances' father didn't manage to ease himself into sleep for quite a long time.

At least it wasn't raining, Frances thought as she stared out the carriage window at the countryside. She'd give anything if she could ride and not be a prisoner in this wretched carriage. She could already feel a headache beginning.

Curse him! He could have at least inquired what she wished to do. But he hadn't, of course. She supposed that in his vast experience—and she never doubted for a moment that all his experience was vast—a lady was to be protected from the elements, even if the elements were pleasant and sunny.

Hawk had said over breakfast, "I wish to continue

until it's dark today. Grunyon tells me we have a good chance of reaching Peebles if we suffer no mishap."

How many hours would that mean closed in this dreadful carriage?

Her headache came on in earnest.

It was dark when the weary horses trudged into Peebles and came to a halt in front of the Flying Duck Inn.

Frances felt so ill that she wanted to vomit. The only thing that saved her from that ignominy was her husband's curt voice coming from the innyard.

She felt dizzy and befuddled when Grunyon assisted her from the carriage.

"My lady?" he asked, seeing her pallor.

"I'm all right," she managed.

Her husband, curse his vitality, strode over to her and announced in a nauseatingly enthusiastic voice that he'd ordered up a neat dinner for them.

"I'm not certain—" Grunyon began, only to be cut off by Frances.

"I wish to dine in my room."

"Do you feel ill?"

"Yes, I do. A headache."

Hawk's lips thinned. Damnable excuse for a wife to present a husband on their second night of marriage. Well, it wouldn't do her any good.

"Fine," he said, and strode into the inn.

A few moments later, he found himself watching her climb the stairs, a chattering maid in her wake.

"You're pushing too hard, my lord," said Grunyon.

"What do you expect me to do? Stop every hour and let her smell the daisies alongside the road?"

"There ain't any daisies."

"Dammit, Grunyon, you know what I mean! Do you so easily forget about my father?"

He saw that his valet would remonstrate further,

and raised his hand. "No, no more. I'm dining now, then I'm going to see to my bride. I fancy she doesn't know that her bedchamber is also mine."

Grunyon stared at him and Hawk suddenly realized that such a speech was most inappropriate. He cursed under his breath and strode into the parlor.

Frances stared at the tray of food and quickly covered it. The headache was ferocious, one of the worst she'd ever experienced. But then again, she'd never been forced to spend ten hours in a closed carriage.

She didn't like to dose herself, but the thought of sleep induced by laudanum was appealing. She searched through her valise and unearthed a small vial of laudanum. She poured several drops into a cup of now tepid tea and drank it down.

She undressed quickly, donned her nightgown, and staggered to her bed.

It didn't occur to her until she crawled to the center of the bed that both the bed and the room were much larger than the one of the night before. She fell back against the soft pillow, too ill to think about anything.

Hawk finished off his meal in fine style. Every few minutes he found himself thinking about the woman upstairs. He had to get it done tonight. He had no idea how many times one had to have sex to bring about conception, but he couldn't be so lucky to manage it the first time. No, he had to get started tonight and keep it up.

He drank three more glasses of brandy. It was close to ten o'clock when he finally made his way up the stairs toward his bedchamber. He was pleasantly drunk, but not too drunk to do his duty. And do his duty he would.

He paused a moment outside the bedchamber, aware

that there was a light coming from beneath the door. So, his bride was awake and waiting for him. He started to turn the knob, and paused yet again. What the devil was that noise? He frowned, then resolutely turned the knob and pushed the door open.

He stepped inside and came to an urgent, appalled halt.

Frances was on the floor, on her knees, vomiting into the chamber pot. Her white nightgown flowed about her and a thick braid fell over her shoulder perilously close to the chamber pot. He felt like a monster. He'd believed her blasted headache all an act.

"My God, what is the matter with you?"

He strode toward her.

7

I was struck all in a heap.

—RICHARD SHERIDAN

Frances heard his voice, but she felt too miserable and too ill to move, much less respond.

"Frances," Hawk said, leaning down over her. "What is wrong?"

She felt his hand on her shoulder, felt his fingers pull back her braid.

"I'll be all right," she said between gritted teeth, and promptly proved herself wrong. Her body shuddered and heaved, but there was nothing left in her stomach.

"Just a moment," Hawk said, now seriously worried. "I'll fetch Grunyon."

But Grunyon was already standing in the open doorway, his face a study of appalled concern, his nightcap askew on his bald head.

"My lord—"

"She's ill. Can you help her?"

"Leave me alone," Frances said. She managed to pull back from the champer pot and come up on her knees. She sent a bleary look toward her husband, then a cramp seized her, and she moaned, wrapping her arms around her stomach.

Grunyon dropped to his knees beside her. "My

lady, did you take anything? Any medicine for your headache?"

Frances managed a nod.

"What was it?"

"Laudanum, I thought, but now I'm sure it was something else. I'm all right now ... no I want to die." She shot a brief look at her husband, who was standing quite close, his eyes narrowed with worry. "Just leave, please."

"Don't be a fool," Hawk said shortly. He leaned down and pulled her to her feet and then into his arms. "Grunyon, get me some water and a clean cloth. She's sweating like a pig."

Frances felt too awful to take more than a passing exception to his words. Another cramp seized her, and she twisted in his arms.

"Shush," he said. "You'll be all right, Frances." He laid her on the bed and covered her shaking body with the blankets. Grunyon handed him a wet cloth and he wiped her face. If anyone could look colorless and green at the same time, she did. Her eyes were tightly closed, her lips pressed firmly together.

"My lord," Grunyon said from behind her, "here's the vial, but I can't tell the contents."

Frances couldn't bear to have this stranger, this husband/man staring down at her as if she were some sort of freak. She forced her eyes open and saw him take the vial from Grunyon and sniff the contents. She turned her face away and said, "I think it was a medicine I packed for colic."

"Colic?" Hawk asked blankly. "Why the devil would you pack something like that?"

"Horses get ill. It's a special mixture of herbs, I didn't want to forget it."

Dear God, Hawk thought, stiffening. What the hell

was it? He said, without thinking, "We must rid your system of it. Come, we—"

"There's nothing left in my system," Frances said, gritting her teeth against another cramp.

"I think tea, my lord," said Grunyon, hovering beside the bed. "Lots of strong hot tea."

Frances groaned.

"Fetch it now," said Hawk. He watched Grunyon's nightcap slide off his head as he rushed toward the door.

He continued wiping Frances' face with the damp cloth. He said more to himself than to her, "So, you were really ill with a headache after all."

Anger at him fought with nausea and the anger won for the moment. "You thought I wasn't? You believed me a liar?"

"Yes," Hawk said honestly, "but not a liar exactly. I just thought you'd do anything to keep me from bedding you."

"You're right about that," Frances said. The nausea faded and she allowed herself to relax. She sighed deeply, but still kept her face averted. She wasn't wearing her spectacles. That, she decided, in a moment of irony, would have been the final touch. She could imagine what she looked like. Heavens, with the spectacles, he would probably have left her hanging over the chamber pot and escaped the room without a word.

He realized she was on the verge of feeling a bit better and remembered well enough that distraction was a good thing for a sick or wounded soldier. For anyone, he supposed. "But why?" he asked after a moment, wanting to distract her, but also utterly serious.

He doesn't even realize how arrogant and conceited he is, Frances thought.

"We are married, Frances. You know that we must sleep together and make . . . and be intimate."

He sounded so genuinely confused that she wanted to laugh. "I saw you naked, you know," she said.

"What?" He quickly placed his hand on her forehead, wondering if she'd lapsed into delusion.

"When you were bathing in the loch, the day you arrived at Kilbracken. I was there. I didn't know who you were, at first."

"Ah," he said, and grinned. He remembered clearly the shock of that icy water. "In that case, you must know from your firsthand observation that I'm not ill-formed."

"No," she sighed. "No, you're not. Not excessively, in any case, save perhaps for the hair. You've a lot of it and it's black."

Hawk stared down at her, bemused. Just to keep her distracted, he said smoothly, "At least I provided you the opportunity to see what you were getting in a husband. I wish I had enjoyed the same opportunity and assurance."

She sucked in her breath.

"My lord, here is the tea."

"Thank you, Grunyon. I'll see that she downs all of it. I'll call if I need you."

Grunyon gazed a moment at his mistress, lying in a wretched huddle in the center of the large bed. Poor little mite, he thought, shaking his head. Then he looked at her, really looked. Without the spectacles, she wasn't at all homely. Not at all. Even though her hair looked sweaty and lank in its braid, it was a lovely color and the braid thick as his wrist. Was the earl blind? He stepped back and watched his master gently lift his wife and put the teacup to her pale lips.

"It's not too hot," Hawk said, feeling her resist him. "Come on, drink it."

She felt too weak to argue with him. She drank, all of it. He eased her onto her back, turned, and poured another cup.

"Please, please, just leave," Frances said. He'd seen her vilely ill; it was mortifying.

"I can't. This is my bedchamber as well as yours. Come on, my girl, drink some more."

"No, no more."

Her refusal had no effect on him. She drank two more cups of the bitter hot tea, but with ill grace. "Well done," Hawk said.

It needed but this, she thought, realizing she had to relieve herself. At that moment, she wished she could throw up the damned tea. But she didn't. It had washed right through her.

"Sir," she began, "I would ask that you leave me for a while. Please."

"Sir? Why? Really, Frances, I'm not such a cold-blooded brute to leave you alone when you're ill."

"I have to use the chamber pot," she said baldly, beyond niceties.

"Again? Ah, good. Grunyon emptied it. Come along, I'll help you."

"Sir . . . Philip . . . Hawk, please. Go away now."

"Frances, stop being an ass." He was getting impatient with her. "For heaven's sake, my sensibilities won't be unduly lacerated by your vomiting, for God's sake."

"It's not my mouth that needs the chamber pot!"

He laughed, he couldn't help himself. "I see," he said, and quickly rose. "Can you manage alone?"

"Get out!"

"You have five minutes. I don't want to take the chance of finding you sprawled unconscious in a heap on the floor." With that, Hawk strode out of the room, closing the door behind him.

"My lord, why are you leaving her ladyship?"

"You still up, Grunyon? Of course you are, I'm turning into a blithering idiot. Yes, I left her alone. She had to use the chamber pot."

"But in that case . . ." Grunyon headed toward the door. "I'll help her, my lord, I'll—"

Hawk laughed. "She had to relieve herself after the three cups of tea."

"Oh," Grunyon said, and surprised Hawk by blushing right to his eyebrows.

Hawk grew abruptly serious. "Do you think we should fetch a doctor?"

Grunyon shook his head. "If she managed to keep the tea down, she will be all right, I believe."

"Down and through," said Hawk.

"My lord!"

"Sorry," Hawk said. He thrashed his fingers through his hair. "This has been the strangest two days of my life. I really thought she was lying about the headache to avoid . . . well, to keep from—"

"Yes, my lord," Grunyon said quickly. "I do understand."

"I think her five minutes are up. Go to bed, Grunyon. I intend to." He grinned. "Hell, a first time for everything. Sleeping with a woman and not making love to her."

"My lord!"

He quirked an eyebrow at his valet, then quickly entered the bedchamber. Actually it was also a first time to sleep with a woman who had been vilely ill. There was but one candle lit on the small table beside the bed. Frances was turned on her side away from him, the blankets drawn to her nose.

"How do you feel?"

"All right," she said, not emerging from the warm and protective cocoon.

He wanted to leave but knew that he couldn't. He said, "Look, Frances, I'm staying with you tonight. If you get ill again, you don't want to be alone."

"I won't get ill again."

"You won't, huh? If you're so smart, then why did you drink down horse-colic medicine?"

"Go the devil," she said very clearly.

Hawk was taken aback for a moment. So she wasn't all dimness and diffidence. There was a bit of bite to her when pushed hard enough.

"Go to sleep," he said. "You may be certain that I shan't ravish you tonight."

Tonight.

Hawk turned away and stripped off his clothes. Out of long habit, he neatly folded them over the back of a chair. When he returned to the bed, he saw that Frances was hugging the far edge, so close that he expected her to crash to the floor at any moment. It would serve her right, he thought, feeling suddenly completely out of charity with her. Silly twit. Did she find his hairiness that repugnant? Now, if she was really against male hair, she should have met his old sergeant, Dickie Hobbs. Lord, the man had a mat of hair on his damned back! The jest among his men had been to the effect that woman could run her hands through Dickie's hair and never finish until she'd reached the soles of his feet.

Frances felt the mattress give when he got into bed. She held her breath, but he stayed on his side. How odd, she managed to think some minutes later, finally secure in her belief that he would keep his word. She was lying in bed with a man. She was so nervous that it took her some minutes to realize that her stomach was back to normal and that her husband was asleep.

He turned onto his stomach.

He began to snore.

Frances gritted her teeth and clamped the pillow around her ears.

She awoke to find herself quite alone. She queried her body and found a neutral response. No more cramps, no more nausea. But the thought of another interminable day spent riding in that lurching carriage gave her considerable pause. At least her husband, in a spate of good manners, had dressed and left her alone. She glanced toward the small clock on the mantel. It was only six o'clock in the morning.

She sat up in bed and sighed. He would want to leave, and very soon. *I'm being a selfish ninny. His father is very ill and he is anxious to see him.*

She found the basin of water he'd used the previous evening to bathe her face and quickly washed herself. She was dressed, her hair in a severe, dull bun, her spectacles in place, within ten minutes. She came down the inn stairs, only to draw up at the sound of her husband's voice.

"I suppose it would be monstrous of me to ask her to get out of bed," Hawk said. "Damn, I don't wish to waste another day!"

"I can't see that there is a choice, my lord," came Grunyon's voice.

"No, I suppose you're right."

He could at least act a bit concerned, Frances thought, her lips tightening. Show some worry for me. She squared her shoulders and descended the stairs.

"I should like a bit of breakfast before we leave, my lord," she said.

"Frances! What the devil are you doing out of bed?"

"I . . . that is, we . . . well, I think we should continue, my lord."

"Philip," he said.

"Yes, well, Philip."

"Are you certain?"

She flinched a bit, seeing that he was closely regarding her. She remembered to squint at him.

"Of course."

They breakfasted in silence. Thirty minutes later, Frances was standing by the open carriage door.

Hawk, who had just mounted Ebony, saw the look of strain on her face, the dread. He started to say something, when he saw her stiffen and climb into the carriage. She wasn't a bad sort at all, he thought. No weak-willed fragile little lady. She had guts.

Still, Hawk had Grunyon pull off the road at least every two hours during the day.

Frances realized his kindness, but couldn't bring herself to say anything conciliatory to him.

When they stopped for the night in Jedburgh, she didn't have the slightest twinge from her head.

More's the pity, she thought, wondering what the devil she was supposed to do tonight to keep him at bay. She thought of the horse-colic medicine and grinned ruefully.

She was silent as her mouse image all during dinner.

Hawk said at last, "I'm tiring rapidly of haggis."

Frances forked down an extra large bite.

Hawk studied her bent head a moment, then said, "You're feeling the thing now?"

Frances jerked up, unable to help herself. And he saw the wariness, the distaste on her face. She squinted at him and he said sharply, wondering even as he spoke if he would be able to bring himself up to performance snuff, "For God's sake, Frances, 'tis not a question designed to get me in your bed!"

"Yes," she said, eyeing her haggis with grave concentration, "I am feeling much better. Thank you for stopping during the day. I am not used to riding in a closed carriage."

"What are you used to?"

"Riding my own horse, of course, or walking."

"I have no extra horse and you can't walk to York."

"No, I can't."

He eyed her with mounting frustration. Why the devil couldn't she carry on a civil conversation with him? Then he wanted to laugh at himself, remembering clearly his reasons for selecting her over her sisters. She didn't chatter. She was quiet and homely as a mouse. She wouldn't bother him or make demands on his time or ask for attention.

He said suddenly, "Was I the first man you'd ever seen?"

She understood him very well, but she said slowly, "Perhaps you believe Kilbracken to be isolated, my lord, but both sexes were present from time to time."

"Philip," he said.

She said nothing, merely toyed with her wine goblet.

"Naked, I meant."

"Of course not."

That drew him up short. "You've seen a lot of naked men?"

"No, a couple of boys, that's all. And my little brother, Alex, of course. They didn't have any hair."

For a moment he thought she was mocking him, but no, that couldn't be true. She was too timid, to damned dull for that. And far too ugly. No, not really ugly, just . . .

"Frances, you'll have to accustom yourself to me sooner or later."

"I suppose that's true enough."

"Just as I will have to accustom myself to you."

Aha, she thought, wishing she could smack his handsome face, it's a thought that turns your stomach, isn't it?

"I hope that you will not," she said in a flat voice.

Hawk said, his voice equally flat and emotionless, "Well, you needn't worry about it tonight. You have your own bedchamber."

"Excellent," said Frances, and squinted up at him. She saw him stiffen and quickly lowered her head to hide her triumphant smile.

They reached York two nights later, near to ten o'clock. The horses were exhausted, as was Hawk. It was still a fifteen-mile trek to Desborough Hall. He wanted to push on but knew he couldn't.

Frances was so bored she wanted to scream. And she was ravenous.

English fare, she thought, staring some thirty minutes later at the boiled beef and tasteless potatoes. But she ate.

Hawk had made up his mind. He had let her be for the past two nights. Tonight, he thought, he had to consummate their union. The last thing he wanted was for his servants at Desborough Hall to find her virgin's blood on the sheets. They'd been married five days. It was time. I will make her relax, he thought, and said, "Tomorrow before luncheon, we'll arrive at my estate, Desborough Hall."

"Hmmm," said Frances, not looking up.

"It belonged to my older brother, Nevil, you know. Indeed, he was the Earl of Rothermere until his death some fifteen months ago."

"I am sorry," said Frances.

"It was very odd," Hawk continued, speaking now for his own peace of mind rather than to her. "It was a yachting accident, near to Southampton. He drowned. I've been to Desborough Hall only three times since I returned to England."

"Why?"

A woman of few words. He fiddled with his brandy snifter for a few moments, then shrugged. "I don't know. I suppose it's because Desborough Hall was never mine, never meant to belong to me. I suppose I'm still not used to being my father's heir and the Earl of Rothermere. It's a beautiful estate."

So, Frances thought, now seeing the light clearly, this is where I'm to be immured. Well, it could certainly be worse.

"Gentlemen in London will call me Rothermere and I won't respond. I feel like an interloper, I guess. As I mentioned to you, most people call me Hawk." He grinned and she noted with dissatisfaction that he had very straight, very white teeth. "Thank God for the number of army friends. They got it started, you see. The Hawk part, that is."

He was sounding positively human, and it made Frances uncomfortable. As long as he acted arrogant and conceited, she could keep him in excellent perspective.

She managed a sound that gave him the impression that she was listening, and he continued, "I'd always assumed that the army would be my life. I found it somewhat difficult to adjust to the demands of a gentleman of leisure."

Ah, but you have adjusted, haven't you, beautifully?

She merely nodded this time, biting her tongue to keep her sarcastic words behind her teeth.

"You will like Desborough Hall," Hawk continued after he'd cracked a walnut between his long fingers. "It is a well-run estate."

Does he believe me utterly stupid? she wondered. She wanted to tell him that she knew his intentions well enough.

"We will stay but one day. Then we must leave for Chandos Chase, my father's estate in Suffolk. I'm sorry, Frances, that there won't be more time for you to rest, but—"

"I understand, my lord. You wish to see your father as quickly as possible."

"Philip."

"Yes. If you wish, I shouldn't mind continuing directly to your father."

"No. We must stop. The horses are blown. I'm certain you'll appreciate not riding in a closed carriage for a while."

A very short while, she thought.

He fell silent, and Frances, after some minutes, decided his confidences, such as they were, were at an end. She carefully folded her napkin and placed it beside her plate.

"I will bid you good night, my lord."

"Philip."

"Yes, in any case, I am tired. I will see you in the morning."

Hawk watched her rise, and his eyes went over her body. It won't be too bad, he thought. He elected to say nothing to her. He would simply appear and get the damned business over with.

"Good night," he said, and watched her walk from the private parlor.

To Frances' delight, a tub of hot water was waiting for her in her bedchamber. At least there was one good thing about being in England. And there was a maid, whose name was Margaret. She sank into the water with a blissful sigh.

Margaret washed her hair for her. I've died and gone to heaven, Frances thought. No one had ever washed her hair for her before, save for that one time when she was twelve and ill and Adelaide had assisted her.

She thought of Desborough Hall, her future home, while Margaret combed her hair before the fireplace.

She tried to imagine living there, not knowing a single soul, and shuddered.

"You're cold, my lady?"

"No, Margaret. Is my hair dry yet?"

"Almost, just a few more minutes. You have beautiful hair, my lady."

"Thank you." I'm in England, she thought, and shuddered yet again. A foreign country. A foreign husband.

She wanted to cry, but she didn't. "I wish to go to bed now, Margaret."

She began to braid her hair, but stopped at Margaret's gasp.

"I shouldn't, my lady. I'll comb it for you tomorrow."

"Very well," Frances said.

Ten minutes later, she was lying in the middle of her bed, her hair spread on the pillow, the room utterly dark.

She heard footsteps in the corridor outside her room, and frowned. Then the doorknob turned.

Heart pounding, Frances sat up, jerking the covers to her nose.

Her husband walked into her bedchamber and closed the door behind him.

❧ 8 ❧

Great souls suffer in silence.
—FRIEDRICH VON SCHILLER

"What are you doing in here? What do you want?"

Her voice rang out shrill and hoarse. Hawk saw her outline in the bed from the dim corridor light. She was sitting up, the covers pulled to her chin. He closed the bedchamber door and calmly walked into the room.

"Get out of here, my lord! You shouldn't be here, 'tis not your bedchamber!"

He could hear her breathing—fast, nearly gasping. "Frances," he said, trying to sound reassuring, "I am here to consummate our marriage. It won't take long, I promise you. All you have to do is—"

"No! Get out!"

"—lie quietly. I'll try not to hurt you."

Frances heard the determination in his voice. She stuffed her fist in her mouth at the sounds of him undressing. When his boots hit the floor, she nearly shouted, "I won't have it, my lord, I—"

"Philip," he said. "Hush now, Frances. You are my wife and you will obey me. Let me remind you that this is your duty as a wife."

She knew all about duty, but she'd hoped that he believed her ugly enough to forgo this whatever-it-was for a while longer.

"I really don't feel well," she tried, and flinched at his chuckle.

"Did you drink more horse-colic medicine?"

"No, but I wish I had!"

He suddenly sat down on the side of the bed, and Frances scrambled away. He reached out his hand and touched soft, slightly damp hair. He wondered, not at all amused, if she wore one of her ridiculous caps to bed.

He could hear her breathing again, nearly feel her fear. He wished he'd left a candle burning, but imagined ruefully that he'd be unable to do his duty if he had to look at her.

"Frances," he said, his voice still calm and gentle, "you must trust me. I know that you are . . . worried about this"—that was a seemingly vast understatement, he thought—"but it won't be so bad, I swear it. I know what I'm doing, and if you'll just cooperate, it will be much easier for you. Don't fight me, Frances."

Frances thought suddenly of the dreams she'd had as a girl. Dreams of a man who would love her and woo her and respect her and want all of her. It was nearly too much, this cold deliberation, this ghastly objective of his. She closed her eyes, knowing well enough that there was no hope for it.

"All right," she managed in a thread of a whisper.

"Just lie still."

"All right." And she did, on her back, her eyes tightly closed even though the room was completely dark. She felt him draw back the covers, felt him lightly touch her cheek with his fingertips. She flinched away.

I had more fun in a raging battle, Hawk thought. He quickly grasped her nightgown and pulled it up to her waist.

"Hold still," he said, his hand coming down on her

stomach. She was very soft, he thought, his fingers
seeking lower. He felt the nest of curls between her
thighs and paused a moment. He heard her suck in her
breath, and quickly moved down and parted her legs.
Her flesh was soft, her thighs slender. He paused a
moment.

"Frances, you do know what we will do, don't you?"

We? She wanted to spit at him, tell him to go to the
devil, but the words stuck in her throat.

Hawk waited a few more moments for her to answer, then said, "You are a virgin, aren't you?" *Of
course she is, you damned fool!* "Frances, I understand that it is natural to be afraid of something you
don't know about—"

"I understand," she whispered, just wanting it to be
over with and him gone.

"Good," he said for want of anything better.

His fingers stroked up to find her and he realized at
that moment that he would hurt her if he came into
her now. Not just because of her virginity. She wasn't
ready for him. She wasn't fighting him, but her body
certainly was. How did one make one's wife ready?
He certainly couldn't caress her like he did his mistresses; it would embarrass her horribly and make
matters but worse. He shook his head, wishing now
that he'd thought to cover his member with cream to
ease his way into her.

Still, he touched her lightly, his finger gently seeking her entrance. Her flesh was soft and cold. She
jerked away and made a soft, frightened cry.

I can't do it, not this way, he thought, and retreated. "Lie still, Frances, I'll be back shortly."

He quickly pulled on his trousers, then he was gone.

Frances jerked her nightgown down, then lay back
again, not moving. Where had he gone? What was he
doing? She looked wildly toward the area where the

window was and considered jumping. Ninny! She swallowed, her body tense, her mind whirling.

There's nothing you can do, save bear it. Nothing at all. Don't carry on like a silly fool. He told you to lie still and that it would be over with quickly.

But where had he gone?

The bedchamber door opened again, then closed.

"Frances?"

"Yes?" she managed on a croak.

"Just stay put."

What he had expected? That she would be cowering in the corner? That she would have jumped from the window? That she had a pistol and would shoot him? She had a sudden picture of him pulling her out from under the bed.

Hawk rubbed himself with the cream and approached the bed again. Hell, he thought, when he realized that she'd pulled down her nightgown. He worked it up again over her hips to her waist.

"Don't be frightened," he said, his hands pulling her legs apart.

He was hard and ready—surprising, considering this was the last woman on earth he wanted to take.

Frances felt him press against her. He was naked. She could feel the hair on his legs against her. She felt his large hands clasping her hips and drawing her up.

"Just hold still," he said again, almost a litany now.

Hawk had never before made love to a woman in the dark. It was damned difficult. He parted her quickly with his fingers, feeling her flinch, then guided himself forward. He eased inside her and stopped when she cried out. Had he hurt her already?

"It's all right, Frances," he said. "I'll go slowly." And he did, just a bit at a time. He felt how small she was, how she was stretching to accommodate him. He wanted suddenly to thrust deep, but kept himself in check. Taking a virgin was a heady thing. No, not just a virgin, for God's sake, he told himself. She was a lady and his wife, and she deserved to be handled as gently as he could manage. He was glad he'd gotten the cream. He'd been thoughtful and spared her unnecessary pain. Why did he want to drive into her, fill her with himself? He bit down on his lower lip. He was doing just as he ought, and he would continue to. Slowly, very slowly, no sudden movements.

Frances felt frozen and tense, her hands fisting the sheet at her sides. She didn't feel any sharp pain, just a tremendous fullness and stretching. *But he's inside your body.* Then she felt a jolt of pain. He butted against her maidenhead.

"Frances," he said, wishing yet again he could see her to judge if he were hurting her. Hell, she couldn't wear her spectacles to bed, could she?

"Yes?"

She sounded calm enough, resigned, in fact.

"You're going to feel a bit of . . . discomfort. It's your maidenhead and I've got to get through it. Just relax, all right?"

"No," she said very clearly. "No, please stop. Please, just go away."

"I can't," he said, and before she could catch her breath, he tore through the small barrier.

She screamed at the sudden tearing pain, her body bucking wildly to be rid of him.

He came down on top of her to hold her still with his weight. "Hush," he said, his face pressed against hers. "The rest won't be so bad, I promise."

She hurt, deep inside, raw hurt. And he was the cause of the hurt and he was inside her, so deep. She hadn't known, hadn't realized that her body could allow for such an invasion.

She didn't want to cry, but besides the pain, she felt

defiled and used and angry. And helpless. She stuffed her fist into her mouth, but the sobs broke through. She couldn't help it. She tried to shove him off, but her hands come in contact with his naked shoulders. She dropped her arms back to her sides and clutched at the rumpled sheet beneath her.

She felt him rear above her, felt him moving inside her. Back and forth.

It hurt, but not as much now.

"That's it, Frances," Hawk said between gritted teeth. He felt himself ready to burst, and because there was no reason to draw out this damnable encounter, he thrust deep, letting himself go, spewing inside her.

She felt him tense, heard a deep sort of growl come from his throat. Then she felt the wetness, and knew it was from him.

She didn't move.

She hated him. This thing he'd done to her was vile, unforgivable.

Hawk caught his breath, feeling her flesh convulse about him, and quickly withdrew from her. He felt her flinch, and was sorry for the pain he'd caused her, but dammit, he'd done it quickly, as efficiently as he could manage it.

"Next time, it won't hurt," he said. Did a husband always have to use a cream when he took his wife? He supposed so. Since ladies and wives experienced no passion, a husband simply had to make things as easy as possible. He rolled off the bed and rose. His heart was still pounding from his release.

"Are you all right, Frances?" he asked, suddenly concerned at her silence.

"Yes," she said, her voice dull and utterly lifeless.

He frowned toward her, then sighed. Suddenly he wondered how little she knew. He cursed softly, then said, "When I came into you, I broke through your maidenhead. Please don't be worried if tomorrow you see blood. It happens like that the first time. There won't be any pain for you the next time, or blood." At least he hoped not. He'd never taken a virgin before, and was uncertain.

With those comforting words, he quickly dressed and strode toward the door.

"I will see you in the morning, Frances," he said. "Uh, sleep well." And he left her.

Now, Frances thought, now I shall jump through that window. But she didn't move. She felt sore, her body ached. And there was wetness between her legs.

Blood? His seed?

She didn't want to know.

There won't be any pain for you the next time. Next time! How long did it take to make a child?—for surely that was his only reason for doing this to her. How many times would she have to put up with being used like an animal? She wondered if he had really hurt her badly, and only pretended it was her maidenhead. She pictured herself as a castle being breached by a huge battering ram. She didn't smile at the image.

She was angry with herself when she tasted salty tears on her lips. "I hate you," she whispered into the darkness.

She wasn't certain whether it was her husband she hated, or herself.

She rose slowly and padded to the basin atop the commode. She didn't want to see—anything—and quickly pressed the wet cloth against herself.

Once in his own bed, Hawk stretched his arms over his head. All in all, he was pleased with himself. He'd treated his wife with all the respect she was due. He had hurt her, but it was to be expected that first time.

She'd been very small. He frowned as his body reacted to the image of thrusting inside her, filling her. He'd leave her alone for a couple of nights. She would probably be very sore. After all, he was a man, and large, and she was unused to sex.

But did she have to act as if he were killing her? Abusing her, for God's sake?

I can't face him, Frances thought, her hand on the knob of her bedchamber door. I simply can't.

What are you going to do, then, ninny, stay like a coward in this ridiculous room?

She drew a deep breath and opened the door. She cannoned into the corridor while she still felt courageous. She cannoned right into her husband.

"Frances!" His hand clasped her upper arms. "Are you all right?"

God no, I'm not! She said nothing. She wished he would suddenly, magically disappear—from the face of the earth. To her utter chagrin, when he released her, her eyes fell downward, to his belly and groin.

He'd been so large the night before. Where was it? How . . . Was he like a stallion? Did he increase in size only when . . . ?

Hawk chuckled, he couldn't help himself. Her thoughts were so clear on her face.

Her eyes flew upward. Belatedly, she squinted.

But he was too amused to notice the small distorted eyes behind the thick lenses. He said, rumbling laughter still deep in his chest, "I thought you said you saw me naked in the loch."

"I did," she said, choking with embarrassment.

"I'm certain you realized that the water was damnably cold, frigid in fact."

What did that have to with anything? "Of course the water is cold this time of year," she said, hoping her voice was as cold as that water. "I enjoyed watching you shiver." Ah, that sounded nice and nasty.

But still that wretched smile was on his face. "Then you must know that men aren't always ready to, well, to, ah, indulge in—"

"I didn't look at that part of you! Oh, stop it!" She flung up her hands to ward off further drawing comments from him. She quickly turned on her heels and fled down the inn stairs. She heard his laughter behind her.

"You miserable animal . . . stallion," she said under her breath. She met Grunyon at the foot of the stairs, and flushed to her puce cap.

He smiled at her with grave understanding. "Good morning, my lady. Breakfast is served in the private parlor."

Hawk joined her some minutes later. He was no longer laughing—or smiling, for that matter. He was looking quite serious. "Frances," he said gently, for he was now writhing in guilt for embarrassing her and baiting her, "are you all right? No . . . aftereffects?"

"No," she said coldly, "I bathed. In the dark. After you took yourself off."

So much for my concern, he thought, and seated himself. He looked with satisfaction at the array of food on the table. Ah, thick sirloin. Rare, just as he liked it.

As he chewed on the delicious beef, he remarked upon the disgusting cap that covered most of her head. He could just imagine the reaction of the staff at Desborough Hall, much less his father's reaction. He cleared his throat, wondering how to tell her that she looked deplorable.

He shook his head at himself. He couldn't bring himself to criticize her, not just yet.

"We will go immediately to Desborough Hall," he

said after a long, strained moment. "Soon, I will bring you back to York. It's a lovely city and boasts many sites you would enjoy."

She said nothing, merely spread her scrambled eggs about her plate.

He forged ahead, taking her silence as a positive sign. "There are, uh, very nice shops here. You know what I mean. The modistes are excellent."

Frances silently vowed to wear this gown until it rotted off her body.

"It's also very probable that there are competent medical men here. Perhaps we could see to your getting some more . . . well, new spectacles. Is your eyesight very bad?"

She gave him a particularly vicious squint. "Yes," she said, "terrible."

Hawk eyed her with growing impatience. Didn't she realize how very kind he had been to her? He'd spared her all the embarrassment he could. Well, he amended to himself, he had been a bit rough with her this morning in the corridor, but damn her, why didn't she say something, anything, to show that she was at least thinking?

Couldn't she at least be a bit civil?

He downed some excellent English ale, then slammed down his mug. "Are you ready?" he asked, his voice curt.

"Certainly," Frances said. She wished she had something to bang on the table.

Frances didn't realize that ladies and gentlemen of the English *ton* viewed northern England, this county in particular, as the wilds of Yorkshire. It was beautiful, she thought. Rough and wild, with rolling hills. Untamed, like Scotland, like home. She felt tears sting the back of her eyes and quickly sniffed them back.

They traveled due south, close to a winding river,

the River Ouse, Grunyon told her when they stopped for a rest near Naburn Moor. The moor fascinated her. It was desolate, so unlike the neat farmlands that surrounded it.

"Desborough Hall," Hawk continued to her, "is near Stillingfleet. East, to be exact, quite close to the river. Our closest town is Acaster Selby."

They rode another thirty minutes through farming country and several small villages.

Then Desborough Hall came into view.

France's jaw dropped as the carriage wended its way down the long tree-lined drive. It was a stud! She saw the huge stables, their red slate roofs gleaming in the late-morning sun.

Not only a stud, she thought, but racing stables as well. There were huge paddocks, enclosed with white fences, for exercising and training. For the first time since she'd left home, Frances felt a spurt of excitement. She'd heard that northern England was renowned for its studs and racing stables, but hadn't thought to ask if Desborough Hall was amongst them. Why the devil hadn't her precious husband mentioned it to her? Well, she decided, craning her neck to see the Hall, if she had to be dumped somewhere, this was the place to be dumped.

9

> *There is a wicked inclination in most people to suppose an old man decayed in his intellects.*
>
> —SAMUEL JOHNSON

"Father! What are you doing here? You're ill . . . you're supposed to be . . ."

Hawk broke off in speechless confusion.

The marquess beamed down at his disconcerted, gape-mouthed son from the steps of the Hall.

"Glad you're home, my boy," he said, and bounded down the deeply indented marble steps to the drive. He clapped Hawk on the shoulder.

Hawk managed to grit out, "You're the picture of health. You're positively blooming."

"You sound disappointed, son." A thick white eyebrow soared upward. "Did you expect me to have cocked up my toes? No, couldn't do that. Too much to be done, you know."

"Of course I'm not disappointed! I'm happy, I'm ecstatic and astonished."

"That's a relief, Hawk. Now, where's your bride?"

Grunyon was letting down the carriage steps. Frances emerged, to see an older version of her husband striding toward her. No, she quickly amended, not all that exact a copy—his nose was a veritable beak. He was the one who deserved the name Hawk. His hair was white and very thick, just as, she imagined, her

126

husband's would be in the years to come, and his very sharp, piercing eyes were just a shade or two darker than his son's. He was built on more slender lines, not big-boned and massive like Hawk.

"It's Frances, isn't it?" said the marquess, stepping forward to hug her close.

"Yes, my lord, I am Frances Kilbracken."

"Nay, lass," said the marquess, in a broad Scottish brogue, his eyes twinkling down at her, "you're the Countess of Rothermere, Frances Hawksbury. I trust you left your father—that rascal!—quite up to snuff?"

"Father is up to it, sir, as well as takes it," Frances said. How did he know who she was? What the devil was going on here? Her husband had told her his father was gravely ill. Just an hour before, when they'd stopped for a few minutes, he'd informed her again, his voice low and worried, that they would leave at first light on the morrow to travel to Chandos Chase.

"I don't understand, sir," she said.

"I do," said Hawk, his voice grim. "Oh, indeed I'm beginning to understand quite well."

Frances' eyes swung to her husband. He sounded utterly furious. He sounded almost . . . betrayed. If a man could be said to gnash his teeth, Hawk was doing it.

The marquess ignored his son, and wrapped his arm about Frances' shoulders, giving her another affectionate hug. "All the staff is waiting to meet you, my dear. Come along. You too, Hawk. I hope the staff hasn't forgotten who you are! Here only three times in the past year, isn't that all? Grunyon, don't strain your back! Here is Ralph to assist you with the luggage!"

Indeed, Frances saw with a sinking heart, there were at least twenty servants lined up in front of the great double doors of Desborough Hall, the women on one side, the men on the other. She saw vaguely the Hawksbury crest above the door and remembered the motto: *With a strong hand.* And her snide remark about a strong fist. Whose fist here was the strongest? she wondered, darting a glance from her husband to her father-in-law.

How does he know which daughter I am? she wondered yet again, her feet dragging as the marquess walked beside her toward the array of well-dressed servants. English servants. They would hate her, despise her.

She looked hideous, she well knew it. But the marquess didn't seem to have noticed. If he had noticed, it hadn't fazed him in the least. Her hand went up to pull off the spectacles.

"My damned servants are garbed better than you," she heard Hawk say in an angry undertone. "God, I don't believe this!"

She left her spectacles firmly balanced on her nose, and thrust her chin upward.

What didn't he believe? Why wasn't he delighted that his father wasn't dying? Why was he acting like such a boorish lout?

The marquess said jovially, "This devout personage, my dear, is Otis, the butler of Desborough Hall. Otis, this is your new mistress, Lady Frances."

Not a muscle moved on that lined, austere face, but to Frances' sensitive eye, there did seem to be a slight spasm of distaste about the man's thin lips. An English butler, she thought, the most terrifying of God's creatures.

"Hello, Otis," she said in a clear voice.

"My lady," Otis said, bowing from the waist. "Welcome to Desborough Hall."

"And this, Frances, is Mrs. Jerkins, a gem of a

housekeeper. She and I are growing into dotage together."

Mrs. Jerkins, looking stolid and terribly efficient in an array of black bombazine, proffered Frances a curtsy. She looked to be a long way from the state of dotage, as did Frances' exuberant father-in-law for that matter. "My lady," she said in her low, somewhat hoarse voice.

"A pleasure, Mrs. Jerkins." Goodness, Frances thought, her courage dropping to her toes, the housekeeper should be on Wellington's staff. She looked formidable, her will iron.

"I will introduce you to the staff tomorrow, my lady," said Mrs. Jerkins, and clapped her hands. Like magic, the long line of women faded away. Otis, taking his cue from the marquess' nod, dismissed the men.

"Don't know why we use the 'Mrs.,' " the marquess whispered in Frances' ear. "Never been married. I suppose she added it for dignity's sake. Must have been decades ago."

Hawk suddenly cleared his throat. He was furious, so furious he wanted to spit. And here his damned father was introducing Frances to *his* servants, as if Desborough Hall belonged to him!

"Otis," he said in an overly loud voice, "have another footman assist Ralph with the luggage."

"Yes, my lord," said Otis, and snapped his fingers.

"He," Frances said, looking briefly over at her husband, "did not tell me that Desborough Hall was a stud. It is also a racing stable, isn't it, sir?"

"Yes, indeed," said the marquess. "At least it was until Nevil died. Hawk, more's the pity, has no interest in it. It's falling to bits now. Well, my dear, what do you think of your new home? The old Hall—called the Grange—was gutted back under Queen Anne.

The present Hall dates from about 1715, not old at all, built by a fellow called Sir John Vanbrugh. All that classical nonsense, you'll see. Palladian, I believe it's called. Don't have the foggiest idea what that means, though."

"Palladian," said Hawk in a ferociously calm voice, "refers to the classical Rome style of Palladio."

The marquess shrugged good-naturedly. "Nonsense," he said, winking at Frances.

"Who was Palladio?" Frances asked.

"An Italian architect," said Hawk curtly.

"Sixteenth-century," Grunyon said as he trudged by them with a heavy valise.

I don't believe this is happening, Frances thought, so confused that she wanted to yell. She felt as though she were sitting on a very narrow fence and a battle was raging on either side of her.

"Fellow should be forgotten," said the marquess. "He stuck his spoon in the wall long enough ago. Come along, Frances, I'll show you a bit of Desborough Hall, then you must rest." He sent a rueful glance toward his glowering son. "I imagine that your journey here from Loch Lomond was a bit . . . hurried."

"At the very least," said Hawk. "Going, staying, and coming back."

"The name Desborough Hall harks back to Queen Anne's time again," the marquess said, ignoring his son. "Charlotte Desborough was a great heiress. She brought this magnificent house with her as a dowry."

I didn't even bring a sou, Frances thought, staring up at the huge two-story rectangular edifice.

"It always belongs to the eldest son. The second-generation son started the stud and racing stables. The Desborough stud has been revered and quite famous for many years, not to mention the famous race horses produced here. I'll never forget Fortune, a great stallion who swept all other horses off the tracks. Yes, it was back in 1785, as I recall. Nothing to match him at Newmarket. Not to compare to the famous Eclipse, of course, but no racer compared to him! Fortune was bred off a thoroughbred dam and a Barb sire. Strong as the devil, he was."

Frances was certain now that she heard Hawk grinding his teeth again.

She was led into the grand entrance hall, actually an elaborate drawing room, its ceiling the full height of the mansion, with a fireplace and balconies guarded by wrought-iron gratings. White columns soared everywhere. She followed the marquess into the Western Corridor, through the Smoking Room, and finally into the West Drawing Room. There were George Stubbs paintings of horses on many of the walls. She was aware of elegant furnishings, of so many white walls that it was nearly blinding. "Look closely at the pilasters," the marquess said, and Frances, thankful that he was pointing to something, realized that it meant the innumerable sculptured columns. "And of course the arcadings are famous, you know." Arches, Frances thought, pure-and-simple arches. Cornices, she knew, grateful that she knew *something,* comprised all the ornamental moldings at the tops of the walls. For someone who said "nonsense" about Palladian, the marquess certainly seemed to know his architecture.

Frances murmured again and again, her voice becoming more dazed by the moment, "So elegant, my lord. So very exquisite. So very . . . ah, nice."

She was most aware of her husband's furious silence.

The marquess came to a sudden halt. "Frances, my dear, you are ready to rest now, are you not?" At her silent nod, he continued, "I have asked Mrs. Jerkins to assign a maid to you." He pulled on a bellcord, and very quickly a young woman appeared, fresh-faced, shyly smiling. She gave Frances deep curtsy. "My name's Agnes, my lady," she said.

And the old reprobate has the gall to assign my wife a maid, all without consulting me! Hawk stood silently, fuming.

Frances nodded, then turned to her father-in-law. "Thank you, sir," she said, and he smiled at the obvious gratitude in her voice.

"You rest until dinner, my dear," the marquess said, and patted her cheek. She looked toward her husband, but his face was a closed thundercloud.

As Frances followed Agnes out into the main entry hall, she heard Hawk say furiously, "You damned old bounder! You planned this whole thing, didn't you? You wanted me married, so you pretended that affecting final illness! God, I don't believe it!"

"You will forgive this pious old fraud, son?"

Frances stiffened, Hawk's words flowing through her, but she continued to follow Agnes up the wide staircase toward the vast Eastern Corridor.

"Your rooms . . . well, they're called Lady Dawnay's Rooms—and of course, they adjoin the earl's suite."

"Marvelous," Frances said under her breath. She felt as though she'd wandered into Bedlam, and now she was, willy-nilly, one of the inmates. At least Agnes didn't give her a lecture on pediments and pilasters.

In the Smoking Room, Hawk was still raging in fine form.

"Well, it's the truth, isn't it? All that damned illness of yours was just an act, a ruse."

"A son should never underestimate his father," said the marquess, not visibly moved by his son's tirade.

"Now you cite me a damnable platitude!"

"Not really. I just made it up, but perhaps it is worthy of being remarked upon in future generations.

Now, Hawk, there's no reason for you to get so riled. Really, my boy—"

"No reason!" Hawk thrust his hands into his pockets and began to pace the length of the room. His father regarded his progress with mild interest.

"You manipulated me!"

"Well, yes, I suppose you could say that," the marquess conceded. "In a more felicitous manner, perhaps. But it was time, Hawk, time for you to marry and set up your nursery. You're not getting any younger, you know."

"I'm twenty-six! Not exactly in my dotage with you and Mrs. Jerkins!"

"Nearly twenty-seven," the marquess said.

"Another thing," Hawk said, "how the hell did you know that she was Frances? There were three daughters. No one ordered me to marry any one of them in particular."

Now, the marquess thought silently, studying his sons' flushed face, I have set myself a problem by making her so warmly welcome. He said slowly, "Well, I knew that Frances was Ruthven's favorite daughter. I imagined, well, perhaps Ruthven pressed a bit more in her direction."

"Like hell he did! Didn't you *see* her? My God, Father, she looks a fright, a hag! I was worried that when I brought her to meet you—on your death bed, of course—that you would have spasm at the very sight of her. Indeed, in deference to you, I was going to make her remove those ghastly spectacles."

The marquess wondered if he should tell his son that he'd seen a miniature of Frances, painted only a year before. He'd hoped desperately that Hawk would select her from among the sisters. Interesting, he thought. Why had Frances donned the guise of a hag?

—for that was indeed how she appeared. And Hawk hadn't seen through it. Most odd, the entire situation.

"Why did you marry her if she repels you?" he asked. He hoped at least his son's part of the puzzle would solve itself.

Hawk fidgeted with a fleck of dust on his blue sleeve. He flushed, and was furious with himself for doing it, for his father, that old dog, had the keenest eyesight imaginable.

"Why, Hawk?" the marquess asked again.

Hawk cursed, and flung his hands out before him. "All right, I'll tell you. Her sisters, Clare and Viola, were both quite lovely as a matter of fact. And witty and charming. And they wanted, nay expected, that if I married them I'd introduce them into London society and allow them to hang on my sleeve. I just happen, Father, to like my life the way it is. Frances, for all her wretched appearance, was preferable. She is quite shy and timid. She doesn't chatter. Can't you just imagine beautiful silence at the breakfast table? She doesn't like crowds or gaiety of entertainments. So, despite her looks, she is perfectly suitable, and she won't . . ."

Hawk faltered, and his father said in the driest voice, "And you expect to leave her here, don't you, and continue with your ways in London?"

Hawk cursed again.

The marquess wanted to tell his son that his motives were those of a bourgeois, but he didn't, for the simple reason that Frances was, according to Ruthven, beautiful, charming, witty, intelligent, and a handful. No matter his son's motives, he had ended up with the right daughter. He suddenly wanted to laugh at his son's folly, his blindness, his gullibility.

But Frances did look awful.

Well, he would take care of that . . . eventually.

First, he had to find out from his new daughter-in-law the reason for her elaborate charade.

Then he would deal with his son.

He was not allowed any conversation with Frances that evening, for she sent word through Agnes, who informed Mrs. Jerkins, who very straightly told Otis, who in turn announced to Hawk that "Her ladyship is not feeling well, my lord. She begs to be excused."

"Just as well," Hawk said. He could enjoy his dinner without chancing to gaze upon that fright in the middle of a bite.

"Pity," said the marquess, frowning a bit. "I trust Frances is not sickly?"

"Nary a bit," Hawk said, then frowned. "Well, she was ill during our journey from Scotland. She mistakenly quacked herself with horse-colic medicine—thought it was laudanum. Lord, what a fracas!"

The marquess appeared thoughtfully silent throughout their very formal dinner, and Hawk, still peeved with his sire, said little to enliven things. No, he was thinking, Frances wasn't ill, not this time. What she was was a damned coward.

After three snifters of brandy, consumed in splendid solitude in the Smoking Room, Hawk was in a proper way of blaming Frances for all his misfortunes. "I want nothing more than to escape this place," he said aloud to the empty room. His voice reverberated off the high ceiling. "But I can't, not until she's conceived."

He had to do it and keep doing it. Hawk rose, doused the candles, and made his way to the Eastern Corridor.

He stripped off his clothes in his own bedchamber, shrugged into a velvet dressing gown, and strode purposefully to the connecting door.

If it weren't for her, everything would be as it should be.

He opened the door and strode in.

The room was in darkness.

"Who is it? Who's there?"

Hawk heard her sit up in her bed, heard the shrillness in her voice.

"It's just me," he said.

"What do you want?" Frances felt her heart begin to pound, felt herself begin to sweat. Not sweat, she thought wildly, perspire. She could picture Adelaide in her mind's eye, lecturing her in her placid way.

"Just be still, Frances. I'll be gone in no time at all."

"No!"

"You certainly cozied up to my father, didn't you? Did everything he asked of you?"

"My lord—"

"Philip."

"I want you to leave me alone . . . please!" How she hated herself and the damned pleading, nay, begging. "Go away!"

But he was now standing beside her bed, and she could hear his breathing. "Just lie on your back," he said. "It would help if you pulled up your nightgown."

Bastard! Cold, unfeeling, selfish oaf!

"No," she said, and quickly scurried to the far side of the immense bed.

Hawk gritted his teeth, all thoughts of treating her gently fleeing his mind. "This gives me little pleasure, Frances. It must be done. Now, just lie still!"

She sucked in her breath on the helpless sob. "God, I hate you," she whispered.

He grunted, but she wasn't certain whether or not it was a grunt to signify he'd heard her and didn't care, or just an isolated male sound.

She felt the bed give under his weight, felt his hands clasp her about the waist and pull her under him.

"Oh damn," Hawk said. He'd forgotten the wretched cream.

He frowned into the darkness, but was loath to leave her to fetch it from his bedchamber. He'd just have to make do.

Without further words, or sounds, he jerked up her nightgown and pulled her legs apart. He could feel her trembling, and that slowed him a bit. "Just hold still," he said, beginning to feel like a half-wit.

He eased his hands between her thighs, his long fingers finally touching her. He slipped his finger into her, and began to move. To his relief, he felt her accommodate him, felt her small body becoming damp.

"Don't move," he said, and without another word, came into her.

Frances cried out, and pounded his chest with his fists.

He could feel her pain and for a moment cursed himself for treating her badly. She was so damned small, and he prayed he wouldn't tear her. Then he was seated to the hilt within her. He stopped and waited.

She was filled with heat and pain and fullness.

"I hate you," she said, her voice a hissing sob.

He ignored her words and began to move within her.

"You animal!"

He thrust deep, arching his back, and groaned as his seed spewed within her.

He fell on top of her, not really from the strength of his release, but from the vague knowledge that he shouldn't leave her, not yet. His seed had to take hold in her body.

She lay still as a stone beneath him, her only sign of life the occasional bursts of rasping gasps.

His breathing slowed, and he felt himself retreating.

He pulled out, felt her flinch with pain, and rose.

"Don't bathe just yet," he said. "I'll see you in the morning, Frances."

Even before he'd closed the adjoining door behind him, he heard her scrambling out of bed and knew she was running to the basin of water on the commode.

So much for wifely obedience, he thought, but said nothing.

He was tired, he realized, very tired indeed. And he was still furious at his father's duplicity. And Frances was the result of that duplicity.

He sighed and eased himself between the cool covers on his bed. It wasn't her fault. He'd acted a rutting bastard. Tomorrow night, he would use cream. He wouldn't hurt her again.

I hate you.

She hadn't meant that, not really. Still, it bothered him. A wife shouldn't say such things to her husband, much less mean them. A wife owed her husband respect and obedience.

Life had become excessively grim. Hawk finally fell into a deep sleep, but his dreams were filled with shadowy women who shrank away from him whenever he approached them. He couldn't make out their faces, but he *knew* that they were fearful of him, that they wanted to escape him.

10

The march of the human mind is slow.
—EDMUND BURKE

"You have the brain of a damned turtle! No, that isn't quite true—a turtle keeps his head tucked inside, while yours, Philip Hawksbury, is aboveground and sticking out of your collar!"

Hawk eyed his father with faint interest.

"A village idiot, that's what I begat!"

"Father, you will cease insulting me. I am going riding now."

"Damn you, boy, what did you do to her?"

Hawk looked his father over very coolly, an expression he had perfected in his army days. It was nearly always effective, particularly with recalcitrant troops.

"I did nothing to my wife," he said finally, his voice as forbidding as the wretched cold water in Loch Lomond.

"Oh yes, you did," the marquess said, his eyes gleaming with fury. "Her maid told Mrs. Jerkins, who just happened to let slip to Grunyon, who told me, as is proper, that there was blood on her bedsheets and that she was pale as a ghost this morning!"

Hawk cursed very softly.

"Surely your wife wasn't a virgin until last night?"

Hawk was silent.

"No, I can't believe that, not with you, you randy young goat."

Goaded, Hawk said, "No, no, she wasn't."

"Then why blood, damn you? What did you do to her, you half-wit?"

"It's what I didn't do," Hawk said. He wondered vaguely if a village idiot was worse than a half-wit.

"And that being?"

Hawk shrugged, and walked to the long windows in the drawing room. "I didn't use any cream," he said over his shoulder. "I forgot."

The marquess closed his eyes. Why the devil would a husband have to use cream with his own wife? It was ridiculous, unless he was rough with her and uncaring.

He looked over at his beautiful son. He was standing tall and straight, his eyes locked on the elm tree outside the window. His Hessians gleamed in the morning sunlight that poured into the room. He was wearing buckskins, and a gray sporting jacket.

"A husband shouldn't hurt his wife," the marquess said slowly.

"I didn't mean to," Hawk said, turning to face his father. "I thought that if I left her to get the cream, she would hide herself somewhere in this tomb of a house to escape me."

"Well, that's truth of a sort. What are you going to do about it?"

"I'm going riding."

The marquess frowned, his most baleful frown, and Hawk suddenly realized that his own practiced expression came from his father. He wondered suddenly if his own son would carry the same expression.

"You shouldn't, you know."

"Look, Father, I'm weary to death of all this idiocy. If you're so concerned about Frances, why didn't you marry her yourself?"

"I did consider it," the marquess said frankly.

Hawk looked surprised.

"But, Hawk, I realized it wouldn't be fair. What young girl would want to be bound to an old man?"

Hawk threw up his hands. "Quite a rich old man," he said. "I'm quite certain Ruthven would have been delighted."

"I never believed—until this moment—that you had more of your mother's brains than mine." With those blighting words, the marquess strode from the room.

Hawk went riding. He returned late in the afternoon and closeted himself with his new steward, Marcus Carruthers. An intelligent young man, the son of a vicar, Marcus felt his head reel with all the bits and pieces of gossip he'd heard since the earl's return to Desborough Hall with his homely little wife.

"Well?" Hawk asked as he seated himself behind the huge mahogany desk in his estate room.

Marcus cleared his throat. Why, he wondered silently, was this man, younger than he, so intimidating? Marcus took his time gathering the appropriate papers. "My lord," he began, "it's about the stud."

"What about it?"

"It is not being used. The estate is losing a good deal of money. There are three superb stallions, their bloodlines as grand as the king's, who are moldering in the fields. Two are thoroughbreds, one is an Arab. Stud fees would be enormous."

"Speak to Belvis if you wish," Hawk said, but not caring one way or another.

"Very well, my lord," Marcus said. He wasn't up to telling the earl that Belvis, a crusty old man and an excellent trainer and manager, had left the estate some three months before, mumbling to Marcus that there was nothing for him here, not anymore.

Hawk laughed suddenly, very harshly.

"My lord?"

"Nothing, Carruthers. If we wish to treat our stallions as trollops, and charge for their services, who am I to quibble? Any worthy lightskirt, or mare in this case, would do the same thing."

Marcus had nothing to say to that observation. Their meeting continued for another hour, and by the end of it, Marcus was ready to pound his lordship into a desk drawer. The man was infuriating, and utterly uninterested in the running of his own estate. No, Marcus amended to himself, it wasn't lack of interest exactly, it was a barely suppressed abstraction. His lordship was miles away in the middle of more pressing problems.

"It is teatime," Hawk said finally, rising. "I will have the dubious honor of sharing this precious time with my . . . family. I will see you sometime tomorrow, Carruthers."

Marcus shook his head as the earl strode from the estate room.

Hawk found his father and Frances seated comfortably in a cozy room called the Double Cube. He'd never understood the genesis of that particular name, and although he was interested, he didn't feel this was precisely the right time to seek enlightenment.

Frances looked her usual self, perhaps even more so, for when she looked up at his entrance, she paled to the color of the white walls.

"Good afternoon," Hawk said, nodding to the two of them. He walked to the ornately carved fireplace and leaned his shoulder against the mantelpiece.

"Tea, my lord?"

"Philip," he corrected loudly.

"With or without milk?"

"Hawk likes his tea strong and plain, Frances," the marquess said. "Doubtless because there weren't enough goats to milk in Portugal."

"Exactly, sir," Hawk said, giving his father an ironic nod.

"I was just speaking to Frances of bridal visits. Your neighbors will want to meet her, of course."

The horrified look on her husband's face was enough to make Frances thrust up her chin and declare, "I should enjoy meeting everyone, my lord."

"Not," Hawk said very slowly and very precisely, "until you do something with yourself, Frances."

Frances gave him a long, squinting look, rose, and walked out of the room, her back ramrod straight.

"She's still wearing that same ghastly rag," Hawk said to no one in particular. "Twenty years out-of-date if it's a day. And that cap—it should have been burned before it was sewn."

The marquess wanted to plant his beloved son a facer. Stupid half-wit! Stubborn idiot! He'd tried to speak with Frances before Hawk's belated arrival, but hadn't gained much ground. In fact, he hadn't gained anything. He hadn't known what to say to her.

"What do you plan to do, Hawk?" he asked finally, waving a cup of tea toward his son.

Hawk walked to his father, took the tea, and downed it in one gulp. "Do, Father? Why, I plan to get my wife pregnant as quickly as possible."

"And then?"

"I will return to London, where I belong."

"That is what you said yesterday," the marquess said, "more or less."

"Yes," said Hawk, pouring himself another cup.

"Belvis is gone, left some months ago."

Hawk blinked at his father. "Marcus didn't tell me."

"You probably had the poor young man quaking in his shoes. I told you because nothing you do or say makes me quake."

"I suppose not."

"Belvis is not someone to lose lightly."

Hawk shrugged. "I told Marcus to do what he wished about the stud. If he wishes Belvis back, he can fetch him."

The marquess rose. He was a meddler; he freely admitted it to himself. He wondered if it wouldn't be for the best if he left the two of them alone and returned to Chandos Chase.

No, he couldn't do it. He had to get the truth out of Frances first.

Frances pulled her shawl more closely about her shoulders and escaped through the garden door off the immensely intimidating library. It would take three lifetimes to read all those vellum tomes. She breathed in the sweet, clean air. Spring was making itself felt. There were full buds on the trees and some flowers were coming back to life. It would be lovely here in the summer. She tried quite successfully for the next ten minutes to extol the virtues of the estate. After all, it was now her home. She felt a wave of homesickness and sank down under a very old, gnarled oak tree, leaning back against the rough bark. She closed her eyes and saw her husband, and heard his hateful words play over and over in her mind. *Well, what he said is only the truth. You look ghastly. Do you expect that he'll want to introduce you as his wife?*

She was on the point of pulling off her spectacles and taking the cap from her head when she saw Hawk striding toward the small ornamental lake. His head was lowered and he appeared lost in thought. His thick black hair glistened under the afternoon sun. She let her eyes rove down his body, looking at him with complete objectivity. He was a handsome man, a powerfully built man. There, she thought, she would allow him that. But nothing more.

It was as if he sensed her presence, for in the next moment, he whipped about and stared at her.

"Frances," he said.

"My lord," she said.

"Philip."

"Yes. It is a lovely prospect, is it not? Do you know when the lake was built?"

"In the early part of the last century. One of my late, unlamented ancestors with a head filled with foolishness." He paused a moment, raking his fingers through his hair. "Look, Frances, I apologize for what I said to you. It wasn't fair of me. After all, it's not your fault that you . . ."

"Yes?" she pressed in a very sweet voice.

"Well, quite a bit of it is your fault."

"I should say that it is all my fault. But it matters not, at least to me."

"I don't understand," Hawk said slowly.

Frances shrugged, not looking up at him.

"Look, Frances, I'm sorry about last night. I won't do that again . . ."

She shot him a look of undiluted relief. "You won't touch me again? You're leaving Desborough Hall, then?"

"Not just yet. What I meant to say was that I won't ever approach you again without some cream. I did not mean to hurt you."

Cream, she thought dully. She found herself looking at his firm mouth for a moment. He had never kissed her.

"Should you like to go riding with me tomorrow morning?"

An olive branch. "Yes, I should like that, my lord."

"Philip."

"I don't have a riding habit."

Hawk paused at that daunting bit of news. Then he

said, "Tomorrow evening, Lord and Lady Bourchier are coming to dinner. As I recall, Alicia is about your size. Perhaps she would lend you a riding habit until you can have several made. We will just have to postpone your ride for a day or two. I will go see Alicia and John now and borrow one for you."

"There are guests coming tomorrow evening? To dinner?"

Hawk frowned at the sound of her set voice. "Why not? They've been friends of mine since we were children. I suppose you should meet with Mrs. Jerkins and plan the menu." He didn't tell her that this damned dinner hadn't been his idea. His father had taken the liberty of doing the inviting.

"Yes," Frances said, coming gracefully to her feet. "Yes, I suppose I should. Another wifely duty."

"You will come down to dinner this evening, will you not?"

"I haven't yet decided," she said over her shoulder.

Hawk watched her stride back toward the house—like a damned man, he thought. Not a feminine bone in that body of hers. But her body was very soft, her skin smooth and sweet-smelling. He clearly remembered the feel of her thighs, their slenderness, their long, graceful shape, and the softness of her between her thighs. He found himself wondering about her breasts. Tonight, he thought, he would satisfy his curiosity on that score.

Frances, knowing she had no choice, dutifully rang for Mrs. Jerkins when she returned to the house.

"Yes, my lady?" came the formidable response.

"Mrs. Jerkins, my husband informs me that we will have two guests for dinner tomorrow evening."

"Yes, my lady. His lordship—that is, the earl's father—informed me of the invitation. I have the menu planned. Here it is."

So, she thought, the marquess had done it. She was surprised that her husband hadn't pleaded a vile illness to keep his friends from coming. She lowered her eyes to the paper. It was the first time she'd tried to read with her spectacles on. The words blurred. She couldn't make them out. She shot Mrs. Jerkins a look, but knew it would be odd in the extreme to that intimidating woman if she were to remove her spectacles in order to read. She sighed, forced her eyes over the blurred words, then said, "This is fine, Mrs. Jerkins. Thank you."

Mrs. Agatha Jerkins nodded, and took back the paper. She didn't realize until she had left her new mistress that she hadn't given her the menu. She'd given her a list of the linens that needed to be replaced.

She told Otis, " 'Tis exceeding odd, James. Do you suppose that in Scotland they don't teach people how to read?"

"It is a brutish, uncivilized country," said Otis.

"Our poor master," she said, shaking her gray head. "To be tied to such as her . . ." Mrs. Jerkins broke off suddenly, quite aware that it was not at all acceptable to speak thus of her betters, particularly to Otis, the stiff-necked old goat.

"I shall contrive," she said, and hastened away.

That evening at dinner, Frances said not a word. She listened to the marquess relating tales from bygone days, scandals of this lord or that lady, fortunes won or lost at the gaming tables.

When she'd come into the drawing room, Hawk had taken one look at her and become as silent as she.

The marquess carried on manfully. He wasn't a military man like his son, but he knew well enough when the battle was well lost.

Frances excused herself at the first moment possible

and returned to her room. Agnes was seated next to the fireplace stitching one of Frances' impossible gowns.

"That won't be necessary, Agnes. You may go now."

Agnes brightened. "You are expecting new gowns, my lady?"

"No," said Frances. "Please, Agnes, go to bed."

Frances was wide-awake when she heard the adjoining door open some two hours later.

"Frances."

"Yes," she said. "Just a moment, my lord, allow me to raise my nightgown for you. There."

Hawk felt a frisson at those empty, dull words. He plowed his fingers through his hair. "Frances, look, I—"

"I quite understand, my lord. You wish me to conceive. I am ready. Please, just get it over with."

He did. He didn't hurt her, for the cream eased his way. She didn't move, nor did she say another word. He finished quickly, and retreated to his own rooms.

He realized later as he lay in his own bed that he hadn't touched her breasts.

The small dinner party with Lord and Lady Bourchier from Sandbury Hall could have been worse, Hawk thought. Alicia, bless her sweet heart, had been most kind to Frances, once she'd gotten over her shock. As for John, he was a man who could charm termites out of walls, if he so chose. The marquess had been in fine form.

Frances had been so quiet and reserved that she might as well have not been present. Hawk found himself wondering during the lengthy meal how Clare or Viola would have responded. They would have been charming, he thought, and well-gowned and lovely.

But he'd married Frances. And she detested him. He shrugged as he mounted the stairs after bidding his father a good night, and set his jaw. Frances obviously wanted to see the back of him, and he resolved to give her her wish.

Why couldn't she try, just a bit, to make herself more presentable? He'd held his breath when all of them had adjourned to the drawing room after dinner and the marquess had begged Alicia to play for them. Hawk couldn't bear the thought of Frances playing, particularly after Alicia, who was blessed with a soft clear voice and nimble fingers. He didn't want her to embarrass herself. His father had asked her, and Hawk sent an agonized plea heavenward. It was heard; Frances refused, her voice emotionless.

Had the woman no feeling at all? He knew she was shy and diffident, but he hadn't quite realized to what extent it was true. She was shy almost to the point of rudeness.

He sighed, dismissed Grunyon, and stripped off his clothes. When he quietly opened the adjoining door, he heard Frances say in a weary, bored voice, "Again, my lord? Are you not too fatigued?"

"Yes," he said, "but it doesn't matter."

"Very well," she said.

"You know, Frances," he said as he drew closer to her bed, "you could have made a bit of a push to be more pleasant to my friends. Both John and Alicia are quite nice."

"I'm sure they are."

Her heard her moving about in the bed, and could picture her pulling up her nightgown. This is not right, he thought, suddenly miserable. Life shouldn't be like this. He sat down on the edge of the bed, his hands clasped between his knees. "I would that things were not so difficult between us, Frances."

"I would that there were no things at all," Frances said. "Between us, that is."

"Are you homesick?"

"Yes."

"I'm sorry, but . . ."

He heard her draw a deep breath. "Yes," she said quietly, "there is always a 'but,' isn't there? I am tired. Cannot you be done with it?"

"Very well," he said, his voice curt.

It relieved him that he was able to enter her immediately. He had an awful fear of impotence with her. That would demolish him utterly. When he spewed his seed deep inside her, he heard a muffled sob, and froze. He closed his eyes, even though the room was in complete darkness. He hadn't hurt her, had he? She was very small, and he had thrust deeply into her, repeatedly. He started to ask her if she were all right, but he couldn't bring himself to. He could just hear her flat, emotionless voice telling him a lie.

He pulled out of her quickly, feeling her flinch as he did so.

Frances didn't move. She heard him stride quickly from her room, heard him firmly close the adjoining door behind him.

It isn't so very bad, she thought, lying very still. It doesn't hurt. But it was so empty, so cold and inhuman.

She suddenly saw her life laid out before her. It was all loneliness and darkness. It was a man who was her husband who would visit her when he was forced to. She rolled over and buried her face into the soft pillow. She wanted desperately to go home. She wanted desperately to be free again, to be herself, to laugh and visit all the Kilbracken crofters, to swim in the loch, to sun herself in the midst of heather during the summer.

Silly weak twit! Your whole charade was designed to have him leave. And it's working, indeed it is. He can't bear to look at you, much less be in your company.

Soon she would be free again. Soon he would be gone. *And then what will you do?*

She awoke the next morning with no answer to her question.

She realized soon enough that she would not be riding. Her husband hadn't inquired about a riding habit from Lady Bourchier.

11

Brevity is the soul of wit.

—SHAKESPEARE

"No," Hawk said.

"What, nothing else to say? You proffer this rackety reason, unbelievable, and you know it, and then say no?"

"Correct," Hawk said.

If a look of absolute ire could destroy, Hawk would have collapsed, slain at his father's booted feet.

"This is all nonsense, my boy," the marquess said after a moment in which he'd failed to reduce his son to filial obedience. "See your man of business in London? Absurd! He had to beg you to pay him a call after you returned to England. I tell you, Hawk, I forbid you to leave now."

"Not now, at dawn," Hawk said.

"And just what does your wife think about this? Does she even know that you plan to leave her?"

"No, not yet. I will speak to her when I find her, which is difficult, since she hides whenever I am in the vicinity."

"Except at night," the marquess said with lowered brows.

"That is right."

The marquess threw up his hands. "I'm going to breakfast now."

To Hawk's surprise, Frances was seated at the breakfast table when he and his father entered the small breakfast room. She was wearing what he now recognized as the ugliest of her three gowns, a dull brown wool that could have had no style the day it was conceived. On her head sat a cap of bilious yellow.

She looked up briefly, nodded, then lowered her head again to her plate of eggs.

The marquess looked from one to the other, and announced, "I think I shall breakfast a bit later." He left, a brief prayer on his lips that his son would bend one way and Frances would not run.

She looked like a pinched, pale, very homely shadow, Hawk thought, except for those awful spectacles that brought everything into sharp focus. He suppressed the unacceptable feeling of guilt and set himself to his trencher.

When Otis retreated from the room, taking the serving maid, Rosie, with him, Hawk sat back in his chair and folded his arms over his chest.

"Good morning, Frances."

"Good morning, my ... Philip."

"I am pleased with your verbal progress."

"Thank you."

He wanted to shake her until her teeth rattled. Instead, he said, "Do you think you could be with child?"

Frances dropped her fork. She wanted to hurl her cup of very hot tea into his face. She wanted to scream the best of her invectives at his head. She said in a low, tight voice, "It certainly seems possible. You have, after all, done your duty quite assiduously."

"That is quite a number of words you have strung

together," Hawk said. "It pleases me that you realize I deserve more than a nod or a shrug from you."

"Oh yes," she said. "You deserve much more."

Hawk frowned. Her voice was flat, utterly emotionless. Didn't the woman have a shred of sensibility? But perhaps her words had held a shred of sarcasm?

"I am leaving in the morning."

"I wish you a good journey."

"Do not you care when I shall be back, or where I am going, for that matter?" His tone was irascible, his words perverse, and he knew it.

"No," she said. She began to spread the soft sweet butter on a slice of bread, concentrating to her full powers on the strokes of her knife.

His hands clenched, and he said in a nasty voice, "I shall visit you again tonight. I wouldn't want to be at all remiss in my duty, now, would I?" '

Frances felt her heart plummet to her toes. She had begun her monthly flow. Oh dear, what was she to do? It was time to attack, she knew it. The mouse couldn't lie still for this. It was her only hope. She said very coldly, "Why do you not leave a list of eligible gentlemen who live in the neighborhood? If you have indeed not succeeded in your ... husbandly endeavors, perhaps one of them will."

Hawk stared at her, for a moment completely taken aback, then threw back his head and burst into laughter. "Look, Frances," he said at last, seeing her sitting there rigid as a statue, "even if one of the gentlemen could be induced to bed you, he wouldn't treat you with as much, ah, respect as I do. Lord, he might even expect, nay, insist on seeing your body, perhaps thrust his tongue in your mouth. You would detect that, wouldn't you? He would, I venture to point out, even force you to touch him. A ghastly prospect, wouldn't you say? All that disgusting hair?"

It was difficult, but Frances maintained a hold on herself. He was a conceited, selfish beast, a bounder, a ... "Why do you not leave today, my lord? The weather is quite acceptable for travel, I think."

Hawk regarded her in thoughtful silence. He supposed that a homely, very dowdy female would feel some bitterness about her looks, but this very agile sarcasm? It didn't set right on her hunched shoulders. Somehow it didn't fit her nondescript character.

Frances realized she'd make a mistake. She bit her tongue. Fool, don't give him reason to question you, to bait you into anger. Give him no reason to stay. She tossed her napkin beside her plate and quickly rose.

"Perhaps I shall see you before you leave, my lord," she said, and nearly ran from the room.

Hawk sat quietly, looking at nothing in particular. What the devil was the matter with her? Hell and damnation, he'd picked her instead of her sisters, given her a title, given her a home, given her consequence. And she detested him. And he did treat her well at night. Didn't embarrass her or insist upon seeing her naked or demand that she touch him. He decided at that moment that he *would* leave today.

But it wasn't to be.

Two hours later, Grunyon interrupted him in his bedchamber. "My lord, Otis informs me that you have a visitor. It is Lord Saint Leven."

"Good God," Hawk said blankly. "I wonder what Lyonel is doing here. I thought he was firmly ensconced in London."

"I heard him mention to your father, my lord, that he was visiting a great-aunt who lives near Escrick."

"Oh yes," Hawk said, dredging up a bit of memory. "It must be his Great-Aunt Lucia, an old tartar, he told me once. He likes her immensely."

He joined his father and Lyonel Ashton in the Smoking Room.

"Hawk, old fellow," Lyonel said, coming forward to clap his friend on his shoulder, "you are now a married man. My congratulations. About time, I should say."

"You say, Lyonel? You, as I recall, arrived on this earth only one year before I did."

"Some of us fellows mature more quickly, Hawk," said Lyonel, his dark blue eyes twinkling. "Where is your lady wife? I should like to meet his paragon who pulled you into the parson's mousetrap."

Mouse. Hawk felt as if his tongue had become dead meat in his mouth.

Lyonel frowned at the sudden silence. He heard the marquess clear his throat, but still Hawk stood there like a stupid puppet.

"Where is Frances, Father?" Hawk said finally.

"I don't know," the marquess said. "I sent word to find her, but no one has yet succeeded."

Hawk remembered the awful scene at breakfast and imagined that Frances had indeed escaped.

"Frances," Lyonel said. "A very nice name. Who is her family, Hawk?"

"Her father is the Earl of Ruthven, a Scot. She lived near Loch Lomond until a week ago."

Lyonel felt at least a score of questions hovering, but he held himself silent. Not in front of Hawk's father. There was a mystery here.

"Brandy, Lyonel?"

At that moment, Frances slithered into the room. That was the only word for it, Hawk thought, frowning at her. Damnation, she looked ready to be whipped.

He cleared his throat. "My dear," he said in his most pleasant voice, "please come in. I should like you to meet one of my best friends, Lyonel Ashton, Earl of Saint Leven. Lyonel, my wife, Frances."

Not a clue to his thoughts appeared on Lyonel's face. "My pleasure, ma'am," he said smoothly, and raised Frances' hand to his lips.

Lord, Frances thought, staring at the bent head, she had believed Hawk the most handsome man she'd ever seen, but this elegant male creature easily rivaled him. His hair was a rich, thick dark brown, nearly the color of Hawk's mahogany desk in the estate room.

When he straightened and smiled down at her, she realized he was even of Hawk's size. Warily she met his eyes, but saw no distaste in them; indeed, she saw only pleasure and intelligence. She ran her tongue over her suddenly dry mouth, terrified of his perception, and muttered, "Yes, indeed a pleasure to meet you, sir."

She sent an agonized look toward her father-in-law, and obligingly, the marquess said in a very relieved, quite loud voice, "Let's have that brandy now."

"Excuse me," Frances said, retreating, "I do not drink brandy, truly, I . . ." She quitted the room before anyone could say a word.

Lyonel said thoughtfully when the marquess handed him the snifter, "Let us drink to your marriage, Hawk."

They did.

It was close to thirty minutes later before the marquess left the two longtime friends alone.

Lyonel sat back in the comfortable leather chair and stretched his long legs before him. "This is all most interesting, Hawk."

"Go to the devil," Hawk said.

"Always brief and to the point. I am blessed in my friends."

"How is your sainted Great-Aunt Lucia?"

"She bastes me with her ire as thoroughly as the

cook bastes the Christmas ham. She is in rare good form, healthy as a stoat, her tongue whirling faster than your carriage wheels."

"I had looked forward to seeing you in London."

"Ah. Soon? You will introduce your bride to the *ton*?"

"No. Frances stays here, that is, she wishes to stay here, in the country—she is more comfortable here, you know."

"I see," said Lyonel. He waited, but there seemed to be nothing more forthcoming. "I suppose you will confide in me when it pleases you."

"There is nothing to confide," Hawk said.

"Probably nothing of interest," Lyonel agreed, his deep voice sounding lazy and bored."

"How long do you intend to stay?"

"I have but just arrived, Hawk."

Hawk gritted his teeth. "You know what I mean, Lyon!"

"Ah, now we're back to the animal world. My father never approved of that particular nickname, you know. Believed it undignified, not at all worthy of Viscount Beresford. You will recall, old fellow, that that was what I was called before my father's unfortunate demise last—"

"It is not a love match, curse you!" Hawk said harshly, breaking into this fascinating blather on Lyon's antecedents. "You aren't blind. You met her. You *looked* at her."

Lyonel shot him an odd look, then said mildly, "Then I would suppose that she is a great heiress."

"Nary a bit."

"Not twenty thousand pounds a year?"

"Not a bloody sou."

"I brought a valise, Hawk. I had intended to spend the night, but if you wish, I shall take to my heels and endure Lucia's insults. Poor woman, she thought she'd seen the last of me for a while."

"Stay. We can return to London together—tomorrow—if it is convenient with your plans."

"That will be pleasing, no doubt. I trust, dear boy, that you have sent an announcement of your marriage to the *Gazette*?"

"I imagine that my father has done that."

"I wonder," Lyonel said, his voice a lazy drawl, "what the fair Constance will make of it?"

"I would never have married her," Hawk said. "Even if I had wanted to, well . . ."

"Yes, I understand. Your Scottish lass. As for your Amalie, she is certain to be devastated."

"No, I daresay she won't be. Why should she be, after all?"

"It is like that, is it?" Lyonel said easily. "Odd, but I have always believed that when I marry, if I ever find a woman to bear up with me, that I should show my mistress to the door. Of course, Amalie is a charmer . . ."

He paused a moment, seeing Hawk eye him with frank surprise.

"I've said something that your intellect can't grasp?"

Hawk said slowly, "I have never believed that any gentleman would forgo his pleasures for the sake of a wife, particularly if the wife in question is merely a . . . duty."

"Perhaps that is true of many of our acquaintances," Lyonel agreed. "I imagine, though, that there are some love matches. I hope I shall be so lucky."

Hawk said something quite crude.

"Then a gentleman wouldn't be inclined to poach elsewhere," Lyonel finished.

"Not for a twelvemonth in any case," Hawk said, his voice as cynical as his raised eyebrow.

"If that is your belief, my friend, then wouldn't the same thing apply to a wife? Lady Constance—well, she has a great deal of self-consequence, as well as stunning looks. She is also an accomplished flirt. I am certain her flirting wouldn't go to the bedchamber until she'd provided an heir for her husband, but then. . . ?" Lyonel shrugged elaborately. "I suppose you have excellent reason for cynicism. Sometimes I find myself wishing that . . . Well, no matter, here I am carrying on like a gabbleseed. Come, old fellow, let me show you my new cattle. My bays will beat your grays to flinders."

"And your Great-Aunt Lucia will become mute! You know I got those grays from Kimbell when he went all to pieces, the damned fool. Nothing can beat them."

Frances was standing by the window of a small sewing room that faced the drive. She saw the two men stroll companionably toward the stable. Both large powerful men, both filled with all the confidence only a man of title and wealth could possess. But appearances could be deceiving, she knew. She could imagine how the Earl of Saint Leven would treat her if he had to suffer looking at her a second time. Surely he couldn't hide his true feelings again. But he had looked at her so very oddly.

Would she have to suffer another night of Hawk's amorous bouts? Amorous, ha! Husbandly bouts was more like it. Duty bouts, heir bouts, damn him.

She saw Lord Saint Leven throw back his head and laugh at something her husband said. Had her husband made a jest about her? No, he couldn't be that great a bounder. She turned away from the small window, her shoulders hunched.

She pleaded an indisposition that evening and stayed safe in her room.

Agnes, eyeing her when she brought her a tray, wondered just what this indisposition was. Her mistress was pacing about, looking alternately flushed with anger, then pale as the gravy that swamped the veal on the beautiful gold-edged plate.

"I will not let him do it, not again," Frances said aloud to her empty room several hours later. "Enough is enough."

It was more than that, she knew. If she stayed and he visited her, she would have to tell him that she was far from pregnant. She would have to tell him about her monthly flow. The consequences of such a confession left her mind blank.

She molded a fat bolster under the covers of her bed, and made her way to the small sewing room.

When Hawk quietly entered her bedchamber three hours later, he was more drunk that he cared to admit, but his determination was profound. It took him several moments to realize that the bolster wasn't a woman. He stared down in the darkness, his hands feeling the damned bolster as if it were a woman's leg. Then he felt utterly enraged.

He'd asked nothing of her, damn her! He'd given her everything any woman could possibly want. His sexual demands required but ten minutes of her precious time. And she didn't have to do anything save lie there like a damned log while he did all the work. He realized vaguely that he'd been through all his logic several times before, but it didn't matter. He was certain the list of her shortcomings would continue to grow.

The roar of anger was building in his throat when he realized that Lyonel and his father were in the house. It would cause the most ridiculous scene. He could just hear Lyonel's lazy drawl. "How very odd, Hawk, old man. You say you mistook a bolster for your wife? She's hidden from you, you say?"

He swallowed.

He would leave her to wallow in her own dowdy stupidity. Selfish, silly twit!

It didn't occur to him until he was lying in his own bed, the room spinning dizzily when he closed his eyes, that it was indeed probable that she had unwittingly spared him male embarrassment.

He felt dead, all of him. Not even a twinge of life.

Both men left the following morning, each nurturing a hangover that would dog their heels to Nottingham.

Hawk didn't bid his wife good-bye. She was nowhere to be found.

Frances watched their leave-taking from her post in the sewing room. Good riddance, she thought, twitching the lace curtain back into place. Her father-in-law was waiting for her at the foot of the stairs.

"Good morning, Frances," he said quite pleasantly.

"Sir," she said.

"Did you sleep well, Frances, in your hidey-hole?"

How did he know?

She elevated her chin. "Yes, sir, indeed I did."

"Hawk is gone, Lyonel with him."

"Yes, I watched them leave."

"And that is why you finally are showing yourself?"

"I am hungry."

"And something of a coward also. Come here a moment, my dear. I have something to show you."

Frances shot him a wary look, but obligingly trailed after him into the library. He quietly closed the door, then turned to face her. "Look at this, Frances."

She took the small miniature from his outstretched hand. She stared down into her smiling face.

"My father . . . Why did he send you this? I assume he did send you this."

"Yes, he did," said the marquess. "He hoped I would be seeing a painting of my future daughter-in-law. He devoutly hoped that Hawk would select *her*." He pointed at the lovely happy face. "But instead my son selected you. Now, don't mistake me, Frances, I am not a doddering old fool and I know well enough why Hawk picked you over your sisters. He is incapable of lying to me. His cheek always twitched whenever he tried as a boy. He hasn't tried as a man. No, my dear, my question is: why your elaborate charade? I gather that Hawk met you as you are now."

Frances, at the end of her tether, waved her fist at him and shouted, "It is all your fault! If you hadn't been so foolish as to get yourself captured by bandits, and rescued by my damnable father, none of of this would have happened! I didn't want to marry the Earl of Rothermere. I didn't want to leave Kilbracken or Scotland. I didn't want your precious son to even look at me!"

"It appears that he hasn't—looked at you, that is," the marquess said mildly, pleased by this very Ruthven show of passion. "I begin to understand you, Frances. But I still wonder why you simply don't show your true self when he asked you to marry him."

"He left, curse him! He ran away as quickly as he could for Glasgow. I told my father I wouldn't have him, but my father said that I had no choice. It was all a matter of money, as you well know, since you're the one providing that cursed ten thousand pounds!"

The marquess absently rubbed his chin. What an interesting and amusing coil this was. "I gather, then, my dear, that you maintained the facade in order to . . . nauseate Hawk enough so that he would leave you quickly."

"Exactly," she said in an acid voice. "And it worked." Suddenly she crumpled, lowered her face in her hands, and began to sob.

"Frances!"

"Oh, be quiet," she cried, rubbing her eyes with the back of her hand. "He has indeed left and here I am stuck in a foreign country, surrounded by servants who believe me an utter fool and *unworthy* of my vaunted new position, and I hate it! There is no beautiful loch, no heather, no . . . Oh, I don't know what to do!"

"Of course you do, my dear," he said very gently.

Frances pulled off the offending spectacles and glared at him.

"Yes, that is a start."

"Well?" she demanded.

"You, my dear Frances, are the Countess of Rothermere. There is no one to gainsay you, not a mother nor a father. You are mistress here. This is your home. These are your servants. You can, as a matter of fact, do exactly as you please."

She stared at him a moment, his very calm words sinking into her befuddled brain.

She said very slowly, her brow nit in thought, "You are quite right. I can do exactly as I please, can I not?"

"Most assuredly," said the marquess, hope flaring.

Frances gave him a quite dazzling, beautiful smile. She pulled the cap off her hair and flung it to the floor. She stomped on it.

She next pulled the pins from the severe bun and shook out her thick hair.

She burst into merry laughter. "I believe, my lord, that the dowdy mouse has just died behind the wainscoting." She threw the spectacles into the air, and when they landed, she ground her heel into the lenses.

"My lord, do you know of any acceptable modistes in York?"

"We will invite Lady Alicia Bourchier to tea, Frances. She will know of a top-of-the-trees modiste, doubt it not. As for funds, as the mistress here, you have all you need. Now, my dear, I know of a trunk that holds some of Nevil's clothing. Perhaps we can find a pair of trousers for you. You would like to go riding, would you not?"

Frances threw her arms around the marquess's neck. "You are a wicked old man, sir!"

"And you, my dear daughter, are a minx."

Frances laughed gleefully, and didn't hear the marquess add under his breath, "My poor son. You haven't a chance, not now."

He wondered as he rode beside a laughing, carefree Frances, how long he should allow Hawk to absent himself. Well, he would just wait and see how Frances settled in. Then he would decide how to bring his son about. If it were not for wicked, meddling old men, he thought, heedless young men would not gain their just deserts.

As for Frances, didn't she realize that her husband would return? He wondered what she would do when that realization struck her between the eyes, as it surely would, sooner or later.

12

She lays it on with a trowel.
—*WILLIAM CONGREVE*

Mrs. Jerkins gawked at the vision, her mouth opening in a most undignified manner. Agnes had gasped that her ladyship had *changed,* but Mrs. Jerkins was of a tenacious, unchangeable nature, thus retrenching proved difficult.

"I .... my lady, what ... ?"

Frances gave her a sweet smile and said gently, "Please be seated, Mrs. Jerkins. I believe that you and I have some plans to make."

"But here, in his lordship's estate room?' No lady in Mrs. Jerkins' experience would ever poach in a masculine preserve.

Frances understood well enough, but her smile never faltered. Mrs. Jerkins was quite used to being the oracle of housewifely behavior at Desborough. But Frances was taking over Delphi, and without further delay. She'd delayed too long as it was.

"Please be seated," she said again, and Mrs. Jerkins sat, the keys at her waist jingling loudly.

"Now," Frances said, "here is what you and I shall do. First of all, I will go over the menus for the week each Monday morning—"

"But," Mrs. Jerkins sputtered, "you can't read!"

Frances laughed at that. "What a poor impression I first gave you of my countrymen, Mrs. Jerkins. I assure you that I can read, it was just that I was in my, er, spectacle mode and thus was quite blind. I gather that menu you showed me wasn't for a dinner?"

"It was a linen list!"

"Ah, I trust you still have it, for I should like to see to that this morning. Then, a complete tour of the house."

Mrs. Jerkins was still looking like a full-ballasted three-rigger floundering in the shoals. Frances sat forward, her hands flat on the beautiful mahogany desk. "I believe that you and I will deal quite well together. It has been difficult, I would imagine, not having a mistress here. A household of men must have made your life less than harmonious."

That hadn't been the case at all, but Mrs. Jerkins wasn't stupid. She thought suddenly of the chipped dishware, of the linens that were tattered and moth-eaten, of the draperies in the Crimson Room that had seen better days a generation ago.

"Well, perhaps," she began, her tone grudging. After all, this still was a savage little Scottish girl ... well, perhaps not savage. "There are the dogs, my lady!"

"Dogs?" Frances repeatedly blankly. "What dogs?"

"His lordship ... his former lordship's hunters. His new lordship normally brings them into the Hall, but he didn't this time, for what reason I don't know, but still—"

"I perceive the problem, Mrs. Jerkins. There will not, of course, be any more animals allowed to frolic in the Hall."

Mrs. Jerkins pulled her scattered wits together by a

thread. Everything was changing so quickly, at a dizzying pace. She could but nod.

Their tour of the vast house produced a surprise for Frances. Mrs. Jerkins was marching her through the long, narrow portrait gallery in the West Corridor when Frances spotted the painting of a young woman who looked like the feminine counterpart of her husband. She walked to the picture and stared up at it blankly.

"That is Lady Beatrice, my lady," said Mrs. Jerkins, "his lordship's older sister."

I can't very well tell her that I never heard of a sister, thought Frances. She said instead, "Tell me about her, Mrs. Jerkins, since of course I have yet to meet her."

Mrs. Jerkins' lips thinned a bit, but blood loyalty was strong. "Well, you know of course that Lord Nevil was the eldest, would have been thirty-one had he not drowned. Lady Beatrice is twenty-eight and his lordship twenty-six. Lady Beatrice was a very high-spirited young lady, married against her father's wishes when she was nineteen to a man older than her father, a Lord Dunsmore."

Frances frowned a bit at that. It wasn't as if Beatrice—her sister-in-law!—was impoverished. "Why did she marry this man?"

"I shouldn't know, but old Lord Dunsmore was quite wealthy and Lady Beatrice wanted to be her own mistress."

"Where do she and her husband live now?"

"Lord Dunsmore died two years ago. Lady Beatrice is in London, I believe, now betrothed to a much younger gentleman, a Viscount Chalmers."

Frances didn't wonder why Hawk hadn't mentioned he had a sister. Heavens, he hadn't told her anything about himself or his family, for that matter. She wondered now if she would ever meet Lady Beatrice, particularly since her husband wanted her in the north of England, out of his way.

She forced a bright smile. "Onward, Mrs. Jerkins."

Mrs. Jerkins said later to Mr. Otis, in the privacy of her small sitting room, "Just like a whirlwind she is, James. And her looks! I don't mind telling you that I was bowled about the head!"

"*She* informed me," said Mr. Otis, unbending just a bit at this confidence, "that she doesn't care for the footmen's livery! She said she's been studying the Rothermere coat of arms and that our colors aren't quite right."

Mrs. Jerkins clasped her bosom in instant commiseration.

"What his lordship will say, I can't begin to imagine. The change in her, 'tis astounding, though."

The two old martinets drank their tea in silence for some minutes, each thinking that life as they had known it was long gone and wouldn't likely return.

"More milk for your tea, James? No, well, I tell you, *she* needs to be put swiftly and firmly in her place, that's what I think! Why, his lordship left her without a backward glance! It's all very odd, you know. And her appearance, her *former* appearance—very smoky, I say."

"Agatha, she is the mistress, no matter what his lordship has done, no matter what she has done to herself. It is very odd, but it appears that she has just realized the fact that she is mistress here. It is the marquess's doing."

"She knows how to read," Mrs. Jerkins exclaimed as if it were a mortal sin.

"That is a relief," Mr. Otis said, sipping his tea. "A bit more milk, please, Agatha."

"More dresses and gowns and riding habits arrived for her this morning from York. Agnes is all agog. What his lordship will say with her spending all his blunt—"

"Her need was most pressing, I should say," said Otis.

Mrs. Jerkins glanced toward her small clock on the table beside her. "Oh dear, I believe that Lady Bourchier is to arrive shortly. Her *ladyship* requested a special tea."

"I believe," Mr. Otis said calmly, a glimmer in his rheumy eyes, "that Mr. Carruthers is to join her ladyship for dinner. She has given orders that only the second dining room is to be used."

"Scandalous, I call it!"

Lady Alicia Bourchier was a very pretty woman who had been much infatuated with Lord Philip Hawksbury some six years before when he was in London at the Hawksbury town house on leave, his arm in a sling. He'd flirted with her, healed, then left again. She'd met her childhood friend John again after a distance of two years, fallen in love, and now felt only an occasional twinge of regret when thoughts of the handsome Philip took her unawares.

She looked over her teacup at Philip's wife. She had felt so sorry for him upon her first meeting with Frances. Perhaps, she thought ruefully, she should feel more sorry for him now.

"So, Alicia, you must come see the rest of my new wardrobe when we finish our tea. I do thank you for all your help. Ah, I must tell Mrs. Jerkins that the tea is much too weak!"

"Frances," Alicia said suddenly, "I really do not understand, you know."

"It doesn't matter, truly. And to be frank, I do not wish to discuss it. Now, you haven't told me what you think of this gown."

"You look beautiful," Alicia said quite honestly. Indeed, she did, Alicia thought to herself. It was a round dress of thin jaconet muslin over a lemon-colored sarcenet slip. The bodice was trimmed with a triple fall of lace at the throat, the hem flounced with matching rows of like lace. The fitted bodice, though quite modest, did nothing to deceive the viewer of the abundant bosom beneath.

Frances was elegant, there was no other word for it, Alicia admitted to herself, from the tip of her glossy chestnut curls—or was her hair more auburn or perhaps blond—she couldn't decide.

She realized for the first time that she was Frances' elder by at least three years. It was a daunting thought, and one that she tried earnestly to dismiss. She wanted to be Frances' friend, after all, for Philip's sake. Even though she was from Scotland. Even though she was Philip's wife. However had she attracted him in the first place? Why had she played the shy dowd?

It was a mystery Alicia did not despair of unraveling, in time.

She said brightly, "Have you heard from Philip?"

"No," Frances said, sounding not at all downcast.

"But it's been nearly two weeks, Frances! Whatever is he doing in London?"

Frances shrugged, a glimmer of a smile playing about her mobile mouth. "I am fairly certain that he amuses himself."

"I shouldn't approve of that if I were you!"

Frances said very gently, "But you are not me, Alicia. Ah, here are my dear father-in-law and Marcus! Come in, gentlemen, and make your bows."

Amenities were the order for the next few minutes.

"You've a letter from your father, Frances,"the marquess said, handing her a rather disreputable, wrinkled envelope.

"Thank you, sir. Now, here is your tea. Marcus, you like milk, do you not?"

"Yes, my lady," Marcus Carruthers said. He felt still in something of a state of shock. The new countess had turned from a toad into a prince—or something along that order, he amended to himself—and she was charming to him. She'd requested his assistance for the following day. He didn't yet know what to make of it.

Frances saw that her father-in-law was gazing pointedly at the letter she'd laid on the tea table. "I shall get to it later, sir," she said. "All outright lies and jests and advice I shall pass on to you, you may be certain."

The marquess nodded. "I like the gown, Frances. It suits you quite nicely."

That was an understatement, thought Marcus.

"Thank you," Frances said in a very demure voice, but there were demons dancing in her gray eyes. "Incidentally, sir, I saw a portrait of Lady Beatrice in the gallery. She is quite lovely."

The marquess said nothing for a long moment; then he shrugged. "That's as may be," he said obliquely, and Frances' left brow arched upward.

"I haven't seen Beatrice for a goodly number of years," said Alicia. "She goes well, sir?" At his nod, she continued to Frances, "She is recently betrothed to Edmund Lacy, a quite charming gentleman, from all I hear. He was a good friend of Nevil's and now a friend of Philip's. He owns quite a respectable stud and racing stable. Isn't it in Devonshire, sir?"

"So I hear," the marquess said.

Frances wasn't blind. She saw that the marquess was discomfited by this talk, and though she didn't understand why, she took pity on him and quickly changed the topic. "I was just on the point of asking Alicia how one goes about meeting all our neighbors. I believe I am ready for the assault."

"Indeed you are," said Alicia. "Now, we must have your visiting cards made up. Mr. Crocker in York is quite accomplished. Something simple yet elegant, I think."

"An excellent combination," said Frances, thinking that she'd been through the simple, and now elegant was the order of the day.

"But I shall spread the word that you are now receiving. You do not need the cards until you wish to visit."

"Yes, I know," said Frances. "I wasn't raised completely bereft of proper social behavior."

"No, of course not!"

Frances grinned at her.

It had begun to drizzle by the time Alicia left Desborough Hall, and Frances, concerned, said, "Should you wish to remain to dinner, Alicia? I could send a footman to tell John."

But Alicia refused. Frances, rather than returning to the drawing room, sought out Otis.

"Tomorrow, Otis, I should like you to accompany me to York. I wish your assistance in choosing new livery for the men."

Otis was stunned by such an invitation. He felt immensely flattered, and his impassive features showed it. "I should be delighted to assist you, my lady," he said. His opinion, without his conscious realization, had just shifted markedly.

"Yes," he said later to Mrs. Jerkins, "her ladyship has asked me to help her. What do you think, Agatha? Shall it be wool or broadcloth? Perhaps both. Her ladyship does not stint. I rather fancy her color selection. The crimson and blue will be most elegant, yes indeed, most elegant."

Agatha was jealous as could be until Frances summoned her and asked her advice on new linens. "You know, we need to do quite a bit of refurbishing, Mrs. Jerkins. You have done so well all this time, but now it is appropriate to lay out the funds. I trust your experience in this matter."

Mrs. Jerkins expanded under Frances' twinkling eyes.

"Ah, another thing. The dishes the staff use—they're in deplorable shape. You and I shall select a new set. Something that is sturdy and will last awhile, but also something nice. What do you think?"

Tomorrow, Frances thought, I shall beard you, Mr. Carruthers, in your den. She returned her wandering attention to Mrs. Jerkins' excited suggestions. The woman was actually smiling at her, for the first time.

> *Let us have wine and women,*
> *mirth and laughter,*
> *Sermons and soda-water*
> *the day after.*
>
> —LORD BYRON

Hawk smiled down at Lady Constance, pulling her just a bit closer as he twirled her about the ballroom. He'd forgotten how lovely she was, how her breasts pushed so seductively against his chest, how her fingers tightened on his shoulder.

But she was in the devil of a snit. He supposed he couldn't blame her.

"I would speak to you, my lord," she said in a throbbing voice that gave him pause.

"Continue," Hawk said. "I am at your service."

"Apparently not. The question, my lord, is why you are here without your bride."

"That is not part of the service, Constance. Is there anything else?"

"Well, you know there are the strangest rumors going about."

"There always are. Mine aren't terribly interesting or titillating, I wouldn't imagine."

"Sally Jersey doesn't agree with you."

"She will grow bored soon enough," said Hawk, trying out Lyonel's lazy drawl.

Constance managed to make her chin tremble just a bit. It was, in her experience, a very effective ploy. "I had thought, indeed hoped, my lord . . . Hawk, that there were something more between us, something that—"

"Ah," said Hawk, "the music has come to a halt. Would you like a glass of champagne, Connie? An old married man like myself would be most gratified."

She drew a deep breath, one so profound that his eyes were drawn to her very ample bosom. He still wanted her, she knew it. Why this ridiculous marriage? Why had he left his bride in Yorkshire?

They were sipping their champagne when Lyonel strolled by.

"Quite a crush," he said, lazily surveying Lady Bellingham's ballroom. "Your servant, Lady Constance, Hawk—but not your servant, old fellow."

Constance wondered if she would try for Saint Leven. It was her second Season, and she knew her parents wanted her to make a push to attach an appropriate gentleman. He was handsome, she thought, and seemed pleasant enough. She listened with half an ear to the gentlemen's conversation, pausing, her eyes widening when Lyonel said, "I should think Frances would much enjoy herself here. Does she enjoy the scandalous waltz, Hawk?"

Frances. So that was the bride's name! Lord Saint Leven had met her?

"I don't have the foggiest notion," said Hawk, trying his best to frown Lyonel down.

To his relief, Lord Bellamy minced up at that moment to claim his dance.

"Silly fop," said Lyonel, watching the baron lead Constance into a country dance.

"Please drop that damned eyepiece of yours, Lyonel, it reminds me of Frances in her spectacles."

"Miss her already, do you, my boy? And this only your second day, er, night, in London."

"What I miss," Hawk said, "is Amalie. If you will excuse me, Lyon, I'm off to Curzon Street. Amalie, unlike others, is awaiting me, with great sweetness, no doubt."

"Sweetness," mused Lyonel. "What an odd way of putting it. Do enjoy yourself, old fellow."

Hawk had every intention of enjoying himself immensely. When he arrived at Amalie's very charming house on Curzon Street, a house he'd allowed her to select and furnish, at his expense, of course, he was greeted by her pert little French maid, Marie."

"Madame is expecting you, *monseigneur.*"

Hawk felt himself becoming aroused even as he strode up the stairs to her bedchamber.

Amalie was lounging in the center of her pink frilled counterpane, her favorite book open on her lap. Ah,

Diderot, she was thinking, a man of talent, a man of wit. She heard Hawk's footsteps, and quickly stuffed Diderot's thin volume under her pillow.

She'd missed him, no question about that. She wondered if his father had died. Hawk had been distraught when he'd left London for his father's estate. She should have read the *Gazette,* but she found it boring, much preferring her countrymen's elegant writing.

He appeared in the doorway, beautifully handsome, his large body filling her very feminine bedroom.

"*Mon faucon!*" Amalie cried, and jumped off her bed. She was immediately enfolded in his strong arms, her face pressed against his shoulder.

"I never get used to being a hawk in French, Amalie," he said, his hands moving down her back to her hips. He breathed in the sweet scent of her—female and attar of roses. A heady combination. "I want you, now," he said, his voice deepening.

She moved against him and felt his hard manhood straining at his breeches. "You do indeed, *mon amour,*" she whispered, and stood on her tiptoes to kiss him.

"And you, Amalie? Do you want me?"

That made her cock her head to the side. "What a question *ridicule!*"

She felt his hand slip inside her peignoir, his deft fingers stroking down her belly until he touched her intimately.

"Ah, how nice," Hawk said, feeling her warmth, her wetness.

"What do you expect, *mon faucon*? Coldness?"

"I don't know," he said, and lifted her easily into his arms. Frances would have been cold and dry and stiff.

He was undressed so quickly that Amalie had little chance to admire his beautiful body. Then he was on the bed beside her, drawing off her pink silk peignoir.

"God, I've missed you," he said, burying his face in her breasts.

"And I you," she whispered, gently clasping him to her.

"I fear I cannot wait, Amalie," Hawk said, so tense that it was almost pain.

"You can see to my pleasure later," Amalie said, and shifted her body to receive him. She closed her eyes when he thrust deeply into her. "Ah, yes," she said, arching her hips upward.

Hawk felt her thighs close about his flanks, felt her hands grasp his buttocks, and he was gone in the next instant, his head thrown back, gasps of pleasure erupting from his throat.

He fell against her, his head beside hers on the pillow.

She smiled as she gently stroked his head. "I give you thirty minutes, my Hawk. Then you must become my lover again."

"And not your husband," he muttered, aware of that damned niggling guilt.

"I do not understand," Amalie said.

"Later," Hawk said.

"Your father?"

"Healthy as you, my dear, more so in fact."

"Ah, good."

Hawk fell asleep sprawled atop his mistress's body. Amalie stroked his back very lightly, her brow furrowed in thought. How to tell this beautiful man that she wished to return to Grenoble, that she had a marriage proposal from a man she'd known for years, now a prosperous farmer. She had sufficient funds to buy all the books she craved, and she wanted to settle down. She wanted Robert and she wanted children. Ah, but it was a difficult thing to decide.

There would be no more luxury, not like this. Robert would make vigorous love to her, of that she was quite certain, but he wouldn't be a lover, not like Hawk.

But there would be respectability, and Amalie's French soul wanted respectability more than anything. And Robert Gravinier need never know that she had been any man's mistress.

Hawk awoke with a start some two hours later. "Oh my God," he said, realizing that he was crushing Amalie beneath him. "I'm sorry, you should have awakened me."

"Ah no," Amalie said, kissing his chin, "I fell asleep also." It wasn't true, she'd finished readying the next chapter in Diderot's *Encyclopedie,* and her body was quite numb.

Hawk rolled off her and rose. She watched him stretch, and immediate yearnings for the respectable Robert faded. "You are magnificent," she said. "It has been too long."

"Allow me to bathe myself, Amalie, then I will pleasure you until you scream."

"I should like that," she said, her dark eyes twinkling at him in anticipation.

Hawk loved a woman's pleasure. It made him feel immense satisfaction when a woman made those breathy little cries and her body tensed and convulsed. A woman, not a wife, he thought to himself as he spread kisses down Amalie's soft belly. When his mouth found her, she lurched up, reaching her pleasure very quickly.

He raised his head and gave her a lazy smile. He slid into her warm body and felt her close tightly around him. He stretched over her, kissing her deeply, his tongue foraging in her mouth just as his manhood thrust deep in her belly.

It was near to two o'clock in the morning. They were eating sweet rolls and drinking tea, seated naked on Amalie's bed.

"I'm married," Hawk said abruptly.

Amalie's sweet roll fell onto the bed between her crossed legs. She stared at him, certain she'd misunderstood. Her English was good, but . . .

"I'm married," Hawk said again, and sighed deeply.

"I do not understand," said Amalie slowly, her dark eyes fastened intently on his face. "It is most curious . . . yet so fascinating."

Because she was serious, and not a gossipmonger, because her voice was soft, her eyes wide with concern, he found himself pouring out everything that had occurred, from his race to his father to his race to Scotland. When he completed his recital, he felt drained and exhausted.

"You have left your lady wife in Yorkshire?"

He nodded.

"She will fall in love with you, *mon faucon*. No woman could resist you for very long."

"Ha! She detests me, she spits on the ground I walk, she—"

"Bosh. You bring her pleasure and she melts all over you, *n'est-ce pas*? After all, you are an excellent lover, and not at all a *bête*."

Hawk realized it was most odd to be speaking of his wife to his mistress, but the floodgates had burst open. "Amalie, you must realize that a gentleman doesn't treat his wife as he would his mistress."

"He doesn't? How very curious."

"It isn't curious at all. A wife is a lady and isn't . . .

well, she doesn't want to be bothered with sex. I have been most respectful of her feelings, I promise you."

Amalie could only stare at him. "You do not make her melt all over you, Hawk?"

Hawk shuddered. "I've never even seen her," he said. "I've never even touched her above the waist. As I said, Amalie, things are different between a gentleman and his wife."

Amalie was thoughtfully silent. She saw Hawk gazing intently at her breasts, and stretched lazily, seductively. She was a bit sore, but what matter? She quickly removed the remains of their tea and food. "Come," she said softly.

Hawk didn't leave Curzon Street until gray streaks of dawn were lighting the London darkness.

❧ 13 ❧

She pays him in his own coin.
—*JOHNATHAN SWIFT*

Marcus Carruthers stared at Frances, reminding her forcibly of Mrs. Jerkins' initial reaction.

"But, my lady, I . . . well, I don't think it would . . . no, 'tis quite impossible, his lordship, what will—"

"I am from Scotland, sir, and yet I am capable of stringing together a logical thought." Her eyes twinkled at him, and her tone was teasing, robbing her words of any offense.

Marcus Carruthers mopped his brow with his white handkerchief.

"Now, listen, Marcus. You are new here. I am new here. I am telling you all about my outlay of money, not only for my own wardrobe, but also for household items, and you have no real choice but to agree. After all, my husband isn't present, as I'm certain you notice, nor is he particularly interested in this estate of his."

"We spent a good deal of time together before he left," Marcus said defensively, but he was thinking: *His lordship gives not a damn about Desborough Hall. What am I to do?*

"I see, but now he is gone, Marcus. What instructions did he leave you?"

"He, ah, well, he told me to continue."

"Continue what?"

"Well, keeping things afloat, I suppose."

"That is not acceptable, Marcus." Frances sat forward in her chair, clasping her hands in her lap. "I am taking over management of the Desborough stud and racing stables. I have spoken at length with my father-in-law. I have learned of the former grandeur of Desborough. Indeed, his lordship's brother, Nevil, kept up the tradition until his death. Things are now in utter disarray. It is outrageous and I will not allow it to continue."

She drew to a temporary halt and stared at Marcus Carruthers.

"But you are a lady," he began.

"Thank you for remarking on that, Marcus. Now, I have seen at least four three- and four-year-old colts, thoroughbreds, mind you, that are wandering about the paddocks, getting no training, eating their heads off, in short, costing us money, rather than winning us money. For heaven's sake, the stableboys ride them for sport! Thoroughbreds! In addition, we have two magnificent Arabians and three Barbs, all with impeccable bloodlines, that could be earning us quite respectable sums in stud."

"I know," said Marcus, warming a bit. "I told his lordship that."

"And he said?"

"He . . . well, he wasn't much interested."

"No? Well, I am and you are. The first thing we must do is secure the return of Mr. Belvis. His experience, I understand from my father-in-law, is most impressive, and he *knows* the Desborough stock."

"That is true." Marcus lowered his eyes a moment. "There is something I should tell you, Lady Frances.

His lordship mentioned to me that he'd an offer for the entire Desborough stock—racing stock, stud stock, the Barbs and Arabs you mentioned—everything, all the prize mares as well. None of our mares have even been bred," he added.

Frances sucked in her breath. "What? He would consider destroying a tradition all because he doesn't wish to be saddled with the responsibility? Oh, I could kill him!"

"His lordship, ah, told me he was just thinking about it. He has not made a decision, my lady."

Frances bounded out of her chair and began pacing about the drawing room, her steps a stride, not lady-like and mincing. Marcus watched her perambulations with a good deal of wary interest.

She paused, her hands fisted at her sides, her gray eyes dark with emotion. "I think it is time that I consulted my father-in-law about funds. It will cost a great deal of money to bring the stables back into shape. I do not think I can, myself, authorize such expenditures."

"No, I am sorry, but you cannot. His lordship said—"

"Oh, bother his lordship!" Frances clasped the bellcord and gave it a vicious tug.

Otis appeared as swiftly and silently as an omnipresent genie.

"Is his lordship about, Otis?" Frances asked.

"I shall endeavor to locate him, my lady." Otis remarked her flushed face and wondered what she was up to now.

The marquess, refreshed from his nap, strode some minutes later into the drawing room. "Well, my dear, what bee have you in your bonnet now?"

"No bee, sir. Did you know that Hawk is considering selling all the Desborough stock?"

"The devil you say!"

"The devil's identity is uncertain at this moment. However, I have a proposition for you, sir."

"I believe I'll have a brandy first. Carruthers, will you join me?"

"What about me?" Frances demanded. "I am more in need of the brandy than either of you. After all, it appears that I am now responsible for Desborough Hall!"

The world is made up for the most part of fools and knaves.
—GEORGE VILLIERS

Edmund Lacy, Viscount Chalmers, calmly regarded his betrothed, Beatrice, Lady Dunsmore.

"Not a single word to me about this!" Beatrice raged, her famed pale complexion now in high color. "It is my father's doing, you may be certain of that, Edmund. Didn't you say that my dear brother is here in London, quite alone?"

"Yes, that is what I said," replied Edmund, gently twirling his looking glass on its velvet ribbon. "He is enjoying himself most thoroughly, I should add."

"Back to his mistress?"

"Indeed, it would seem so."

"He could have had the decency to call upon me." Edmund shrugged, and she added, her eyes glittering, "I wonder what Constance has to say to all this nonsense?"

"The lady is . . . perturbed, I gather. I saw her but yesterday, out with her damned Pekingese and her cowering maid. She was most vocal in her dissatisfaction."

Beatrice didn't really care a snap about Lady Constance, the eldest daughter of the Earl of Lumley. The girl was something of a bore, really, at least in the company of ladies. But for Hawk to get himself married, and to a stranger none of them knew anything about! And they were so close, so very close to gaining her heart's desire. She wondered if the new bride had any power over her husband and if she did, what she thought about Desborough. Beatrice shook her head. No, indeed, if this ramshackle marriage had been her sire's idea, then Hawk's presence without his bride was explained: he couldn't bear the sight of her.

"Have you asked him again about Desborough stock, Edmund?"

"One does not press like a tradesman, my dear," Edmund said gently. He saw her flush and smiled. "Soon, Beatrice. Hawk can be stubborn. I will not push him unduly."

"Oh, if only I'd been born a male! 'Tis not fair, Edmund! It would be mine now, all of it. And Hawk doesn't care a penny for the stud or the racing stables!"

"But then, my dear, we would not be betrothed—if you were a male, that is."

That brought Beatrice up short, but only for a moment. "Oh, that," she said, waving a pale, elegant hand, oblivious of the fact that she'd insulted her future husband. "Well, I suppose if my dear brother agrees to the sale, I shall have it in any case."

"Yes, that is quite true."

"You know, all Hawk ever knew was the army, and now he's like a bird let out of his structured cage. He told me once some months ago that he'd never wanted Nevil's title and fortune. Is he gambling much, do you think?"

"He is not a fool, Beatrice. Even if he were, he

would have to lose vast sums at the table before he would have to consider selling the stock."

Beatrice grew silent and Edmund watched her, amusement deepening the rich amber color of his eyes. She was a witch, no doubt about that, but he would control her quite nicely once they were married. And she need never know that he needed her fortune to help pay for the stock, once Hawk agreed to sell. Ah well, they would both be getting what they wanted. Edmund didn't love her, but he wanted to bed her, and planned to do just that very shortly. She was a widow, after all, and he reckoned that her ancient relic of a husband hadn't given her much satisfaction, if any. She was also quite pretty, her features so like her brother's, but feminine at the same time. Her hair was glossy black, her eyes a gleaming leaf green. She was tall, deep-bosomed, and if she was gaining flesh, she would retain her bodily charms for a number of years yet. It occurred to him that there wasn't much love lost between brother and sister. He trusted that he hadn't made a miscalculation. He had assumed that Beatrice would assist him in gaining Hawk's agreement for the sale.

"Why do you not invite your brother to dine, Beatrice? I would be there also, of course. It might prove an appropriate time to broach the subject again."

Her eyes flashed. "An excellent suggestion, Edmund. Would you like to search him out?"

"I cannot pay a visit to his mistress," Edmund said dryly.

"He cannot be with her all the time!"

Edmund merely smiled at her; then he caught her hand, drew it to his lips, and kissed her palm. "Ah," he said with satisfaction, feeling the pulse quicken at her wrist. He looked directly into her eyes, and slowly stroked his hand over her breasts. He felt her nipples harden beneath the thin muslin. "Soon," he said, turned, and left her without another word.

He could hear her quickened breathing behind him. She was a witch, he thought again, but she would be such a passionate witch in bed.

Edmund Lacy tracked his future brother-in-law down at White's, not in the gaming room, but in the immense reading room, whose usual inhabitants were two generations removed from him.

The silence was disconcerting. There was only an occasional rustling of paper, an occasional snore.

"Hawk," Edmund said quietly, lightly touching his shoulder.

Hawk was reading the war news in the *Gazette*, his brow furrowed. "Not going well at all," he muttered under his breath. "Oh, Edmund, how are you? How is Bea?"

"She is well, as am I. In fact, I am here as her emissary. Would you care to dine with us this evening at Dunsmore House?"

More damned impertinent questions about my marriage, Hawk thought, but his face remained impassive. He felt a stirring of guilt that he hadn't yet seen his sister. She looked so much like him that he should have felt closer to her, but he didn't, never had, in fact. Not that he'd ever seen her very much during their growing-up years at Desborough Hall. Then, when his grandfather had died and his father had moved his family to Chandos Chase, he saw even less of her, for he was off at Sandhurst. He realized suddenly that he hadn't replied, and quickly said, "I should be delighted, Edmund."

They chatted amiably about the war, and Hawk found himself impressed by his future brother-in-law's knowledge. Neither an empty-headed fribble nor a fool was Edmund Lacy.

When Edmund rose finally to take his leave, he said gently, "Incidentally, Hawk, you needn't worry that Beatrice will quiz you about your marriage. I have assured her that it is none of her affair. Nor, of course, is it any of mine."

"What courage you possess," Hawk remarked, grinning. "I have heard it said that poor old Lord Dunsmore cocked up his toes as his last and only independent act."

"Hawk," Edmund chided, "what a thing to say about your sister. She is high-spirited, 'tis all. You cannot imagine, old boy, that she would drive me to a similar fate?"

Hawk laughed, only to close his mouth at the snorting sounds of disapproval from one of the ancient members of White's.

He obligingly shook his head, sat back in the high-cushioned leather chair, and watched Edmund Lacy leave the room. A fine specimen of a man, Hawk thought. Not a flabby macaroni nor a pompous idiot. Fashionable, yes, but he didn't carry on with excessive rings and fobs. He was trim, his features well-formed. He would make Beatrice a good husband, keep her in her proper place.

Frances. Oh hell, he thought, rising, disgusted with himself. He didn't want to think of her. He wondered, as he strolled out onto St. James, if his father were still at Desborough Hall. He probably was, Hawk thought, holding her little hand and trying to make the servants regard her as something of a mistress. Perhaps his father would encourage her to buy some new gowns. Perhaps he would encourage her not to cower and hide. Hawk decided he should write her a letter.

Yes, he would do that. He returned to the Hawksbury town house in Portland Square. There were only two servants in residence besides Grunyon, but it didn't matter, since he never dined there in any case.

Rolland, his majordomo, was older than Otis at Desborough Hall and made Shippe at Chandos Chase look like a frisky young pup. He managed to answer the door knocker, but other duties beyond that were, at the very least, a decade behind him. Thus, it was Grunyon who brought him a quill and paper in the library.

"Is Rolland still breathing?" Hawk asked, grinning at his valet.

"After a fashion," said Grunyon.

"I'd put him out to pasture, but he has no relatives. Lord, he's outlived the lot of them, and he was, as I hear my father tell, the ninth of twelve children."

"A case of longevity," said Grunyon. "You are writing to Lady Frances?" he asked with the assurance of a longtime retainer who knew quite well his head wouldn't be removed from his shoulders.

"Curse it, yes," said Hawk, dipping the quill into the ink pot. "I shall be dining this evening with my sister and Lord Chalmers. See to my togs, will you, Grunyon?"

"Yes, my lord. Ah, do give Lady Frances my, er, best wishes."

"Impertinent fool," Hawk said.

"Sartorial splendor," Grunyon said that evening, regarding his lordship with approval.

"What?"

"I heard that said of you, my lord."

"What utter nonsense. Damnation, I don't even know the meaning of that word."

"It refers, my lord, to the elegant appearance you present in your evening clothing."

Hawk snorted, accepted his cape, gloves, and cane, and took his leave.

He took a hackney coach the short distance to Grosvenor Square. He was met by a charming, gay sister at Dunsmore House, a sister filled with enthusiasm for his presence, and suffered her kiss on his cheek. Edmund shook his head at her display, and retreated, allowing Beatrice full rein.

Dinner concerned itself with exquisitely prepared French dishes—veal in a delicate wine sauce, partridge stuffed with raisins, chestnuts, and rice, lamb so tender that it melted when touched by teeth.

"I think we should both visit Gentleman Jackson tomorrow, Edmund," Hawk said, sitting back in his chair, sated.

"I agree," said Edmund. He gave Beatrice a nod, and she dutifully rose from her chair.

"I shall see you gentlemen after you've imbibed your port," she said, and left them to themselves.

"Congratulations again," Hawk said, and toasted Edmund.

"Thank you. We will deal well together, you know. It is my feeling that your father is . . . relieved."

The marquess rarely spoke of his daughter, and upon hearing of the engagement, had merely snorted and muttered under his breath, "Maybe the chit will have the good sense to have some children now." And then he'd said something that had made Hawk frown. "The only thing that concerns me about Lord Chalmers is that he was one of Nevil's closest friends." Odd, that. Not what one would expect from a father.

"Perhaps," Hawk said. He suddenly grinned at Edmund. "I also congratulate you on your strength of character. Beatrice has said not a word about my unfortunate alliance."

Unfortunate? Edmund let it pass. He poured Hawk another glass of the excellent port, leaned back in his chair, and said in a meditative voice, "Did you hear what happened to one of the Earl of Egremont's prize racers?"

Hawk wasn't particularly interested, but he shook his head and leaned forward a bit.

"The horse's name was Falcon and he was lamed by his trainer before a quite important race at Newmarket. The trainer has taken to his heel, to the Continent, one supposes."

"Unfortunate," Hawk said.

"I mention it just to remind you that the racing world isn't one of unblemished character. One must really be utterly committed to succeed, like the Duke of Portland and the Duke of Richmond, for example. The men live their lives for their horses and their races. It is the only way." He paused a moment, then added, "Nevil was the same way. He lived and breathed his horses. There was nothing else that gained his attention."

Hawk, to Edmund's brief chagrin, responded, but not as he had hoped. "It is odd, but you knew my brother much better than did I. I scarce ever saw him for the last six or seven years of his life. Was he successful at Newmarket and Ascot?"

It was on the tip of Edmund's tongue to say that his racing stock wasn't of the best, but then, that wouldn't make logical sense. For if that were the case, then why would he, Edmund, wish to buy all the stock? "Yes," Edmund said, "he was."

"And you, I take it, are an avid racer?"

Edmund nodded, searching frantically for the right

opening, the right thing to say. "That is why I would like to breed your stock with mine. It is my fondest ambition, I suppose you would say. Incidentally, your sister is also absorbed with racing. She also shares my ambition."

"Ah." Hawk realized that he wasn't as eager about selling off Desborough stock as he had been but two months before. He was now a married man, and a married man normally, in the course of events, was blessed with children. What would his son think if he were to be informed that his father had sold his legacy? It was a startling, rather unwelcome thought, at least at the moment. He liked Edmund and he didn't wish to deal him such a disappointment. He chose, instead, to perseverate. "I am still considering it. As you know, old man, my life has undergone severe buffeting during the past month. I am still not certain." He shrugged. "But of course you aren't interested in my mental machinations. Shall we see if Bea will play for us?"

Hawk saw the brief questioning look that passed from his sister to her betrothed. What to do? he wondered.

He listened with half an ear while Beatrice regaled them with her talented fingers at the pianoforte. He winced, thinking of Frances' playing and singing.

"Belvis, he is truly magnificent, isn't he?"

"Indeed so, my lady," said Belvis, pleased at the excitement in her eyes as she stroked Flying Davie's sleek neck. "Nearly sixteen hands he is, and a beautiful rich bay. You know that most thoroughbreds are bay, many chestnut. Rarely will you see a gray or a black. From his elegantly curved neck, fine muzzle, it's obvious Flying Davie has much Arab blood in him.

As for the white star on his forehead and the white tufts on his fetlock, 'tis inexplicable.''

"Who were his sire and dam?"

"Odd that you should ask," Belvis said, scratching his thatch of curly gray hair. "His papers seemed to be missing when he was delivered here, nearly four years ago. But he's a winner, you have but to look at him to know it." He didn't add that Flying Davie didn't appear in any of the stud books, due, he supposed, to the former earl's forgetful habits.

"Why didn't his owner replace the papers?" Frances asked, feeling the stallion's hot breath as he nibbled a carrot from her hand.

"The owner had left for India. Died there, from what I understand from his former lordship."

Frances wiped her hands on her old wool skirt. "Will you come back, Belvis?"

"I'm not as young as I used to be," he hedged.

"None of us is. Have the years taken your knowledge and skills?"

"Certainly not!"

Ah, Frances thought, he's weakening. Before she could press him further, he said, "But you know, my lady, the reason I left was that his lordship has no interest. Indeed, he mentioned to me that he just might sell everything."

"He won't," Frances said firmly, her fingers crossed at her sides.

"Well, it appears you're a strong-willed lady, ma'am. But still, it—"

"Please, Belvis." She studied the older man. He must be over sixty, but he appeared as healthy as she. His face was leathery and deeply seamed from his long years out-of-doors. He was short, lean, of a wiry build, but his arms were immensely strong. His eyes were a faded blue, as if the harsh sun had bleached away the color. And the horses seemed to know him and to *trust* him. He was what her father had called a *natural*. Frances raised her chin. So was she, a natural, that is.

She drew a deep breath and blurted out, "I shall pay you three hundred pounds a year, Belvis."

His eyes widened at that. Then he began to laugh, a rusty sound. He stopped just as suddenly as he'd begun, and wiped his eyes with his sleeve. "Tommy tells me that you cured a bruised back leg on Springer, and that he's now in excellent condition."

"He no longer even limps," said Frances. "I . . . well, I spent my growing-up years in Scotland learning about horses, about taking care of them. I have even delivered calves and foals. As for Springer, I simply applied frequent formentations, then some liniment for the swelling."

"Doesn't sound like much of a ladylike hobby to me, ma'am."

"I am a Scot, Belvis," Frances said, her gray eyes darkening just a bit. "I am not a useless creature to be cosseted and— "

"I know, my lady," he said, cutting her off.

"—and it wasn't a hobby, Belvis!"

"Evidently not," he said, rubbing his rather pointed chin. "My lady, don't misunderstand me. 'Tis not that I don't wish to return to Desborough, 'tis just that when all is said and done, it's his lordship who owns everything."

"His lordship isn't here, Belvis."

"Yes, but—"

"I have no idea if he will return within the next six months."

"Ah, and when he does return, you plan something of a . . . surprise for him?"

Frances' smile was radiant. "Yes," she said, "oh yes, indeed I do!"

"And if he sells before he returns?"

That drew Frances up short. She gnawed on her lower lip, considering various possibilities. "I suppose," she said finally, "that I shall have to write to him in London." *I shall beg, plead with him not to sell.*

Flying Davie butted his nose against Belvis' sleeve at that moment. The old man smiled. He said to Frances, "I shall stay until we know—one way or the t'other."

"Excellent," Frances said, and shook his hand. She was smiling until she sat down in the estate room, a quill in her hand, a blank sheet of pressed paper before her. "Oh curse you, my lord!" she muttered, and set the quill to paper.

14

There was all the world and his wife.
—JOHNATHAN SWIFT

Hawk tapped his long fingers against the sheet of paper. He hadn't appreciated being reminded of Frances' existence, and here she had written him a letter! And what a letter . . .

Odd, he thought, frowning as he studied her neat black script. Why the devil did she care about the stud? And she knew nothing of racing, at least he didn't think she did. He felt a moment of sheer perversity, then grinned at himself. He slipped the page back in its envelope and shoved it into his desk drawer. No, he wouldn't sell anything, but not because of her letter.

Such a show of excitement, of passion, from such a little dowd. He shook his head. He simply couldn't imagine Frances interested in his high-strung race horses, for God's sake. Certainly she would cower, afraid that they would bite her. He wondered if his father had set her up to do this, then shook his head at himself. That was not, to his firsthand knowledge, his sire's way.

He toyed with the idea of writing to her to assure her that he had no further plans to sell. No, he decided, memory of her coldness, her ill-mannered behavior toward her husband rekindling his anger at her. Let her stew in her own juices.

He took himself off to another ball that evening, danced with Constance and a multitude of other ladies, flirted shamelessly with his hostess, Aurelia Markham, and left at eleven o'clock.

He thought to go to White's, but changed his mind. He wanted, needed Amalie.

Amalie was ensconced in her favorite chair in her small drawing room reading Voltaire's *Candide*. She was laughing in delight when she heard the door knocker. Hawk, she thought, and quickly stuffed the volume beneath the chair cushion.

Marie was in bed in her small bedchamber. Amalie opened the door, her smile welcoming. "*Bonsoir, mon faucon,*" she said, and opened her arms to him.

"I'm a horny goat," Hawk said by way of greeting, and began to nibble her earlobe.

"You are always that randy animal," she agreed, and lovingly stroked her hand over the ready bulge in his trousers.

He was also a randy animal *husband,* and that bothered Amalie. She wanted to laugh at herself for this most odd display of principle.

Because he was an exquisite lover, Hawk brought her pleasure first even though his own need was urgent.

"Most acceptable for a goat," Amalie said, rubbing her hands over his strong smooth back. He was still breathing heavily, his face beside hers on the pillow.

"Thank you," Hawk said dryly, heaving himself off her. He lay on his back, pillowing his head on his arms, and stared at nothing in particular.

"Something has happened to disturb you?"

He started at that, but shook his head vehemently.

"Come, *mon cher,*" she said gently, speaking before her mind had censored her thoughts, "you know very well that what the famous Corneille says is quite true: *By speaking of our misfortunes we often relieve them.*"

"Corneille?" he repeated in some astonishment. He turned to look at her closely and saw that she was flushing. Actually flushing! He grinned and ran his fingertip over her full lips. "A bluestocking mistress? How very delightful!"

"I am not this bluestocking," she said, frowning at him. "I am no ignorant person, that is all."

That drew him up short yet again. A person. He had always been fond of Amalie. She was pretty, she was gay, and she pandered to his every wish. She wasn't rapacious or greedy, she was loving. She'd feigned pleasure with him but once, but never again. Oh no, he hadn't allowed that. But she was a mistress, for God's sake. Had he been so very blind to her?

"And there is another thing," Amalie said, her lips tightening at what she thought was her lover's amusement. "Voltaire says that *we should cultive our garden.* A noble sentiment. And you, my lord, have left your garden in the north . . . well, untended!"

"The devil you say," Hawk said slowly. "This is incredible . . . a mistress championing a wife?"

She continued frowning at him.

"Done in by a damned Frenchman," he said, running his fingers through his hair. "Look, Amalie, let's not speak of her, all right? Indeed, I don't want to speak at all this moment."

She saw the gleam in his beautiful green eyes and felt her heart quicken despite her principles. "All right," she said, and arched upward to kiss him and press her breasts against his furred chest.

Hawk wasn't feeling particularly urgent now, and took his time. He wanted the woman, his mistress, back, not the *person.* When his mouth caressed her belly, and his fingers found her and stroked her so expertly, so completely, Amalie sighed.

Then she said abruptly, "You should do that to your wife."

His tongue became as still as his mind. He lifted his head to look up the length of her body to her face. "My God, I haven't even kissed my wife! I told you that. One doesn't do *this* to a wife, for God's sake!" He dropped a quick kiss on her damp curls. "She would faint, she would have galloping hysterics, she would expire of lacerated sensibilities on the spot!"

"Bosh," said Amalie. "What a ridiculous notion you men have of women. Is your wife fashioned differently from me?"

"I wouldn't know," Hawk said acidly. "I haven't seen her body."

"So it is your gentleman's belief that a wife, a *lady* born and bred, hates the thought of coupling?"

"Your English is improving by leaps and bounds," he said in the most sarcastic voice he could muster. His desire was as dead as three-day-old ashes in the grate.

"Of course, I told you I am not ignorant. Listen, *mon faucon,* how can you be so stupid?"

"I am not being stupid, thank you! I have treated her with the utmost respect, I have—"

"Stupid," Amalie repeated firmly, warming to her subject. "You are not an ugly man. You have skill in giving a woman pleasure. And that should include a wife."

"She is ugly, however," he said. "She—"

"Is fat?"

"No, quite slender as a matter of fact. But her spectacles, her hair, her clothing—"

"So, *mon cher,* the fact is that you don't wish to pleasure her as you do me? You are repelled by her, thus you hide behind this ridiculous notion that ladies are to be protected from gentlemen's baser needs."

"A damned philosopher," he growled at her. "I don't need you to preach at me, Amalie."

"Spectacles can be removed," she said gently, "and clothing can be removed as well."

"But her hair—she looks like a nun, with her ridiculous ugly caps—"

"Stupid. Quite stupid, as I said. Caps, as well as everything else, can be removed."

Hawk heard himself saying, most inappropriately, "I have wondered about her breasts . . . Oh God, look at what you've brought me to! Just shut up. I wish to tend this particular garden, if you don't mind." He cupped his palm over the curls between her white thighs.

He brought both of them to pleasure again, but Amalie knew that he was abstracted.

A mistress taking a husband to task. She wished she could laugh. It would feel so good. But of course it would enrage him. Men were such sensitive creatures. Still . . .

"Hawk," she said softly, knowing he wasn't yet asleep, "you shouldn't treat her like this nun you speak about, you—"

"Amalie," he said, impatient now, "I don't wish to talk of her. She dislikes me heartily. She wouldn't want me to touch her, even if I could bring myself to."

"That sounds not right, *mon cher*. You can, when you wish, charm even that fat man, that Regent, *n'est-ce pas*? And you have told me about that Brummell person and how you made him smile at one of your jests. You do not wish to spend your life with one who dislikes you. A wife—"

"Enough!" he roared, rolling off her. "It is your duty, Amalie, to see to my pleasure, to make me

happy, not carry on like some sort of fishwi . . . mistress!" He rose, hands on his lean hips, and stared
down at her. Suddenly his eyes narrowed thoughtfully
on her face.

"Why, Amalie?"

Amalie eased herself up, pulling the light coverlet
over her body. "It is not right," she said finally, not
meeting his eyes.

He could only stare at her. "I think," he said slowly,
weariness overtaking him, "that I shall leave you now."

She watched him dress, watched the firelight cast
intriguing shadows on his golden body, playing over
his smooth man's flesh, the planes and angles of chest
and belly. She sighed softly to herself. He said nothing
more until he was fully clothed. He walked to the bed,
bent down and kissed her, then straightened.

"Hawk," she said very softly, "you are a good man."

"Thank you," he said, his voice utterly emotionless.
"I shall see you soon, Amalie. Good night."

She murmured good night after him. She heard his
steps in the corridor, heard him take the stairs two at a
time, heard the door close behind him. Life, she thought
vaguely, feeling drowsiness tug at her, life was not
simple.

Hawk walked down St. James Street, nodding automatically to acquaintances, speaking only when it would
be rude not to.

He felt at odds with himself, a state he was neither
accustomed to nor relished. When he saw Constance
waving to him from her landau, he winced to himself.
He now found her attractions dubious, and that surprised him. He'd known he would never marry her
even if his father hadn't made that ridiculous oath that
had landed squarely on his shoulders, but still, he had
enjoyed her. She was an accomplished flirt.

"My lord," she called to him, motioning to her coachman to halt beside him.

"Good morning, Constance," he said calmly, strolling to her carriage. "You are shopping?" He eyed the mound of packages strewn over her maid, and for a brief instant the maid looked at him. What he saw in that look made him wince again. It was ineffable weariness, a sort of dulled acceptance.

He forced himself to smile up at Constance.

"Yes, as you can see. Teresa, don't let that package fall into the street, you stupid girl! Ah, Hawk, will you be at Lady Esterhazy's ball this evening?"

He didn't want to go to another bloody ball.

"I am not certain," he hedged. "You are looking lovely as ever, Connie, but unfortunately I must forgo this pleasure. I have an appointment." It was a lie, but he was desperate.

He tipped his head, and felt Constance's anger flow toward him.

"I shall look forward to dancing with you," she said, her voice shrill.

He watched the landau pull away, his brow furrowed. Traffic was as thick as usual, and it took some time for the coachman to ease into the flow. All those moments, he was pinned under Constance's fixed smile.

Finally he was free and he continued his meanderings.

"Well, old fellow, you look a thundercloud that doesn't know whether to rain or hail."

"Saint Leven," Hawk said, forcing a smile.

"Yes, I believe so," Lyonel said, cocking an eyebrow at his friend. "I am off to Jackson's. Do you wish to come with me?"

Hawk's eyes glittered. Yes, he wanted violence, he wanted to pound someone or something. It would keep him from thinking.

Hawk readily accepted a challenge from young

Canterley, a loud-mouthed bully from Suffolk who spent most of his time at Jackson's, taking all comers and killing them. Within minutes, he was stripped and in the ring. The sight of Canterley's bulging muscles didn't faze him. Hawk was strong, well-coordinated, and his undefined rage made him formidable. His powerful body was glistening with sweat within minutes. He was destroying young Canterley.

"My lord, hold!"

He pulled back, panting. Gentleman Jackson was regarding him with some surprise. He looked at Canterley and saw blood streaming from his nose.

He shook his head.

"I say, Hawk, well done," shouted Sir Peter Graven. "I had five guineas on you!"

"Come," Saint Leven said, his voice very quiet and gentle.

"I can safely say that you've nipped that odious bully in the bud," Lyonel said after they'd bathed and dressed again. "Do you feel better?"

Hawk rubbed an abstracted hand over his ribs. "He scored once, and it hurts."

"When are you leaving?" Lyonel asked abruptly.

Hawk stared at him. "What the devil does that mean?"

"I mean that you've been in London for nearly two months. When are you returning to Yorkshire?"

"I have no intention of going back there." But he did, he simply hadn't realized it until Lyonel had pointed out the obvious. No, dammit! "There is no reason for me to, there is nothing there, I—"

"You're a miserably unhappy bastard," Lyonel said, interrupting him smoothly.

"I wasn't until quite recently. I'll thank you to keep your tongue in your mouth, Saint Leven!"

"Friends should be good for something," Lyonel

said, brushing a fleck of nonexistent dirt from his elegant sleeve. "You do have a wife now, you know."

"Why the devil is everyone so concerned about Frances? You *saw* her, Lyon. Christ, would you return to that?"

"Yes," Lyonel said very quietly, "I saw her. Quite clearly, as a matter of fact."

"Just what does that cryptic bit of wit mean?"

Lyonel shrugged. "Go home, Hawk, that's all I meant."

He expected his friend to rage at him, perhaps plant his fist in his face, but Hawk did nothing. They strolled through Piccadilly in silence.

"It is going to rain soon," Lyonel remarked, glancing up at the darkening sky.

Hawk grunted. He kicked a stone out of his path.

"Have you heard anything from your father?"

"Not a blessed word," Hawk said, then frowned. That in itself was odd, most odd. His father should be urging him to return, piling recriminations on his head, but there had been no word from that wily old autocrat.

The marquess was playing a deep game, Lyonel thought.

"All right," Hawk said finally, and there was a measure of relief in his voice.

"All right what?" asked Lyonel.

"I shall leave in the morning." *And I will court my damned ugly wife and take off her glasses and her ugly cap and her clothes. I'll kiss her and see her breasts and . . .* He shook himself.

"She doesn't like me, you know," he said more to himself than to Lyonel.

"No, probably not," Lyonel agreed. "But, my friend—"

Hawk threw up his hands. "No, don't say it. Amalie

says I can charm even the fat person known as the Regent."

"All right, I won't say another word," Lyonel said agreeably. "However, this *person* is a trifle different from the Regent. I trust she is still at Desborough Hall."

"Where else would she be?"

Lyonel shrugged. "Who knows? Back in Scotland?"

"No, if she had shuttled the pike, my father would have sent me a message so quickly your head would twirl on your shoulders. I have much to do, Lyon, and it looks about ready to rain."

"Does it really?" Lyonel asked, seemingly startled by this bit of information. "Go easy, Hawk," he added, shook his friend's hand, and strolled off, a slight smile on his lips.

Go easy, Hawk thought with some disgust. What did Lyonel expect him to do? Fling his wife onto the ground and ravish her?

What an odd thought, he realized later as he absently watched Smallpiece pack his valises. Seducing one's wife. Wooing a wife.

❦ 15 ❦

All hell broke loose.

—MILTON

"My lord! We weren't expecting you! You have—"

"Good day, Otis. Where is my wife?"

Hawk was slapping his fine gray leather gloves against his left hand, waiting for a response. There wasn't an immediate one and he looked intently at his butler's unbelievably distraught face.

"Well, my lord," Otis began, wishing he could wipe the sudden perspiration from his brow.

"Yes, Otis?" What was going on here? Otis *sweating*?

Otis pulled himself together. "I believe, my lord, that Lady Frances is in the estate room. She—"

"Estate room? How strange. Well, no matter. See to my things, will you, Otis?"

What the devil was Frances doing in *his* estate room? Was she hiding from his staff? Had she taken over the small chamber as a refuge? Why was Otis acting so particularly? He strode across the vast entry hall toward the back of the house. He was vaguely aware that fresh flowers filled every vase on every surface. Their sweet scent permeated the air. It was spring, he thought, then dismissed it.

The door to the estate room was closed. He frowned at it a moment. Little fool, was she so diffident, so timid that . . . ? He caught the knob, half-expecting it to be locked. It opened smoothly, and Hawk stepped into the room, coming suddenly to a complete and utter halt.

He stared, his mouth dropping open. There was a woman seated behind his desk, a beautiful woman, and Marcus Carruthers was standing beside her, speaking quietly, his finger pointing to a piece of paper on the desk in front of her. Hawk blinked, not understanding, completely at sea. The woman . . . her hair was a rich, streaked chestnut, with delicate wisps trailing down her graceful neck. Her gown was exquisite, a pale lemon yellow, fitted perfectly to her lovely bosom . . .

"Oh my God!"

Frances, intent on Marcus' explanation, looked up to see her husband standing inside the door, a look of utter confusion and chagrined disbelief on his face.

He had to come back sooner or later, she thought, drawing on a thin thread of poise. She had wished, devoutly prayed that he would give her warning, but then, Hawk never did the expected. Oh heavens!

She said in a calm voice, "Good day, my lord. You have just arrived?"

"Frances?"

"Yes, my lord."

Hawk continued to stare at her, stunned. "Where are your spectacles?" he asked stupidly.

She shrugged and gave him a small smile.

At that moment Hawk became completely aware of Marcus Carruthers. He had managed to move a bit closer to Frances, as if protecting her. His look, his posture, looked intimate. Hawk felt rage rise in him.

"What the devil is going on here?"

Frances blinked at his outburst. A jealous husband's outburst? It was all too absurd. Very slowly she rose. "Nothing at all untoward, I assure you, my lord. Marcus, thank you very much. We will make a decision on this matter a bit later."

Marcus Carruthers saw the incredulous expression on the earl's face and for a moment he was very afraid of the man. But he was more concerned about Lady Frances. Did he dare leave her alone with him? Fool, he reminded himself, the earl was her husband.

He cleared his throat. "Welcome home, my lord," he managed on a croak. "I will see you later," he added, but neither party knew exactly to whom this was addressed. He slipped out of the room, noting as he walked past the earl that his hands were fists at his sides. Reinforcements, he thought. He needed to bring reinforcements.

"As I said, welcome home, my lord," Frances repeated, her mind a whirling morass of stray thoughts. She didn't move from her post behind the desk.

"Where is my father?"

"He left for Chandos Chase last week." She added silently that he had waited until she was well in control of everything at Desborough Hall before taking his leave. She wished he were here now. Her errant husband was the only thing, the only creature, she couldn't control.

"I believe, Frances, that you owe me an explanation." His voice was very soft, gentle almost, but Frances wasn't fooled, not for a minute. He was furious, very probably wanted to strangle her, and was barely in control of his temper.

"Someone must see to things here, my lord," she said mildly. "You weren't here. I was."

"Damn you, you know that isn't what I mean!" He strode toward her, his eyes growing wider as he neared her. "What the hell happened to you?" He still couldn't believe it. She was lovely enough to make a man ache just gazing at her. Her eyes were large and gray, fringed with thick, dark lashes, eyes grayer now, cold like the North Sea in winter. Her delicate chin rose, as if in challenge. No, he silently amended, not just delicate, stubborn as the devil. Who and what had he married?

"I see that someone took you in hand," he said, his voice a sneering drawl.

"Yes," she said calmly, willing herself not to react to his baiting. "I did, though it didn't really require much of a hand-taking."

She smiled at him then, and he sucked in his breath. His eyes roved over her face, noting the high cheekbones, the beautifully shaped brows, the high smooth forehead. How could he have thought her eyes looked like tiny mean raisins? How could he have believed her complexion sallow as a dead prune? His eyes fell to her breasts and he saw their fullness.

"Why, damn you?"

Frances cocked her head to one side as if in question, but she knew well enough exactly what he meant. She had known that when she saw him again he would ask, and her response was well-rehearsed. She realized now that she'd never intended to retreat into her dowdy shell again, even though she'd told herself she would. Oh no, she had lied to herself. She'd consigned the dowdy mouse to oblivion, once and for all.

She said straightly, "I didn't want to marry a Sassenach, that is why."

That drew him up and he stared at her in stunned silence. He couldn't quite comprehend that. He spoke aloud his confusion. "But I am an English nobleman, I am not a pauper, I am neither old nor ugly, and I have all my teeth. There could be no woman who wouldn't want my hand in marriage."

Frances laughed, she couldn't help herself. "You

have an excellent opinion of yourself, my lord, not that I ever doubted it for a moment."

"Philip," he said, his voice filling with rage.

"Well, yes, as you wish," she said. "You are correct. You have excellent teeth. Very white and straight." She smiled, an ironic smile, showing him her own very white, straight teeth.

"What was Carruthers doing hanging all over you? Is he your damned lover?"

That was straight talking, but no more than wounded male vanity, of which he had more than his fair endowment. "No," she said, the smile still fixed, her eyes now a lighter gray, mocking him.

"You have made a fool of me, Frances!" There, he'd said it, said what he really thought. He felt enraged, so angry that he wanted to spit nails.

"It wasn't difficult," she said, enraging him all the more. He took a step toward her, and she took a quick step back.

He saw the length of her now, and his face paled even more with anger. God, had he seen her in London as she was now, he would have been sniffing after her like a rutting stoat, along with all the other gentlemen of his acquaintance.

"You didn't want to see anything more than I presented," she said quickly, alarmed by the steely narrowing of his eyes.

Yes, I saw her. That was what Lyonel had said. "Damn you," he said aloud. "No woman has played me false."

"I told you that Marcus Carruthers wasn't my lover," she said, a bit of a sneer in her voice.

"And you're no timid little mouse, are you? Not a diffident bone in that body. Did you build a bonfire, Frances? Did all your ugly gowns and caps go up in flames? Were you laughing at me as you did it?"

"No, actually, I donated all those gowns to the rector. He was most grateful, I assure you."

"I am not a blind man," he said, knowing that he had been, knowing that he'd not only been blind, he'd been an abject fool.

"No, I am certain you are not, at least not in the normal course of events," Frances said, willing to be a bit conciliating now. "Your being forced to come to Kilbracken wasn't at all normal, however, but you see—" she continued, only to break off abruptly when Otis appeared in the doorway.

"My lady, is there anything you wish? Tea perhaps?"

Hawk swung around to see Otis, standing tall and unintimidated in the doorway, his eyes fixed on Frances.

Frances smiled. "That would be quite nice, thank you, Otis. My lord, should you like tea now?"

Hawk couldn't believe it. There was *his* butler, looking as stolid as a rock, speaking to *her*, protecting her!

"Yes," he nearly roared, then said, more quietly, despising himself for allowing this ridiculous situation to rile him, "Yes, I should. In the drawing room, Otis."

To his further chagrin, Otis looked toward Frances. He saw her nod. The damned butler, *his* damned butler, was looking at her for her approval! He never should have left; he never . . .

"In the drawing room," Hawk said again, his voice as icy as a winter Yorkshire frost.

"Very well," Otis said, and withdrew with all his dignity still intact. Hawk's dignity was in tatters and he knew it. Suddenly he smiled, an evil smile.

"Come here, wife," he said, very quietly.

Frances froze, her eyes widening. She didn't move a muscle.

"I said to come here. Now."

"No," she said, backing up another step. "However, I will have tea with you now, if you wish."

"Before I have tea, I wish to . . . look more closely at my wife. Come here, Frances."

She began to walk toward him, then at the last moment ducked away, and nearly ran from the room. He whirled about, but she was too fast. His hand caught air, not her arm.

"Frances!" he roared.

But she was gone. He heard the rustling of her skirts and the clicking of her slippers in the corridor.

He strode from the estate room toward the drawing room. He came to a disconcerted halt when he stepped into the room. Both Otis and Mrs. Jerkins were flanking his wife. He suddenly felt as though he'd stepped onto the stage of a very bad comedy. The blind fool of a husband, and he didn't know his lines.

"My lord, welcome home," said Mrs. Jerkins, a tight smile on her lips. "Tea is ready, my lord. Won't you sit down?"

"If the general will dismiss her soldiers," Hawk said acidly, and saw Frances stifle a smile.

She said in that damned calm voice that infuriated him to the point of insensibility, "Thank you, Otis, Mrs. Jerkins. I will serve his lordship."

Both old retainers took their blessed time leaving the drawing room. Otis didn't close the doors. Hawk strode to the doors and pulled them closed with a snap.

He turned to see Frances calmly pouring tea. "The scones are quite tasty," she said, all her concentration on the teacups. "Cook has got them just right. There is sweet strawberry jam I believe you will enjoy."

"Frances, shut up."

"Very well," she said, not looking at him. As if she didn't have a single bloody care in the world!

She simply stuck out the cup of tea in its saucer, and he took it, out of habit. He sat down opposite her, his long legs stretched out in front of him. He sipped the tea, getting a hold on himself. He said, "I didn't want a beautiful, frivolous wife."

"I know you didn't. That is what I was on the point of telling you when Otis . . . my general . . . interrupted me. "Had you had the courtesy to give me warning, I would have appeared as you . . . expected."

"You said you gave your clothes to the rector."

"I lied." She shook her head ruefully and his eyes were drawn to her quite beautiful ears with the soft tendrils of hair caressing them. "Well, I did lie, but not about that. I didn't want to go back to the diffident dowd, as you called me. However, I would have preferred warning of your arrival. Then I should have thought about it quite diligently."

"You will not put on those damned spectacles, ever again!"

"No, I shan't. Poor Mrs. Jerkins believed I couldn't read, for I truly was unable to see clearly with them perched on my nose."

"As I said, I didn't want your kind of wife."

"My *kind*?" She arched a brow at him.

"You know damned well what I mean, Frances!"

"Oh yes, I guess I do. You didn't want to be leg-shackled to a woman who would demand your time, your attention, indeed, venture to London with you and ruin all your . . . pleasures. But I didn't, my lord—venture to London and spoil all your pleasures, that is."

"I detest liars and frauds."

"And I detest conceited, arrogant, bullying idiots!" She rose jerkily to her feet and began pacing the room. Hawk's eyes followed her progress. Very nice, trim ankles, he thought. Long, elegant legs. She whirled about to face him. "As I said, my lord, I know you didn't, but I didn't realize it until it was too late."

"So, your whole charade backfired on you, eh?"

"I should say so, yes. And yours too, of course. I would have told you the truth of the matter, but you rushed from Kilbracken as if the very devil were on your heels, so I didn't have the opportunity. Then my father and Sophia wouldn't allow me to say a single word."

"Why did you continue the charade?"

"Because, as I told you, I didn't want to marry a Sassenach. I didn't want to leave my home or Scotland. Since I couldn't avoid it, I knew you would leave me alone as soon as possible if I appeared the ugly dowd. And, of course, you did."

Hawk was silent for many moments. He stretched his arms over his head and lounged back in his chair. He looked indolent, and in perfect control. She felt a frisson of alarm. What was the wretched man thinking now? Something evil, no doubt.

He said finally, "You are quite beautiful."

"Thank you."

"And you are everything I didn't want in a wife."

"You, my lord—"

"Philip," he said mildly.

"—you are everything I don't want in a husband!"

"Then it appears we are even. I imagine that you had a difficult time keeping that sharp tongue of yours in your mouth when I was about."

"A very difficult time, you are quite right about that."

"I got the sister who was the worst, didn't I?"

"Worst? I beg you to define that!"

"I should say," Hawk said thoughtfully, stroking his fingertips over his jaw, "that you are headstrong, willful, too independent, and quite used to having men fall all over you like panting puppies."

To his fury, she grinned at him. "You sound just like my father. And on such short observation," she marveled aloud. "Most impressive, my lord."

"Frances, I can beat you, you know, and indeed I shall if you don't cease your sarcasm."

"No, you can't. If you tried such a thing, I should lay you low, I swear it."

"I should be curious to know just how you could bring me low. You're half my size."

"I would think of something."

Yes, oh yes, she would, he knew. Hawk swept his mind nearly clean to find something that would intimidate her, put her back in her woman's place where she belonged. He sat forward suddenly and bestowed upon her his most leering smile. "Would you like to know why I came back unannounced?"

"No, but you will tell me, I suppose."

"I came back to seduce my wife. My guilt drove me back. I wanted, finally, to see your breasts."

To his immense satisfaction, a flush started at her shoulders and spread upward to her eyebrows.

"My mistress informed me very tartly that spectacles, ugly caps, and gowns could be removed. That is what I intended to do. That is what I now plan to do, very soon."

Frances licked her lips. She stared at him. "No," she said, shaking her head, her voice a thin, high sound.

"You are my wife. You will obey me both in our bed and out of it."

He had terrified her, he knew it, but something deep within him was angered at her immense and obvious distress at him bedding her. He wasn't ugly, for God's sake. He was an excellent lover.

And you've got excellent teeth, stupid sod!

"Go back to your mistress, my lord!"

"No."

"I want nothing to do with you!"

"How very curious," he said thoughtfully, drawling out his words so his brain could formulate more. "The dowdy mouse lay as still as a martyr, suffering my attacks on her body. But the beautiful woman now believes to deny me my husband's rights?"

Frances was silent. Why hadn't she realized that he would be far more interested in sex with her new appearance? What would he do? Would he treat her as he had before—abruptly, quickly, with determined silence save for his curt instructions?

"I don't know," she said, her shoulders slumping for the first time.

He'd won, and he smiled. He had her now where he wanted her. He realized that he wanted to take her upstairs this very moment, strip off her clothing, and throw her on his bed. He wanted to kiss every inch of her, he wanted . . .

"I shall give you until this evening to think about it, Frances. You know," he continued thoughtfully, "I have never had a wife. Perhaps I will enjoy sleeping with you the entire night, perhaps waking you to love you, perhaps—"

"Shut up! I don't have to listen to your . . . cruelty!"

"Cruelty? Making love to my wife is cruelty?"

"Making love?" she nearly shouted at him. "Is that what you wish to call it now? Now that you don't regard me as beneath your exhalted notice? Now that you don't believe you'll become ill touching me? You, my lord, are a despicable animal!"

"I suppose you are a bit justified in saying that, all save that final insult, of course."

Frances saw that he would rise, and quickly retreated. "I have much to do. You will excuse me, my lord. We have . . . guests for dinner. John and Alicia Bourchier are to arrive. I must speak to Cook, I must . . ."

It was a lie, he knew it, but said nothing. He watched her rush from the drawing room, and knew her next task was to send a plea to Alicia and John to come to Desborough Hall.

He couldn't wait. The evening should prove to be like the second act of the bad comedy. Only this time, he knew his lines, and Frances didn't.

He was grinning broadly as he rose and left the room.

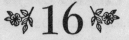

The best laid schemes o'mice and men
Gang aft a-gley.

—ROBERT BURNS

"It's not fair, Alicia! Oh, why did he have to come back? I had thought that he wouldn't return until Christmas! All my plans, everything is in a heap!"

"Now, Frances, calm yourself," Alicia said, gently patting Frances on her bare arm. "I'm pleased that you didn't retreat again—indeed, my love, you look quite lovely. The blue silk does wonders for your eyes. I am not certain what color they are now. I am almost persuaded to be jealous of you. John looks at you like he does at a lovely dessert."

"So will Hawk," said Frances, her voice sounding as dispirited as she felt. She banged her fist against her dressing table and her hairbrush jumped and slid onto the carpet. "He told me it was guilt that brought him back! Likely tale, that!"

Indeed he would think her beautiful, thought Alicia. What a marvelous tangle! So Hawk had told her he felt guilty? Most curious. She said, "Come along, Frances, we must go downstairs. The gentlemen will be waiting. You don't wish to take the chance of Hawk coming up and dragging you down, do you?"

"He would, wouldn't he? Alicia, stop laughing! None

of this is in the least funny! Oh, very well, let us join the precious gentlemen!''

John Bourchier, a slender, somewhat myopic young gentleman, was standing next to the fireplace, speaking in his measured way about his estate. He had said nothing about Frances' transformation. He was a gentleman. Still, he couldn't wait to observe Frances and Hawk together.

He droned on about drainage problems in his northern acres, and Hawk, barely concealing his impatience with his longtime friend, downed more sherry.

"Good evening again," Alicia said gaily, sweeping into the drawing room. She trusted that Frances was following her. "John, dear, may Frances and I have a glass of sherry?"

"Certainly," said John, not daring to look at Hawk's face.

Frances looked so lovely it was like staring directly into the sun. Hawk felt something deep inside him tighten, but he was easily able to ignore it at the sight of two angry spots on her cheeks and the wary, irritated look in her eyes. Were they more blue than gray? His eyes fell to her bosom. "How very charming, my dear," he said, his voice honey smooth, his gaze moving reluctantly from her breasts back to her face. Frances merely nodded, and let him lift her hand and plant a light kiss on her wrist. He held it and she shot him a look that could kill were it a pistol.

"Most fetching," John agreed, nodding to both ladies.

"I fear that Frances has quite outdone me," Alicia said provocatively, her eyes twinkling at Hawk.

"She has outdone all of us, it would seem," Hawk said to no one in particular.

Frances knew her hands were sweaty and she rubbed them on her skirt. She looked up to see Hawk gazing at her with such a knowing look that she wanted to strike him.

"Ah, Otis!" Her relief at the butler's presence was as palpable as a Christian being rescued from the lions.

"Dinner is served, my lady."

Hawk proffered his wife his arm. She looked at it like it was a snake. "Frances," he said very quietly, but she heard the warning, indeed she did. She thrust up her chin and lightly laid her hand on his arm.

"My dear wife," Hawk said after he had seated Frances, "has doubtless ordered up my favorite dishes. She is so very delighted at my homecoming."

There was dead silence. Otis hovered. The three footmen looked blank. Otis had trained them well. In fact, he had particularly threatened them for this evening.

"Aren't you, my dear?" At her grim silence, he added, "Delighted to see me, that is."

"The soup, if you please, Otis," Frances said, ignoring him. "Julienne," she added as the footmen served.

"My favorite," Hawk said fondly. "Such a caring wife."

"It is John's favorite," Frances said.

"Yes, indeed it is," Alicia added, and quickly spooned a mouthful to keep herself from giggling. Poor Frances!

Only the sound of spoons dipping in and out of their bowls broke the silence.

Hawk said, "My dear wife has quite charmed all the staff. I have nothing to do save bask in her adoration."

Frances' spoon hit her bowl and some delicious julienne soup splashed onto the white tablecloth.

A footman rushed forward, and tripped against her chair.

Otis drew up stiff as a poker.

"It is all right," Frances said quickly. "No harm done."

"John was telling me all about his draining problems," Hawk said.

"A subject doubtless close to your heart," said Frances, her voice so acid it would have curdled the soup.

"Indeed," Hawk said blandly. "I am always most interested in problems, of all sorts. There are usually so many solutions available to one. It is just a choice of selecting the most appropriate, don't you agree, Frances?"

He is doing me in quite well, Frances thought, her lips tight. I can't allow him to continue. She raised her face and met his eyes head-on, saying in a clear, honeyed voice, "I have found that to be true, particularly in running this estate. Marcus"—her voice softened markedly—"he is such a help! Such insight from a man so young."

Hawk froze, frowning before he could stop himself.

Alicia said quickly, "Our steward is equally efficient. I was just telling John the other day—" She broke off abruptly, sending a heartfelt glance toward Otis, who was serving fried whiting and red mullet.

"How is Beatrice, Hawk?" Alicia asked. "And her betrothed, Lord Chalmers?"

"She is as she always was, perhaps more so," Hawk said easily, gently setting down his fork. He looked toward his wife. "I believe that Edmund Lacy will handle her quite well, however, after they are wed. It is a husband's responsibility, after all, to see that his wife heeds his wishes, and he sees to her well-being. Don't you agree, Frances?"

Frances raised her empty wineglass and it was immediately filled by Otis.

"Frances?" His voice soft, almost intimate.

"I believe," Frances said, her voice hard and impersonal, "that husbands are, in the general course of things—" She broke off, realizing that she had to curb her tongue, at least in front of the servants and John and Alicia.

"Yes, my dear?"

"Husbands are husbands."

"Ah, an indictment or a compliment? I wonder."

John, quite aware of the footmen's rampant interest, turned the topic neatly back to his drainage ditches.

Once Otis had directed the footmen to serve up the lamb cutlets, rissoles, roast ribs of beef, neck of veal in béchamel, and the multitude of vegetables, Hawk gave him a dismissing nod.

Hawk's jaw tightened when Otis looked toward Frances. "Thank you, Otis," she said calmly, not missing her husband's look. "We will see to ourselves now." She didn't know him well enough. Would he create a scene, jump up from his chair and roar and embarrass all of them?

"Excellent," Hawk said as he chewed on the veal. "Do you have veal in Scotland, Frances?"

"Only at Christmas, my lord," she said. "And then only a small portion, of course."

"How very odd," Alicia said. "Doesn't veal grow in Scotland?"

John laughed. "A city-bred wife," he said, patting her hand. "Veal is not like potatoes, my dear. Young cow, you know."

Alicia's eyes twinkled. "Really, dear?"

"You see how informative husbands can be, Frances?" Hawk said. "We can be most useful, I assure you. In many areas."

Frances' beef could have been the buttered potatoes for all she could taste. It was too soon for her to rise and leave the gentlemen to their port. And if she did rise, Hawk would in all likelihood leap across the table and strangle her. Damn Alicia, she thought, she was enjoying herself immensely!

Frances was well-bred; good manners had been pounded into her by Adelaide since she was twelve years old. But this situation called for drastic action. She couldn't allow Hawk to continue with his veiled innuendos. He was not being a gentleman. There was no reason for her to be a lady.

"I have heard so much about the pleasures of London," she said to the table at large. "I am most excited about visiting with you, my lord."

She saw him scowl and grinned at her buttered peas.

"Just think of all the balls, the soirees, the routs— isn't that what they are called, my lord?"

"Yes," Hawk said. Damned little minx! Trying to turn the tables on him, was she?

"My father-in-law told me all about Hawksbury House. I am most anxious to refurbish the house and hire more servants, settle in for the remainder of the Season. And of course, my lord, I want to meet all your *friends*."

"Lyonel sends his regards," Hawk said.

"Such a charming gentleman," Alicia said. "Frances told me he visited just before you left, Hawk."

"It appears," Hawk said, "that Lyonel saw a good deal more than did I. He was most surprised by Frances and doubtless wondered about her ridiculous charade."

"As a *gentleman* I don't suppose he would remark on it" said Frances.

"No, he didn't. About traveling to London, my dear Frances, perhaps your . . . health won't allow for it."

John looked up from his plate, clearly startled. "Why, Frances, I had no idea you weren't feeling up to snuff!"

"I am quite well, John." But her eyes were wary on her husband's face.

Hawk said in a tender, most solicitous voice, "My dear, you are not overly ill yet in the mornings?"

Alicia cried out in excitement. "Frances, you didn't tell me! How every marvelous!"

Frances gritted her teeth. "I am not with child, Alicia. My husband doubtless refers to the . . . Scottish fever I occasionally suffer."

"Do I? Not with child, my dear? How depressing. As I said, a husband has so many duties and responsibilities."

John sent his wife an agonized glance. He was acutely uncomfortable. He wanted only to leave and let the two of them fight it out. Alicia had been gleeful about the evening. Even she looked doubtful now. John wondered briefly if Frances would leap out of her chair and plant her husband a facer.

As for Frances, she had had quite enough. "Alicia, shall we retire now? The lemon pudding and the rhubarb tarts aren't to your liking, I know. But they are his lordship's favorites, as I'm certain he'll tell you. Gentlemen, excuse us."

There was no footman and no Otis to pull out her chair. John quickly rose from his chair to assist his wife. Hawk merely stared at Frances down the length of the table. His look promised full retribution, but she tossed her head and marched in full-blown regal manner from the dining room.

"My lady!" Otis stared at her, aghast.

She forced a smile at her ally. "See to the gentlemen, please, Otis. Lady Alicia and I will be in the drawing room."

"My, my," said Alicia. "Hawk is in a rare taking."

"He is an objectionable brute," said Frances, so furious that she could barely gather her woefully scattered thoughts together.

"You did deceive him, Frances," said Alicia in a very tentative voice.

Frances looked positively fierce. "I hope he chokes on the pudding!"

"He looks so outrageously handsome in his evening togs, don't you agree?"

"Alicia," Frances said in a warning voice, "you are giving me a headache."

Alicia tripped onward. "His hair is so thick and shiny, don't you agree? And his beautiful green eyes." She gave a delicious shudder, daring a sideways glance at Frances' glacial face. "And he is so very . . . virile and strong."

"I will strangle you, Alicia!"

"He is your husband," Alicia said reasonably. "I like rhubarb tarts," she added.

"Curse you, Alicia! Whose side are you on?"

"I think I shall play some ballads. You listen, Frances, it will soothe your savage, er, feelings."

The gentlemen joined them all too soon. Hawk strolled to where Frances sat in splendid isolation and moved behind her chair. She felt his hand on her shoulder, and froze. She felt his fingers curl and uncurl in her hair.

"Leave me alone," she hissed between her teeth.

"Oh no, my dear, I shan't do that. Not until I wish to, at least."

John and Alicia escaped. That was the only word for it, Frances thought, as she and Hawk walked with them to the front doors. Alicia gave Frances a quick hug. Otis hovered, to Hawk's displeasure. He took Frances' hand and drew her back into the drawing room. He closed the door firmly and stood against it.

"Now," he said, grinning at her. "We are finally alone."

"So?"

"You present a lovely picture. I am most anxious to see more of the picture, perhaps with less . . . paint."

He spoke in a most normal tone, but it took Frances but a moment to glean his meaning. She stared at him, her eyes widening.

"I dislike you intensely," Frances said.

He arched a black brow, but said nothing.

"You are no gentleman!"

"I also suspect that you, my dear, despite being the daughter of an earl, are no lady. A hoyden, perhaps."

"I am going to bed!" She squared her shoulders and walked resolutely toward him.

"My idea exactly," he said. "Come, my dear. I wish to begin my knowledge of the real Frances Hawksbury."

What to do? He was standing in front of the door, blocking her way. Pretend, she thought. Yes, pretend. She said in a very shy, frightened voice, "I . . . well, all right, my lord."

"Philip," he corrected, smiling down at her. He felt a surge of lust so strong that it startled him. She was his, his wife. She belonged to him. And now she was obeying him. He stepped aside. "I shall be up shortly, Frances."

"Very well, my . . . Philip," she said in that same shy little voice, darting him a quick embarrassed look.

"Frances," he said, touching his fingers lightly on her shoulder. He felt her tense, hastened to reassure her. "It will be different this time, I promise you."

She lowered her head and stood silently. He leaned down and lightly pressed his lips to hers.

He raised his head and studied her face. "You are very lovely," he said almost absently. "I am pleased with you."

She said nothing, and he allowed her to walk from the room.

"Soon, Frances," he called softly after her.

He walked into the entrance hall and watched her progress up the stairway. He pictured those long legs of hers wrapped about his hips and swallowed. How could he have been so blind? He shook his head. He wondered if he would have approached her sexually in the same manner had he seen her the way she was now on their wedding night. He didn't know. Ah, Amalie, he thought fondly, tonight I shall follow your instructions to the letter. He thought of Frances squirming with pleasure in his arms, perhaps crying out softly, and he shook again with lust.

He drank a brandy, then quickly made his way upstairs to his bedchamber. Grunyon was there, fussing about, with nothing in particular that Hawk could see. "You may seek your bed," he said shortly.

Grunyon darted a quick glance toward the adjoining door, a glance filled with concern that was not lost on Hawk. Damnation, didn't he have anyone's loyalty? "Go to bed," he repeated.

"Yes, my lord." Grunyon walked as slowly as a snail across the expanse of the bedchamber. He turned, swallowed at his master's cold, determined look, and left, shaking his head.

Hawk waited only until the door was firmly closed before he stripped, donned a dressing gown, and softly knocked on the adjoining door. His hand on the doorknob was shaking a bit. Randy fool, he said to himself.

He opened the door. There was but one lone candle flickering on her dressing table. Good, he thought, he wanted to see her, really see her. "Frances?" He looked toward the bed, and smiled. She was burrowed under the covers, in all likelihood embarrassed and a bit frightened. He would soothe her, make her comfortable with him. He would forgive her her charade, perhaps.

"Frances," he said softly again, and eased down beside her. His hand touched her shoulder and froze.

He roared with anger. He jerked back the covers and stared with fury at the same damned bolster.

"Frances!"

He bounded out of bed and strode across her room. He halted suddenly, frowned, and lowering himself, peered beneath the bed. Nothing. Not even dust balls.

He pulled himself together by a thread. He couldn't go yelling through the house for her. It would awaken all the servants, and he could just imagine the ensuing fiasco.

"I'm going to murder you, Frances," he said, his voice deep with building rage. Where could she be hiding? His mind was set. He would search every damned room! Oh yes, and when he found her . . .

He grabbed the candle and left her bedchamber. His anger increased as he entered and left each empty room.

He approached a small room, crookedly set off the corridor, facing the main entrance to the Desborough Hall. He opened the door, raised the candle high, and peered about.

Then he saw her, huddled on a pile of different materials. There was a loom nearby, and tables. It was the damned sewing room! Had she hidden from him in here the last time?

The light of the candle fell on Frances' face, and she stared at him.

❧ 17 ❧

I am at the end of my tether.

—ROYALL TYLER

"You have pushed me too far this time, Frances. No more."

"I should have gone to the stables," she said, and he drew up a bit, for she didn't appear to be speaking to him in particular."

"Yes," he said, "you probably should have."

"I am stupid."

He smiled at that observation and let his mind rest briefly, very briefly, on the notion that perhaps she had wanted him to find her. Then she said, "Go away, my lord!" in a strong, very certain voice, and his own stupid notion disappeared in a flash.

"No." He strode toward her and she jumped to her feet, scurrying behind the bolts of material until her back was pressed against the wall. Hawk stopped.

"Come to bed, Frances. Now."

She shook her head, and her beautiful hair swirled about her pale face. "No," she said, her voice a small whisper. "No," she repeated, her voice stronger, more assured.

"You really have pushed me too far this time. Now you will willfully disobey me?"

"I have never pushed you, far or otherwise," she

230

said. Striving for calm, striving for some way to . . . to what? She looked at the scissors on one of the tables, and smiled pitifully. She met his eyes in the wavering candlelight and moistened her lips.

"You hid here before, didn't you? You do not count that act as willful, or pushing me?"

"I am not willful."

"So you give me *un*willful disobedience?"

She drew herself up. He was toying with her, baiting her. "I do not want to give you anything. I want you to leave me alone. I want you to leave Desborough Hall tomorrow and return to London, to your mistress."

"But you are not yet with child, wife," he said very softly.

"Not for want of your trying!" Her voice neared a shout, and Hawk quickly turned and closed the door.

"If you do not lower your voice, I will gag you. I will have no talk amongst the servants, do you understand me?"

"Go away!"

She saw him look thoughtfully at some strips of cloth on one of the tables, and she lowered her voice, repeating, "Please, just go away."

"Ah," he said, "there is some obedience in you. Come." He held out his hand toward her.

She didn't move a muscle. Her eyes were wide and frightened. That bothered him, but not that much. He felt his sense of ill-use surge to the fore, and said coldly, "Now, Frances, I will not tell you again."

"You are an animal!"

"So you have the grave misfortune of allying yourself with an animal. It is done."

Still she didn't move. Hawk laid the candle on a table and walked slowly toward her. She tried to duck past him, but he was prepared this time, and jerked her against him. He felt her fists pounding against his chest, and he shook her until her head snapped back on her neck. "Stop it!" He tried to calm his anger at her, but it was difficult. "Do you want me to gag you?"

She shook her head against his shoulder.

In one quick motion Hawk blew out the candle, hoisted Frances over his shoulder, and left the sewing room. He took her to his bedchamber.

She was shaking. With fear or fury? he wondered.

He said nothing more, merely kicked his bedchamber door shut behind him and carried her to his bed. He dropped her onto her back. She was still dressed in her beautiful blue gown.

"Take off your clothes," he said, staring down at her. "Now."

She hesitated, and he added coldly, "I shall rip them off you if you do not obey me."

But she couldn't manage the long row of buttons. He pulled her to her feet, turned her about, and she felt his deft fingers quickly releasing her from the gown. She felt him pull the gown over her breasts.

"Please," she said, "can you . . . would you please douse the candles?"

"I want to see you," he said shortly. "You may finish," he said, and backed away from her.

It was too much. Her low-cut lace chemise barely covered her breasts. It was very nearly transparent and she saw his eyes roving over her. She grabbed her gown over her, quickly doused the candle, throwing the room into darkness, and made a dash toward the adjoining door.

He caught her in three strides. "All right," he said, his anger overcoming all other emotions, "it will be as you demand."

Hawk pulled her back to the bed, held her with one arm, and quickly stripped off her clothing. When she was naked, he picked her up and tossed her on the bed.

He had set himself a problem, he realized, his breathing coming quickly now. If he tried to light the candles, she would probably try to escape him again. He shrugged. He pulled off his dressing gown, and came down over her.

Her smooth, very soft body beneath him made his mind go blank with desire. Her breasts were heaving, full and soft against his chest.

There was no hope for it, Frances realized. She had been a fool. Such a fool. Had she really expected him to shrug and forget about her? An idiot, that's what she was. She said, "I shall lie still. Do as you please. Just be done with it."

She matched words to action.

Hawk was thoroughly enraged. She was limp beneath him, even had managed to slow her frantic breathing. "Very well, wife," he said, and jerked her legs apart.

He realized quickly enough that he couldn't enter her without hurting her. She deserved it, damn her! But he couldn't. He frowned in the darkness, trying to remember what he'd done with the wretched jar of cream.

He rose and said very softly, "Do not move."

She didn't. When she felt his weight come onto the bed, she forced herself to lie very quietly.

"Inside you this time, Frances," he said, and she felt him part her legs again. She lurched upward at the feel of his finger, slick with cream, entering her. She heard him suck in his breath.

He slid his finger slowly, gently, in and out.

He heard her catch her breath in sharp gasps, felt her quiver, but not with desire.

He cursed, reared over her, and drove into her.

Frances felt him deep within her. It didn't hurt. It felt very tight, and she could feel her body stretching to accommodate him, but there was no pain. She lay perfectly still. He would finish with her soon. The few times he'd done this to her, he had finished with her in minutes.

She heard his harsh breathing, felt him plunging deep, pulling away, then plunging again. Then he moaned, deep in his throat, and froze over her. Suddenly he began driving furiously in her. She felt the wetness of his seed bursting deep inside her.

Hawk rolled off her immediately and onto his back. His lust was gone, as was his rage. He felt nothing.

"Go to your room, Frances," he said, his voice sounding dulled and weary.

She nearly leapt from the bed, and he heard her quick footsteps as she raced toward the adjoining door. She didn't slam the door behind her, but closed it very softly.

"Damn," he said aloud to the dark room. *Ah, Amalie, I was a rutting bastard.*

He felt guilt. He didn't like it, and it made him feel very uncomfortable, it made him question himself and his actions. He raged silently. It was her fault too. She'd lied to him, pretended, played him for a fool. She did deserve whatever he meted out to her. Still . . . He felt himself plunging into her small body, felt his mind turn into liquid mush, felt his lust and his anger driving him over the edge.

Frances scrubbed herself until she felt raw. She pulled a nightgown over her head and crept into her bed. *I should have kept wearing my spectacles, my ugly caps, my shapeless gowns. Then, at least, he would have felt honor-bound to continue his kindness to me. Kindness of a strange sort,* she amended silently to herself.

Kindness tempered with condescension, distaste, and boredom.

She drew her knees up to her chest and buried her face into her soft pillow. He hadn't touched her, not *her*. She was safe from him. If he wished to plant his seed in her there was nothing she could do about it. She'd been a fool to try to escape him. She should have accepted him as she'd done the other few times. She realized well enough that her behavior had infuriated him, and she supposed, logically, that what he had done was but to be expected. He hadn't hurt her, after all. He'd gotten the cream. She shuddered at that, drawing her legs even closer to her chest. He'd put his finger inside her. Why had he done that? To humiliate her for having tried to escape him?

Frances shook her head against the pillow. He was a man, and men did as they pleased; men got their way. Her father always did. She found herself wondering, appalled at herself for even thinking it, if her father did that to Sophia, and Sophia bore it in silence and patience. The picture created in her mind made her extremely uncomfortable and embarrassed. Surely her father wouldn't, not now, now that he was older. He already had a son, so there was no reason to continue doing such distasteful things.

Frances resolutely shut her husband out. She would deal with him, oh indeed she would. She even managed a small, smug laugh. She said aloud to her pillow, "I'll see you to the devil before I allow you to touch *me*." Her eyes narrowed. "Never," she said softly. "Never will you touch *me*."

Hawk came to an abrupt halt when he entered the breakfast room the following morning. Frances was seated at the table, calmly eating her breakfast, perusing the *Gazette*.

She looked quite lovely, he thought, eyeing her objectively. She was wearing a muslin gown of pale green with a matching ribbon threaded through her hair. What had he expected? The return of the dowd? No, he thought, frowning a bit, he supposed he really expected that she would hide from him, avoid him at all costs. He felt an appalling surge of lust for her, and was furious with himself. The devil—a husband shouldn't feel such things for his wife. It was nonsensical, ridiculous . . .

"Why, good morning, my lord," Frances said, smiling at him as she folded the paper.

Smiling as if she hadn't a bloody care in the world! His eyes narrowed on her guileless face. What game was she playing with him now?

"Good morning, wife," he said, and seated himself at the head of the table. Rosie, the breakfast maid, quickly began to serve him. When his plate was as he wished, he nodded dismissal. But Rosie didn't take herself out of the room. Hawk watched with narrowed eyes as she smiled toward Frances and said, "Is there anything else you wish, my lady?"

"No, Rosie, that will be fine. Thank you. You may go now."

He watched Rosie bob a curtsy and finally remove herself from the breakfast room. It occurred to him then that Frances' very warm, wifely behavior was due to Rosie's presence. He soon was disabused of that notion.

"Is the sirloin as you wish it, my lord?"

Lord, she sounded so damned cheerful! "I haven't even taken a bite yet, so I wouldn't know."

"Ah, then I shall hold my tongue." She picked up the *Gazette* again and buried herself behind it.

"I am most gratified that the servants treat you as

their mistress," he said after some minutes of grating silence.

"Indeed, most gratifying," Frances agreed, not emerging from her paper.

"What are you reading that interests you so much?"

She started a moment at that. Actually, she wasn't reading anything, nothing at all. She was striving with all her effort to maintain her cheerful indifference to him. She would much have preferred to throw the thick sirloin at his head.

She laughed, a charming, soft laugh. "I am reading all the *ton* gossip, of course! It is so *fascinating*. Why, it says here that a Lady H was seen conversing in the park with Lord R. And Lady H's husband was but a short distance away! So very titillating, isn't it?"

He ground his teeth. "I don't know any Lady H," he said.

Frances didn't either. She had just manufactured the entire tale. "You are acquainted with everyone then, my lord? How very knowledgeable you are, to be sure."

Hawk set his fork down very slowly and carefully. "Frances," he said, "you will cease calling me 'my lord.' My name is Philip or Hawk. You may take your pick, but no more 'lording.' "

"As you wish," she said, and shrugged. She set down the paper, glanced at the clock on the sideboard, and said, "Oh dear! How the time gets away from one! 'Tis nearly eight o'clock! You will excuse me, won't you?"

"Where are you going?"

"Why, there are so many things to do. Desborough Hall doesn't run by itself, you know."

"It did."

"Oh no," she said, giving him a patronizing smile, "it merely maintained itself." With that, she was gone.

He noticed as he left the breakfast room a few minutes later that she hadn't eaten much of her breakfast.

Hawk found himself at loose ends. He considered riding off his ill humor, then changed his mind. He was here, he might as well see to estate business. He strode to the estate room, saw that the door was open, and stepped inside. He came to an abrupt halt.

There was Frances again, seated at *his* desk, with Marcus Carruthers seated beside her.

"I don't know, Marcus," Frances said, her brow furrowed in thought. "I do agree with you that John's approach just might work here, but the funds involved in clearing the timber away—"

"What timber?" Hawk said sharply.

Frances froze, but just for an instant. She raised a guilelessly smiling face to her husband. "Hello," she said kindly. "Marcus and I were just discussing our need for fencing, and the cost of lumber is so very high at present, you know, and we do have an excessive wooded area just to the east of us, and—"

"I do not with any trees to be cut."

"—and since you don't want the trees cut," Frances continued serenely, "of course they shan't be cut. Now, Marcus, if that is all, I have other matters to attend to."

Marcus hadn't uttered a word. He wasn't blind. His lordship was in a royal snit. He wished he could escape with Lady Frances. He watched her walk past her husband, toss him a sweet, totally false smile, and leave the estate room. Leave *him* alone. He tugged at his collar, adjusted some papers on the desk, and endeavored to look industrious.

To his utter relief, his lordship said curtly, "Carry on," and was gone. He stiffened again in some alarm when he heard the earl's voice outside, roaring, "Frances!"

He wiped the perspiration from his brow, wondering as he did so if his father, a very calm, utterly serene gentleman, was ever in a snit with his mother. He felt himself in the middle of a maelstrom and wondered if he could ask for several weeks away from Desborough to visit his parents.

Frances wasn't to be found. Hawk discovered Otis in the nether regions of the kitchen, his presence causing some consternation among the kitchen staff.

"My lord," Otis said, bowing formally. The kitchen staff came to immediate, wary attention.

"I noticed the footmen's new livery," said Hawk. "I should like to know when and why this was done."

"If I could explain, my lord," Otis said very kindly, as if Hawk were still a boy at Eton. He moved away from the staring staff. "Her ladyship believed the staff's appearance could be improved upon. Her ladyship and I ventured into York and disposed of the matter. Satisfactorily, I trust, my lord?"

Hawk grunted.

"The females were also improved upon," Otis added. "Mrs. Jerkins accompanied her ladyship into York for that matter."

"Anything else her ladyship wanted improved upon?"

"You will have to speak with Mrs. Jerkins to determine the extent of the improvements," Otis said, his voice as bland as his visage.

"Curse you!" Hawk said, and took himself off.

". . . and, of course, my lord, new cutlery and crockery and new linens, for the old ones were in a most deplorable condition, and—"

"Thank you, Mrs. Jerkins," Hawk interrupted, his jaw set.

But Mrs. Jerkins, who had known Lord Philip since

he was in short coats, continued undaunted, "Her ladyship is a most proper and efficient young lady, my lord. She has taken a great interest in Desborough Hall . . ." Her tone implied that it was about time someone did.

". . . and she is most kind and pleasant to the staff, my lord, but she doesn't allow laxity, of course, that wouldn't be appropriate."

Hawk let her run her course. When she reached a pause that lasted more than a second or two, he said, more mildly now, but it was a distinct effort, "Thank you, Mrs. Jerkins. I'm certain her ladyship has been most . . . thorough."

Mrs. Jerkins beamed at him, his attempt at sarcasm floating blissfully over her gray head.

Hawk ran his fingers through his hair, and stared about the drawing room.

"Will there be anything more, my lord?" she inquired, watching him closely.

"No, no," he said absently. "Oh, yes, can you tell me where her ladyship is?"

"At the stables, I should imagine. She always is there this time of morning. Works too hard, she does, but what with getting the stud back into operation and working with Mr. Belvis to determine the racing horses and their training—" She broke off at the sudden, quite unexpected exclamation from the earl.

"*She is what?*"

"At the stable, my lord," Mrs. Jerkins repeated patiently, "with Mr. Belvis. She spends every morning there, sometimes into the afternoon. As I said, my lord—"

"The devil!" he said, but under his breath. At that moment, he wanted nothing more than to have Frances' very pretty neck between his hands. What had she done now?

He strode from the room, leaving Mrs. Jerkins to gawk after him. He galloped down the front steps of the hall and headed for the stable offices. It was beginning to rain, and he thought, very stupidly, that Frances should take a care. She might become ill.

Silly fool. You're the one who should take care.

"Frances!"

His roar brought forth four stablehands as if they'd been shot from a cannon.

"Where is her ladyship?"

Dan, the eldest, said with a very small nervous quiver in his voice, " 'Er ladyship is likely in the training office with Mr. Belvis, milord."

The training area was away from the stables, near the eastern paddocks. It had begun to rain in earnest, and Hawk felt water trickling down his neck by the time he gained shelter.

The office door was ajar, and he strode in. The comforting smell of leather, linseed, and various unguents assailed his nostrils.

"Belvis! What the devil is going on here? I thought you had left?"

The moment of reckoning, Frances thought, trying to hide her nervousness. She should have told him, perhaps over breakfast, when he had sirloin in his mouth.

"Hello, my lord," she said in a ridiculous attempt to stem the tide. "D-did you wish something?"

Hawk looked at Belvis. He was a short, very wiry little man, balding, his face merry but seamed from years spent working in the out-of-doors. He looked younger than Hawk remembered.

"Yes, Frances," Hawk said, his voice now well-controlled. He even smiled. "I should like to see you, if you please. We will go to the tack room."

I don't want to go!

"As you wish, my lord. I will be back, Belvis. Please continue."

Continue what? Hawk wanted to demand, but he held his tongue.

The tack room wasn't at all as Hawk remembered it. It was, first of all, spanking clean; all the harnesses, bridles, saddles, were shiny with care and fastened neatly in their proper places.

Hawk pointed to an old chair. "Sit," he said curtly.

Frances sat.

"Now, madam, you will tell me what the devil is going on here." His legs were planted apart, his arms crossed over his chest. He was, she realized, spoiling for a fight.

"Yes, Frances?" he asked, his voice silky.

My sentence is for open war.
—*MILTON*

Frances felt as though she was in an open field and the enemy was charging toward her, bayonets at the ready. There was no retreat, of course. She said, pleased at the steadiness of her voice, the reasonableness of her tone, "Desborough Hall is a very respected racing stable and stud, my . . . Hawk. I managed to talk Belvis into returning, as you saw, so that we could bring things up to where they were before your brother died."

"Did Carruthers clear the money for this ambitious project of yours?"

Frances felt a surge of relief. It was an obvious inquiry, and he'd asked it a very calm voice. Perhaps she'd been wrong about the bayonets.

"No, of course not," she assured him. "I would do nothing so improper as that, and neither would Marcus agree to such a thing." She slanted him a wary look, then forged ahead. "I borrowed the money from your father."

"*You what?*"

So much for calm and reason, she thought. "Your father lent me—us—the money," she said again.

Hawk wanted to roar, but he managed to contain it,

and said with his patented sneer, "I suppose my precious sire also lent you the money for all the wasted expenditures in the house? Crockery? Linens? Uniforms? My God, madam how much blunt do I now owe my father?"

"Of course not! That is, I did not borrow money from your father for the household. Why, as household expenditures, I assumed, and Marcus agreed with me, that such decisions were mine to make. The household is, after all, my responsibility."

"How much money did he give you to start things up again?" He waved his hand about.

Frances gulped. She looked down at her hands, stared over at a bridle, at the harness beside it. "Five thousand pounds," she said to the floor.

He cursed, quite fluently. He calmed and then sneered onward. "I suppose you feel that the racing stock and the stud are also your blessed responsibility?"

She flushed a bit at that. "Well, not exactly, but, my . . . Philip, I—"

"Would you kindly make up your mind, Frances? Is it to be 'Philip' or 'Hawk'?"

"Since I wish devoutly for you to take yourself off, I think I shall select 'Hawk'!" She immediately regretted her insult, for his face hardened with fury.

She rushed into speech. "I couldn't just stand by and watch everything continue to rot!"

Hawk stroked his hand over his jaw. He was well in control again. "Marcus informed you that I was considering selling off everything. You knew, it was all in that letter of yours."

"Yes, but I couldn't . . . that is, I didn't think you really *meant*—"

"How the devil would you know what I meant or didn't meant . . . *mean?*"

She stared stonily at the toes of her stout walking shoes.

"You have taken much onto yourself, Frances."

"Someone had to," she said, still unable to meet his gaze.

"Then you now take it upon yourself to inform Belvis that his services are no longer necessary."

Frances swallowed. "I have already spent the five thousand pounds."

"On what? New uniforms for the horses? New troughs for their endless eating? What, may I ask, do you—a woman—know about anything?"

She bounded to her feet and shook her fist at him. "I know much more than you do! And I care, unlike you, who only wish to waste your time and your inheritance on your damned pleasures in London!"

"Back to my mistress again, are we?"

"Back, yes—that is where I wish you to be!"

His eyes fell to her heaving breasts and she saw his eyes falling. She backed away. To her misfortune, she stumbled over a saddle that was in the process of being repaired. She tumbled over it, onto her back, her skirts flying up.

"Frances," Hawk began, rushing toward her. He stopped, seeing she was quite all right, and said in a leering voice, "How lovely. Do you wish to seduce me here, of all places? Can you not wait until this evening?"

Frances slapped her skirts down as if they were bees to bite her. She came up to her knees, then to her feet. The unmended saddle was between them. She had to try a different tack, she knew. She drew on almost nonexistent patience and said, "Please, Ha . . . Philip, it means a lot to me. I know we can bring Desborough back to its respected position. If you are not interested in it, please let me continue. I can make money, I know it. Your father knows it, he trusts me. He . . . Please, please don't sell out."

"*You* make money? I beg to differ with you, Frances. To date all you've done is spend it, waste it."

"I have not! It is to be considered an investment. As for the household expenses, I had to do something!"

"Do you know that it is my sister and her betrothed, Lord Chalmers, who have offered to buy?"

"No, I didn't know. What does that possibly have to do with anything?"

Hawk didn't know, but he didn't say so. He continued rubbing his thumb along his jaw. To Frances' surprise, he asked, "What do you know about horses?"

She brightened and her eyes grew intense with ill-suppressed excitement. "I grew up with horses. I have . . . well, I seem to have an affinity, a natural ability to sense if anything is wrong with them. I also know how to care for them when they are ill. I am not stupid, Hawk."

He said nothing to that. So, he thought, he was to be Hawk again. Did she hope he would fly off if she kept calling him that?

"How have you spent the five thousand pounds?"

"Three new trainers, new equipment, Belvis, repair of the paddocks—"

"I see," he said interrupting her. He turned away from her and pretended a concentrated study of a saddle. "Did you know," he said thoughtfully, "that a woman shouldn't hunt?"

She frowned at that, ready to take exception to his ridiculous male pronouncement.

"A sidesaddle allows no control," he continued. "A woman can't bring her legs to bear, she is effectively controlled herself, not the horse. It is dangerous, as a matter of fact."

"I hunt and I have never before used a sidesaddle. My father wouldn't allow it."

He raised his head and smiled at her, just a bit. "Odd, isn't it, that that doesn't surprise me. At least *now*, knowing you as you really are, it doesn't surprise me."

"Hawk, what will you do?"

The wind was out of her sails now, he thought vaguely. He disliked the pleading tone in her voice. "My sister, Beatrice, is a smashing rider, at least she was in the old days. She refused to use a sidesaddle after she'd been tossed in a hunt. It was she who pointed out the danger of them to me. I couldn't have been more than ten years old at the time."

"Hawk—"

"Of course, my father, being of the older generation, raised a bit of a ruckus, but Nevil talked him around."

"Hawk—"

He turned full face toward her. "Very well, let us return to the business at hand. Why are you still here? I told you to speak to Belvis. His services are not required."

All thoughts of conciliation fled her mind and she saw red. "You . . . you *bastard*!" She grabbed up the unmended saddle and heaved it at him. It landed short, and Hawk simply stared down at the saddle, then at his wife.

He laughed. "I am fortunate that women are not allowed in the army. Had you been firing the cannon, the enemy would have been toasting you with champagne."

She looked madly about for something else to hurl at him. "You also wrecked your own protective castle wall, didn't you? Not, of course, that I couldn't have easily scaled that saddle to get to you, but now you are saving me energy." He strode toward her, and Frances, seeing the gleam in his green eyes, turning them brilliant as emeralds, tried to dart around him. He caught her arm and jerked her against him.

"Now," he said, holding her firmly, "what will you give me, wife, to keep Belvis here and your precious project intact?"

She opened her mouth to yell at him, and in the next instant his mouth covered hers. It was the first time he had kissed her and it was a revelation. Her lips were soft, parted, her breath sweet and warm. He felt her struggling wildly against him, but he didn't want to release her. He gentled his kiss, his tongue lightly stroking her lower lip. He allowed his tongue to enter her mouth, only to retreat with great rapidity as her teeth bit down.

His desire for her was powerful even though he realized she would willingly have removed the tip of his tongue had he not been quicker. He continued kissing her until she finally quieted. He raised his head and stared down at her. "Have you never been kissed before, Frances?" he asked quietly.

"No, damn you! I don't like it. It's wet and disgusting and degrading—"

He kissed her again, drew away, and pressed his hand against the back of her head, drawing her cheek to his shoulder. He simply held her like that, listening to her harsh breathing. He released her and she jumped back, swiping the back of her hand across her mouth.

"Shouldn't you speak to Belvis, my dear?" he said.

Her hand dropped. "No! You can't, Hawk, you—"

"And, Frances, you will accustom yourself to my kissing you. Tonight, I fully intend to kiss every inch of you."

She stared at him aghast, all thoughts of the stud fleeing her mind. "You can't! It's . . . impossible!"

"No, it isn't, I promise you."

"I don't want you to! Hawk, I swear that I won't fight you again, or . . . hide. I will lie quietly and allow you to . . . well, you can do as you wish."

"And very quickly? In the dark? Without touching you or caressing you?"

"Why would you want to? You want your precious

heir, that is all! Why do you want to torment me? I didn't trap you into marriage, my lord! I wanted nothing to do with you."

"And you still don't, is that right?"

"No—I mean yes, I don't want you!"

"There won't be any further need of the cream either," he continued, his voice deep and certain.

The red flush started at her knees, she knew, and traveled quickly to her hairline.

"Unless, of course, my dear, you much enjoyed my finger inside you, stroking you, easing you, stretching you for my—"

"Stop it! You are disgusting, hateful—"

He laughed. "Would you like to know why we won't need the cream anymore, Frances?"

But she was dashing toward the tack-room door.

He was ahead of her, his hand smashed flat against the door above her head. Her hand clutched uselessly at the door handle. "As I was saying, Frances, we won't need the blasted cream. *Why?* I'm sure you want to ask me. Well, my dear, we won't because when I finally come into you, you will be quite ready for me—wet, warm, and quite wild for me."

"You are disgusting," she said in a low shaking voice.

He drew back his hand and stepped away. "We will see, Frances. I don't think we'll be downstairs for tea this evening." He watched her frantically jerk the door open. "Frances," he called after her, "don't invite any more of our neighbors to dinner."

"The . . . the Melchers are to arrive at five o'clock!"

"The vicar, Frances? You will send a message immediately, my dear. Plead illness, plead anything you like. If they come, Frances, I shall tell them that my beautiful wife and I are anxious to get back to our marriage bed. Don't doubt me, Frances."

She fled. Hawk strolled to the doorway and watched her run in the rain back toward the house. He smiled to himself. He'd regained control and the little witch knew it, and hated it. Still, he thought, frowning slightly, that kiss had surprised him.

It stopped raining in the early afternoon and Hawk took himself off to see John and Alicia. If he remained at Desborough Hall, he feared he would be sorely tempted to attack his wife on the floor of the drawing room.

Alicia, John told him proudly, raising a glass of sherry in salute, was with child. Hawk felt something deep and wonderful clutch at his insides.

"Hawk!" Alicia exclaimed, a bit pink. "You're grinning like a fool! 'Tis not your child!"

He was still grinning as he rode back to Desborough Hall.

He was humming as Grunyon assisted him into his evening clothes.

"Most heartening," Grunyon said as he handed Hawk a neckcloth.

"What is?"

"All the changes Lady Frances has made."

Hawk grunted, concentrating on the folds of his cravat.

"The three new trainers she hired seem to be good men, not all that experienced, of course, but willing and eager."

Hawk said nothing, but his jaw tightened.

"Ah, indeed," Grunyon continued, as if he hadn't a worry in the world, "it is about time that Desborough Hall had a mistress, and one who cares about everything. Why, I was speaking to Mr. Carruthers, a most excellent young man, incidentally, and he was telling me—"

"I don't give a farthing for what that excellent young man has to say!"

"I believe, my lord," Grunyon continued, unperturbed, "that you must file down that nail. It's just a bit ragged."

Hawk looked at the fingernail on the third finger of his left hand. He blinked, suddenly afraid that the nail had been jagged the night before. That was the finger he'd covered with cream and eased into his wife. Had he hurt her? "Bring me the file," he said.

When he entered the drawing room, his step was light, his face filled with anticipation. The room was empty.

"Otis!"

The damned man walked like a shadow, Hawk thought, when Otis glided in but a moment later.

"Where is Lady Frances?"

Otis felt a brief shiver of foreboding. He wanted to glide out of the drawing room and go directly to his room and bolt the door. "Ah, my lord, she left this afternoon for York. She had dealings, and I believe that she and Agnes—Agnes accompanied her of course, as well as a footman—were spending the night there. She will return on the morrow, my lord . . . as you should know, my lord."

Otis had known she was fleeing, and at this moment he wished that he had taken the footman's place. He had assumed, more fool he, that she had told his lordship. The earl looked brutal, which was odd, Otis reflected motionlessly, because he hadn't moved a muscle.

Hawk asked very calmly, his voice genial, "Where is she staying, Otis?"

Otis wished he could ease himself behind the wainscoting. Instead, he drew a deep breath. "I don't know, my lord."

"How many inns are there in York, do you think, Otis?"

"I couldn't hazard a guess, my lord. A great many, I should suppose."

"You are doubtless right," Hawk said smoothly. "Fetch Marcus for me, if you please, Otis. I desire his company at dinner, unless, of course, he also accompanied my wife on her little jaunt?"

"No, my lord, Mr. Carruthers is here. He, ah, planned to dine with you, my lord."

"Instructions from Lady Frances?"

"I believe so, my lord."

Marcus didn't like it, not one bit. He wondered if the earl would ask him to remove himself immediately from Desborough Hall. To his intense surprise and relief, the earl greeted him graciously enough, remarking blandly after they were seated at the dining table, "Such a pity that Frances must needs be gone this evening."

"Yes, my lord," said Marcus. A footman served the vermicelli soup and Marcus grabbed his spoon.

"I believe," said Hawk after a moment, eyeing his steward's shaking hand, "that we are to be blessed with a fricandeau of veal and lobster cutlets this evening."

"Most delightful, my lord," said Marcus, wishing he could taste the doubtless delicious soup. It slithered down his throat.

Hawk raised his wineglass, twirled it between long fingers, and said in an interested voice, "Her ladyship has told me of all your plans, Marcus. Is my father charging me interest for the five thousand pounds?"

The soup suddenly slithered down the wrong way, and Marcus coughed. "No, my lord, not to my knowledge. He was, er, most enthusiastic about it all."

"I see," said Hawk, still twirling his wine, seemingly intent on the deep red liquid. "Her ladyship told me of all her expenditures—repair of the paddocks, the new trainers ... ah, I seem to forget the other expenses."

Solid ground, Marcus thought with vast relief. He listed each expenditure, slowly and precisely. When he paused, the earl merely nodded to him to continue. "And, of course, Lady Frances decided to place advertisement about the stud, and—"

The wine stem shattered. "She *what?*"

"Not in the *Gazette* or any local newspapers, my lord," Marcus added quickly, staring at the blood-red wine spreading its stain over the white tablecloth. A footman had started forward, only to come to an abrupt halt at the sight of the earl's face. "In the *Racing Calendar* and the *Turf*—"

"My God, I don't believe it!" Hawk interrupted, his voice so filled with rage that the footman took a hasty step back. "She has reduced me ... Desborough Hall ... to a bloody tradesman?" He slammed his fist on the table and a sauced slice of veal jumped off its platter.

Hawk roared to his feet, nearly upsetting his chair. He drew up suddenly, realizing that there was a servant present. He cursed softly under his breath, then drew himself stiff as a poker at the entrance of Otis.

"Otis," he said pleasantly, "you and the footman may remove yourselves. I will ring when we need you."

"Yes, my lord," Otis said, casting a pitying look toward poor Marcus Carruthers.

The footman nearly raced Otis to the door.

"Now," said Hawk, leaning over the table, his palms flat, "will you tell me that you endeavored to talk her out of this nonsense?"

Marcus licked his lips. He felt a sudden pain in his belly.

"Actually, my lord," he managed finally, clutching thankfully at a sop, "Lord Danvers is due on the morrow with his mare. He wishes to put her to stud with Gentleman Dan. It is a fee of two hundred pounds, my lord," he added hopefully. "He wrote to Lady Frances immediately upon learning that Desborough was again a stud. He was most delighted, my lord. I believe Lady Frances has received other inquiries as well in the past two weeks."

"I see," said Hawk. He stared off into space for many moments, saying nothing more. Then, suddenly, he said in a meditative voice. "I wonder if I would truly go to the gallows if I murdered her?"

"My lord!"

"Yes, Marcus?"

"Lady Frances is a very gracious lady, she truly cares and enjoys . . . well, my lord, she is—"

"You, my dear Marcus," Hawk interrupted his effusions smoothly, "don't have the blessed opportunity of being leg-shackled to the lady. Perhaps," he continued in the same thoughtfully considering voice, "I could poison her tea, or perhaps her scones. She is most fond of scones, you know."

"My lord! Surely—"

"I jest? I wonder. I suppose I could strangle her and pretend she took a toss from a horse. No, that would leave telling bruises on her throat, wouldn't it? Ah, there is much to consider here."

Marcus wondered wildly if the earl were truly serious. He saw the determined gleam in his lordship's eyes, and decided at that moment that he was quite grateful not to be in her ladyship's slippers.

"Yes," Hawk said after a moment. "She will return on the morrow. Then I shall see."

19

Who can refute a sneer?
— REVD. WILLIAM PALEY

"Why, good morning, Frances. How well you are looking. Was your brief trip to York successful?"

Frances' hand fell silent on Flying Davie's silky nose. The stallion tossed his head, and Belvis murmured in that magic voice of his, "Now, old lad, enough nonsense out of you. You mind your manners with her ladyship."

Frances turned slowly to face her husband. It was ten o'clock in the morning, and she had returned at eight o'clock. She had changed quickly, eaten, and gone immediately to the paddocks.

Hawk was dressed for riding in buckskins and buff riding coat. His Hessians glistened in the morning sun. He looked perfectly calm, and his voice showed only mild interest.

"Yes, my lord," she said, tilting her head up just a bit, "it was most successful."

Flying Davie snorted and Belvis chuckled. "This beast is the jealous sort, my lord," he said to Hawk. "He is well-used to Lady Frances' undivided attention."

"Only because he has but to look at me and I feed him shamelessly," Frances said on a smile.

"It doesn't matter," Belvis said. "I've cut down on

his feed, you may be certain. The fellow is too fat for
his own good. His time will increase markedly within
the month, my lord. He will be our fastest racer and
will do you proud at Newmarket."

Newmarket! Hawk stared from Belvis to his wife.
"May I inquire as to your success in York?"

Frances drew a deep breath. "Actually, I had heard—
from Belvis—that a smithy there had come up with a
most ingenious idea. You see, Belvis has told me the
difficulties in getting the horses to, say, Newmarket or
Ascot or Doncaster. It takes days and the horses are
naturally tired at the end of their journey. This smithy
believes he can construct a sort of closed stall with
wheels so that the racers won't have to walk. They, in
turn, are drawn by other horses."

"It is ingenious, my lord," Belvis added. "The
fellow—his name is Cricks—sent the plans back with
Lady Frances. If you would like to study them?"

"Yes, I should like to," Hawk said. To Frances he
continued, a brow raised, "May I inquire if this com-
mission is part of the five thousand pounds?"

"Y-yes," Frances said, but her slight flush betrayed
her. To her immense relief, her husband said nothing
more about it.

"I understand, Belvis," Hawk said, "that Lord Danvers is due with a mare today."

"Yes, indeed, my lord. Gentleman Dan is ready,
you may be certain."

"I am certain that he is. Would you and Flying
Davie excuse me for a moment?" Hawk gently took
Frances' arm and strode away from the paddock.

She waited for the explosion, but instead she got a
very calm, sneering look. She wasn't certain what to
say to that look. She said nervously, plucking at her
skirt, "You will allow this, won't you, Hawk? It is two

hundred pounds. It will cover the cost of the horse stable."

"Oh, I shall allow Gentleman Dan to have his fun." His eyes lit up as from within, and Frances blinked. "Indeed, my dear," he continued, his voice now evilly mocking to her sensitive ears, "I believe that you should watch the process. It is most enlightening, you know. Perhaps you will learn something."

His sneer became only more pronounced at her disbelieving expression.

"You have never seen a stallion cover a mare before, have you, Frances?"

She shook her head, mute. Such a thing wasn't allowed. She'd never considered, never thought that . . .

"You will be present, my dear."

"I can't, you know that! It isn't proper, only men should—"

"Why, my dear wife, I thought you were intensely interested in every facet of this enterprise. It doesn't bother you that only men watch a stallion mount a mare? Such insensitive brutes—the men and the stallion, of course. Perhaps you could demand that the stallion cover the mare in the dark. Spare the poor mare's sensibilities and all that."

"Stop it, Hawk!"

His voice hardened. "You will be present, my dear, and I will stand right beside you. If you have questions, I will be delighted to answer them for you. For example, you might wonder what the stallion uses to impregnate the mare. I will point out all his endowments. Perhaps you will notice some slight parallel, who knows?"

Her face was washed clean of color. It wasn't done, she couldn't imagine standing, watching, with men about, knowing that . . . "I can't," she said. Her chin went up. "I won't."

He was fairly amiable now. "If you refuse me, I shall tie you up and bring you here. Then I wonder what the men will think?"

"This is my punishment," she said slowly, looking toward the paddock.

"A lesson, certainly. When is our mare to arrive for her, ah, experience?"

"Soon," said Frances, "very soon. Lord Danvers will remain the night, of course. He wishes the mare to remain until . . ." Her voice dropped off as a stone from a high sheer cliff.

"Until she is impregnated. Of course, the mare is willing to be impregnated, and even if she weren't willing, she would be forced to accept the stallion. She would be held quite securely so he could mount her. And men, of course, do the holding . . . and the guiding, as it were."

Frances realized there was no hope for it. She couldn't begin to imagine what Lord Danvers would think about a lady's presence at the mating. It was a humiliating thought. Perhaps he would protest, perhaps he would force Hawk to allow her to leave. No, that wouldn't happen.

"Usually, the mare is . . . well, you will observe firsthand, won't you, my dear?" He didn't expect an answer. He released her arm, and she quickly stepped away from him.

"Frances, attend me."

She turned unwilling to face him.

"You will be present. If you flee, I swear that you will regret it. Do you understand me?"

"I understand," she said. She added under her breath, "You miserable bastard!"

Hawk laughed. "Oh, my dear," he said, "of course Lord Danvers won't be present at your education. We will wait until he is well gone from Desborough Hall."

At least, she thought, he was sparing her some humiliation, but not much.

Lord Danvers and his entourage arrived within the hour. He was a bluff, good-natured man in his early fifties. He greeted Frances graciously, then turned immediately to Hawk. "Pleased, I am, my lord, that you've started the stud up again. My Miss Margaret is ready to breed, and I don't mind telling you, I've always wanted Gentleman Dan to sire a foal. Eh, that's a steady fellow, I've heard! Always ready to—" He broke off, reddening just a bit as he realized there was a lady nearby."

"Yes, indeed," said Hawk smoothly. "Allow Otis to show you to your room, my lord," he continued after a moment. "Then we will have luncheon. Is your mare ready to continue this afternoon?"

"Always ready, you know," said Lord Danvers in a low but very carrying voice.

After Otis had escorted Lord Danvers from the drawing room, Hawk said to his wife, "We will journey to the attic now."

She stared at him.

"In preparation for tomorrow. Come, Frances, I cannot allow you to appear as a woman, you must realize that. I fancy, though, that Nevil and I have some of our boys' clothing in the trunks. You, my dear, may garb yourself as a male. A cap also," he added, studying her hair.

Frances didn't tell him that she and her father-in-law had already visited the attic and found her boys' clothes. Unfortunately, there was still quite a selection.

Frances said little at luncheon and ate less. She heard the men carrying on about breeding and racing and hunting. So amiable!

She stayed in the house the entire afternoon. She

wouldn't have ventured out even if the drawing room had caught on fire.

The Melchers arrived for dinner. Nathan, the vicar, was a serious, rather narrow-shouldered man whose wife, Rosalie, was blessed with a large bosom, a lively sense of humor, and six children. She pandered shamelessly to Lord Danvers.

Frances was aware of her husband's gaze throughout the meal. There was no escape, not tonight, she knew, as she took a bit of cabinet pudding, one of Cook's specialities. She imagined he couldn't wait to taunt her with details of the horses' coupling. Sneering wretch!

Frances liked Rosalie. She'd never before known a motherly flirt. When she rose from the dinner table, Rosalie smiled broadly at all the gentlemen, and followed her.

The gentlemen didn't join them for a good hour. They were, in all likelihood, Frances thought, jesting about Gentleman Dan's prowess. As Hawk strolled across the broad entrance hall toward the drawing room, Lord Danvers beside him, talking nonstop about all the damned chicanery and cheating in the racing world, he blinked, hearing the pianoforte. It was a Mozart sonata, played beautifully. He shook his head at himself. The vicar's wife, of course, but Rosalie had such pudgy fingers. He wondered how they could race so gracefully over the keys.

But it wasn't Rosalie, of course. Hawk stiffened as he entered the room, his eyes going to his wife, who was seated gracefully before the pianoforte. Her lovely chestnut hair glistened with red and blond highlights in the candlelight from the branch of candles beside the pianoforte. Her white neck was long and graceful. She wore no jewelry. He wanted to kiss the nape of her neck and strangle her at the same time.

Frances finished, not looking up for a moment, calming the excitement the rapid last movement always brought to her. When she heard the loud applause, she nearly snapped her neck in her haste. She met her husband's eyes. She'd forgotten the prize performance she'd granted him at Kilbracken. Fool!

"How enjoyable, my dear Lady Frances," Rosalie said. "Such talent and ability! I vow you must be very proud of her, my lord."

"Oh, I am indeed," Hawk said in his blandest voice. "When I first heard her play at her home in Scotland, I remember thinking: Now, here is a talent that makes an audience react with unbelievable fervor."

"And such a lovely picture she is, sitting there" continued Rosalie, more motherly now than flirtatious.

"Indeed," agreed Lord Danvers. "You are a fortunate man, my lord." Hawk saw the older man's eyes rest on Frances' white shoulders and he was surprised at the sudden jolt of anger he felt.

"Incidentally," Hawk said, his attention still on Rosalie Melcher, "has my wife sung for you yet? You will not believe that such a voice can possibly exist. Frances, my dear, please give our guests more pleasure."

His look was a dare and a command, and Frances knew he was remembering quite clearly her singing of that night. She nearly shuddered every time she thought about it. Did he believe her voice would crack the crystal on the mantelpiece? Curse him.

"Very well, my lord," she said, sending him a sweet, very false smile, "if our guests are certain they wish to take the chance—"

There was vociferous agreement.

Frances bowed her head a moment, looking at her fingers spread over the keys. I am Scottish, she whispered to herself. Her fingers lightly came down on a soft major chord. Her voice was a gentle contralto, well-controlled, well-trained. She sang:

> O, my luve is like a red, red rose,
>> That's newly sprung in June.
> O, my luve is like the melodie,
>> That's sweetly played in tune.
> As fair art thou, my bonnie lass,
>> So deep in luve am I,
> And I will luve thee still, my dear,
>> Till a' the seas gang dry.

Hawk silently watched her face, letting her gentle voice and the beautiful words flow through him. He was startled when he heard the applause from his guests. It was on the edge of his tongue to tell her how lovely her voice was, but memory asserted itself, and the memory brought anger, and that brought his sneer. "How well you adapt, my dear," he said softly. "Like a chameleon you are, to be sure. Why is it I expect you next to become a snake and strike where I will least expect it?"

Only Frances heard his baiting words. The others were talking, encouraging her to play another song. Slowly she raised her hands from the keys and laid her hands in her lap. She looked up at her husband and said quietly, "I am not a snake. But if I were, I should wish to be a very poisonous one."

His eyes glistened, and he smiled, offering her his hand. "Just where would you bite me, Frances?"

She said nothing, merely rose and took his hand. She knew Rosalie was probably regarding them with dewy, romantic eyes. All are blind, she thought, when it suits them to be, or when the proper picture is presented to them.

"Perhaps," Hawk continued as he lightly stroked his

fingers over her palm, "you would bite me in my most vulnerable male spot. Not that I shouldn't mind your beautiful mouth there, but biting? I think not."

She quickly turned her hand and pinched his thumb.

His smile faded, just a bit.

"Eh, my lord, how about a game of cards?" Lord Danvers' booming voice brought the both of them back to their responsibilities. "I've heard it said you're quite the piquet player. Perhaps I can win back my stud fee, eh?"

"He is an excellent player, my lord," Frances said quickly, seeing a ray of escape light through the fog. "I imagine your game or games would be quite interesting."

The vicar and his wife took their leave after tea.

Lord Danvers neatly trapped Hawk, and Frances, trying desperately not to grin in triumph at her husband, merely nodded and took her leave.

She lay in her bed, stiff as a stone, until finally she fell asleep, her dreams of snorting stallions and whinnying mares, and her husband's face.

It was near one o'clock in the morning when Hawk quietly entered his wife's bedchamber. He walked to her bed, lifted his candle, and stared down at her sleeping face. He reached out his hand, then very slowly drew it back. No, he thought, he would wait. It would be worth it. Indeed it would.

He smiled.

Lord Danvers took his leave the following morning after breakfast. He was jovial, even though, he informed Frances, her husband had quite taken the wind out of his sails over cards.

"A damned shark, my lady, that's what he is!"

Frances smiled pleasantly. "I have thought similar things about him upon occasion," she said.

Hawk and Frances stood on the front steps and waved Lord Danvers on his way. Frances said to her husband, "I see that it is profitable for you to spend so much time in London. How much of the poor man's money did you win?"

"Five hundred pounds," said Hawk absently. He was regarding her closely, and Frances felt herself stiffening, drawing away. He continued, "You look quite innocent and trusting in your sleep. A man could imagine that you are most malleable and charming— with your mouth shut."

She refused to let him draw her, but still, she couldn't prevent the words that blurted themselves out. "You didn't touch me!"

He slowly shook his head. "No. I am sorry to disappoint you, Frances, but I was rather tired, you know. I decided to wait."

"You didn't disappoint me!"

"You know nothing yet, my dear, about disappointment." He shrugged. "This afternoon, Frances. You will be at the stables at precisely two o'clock." He saw that she would protest, and added, "I also remember seeing you striding about in Scotland. I was riding in a carriage with your sisters at the time. I trust you can manage a believable stride today in your boys' clothes."

"I shall," Frances said.

Frances dithered until it was very nearly two o'clock. Even though her husband had told her to come to the stables, she wasn't particularly surprised to hear a tap on the adjoining door. A moment later, Hawk strolled in, stopped, and looked her over thoroughly. "Very nice," he said. "Now the cap."

He watched her finish braiding her hair and pin it firmly on the top of her head. He took the woolen cap and pulled it down over her ears.

"Very nice indeed. You will behave, I trust, else I just might gain the reputation of a pederast."

"What is that, pray?"

"A man who prefers boys to ladies."

"Oh! That is disgusting!"

"I have always thought so." He stepped away from her and studied her. The pants were a bit loose, thank God, but her long, slender legs were quite evident to him. Her shirt was covered with an equally loose jacket. If one didn't look closely at her beautiful, quite feminine face, she would escape detection.

He grinned at her. "Well, Frances, are you ready for your education?"

She said nothing, for her tongue was dead in her mouth. He gave a final tug to her cap, bringing it nearly down to her eyebrows.

"Excellent. Just keep your mouth closed and no one will guess what really lies beneath that garb. Even if anybody does guess, no one would dare say a word."

20

Between two horses, which doth bear
him best . . .

—*SHAKESPEARE*

Frances stared. Two trainers, Henry and Tully, held the mare, Miss Margaret, firmly by her halter. The mare was whinnying and snorting, her flanks quivering, her beautiful bay coat covered with sweat. Gentleman Dan could barely be restrained. His eyes rolled in his head at the sight of the mare, and the four men who held him strained for control.

Hawk watched Frances' face as the stallion was guided behind the mare. He heard Belvis give a sharp command. This was the tricky part. It was always possible for the mare to be injured, and everything was done to prevent it. The stallion's hooves were wrapped in thick white wool. Gentleman Dan was snorting, tossing his beautiful head, so excited by the sight and smell of the mare that Frances believed he would break loose at any moment. She held her breath. Suddenly the stallion was allowed to rear over the back of the mare, and she gulped.

"You are remarking the horse's endowments," Hawk said, regarding her wide-eyed stare.

"He is going to hurt her," Frances whispered.

"Perhaps, but we will do our best to see that he doesn't."

The stallion was bucking at the mare, straining forward to bite her on her neck. The mare was trying to pull free of her holders, her hindquarters trembling.

"Now, look closely, my dear" Hawk said. He saw that she had closed her eyes, and roughly shook her arm. "You will look well, Frances."

She opened her eyes to see the stallion thrust wildly into the mare. There was unearthly shrieking from both animals. It was a sight she could never have imagined. The stallion was huge, but the mare pushed back against him, craning her head back, snorting frantically. Frances couldn't have closed her eyes against the sight even if she had thought about it. The horses seemed beside themselves; the stallion was allowed to thrust and withdraw as he wished to. He was enormous and Frances wanted to feel revulsion, she truly did. But the mare suddenly kicked her hind legs upward and the stallion, with a furious cry, drove into her. The mare screamed, and Frances knew, deep down, that it was a cry of pleasure. She felt her palms grow sweaty, her breath grow jerky.

The men were encouraging Gentleman Dan, but there was no leering, no stupid jests. It was only she herself, Frances thought vaguely, who was responding to this incredible scene. She felt a deep stirring, but didn't understand it. She felt a tension building in her belly . . . no, below her belly, between her legs.

She wasn't aware that Hawk was watching her closely, his eyes glittering at the sight of the pounding pulse in her throat.

She wasn't aware that Hawk's hand had clasped her and that her fingers were working spasmodically against his. She drew a deep, shuddering breath when Gentleman Dan gave a wild cry and quivered, then stiffened over the mare's back.

Suddenly she felt Hawk take her hand and lead her away. She felt dazed, utterly out of herself, which was foolish, of course, but she couldn't seem to calm the rampaging feelings deep inside her. She kept pace with him, not looking at him. He finally gained the tack room, and closed the door.

"Frances," he said very softly.

She raised glazed eyes to his face. He slowly turned her around so her back was pressing against his chest. Suddenly his hand was on her belly, kneading her, caressing her very gently, feeling her through the boys trousers. She wanted to object, but her body wouldn't allow it.

His hand, just as quickly, stroked down her, and cupped against her. She gave a jerking start, and cried out. She felt his other hand press against her breasts, holding her still against him. She gave a whimpering cry, not understanding, as the palm of his hand pressed against her. She felt wet and hot and furiously urgent.

She vaguely heard his harsh breathing in her ear, felt his fingers now searching over her breasts, finding her taut nipples, stroking them.

Then his fingers were wild on her in a rhythm that made her whimper and press forward. "That's good," he said, his voice raw and low against her cheek. "Yes, move against my fingers."

She saw the mare thrusting back against the stallion, and as she pressed her hips against him, his fingers followed. She felt blood pounding in her head, felt herself opening and tensing at the same time. His fingers quickened and she cried out, wanting more, wanting so much . . .

"My lord! Belvis needs to speak to you. My lord?"

The knock on the tack-room door, the groom's voice, brought Frances plummeting back to earth. She felt

Hawk's fingers leave her, felt him draw a deep breath, heard him curse vividly.

His hands were on her upper arms now, gently squeezing her, as if trying to calm both of them.

"Just a moment," he called out.

"Frances," he said very softly. He turned her about, saw the dazed shock in her eyes, and pulled her close. His large hands stroked down her back, kneading the tense muscles. "It's all right," he said against her left ear. "I'm sorry about the damned interruption. You were so very close."

Close to what?

He gently set her away from him. "Will you be all right?"

She felt a sudden violent surge of embarrassment. She couldn't bring herself to look at him, to see the look in his eyes. She managed to nod, her head bowed.

Hawk cursed again.

"I must go," he said, his voice taut and angry. "You remain here until you are . . . feeling more yourself."

Frances couldn't have moved in any case. She watched him pause a moment at the door, shake his head, and quickly leave the room.

She sank slowly to the floor, her eyes closed. What happened to me? she wondered. Why did I react like that? For an instant she felt his fingers probing against her and shuddered. She had wanted him to continue, wanted him to make that odd, so strange pressure build within her. Tentatively she slid her hand down her belly to lightly touch herself. She felt dampness and pounding heat and jerked her hand away. She moaned softly, not understanding. She felt weak and tight as a bow string, all at the same time.

"What is wrong with me?" she asked the empty room.

She rolled into a small ball, holding her knees, waiting for her breathing to slow. She didn't move for many minutes.

Frances faced her husband at the dinner table. It had required all her resolution not to plead an awful illness, anything not to have to face him. He had had the absolute nerve to send her a message saying he would join her in her room for dinner if she didn't come down.

She had come down. She fully expected nastiness from him, brazen innuendos, baiting. But as yet he had said nothing.

"Would you like some crimped salmon, Frances?" he asked, his voice as smooth as honey.

She shook her head. She didn't want anything, be it crimped, broiled, baked, or raw.

"Some boiled capon?"

"Yes," she said finally, knowing something had to join the vegetables on her plate. A footman rushed to serve her. Of course, she thought. He couldn't bait her until they were alone.

But he didn't dismiss the servants. Otis hovered.

Hawk spoke of his long association with the Melchers, a most unexceptionable topic to the point of boredom.

When he took a final bite of plum pudding, he shoved his chair back and regarded her. "I don't believe I will drink any port. Shall we go to the drawing room, Frances?"

There was no hope for it. At least she hadn't demanded she go with him to his bedchamber.

Otis helped her with her chair. She gave him a shy thank-you and walked beside her husband to the drawing room.

Frances seated herself close to the fireplace. It had

grown cool and there was a small fire burning. She clasped her hands in her lap and stared at the orange flames.

"How do you feel?" he asked abruptly.

She quivered at those particular words. Get a hold of yourself, ninny! She managed to say with credible calm, "I am quite all right, my lord. Quite myself again."

"A pity," Hawk said, his voice still smooth.

Her eyes met his, and she saw irony in his, and something else she didn't understand.

"Would you play for me, Frances?"

He was offering her escape! She nearly leapt to her feet. "Yes, certainly," she said, her voice so pitifully uncertain that Hawk was hard pressed not to smile.

She launched immediately into a very difficult Haydn sonata, only to discover that her fingers had no intention of obeying her. She slaughtered several measures, then with a grimace lifted her hands from the keys.

Hawk said gently, "I should prefer something more gentle, perhaps. Another Scottish ballad?"

He was standing behind her; she felt his warm breath against the top of her head.

"I don't know if I can," she blurted out, so mortified that she wanted to scream and cry at the same time.

Hawk smiled down at her, a painful smile. He looked at her white shoulders and wanted more than anything to touch her, caress her, ease his hands over her shoulders and downward to her full breasts.

He'd been so close this afternoon, so very close. He closed his eyes a moment, his fingers curling at the memory of her exquisite response to him. It had been in those few moments that he had realized that Amalie was quite right. A wife could be seduced, a wife could experience as much pleasure as a man's mistress. He realized suddenly that he'd been silent too long, and quickly said, "Why don't we play piquet instead? Should you like that?"

Piquet! She was an excellent player, for her father had drummed rules and strategy into her head at the age of ten. She wondered briefly if she would be able to tell the difference between a king and a jack.

"Yes," she said, "I should like that." Why was he being so nice? So very unmenacing?

Frances watched silently as a footman brought in a card table, Otis behind him, holding two decks of new cards.

After Frances was seated, Hawk dismissed the servants. He said to Otis, "Take yourself to bed, Otis. I shall ensure that all the candles are doused in here."

"As you will, my lord." Otis paused a moment, his eyes on Frances. She was behaving very oddly this evening, saying next to nothing, eating less, and her face was pale. He said very gently, "My lady?"

The two words held a wealth of question, but Frances merely forced herself to smile at him. "I am fine, Otis. Good night to you."

Otis bowed and took himself from the drawing room.

"Shuffle and deal the cards, my dear," Hawk said, "and I shall get us some brandy."

At least he wasn't standing over her to see her mangle the deck of cards. By the time he set the brandy snifter at her elbow, she had managed to deal the correct number of cards.

Hawk picked up his cards and sorted them. He said, "Do you enjoy brandy, Frances? Perhaps you would prefer something else?"

"N-no, this is fine." She raised her glass and sipped. The warm liquid slid down her throat and landed squarely in her nearly empty stomach.

She began to sort her own cards, staring at them stupidly, half-listening to Hawk. "I suppose I became quite the successful gambler in the army. There were stretches of inactivity, you know, and not much for the officers to do after drilling the men. Many times we didn't play for money, which was probably just as well, as I remember both winning and losing fortunes."

He looked up and smiled at her. "Four," he said.

Frances managed to consult her hand with some intelligence. "How much?"

"Forty-one."

"Equal."

"Quart," Hawk said.

"That is good," Frances said.

"A tierce also, my dear. Three aces."

Play continued. Hawk found himself a good deal impressed with her skill, but as they continued, she lost her edge rapidly.

His wife, he saw with gleaming eyes, was becoming quite drunk.

"More brandy?"

Frances shook her muddled head and selected a card, a ten of hearts, and blankly watched Hawk gently place a queen of hearts over it. "You did not count," he said.

At the close of the game, Hawk said lightly as he tallied the score, "Pity we aren't playing for money. You are in a dreadful situation, Frances." He dropped the pencil and leaned back in his chair. "A long day."

"Yes," Frances agreed, toying with an eight of spades.

"I find myself quite fatigued."

Her mind sharpened with sudden miraculousness. "I too," she said quickly.

"You held excellent cards, my dear."

She shrugged but was forced to agree.

"Shall we go upstairs now, Frances?"

He watched the myriad expressions cross her face. The expression that remained was one of wariness. "What will you do?"

"I think I should like a bath," he said calmly.

"Yes, I should too!"

"I do not believe that there would be enough room for the both of us, more's the pity."

She stared at him, her tongue at half-mast.

He said nothing more, rose, and stretched. She found herself unwillingly looking at him. He was a magnificent specimen, but of course he knew it. Her eyes dropped to her hands, but she saw him with blinding clarity, striding out of the loch, his muscular body dripping water.

She gulped. He was her husband. There could be no more running away. She would bear it. "Will you visit me?" she asked.

That brought him up short, and he blinked. A direct assault, he thought, smiling to himself. Perhaps, just perhaps she was still in the throes of her experience of the afternoon. With the assistance of the brandy, perhaps, just perhaps . . .

"I shall think about it, Frances," he said. He offered her a brief nod and took himself out of the room. His body was throbbing with lust, and he feared that he would ravish her on the drawing-room carpet if he remained.

Frances stared at the embers in the fireplace. Her mind felt sluggish and quite at ease. Her body felt languid. She rose, doused the candles, keeping but one to take upstairs.

Agnes had her bath prepared, and steaming, scented heat reached Frances' nose as she came into her bedchamber. "His lordship told me you'd want a bath, my lady," Agnes said matter-of-factly.

"How kind of him," Frances said vaguely.

It didn't take Agnes many moments to realize that her mistress was tipsy. She smiled, thinking that her ladyship was going to enjoy herself this night. She gave a delicious little shudder remembering the gleam in the earl's eyes when he had given her instructions. She frowned a bit, seeing that Frances was on the point of sleep in the bathtub.

"My lady," she said softly, gently shaking her mistress' shoulder.

"Am I become a prune yet?" Frances said, grinning hazily up at her maid.

"Very nearly. Come now, let me dry you off."

Frances was a pliant creature, but when Agnes refused to braid her hair, she merely giggled. "I lost at piquet," she said.

"No wonder," said Agnes in a starchy voice.

"I did not play as I usually play," Frances continued, frowning down at her bare toes.

"Probably not, my lady," said Agnes. "Come, let me help you into bed."

Frances was on the point of climbing into her bed when she stopped and spun about. "I am hungry, Agnes."

Agnes sent her eyes heavenward.

"Yes," continued Frances thoughtfully, her greed growing, "I believe I shall visit the kitchen. Surely Cook has left something about."

Agnes sent an agonized look toward the adjoining door. She temporized. "If you wish, I can have something sent up to you, my lady."

"No," Frances announced, searching for her slippers, "I wish to forage for my own food."

To Agnes' utter relief, there came a light knock on the adjoining door. She rushed to open it, saying when she saw the earl, "Her ladyship is hungry."

Hawk grinned at his wife, who was endeavoring with great concentration to put her right slipper on her left foot. He nodded dismissal to Agnes. "I shall see to her," he said, and didn't move until Agnes closed the bedchamber door behind her.

"I understand from Agnes, my dear, that you are hungry?" he asked, coming toward her.

"Why won't this idiot slipper do what it's supposed to?"

He watched her sit on the floor, stick her foot out, and try to fit the recalcitrant slipper. "There," she said with triumphant. "But it looks so very odd. My toes are in the wrong direction."

He wanted to laugh, but for a moment he didn't. He was breathing too hard. Her nightgown was spread about her, and her glorious hair hung loose down her back. He looked at the slender ankle and the foot with its toes in the wrong direction.

"Let me help you," he said, and dropped to the floor in front of her.

"Thank you," she said with great seriousness.

Hawk took the slipper and tossed it over his shoulder. Then he picked up her foot and kissed the tip of each toe.

She stared at him, befuddled. Then she started to giggle. She wiggled her toes in his face and giggled all the harder.

Hawk bit her little toe.

Frances fell on her back, hugging her sides as she burst into merry laughter.

Hawk stared at her for a moment, then grinned unwillingly. After all, it had been he who had encouraged her to down the damned brandy. His fingers began sliding up her leg.

"That tickles!" Frances cried, and tried to pull her leg away from him.

Hawk held her leg firmly and with his other hand pushed up her nightgown. He had a sudden view, a very close view, of two long white legs. Slender ankles and calves, he saw, and beautiful thighs. Lord, even her knees were lovely. Suddenly Frances, still in the throes of drunken giggles, lifted her other leg and thrust her foot into his chest. It took him off guard, and he landed on his rear, still holding her ankle.

He pulled her toward him, grabbing her other ankle. Her nightgown rose higher as he brought her closer. He held her legs apart, enjoying her wriggling and the ever-increasing view.

Her nightgown bunched about her waist and he felt himself perilously close to the edge of his control. He swallowed.

"Frances," he said on a gulp.

She tried to sit up and he released her ankles. She balanced herself on her open palms and stared at him owlishly, her legs widespread, her nightgown tangled about her hips.

"Are you ticklish?" she demanded, her eyes sparkling with mischief.

"I . . . uh, well—"

He got no farther. Frances lurched to her knees and dived for him. She smashed him onto his back, laughed down at his stunned face, and sent her fingers flying toward his ribs.

Hawk was very ticklish, and her fingers found his most vulnerable spots in a matter of seconds. His laughter burst forth, for the moment easing his nearly painful desire. He finally managed to catch her hands, holding them away from him.

He became instantly aware that she was between his spread legs and that his dressing gown was parted. She was naked against him to the waist. He looked up into her laughing face.

"Frances," he said very softly, clamped his hands about her arms, and brought her face down to his.

"Kiss me," he said, and moved his hands to the back of her head, pressing her down.

"All right," she said agreeably, and pursed her lips.

"Not quite like that" he said, smiling despite his growing urgency. He lowered his hand and lightly parted her lips with his fingertip. "Keep your mouth open but don't talk. That's the way it's done, you know."

She obeyed him and he thought he would leap out of his skin when her lips touched his. He wrapped his arms around her back and pulled her tightly against his chest.

Suddenly she raised her head and asked with grave seriousness, "Now what do we do? The kissing part is easy."

"Hmmm," he said, gently fiddling with a long curl that fell onto is face, "You want to do something else besides kissing now?"

Her expression changed abruptly, and he knew that she was thinking about those few moments in the tack room. Her pupils darkened. Hell, so was he. His hips thrust upward without his conscious instruction, and he saw that she felt him, hard and demanding, against her belly.

"Hawk," she said, her voice suddenly uncertain.

"Yes?"

"I . . . this is all very odd, I think."

"Not odd at all, I promise you. Come to bed now, Frances."

Her eyes looked troubled, uncertain, but she was grinning. Ah, the benefits of brandy, he thought as he rolled over, bringing her with him. He grasped her under her arms and brought her to her feet.

He grinned as she had obvious trouble in holding up

her own weight. He hoisted her over his shoulder, lightly patting her bottom with the palm of his hand.

When he eased her onto her back, she said in the most worried voice he had ever heard "Where is the cream?"

He blinked down at her. "I really don't believe that we will have need of it."

"Well," she began thoughtfully, troubled, "perhaps you're right, I feel very odd, you know . . ." To his utter surprise, her hips squirmed.

"Frances!" he said, and gulped.

21

In vino veritas.

—*LATIN PROVERB*

Frances felt her head spinning, and she shook her head back and forth, trying to clear her mind.

"Frances," Hawk said gently. "Hold still." He quickly divested himself of his dressing gown and eased himself down over her.

"I saw you," she said very clearly, staring up into his beautiful face. "You are not nearly so ... grand as Gentleman Dan."

"Lucky for you I am not," he said, and tweaked the end of her nose.

"However," Frances continued, her word so lilting with a Scottish brogue that he could scarce understand her, "however, you are very ... inviting."

"Thank you. Now, if you don't mind, I should like to remove this damned nightgown of yours."

"All right," she said, and helped him ease it up. When the thin lawn was covering her face on its journey upward, she giggled again, and said, "You look so terribly serious, Hawk, even through my Salome's veil."

It's because I want you so badly I'm going to embarrass myself!

"So you have finally decided to make me 'Hawk'?" he said as he tossed her nightgown to the floor.

"I'm beginning to believe that a hawk is a very nice bird," she said, and to his utter amazement, she lurched up, grabbed his face between her palms, and kissed him soundly.

"Can I look at you, Hawk?"

He blinked, so confused at this new Frances that he couldn't gather his wits together.

"Please, lie down."

He complied, feeling very peculiar. He should be easing her, caressing her, whispering encouragement to her. He spread himself on his back. Frances came up on her knees and proceeded to give him serious study, from his eyebrows to his toes.

In his turn, he gazed at her, the intent expression in her gray eyes, the taut dark rose nipples on her full breasts, breasts almost too full for her slender torso, her supple waist. He thought he couldn't control himself when his eyes fell to her thighs and the nest of chestnut curls. He forced his eyes back to her face, and jerked when he saw she was staring at his enthusiastic manhood. He watched her flutter her hand above him, then very slowly descend until she was slightly touching him.

"Oh," she said, blinking. "How very odd. You are soft, like silk, I think, but you're so hard and alive and almost . . . throbbing."

"Frances," he gritted between clenched teeth. "Please."

"You want me to kiss you again?"

Lord yes, he wanted her to kiss him, but he knew it wouldn't occur to her to take him into her mouth. "Yes," he said, his voice very thin. The damned Scottish chit was seducing him!

He came up quickly, and with one swift movement spun her onto her back. He gently smoothed her hair from her face. He brought his thigh over hers, and closed his eyes a moment at the feel of her smooth flesh against his legs.

He thought he would burst from want, but then she giggled again, so he was forced to laugh at himself.

He had to get control again. He said very deliberately, cupping his hand over her, "Remember this afternoon, my dear? Do you remember how you felt when I did this?" His palm pressed against her, and she looked profoundly worried.

"Yes," she said, "I remember."

"Now, give me your hand." She didn't move, merely stared at him with a befuddled expression. He took her hand and brought it down and laid it beneath his, lightly pressing her fingers against herself. "Do you feel how moist you are? How hot and swelled your woman's flesh is?"

She nodded, very seriously.

"Have you ever felt anything like this before?"

She shook her head, her expression unchanged.

"How could I have?" she said reasonably. "You've never done that before."

"Very true," he agreed, smiling just a bit. God, he hurt. He suddenly remembered a saying that one of the dons at Eton adored repeating: *Great men move slowly*. Had the fellow meant in bed? He eased her hand away and began to caress her with his fingers. Then he paused a moment, to judge the effects of his labors.

"Hawk," Frances said, her hips rising off the bed, "I want you to keep doing what you're doing, please."

"You may be certain that I shall," he said with heartfelt sincerity. Amalie, he said to himself, I am finally doing things right.

He deepened the pressure of his fingers, and she cried out. "I . . . I can't seem to think properly!"

"Don't think at all, just feel. Feel, Frances. What do you feel now?"

"I am going to ... explode," she whispered, arching her head back.

As am I, he thought, his body so frantic with need that he bit his lower lip. There was so much of her to enjoy, so much expanse of beautiful white skin. He quickly moved between her legs, widened them more, and put his mouth to her belly.

Frances didn't think anything was funny now. She wanted to yell, she wanted ... She didn't know what she wanted. Her fingers went to his hair and she tugged.

When his warm mouth closed over her, she nearly leapt off the bed. "Hawk!"

"Shut up, Frances," he said, his warm breath cascading over her, making her wild.

God, he thought as he tasted her, scraped her soft swelled flesh with his tongue, she was perfect, utterly perfect. When he felt her legs stiffening, he knew that he wanted to see her face in her climax. Gently he eased his fingers into her and raised his head.

She stared at him, at sea. Her voice exploded from her throat. "Hawk?"

"Yes, Frances."

She yelled, her body stiffening, her eyes looking vague, then bewildered, then blind. It was the most perfect sight he'd ever seen in his life. He watched her teeth grip her lower lip. He watched her back arch up, watched her hands fall helplessly.

He felt the tremors hold her in thrall. He was breathing hard now, his body pounding. He moved up over her, and with one forceful thrust seated himself to his hilt within her.

He felt her convulsive aftershocks of pleasure, the small quivering shudders, felt her arms crushing him to her, and found her lips. He took her shuddering little cries into his mouth, and let his tongue dart into her. He was filled with intense warmth, almost as if, he thought crazily, she was wrapped about him, and inside him. "My God," he said aloud, his body shuddering, and then he was lost in the most intense pleasure he'd ever experienced in his life.

Frances locked her arms about his back, felt his deep moans penetrate deep into her being just as his manhood was throbbing frantically inside her. Then she felt his final shudder, felt him flood her, so very deep, with his seed.

His body was bathed in perspiration, he felt as though his pounding heart would leap out of his body. "Frances, my God," he said in a jerky sigh, and fell atop her, his head beside hers on the pillow.

"You were right," Frances said. "You didn't need any cream." She closed her eyes, and was asleep in the next instant.

Hawk knew the exact moment she was gone from him. Slowly he raised his sweating body off hers and onto his side. "Oh, Frances," he said softly as he gently shoved her damp hair from her forehead. "I think I shall feed you brandy for dinner every night."

Ah, Amalie, he thought, grinning like a fool, you were so right. But of course, he continued in his mind, she was drunk. And drink stripped away inhibitions, he knew. He quickly rose, doused the candles, looked at his sprawled naked wife, and with a grin, climbed back into bed beside her. He drew the covers over them and eased her against him.

His last thought before he fell into a deep sleep was whether or not he should have her watch Gentleman Dan in action again tomorrow.

Agnes said not a word. She'd known well enough

that she shouldn't enter her mistress's room, but she was frankly nosy. She smiled, gazing but briefly upon the man and woman in the bed, their bodies twined together, Lady Frances' head snuggled into the hollow of her husband's shoulder. She left, and her smiling, smug expression gave truth to all the belowstairs gossip.

"Oh dear," Frances said, coming abruptly awake and sitting up. "Oh dear," she said again, gazing down at her still-sleeping husband. His cheeks were dark with morning whiskers, his black hair tousled, and he looked utterly marvelous. She reached out her hand to touch his face, then moaned softly. She became aware that her head was pounding horribly, and she felt as if she had drowned a vat of wine. Brandy, you twit, she corrected herself. She felt stickiness between her thighs, and blushed.

"Oh dear," she said once again, this time so quietly that he couldn't possibly hear her.

But he did, of course.

"Good morning, wife," Hawk said, and grinned at her chagrined face. "How do you feel?"

"My head aches abominably."

"It should. I'll have Grunyon make you up one of his special potions. They are most efficacious, you know. Your breasts are exquisite."

Frances jerked the cover over her breasts, and the abrupt movement made her head spin.

"Unfortunately," Hawk continued blandly, "I didn't have time last night to give them their proper due. You rushed me most thoroughly, my dear. I wonder," he added thoughtfully, "if your breasts are as sensitive as the rest of you."

"Shut up," said Frances, not at all tipsy this bright, brittle morning.

Her husband gave her an inexcusably pleased grin.

"Had you believed me as ugly as you used to, you wouldn't have wanted to even bother!"

"My, my," he said, his voice softly mocking, for he knew well the pain of a head the morning after a night of brandy, "it doesn't say much for my intellect that I actually understand what you mean."

"You are a man and—"

"I am a man, to be sure, and last night you never minded that in the least bit."

"No," she said, frowning toward the far wall, "I didn't mind. I wasn't myself."

"Ah, then I must continue the winning combination, eh? Horses mating and brandy. I will never lose to you at piquet, at any rate. I should probably tally up the score from last night."

"I want you to leave now," she said.

"Why? I thought we were having a splendid morning chat."

"My head is going to burst."

"Then I shall win any argument if you are so silly as to begin one."

Frances clutched the cover against her breasts. She wanted to howl, to punch his smug face, but she said only, "I don't want you to do that again."

"Why?" he asked with great interest, staring at her beautiful white back. Her hair was in tangled disarray nearly to her waist. He reached up a hand to smooth her hair, and she froze.

"It isn't what I am used to," she said.

"No, I don't suppose that it is. But you will become quite used to it, I promise you."

He stretched on his back, pillowing his head on his arm. He realized well enough that she would like to leave him, but was too embarrassed to parade about him in her exquisite natural state.

She remained stubbornly silent, and Hawk continued lazily after a moment, "Would you like another lesson, Frances? Men enjoy morning lovemaking, you know."

That fond suggestion made her slither off the bed with a good deal of haste, dragging the covers with her. When she turned, it was to see her husband, naked, his legs slightly parted, lying on his back, grinning at her.

She stared at him, and she knew that he knew she was staring at him. "Oh," she said stupidly, wrapped herself like a mummy in the covers, and dashed behind her dressing screen.

"Would you like some help, Frances?" he called, balancing himself on his elbows.

"What I would like you to do is have Grunyon prepare that damned potion!"

He sighed deeply. "All right," he said, and rose. "I did promise, didn't I?"

He gazed hopefully toward the screen, sighed again, and took himself to his own bedchamber.

It was only another ten minutes before Agnes entered, bearing the potion. "Mr. Grunyon said you would like to have this, my lady," she said.

Frances downed the entire glass without pause. "That was awful," she said. She sat back in her chair, leaned her head back, and closed her eyes.

It was nearly an hour later before hunger drove Frances downstairs to the breakfast room. To her chagrin, Hawk sat at the table, his plate in front of him, the *Gazette* in his hands. Why couldn't he have been long gone by now? It wasn't fair.

He smiled at her, seeing her hesitate, and slowly folded the paper. "Do you feel better?"

"Yes," she said, succumbing to a fickle fate and seating herself, "it was truly dreadful, but I feel somewhat back to myself again."

He took a bit of toast piled with raspberry jam. He met her eyes, licked the jam from the corner of his mouth, and said, "I wonder if your breasts taste as good as the rest of you."

She felt her eyes begin to cross.

"Don't worry, my dear, only you and I are here," he said in a soothing voice. "Would you like me to serve you? You doubtless have a ravishing hunger."

She said nothing to that drawing comment, served herself, her movements sluggish. He waited until she had a mouth of scrambled eggs, and said, "Your scent is most delightfully, uniquely you. And I do believe that your taste is more invigorating than Cook's jam here. In any case, it drove me wild."

"Shut up," said Frances, her mouth still full of egg.

"Pardon me, my dear? Did you say something?"

Frances finished chewing her eggs, swallowed, and said in a very clear, carrying voice, "I said shut up."

"Ah. How very disheartening. A great lover expects to hear cooing, delighted little sighs the morning after."

She shot him a scowl replete with silent recriminations and focused all her attention on her bacon.

He watched her attack her food with a vengeance. He wondered with a silent laugh if she pictured him as the bacon as she poked and prodded it with her knife.

"I shall meet with Marcus now, I believe," he said, rising. "I imagine that it will take me a while to wrest the reins of management from your white hands."

To his surprise, his jest was met with a distressed look. He said, his eyes narrowing a bit, "Surely, Frances, you don't expect me to be a lapdog of no account?"

She swallowed, seeing everything taken from her, seeing herself alone and of no worth at all.

"It is *my* estate, you know."

"Why don't you return to London," she said evenly. "Surely I must be pregnant after last night."

"If howling pleasure on a woman's part was a sign of conception, I just might in all good faith assume that you would give birth to twins at the very least."

Her fork clattered to her plate. She rose from her chair and faced him, her hands on her hips. Hawk eyed her heaving breasts with a good deal of interest.

"I really can't wait, my dear, to caress your breasts. They look utterly inviting this very minute. Is that what you wish, with that pose of yours?"

Frances hurled her empty teacup at him. He ducked it, laughed, and gave her a leering, knowing look. She picked up her plate, only to quietly set it down again upon the entrance of Otis.

Hawk said to his butler, his voice showing his high good humor, "Well, man, what is it? Her ladyship and I were enjoying a most invigorating morning conversation."

"A letter, my lord," Otis said. "It followed you from London. It is from your father, my lord."

"Excuse me," Frances said, and left the room without another word.

Hawk thought: I will give you until tonight to come to grips with yourself.

"Well, Frances, what are you up to?"

Frances looked up to see her husband leaning over the stall door. She gently finished tying up the bandage on the bay stallion's fetlock, and slowly rose. "As you see, I am attending to Clancy. He's got a speedy-cut, which, of course, shouldn't have happened. It is the result of him striking one leg with the opposite foot. He probably did it galloping, since he has a tendency to turn out his toes. I'll have to to speak to Belvis about this." She saw that her husband was watching her patiently, and raised an eyebrow. "What is it you want, my lord?"

Hawk let that formality pass. Indeed, he was perturbed. He held up the envelope. "The letter from my father—"

"He is all right, is he not?" she asked quickly.

"My sire will live to see us all underground," Hawk said, his voice acid. "Actually, he had expected this letter to find me in London. Its contents are most interesting. He informs me that I should consider bringing myself home quickly, as there is talk about my wife and my steward becoming closer than is proper."

"*What*? He said what?"

Hawk watched the shocked expression deepen the color of her eyes. He had realized quickly enough that it was but another ploy on his father's part to get him back to Desborough Hall. He supposed he was wicked enough to draw her on, just a bit.

"Well, what do you have to say about that, madam? Remember, I saw Marcus leaning all over you on the day of my arrival."

Frances wished she had her breakfast plate. She would surely hurl it at his head. How could he believe such a thing! Then she saw the gleam of mocking amusement in his eyes, and she realized her father-in-law's purpose. Hawk didn't believe it, not a word, but he was enjoying himself at her expense. She lowered her head and began to twist her hands in front of her.

"Frances?"

She lowered her head even more. She heard the tentative uncertainty in his voice and was hard-pressed not to smile. Wretched, mocking man! She said in a halting, very guilty voice, "Oh, dear, how could he! I didn't really mean to . . . well, you know that Marcus is so very nice and handsome and—"

Clancy's Pride snorted and Frances quickly let herself out of his stall.

"What did you say?"

She heard the beginnings of outrage in his voice, and allowed her chin to tremble. Her voice was liquid with guilt and shame. "I didn't mean for it to happen, truly I didn't, it is just that I was so lonely and—"

Hawk grabbed her shoulders and shook her. "What the devil are you talking about?"

"Why, I'm talking about my illicit behavior with your steward, my lord."

His eyes glittered and he realized that she'd turned the tables on him.

Frances fluttered her lashes and said in a sweetly reminiscing voice, "Ah, such a pity, but—"

"I am going to beat you," he said, shaking her again.

Frances couldn't help herself. She started laughing, marvelously mocking laughter that made Hawk see red.

"Frances," he growled, deep in his throat. "Stop it, damn you, or I'll throttle you!"

She did, very quickly, and in the next moment had pulled free of his hands and raced toward the doorway. She looked back to see him standing beside Clancy's stall, his face a thundercloud, his hands fisted at his sides.

"Ah, yes, Marcus is such a grand lover ... so considerate—"

Hawk took a step toward her, and she fled, her laughter floating back to him.

When the marquess arrived early that afternoon, he was met by a tearful Frances, who flung herself in his arms and whimpered in an agonized voice, "Oh, my lord, why did you have to tell him? Hawk, I mean. Marcus and I felt so very safe, until that letter—"

Hawk arrived on the front steps in time to witness his wife's sterling performance. He watched the dazed confusion on his father's face become guilt, then awareness of what was being done unto him.

Hawk applauded. "Bravo!" he shouted. He clapped louder.

The marquess pried himself loose of Frances' clinging arms. "Enough, my girl!" he roared.

He watched Frances fall into a fit of giggles, then turned to meet his son's eyes. Hawk's expression was filled with murderous irony.

The marquess frowned at himself. He was bloody tired, having traveled at top speed from Chandos Chase upon word that Hawk wasn't in London, and that his letter had followed his son northward. "I think," he said slowly, "that I have made a miscalculation."

"You, sir," said Frances, "are an unprincipled old fraud! Now, come along, you must be weary. Your room is ready for you."

"You expected me, hmmm?"

"Of course," Frances said, placing her hand on his arm. She whispered in a wicked voice, "Marcus can't wait to see you, my lord."

"Frances!"

How very odd, she thought. The marquess's voice sounded exactly like his son's.

22

A woman's strength is in her tongue.
—SEVENTEENTH-CENTURY PROVERB

Frances sat back in her chair and regarded the two silent gentlemen. "I suppose," she said quite happily, "that the two of you have realized your foolishness."

"Frances," Hawk said, sounding close to the end of his tether, "why don't you rest your mouth for a bit?"

She blinked at him in guileless surprise, "But, my lord, 'twas you who came galloping into the stables ready to slay me with your false ire." She chuckled. "The cuckolded husband, a marvelous performance, my lord!"

"Frances, be quiet," the marquess said.

"Cook prepared your favorite dishes, my lord," she continued blandly to her father-in-law. "Don't you care for the mutton cutlets? Ah, and the soubise sauce . . . so very tasty, don't you agree? And the mashed potatoes are so very fluffy, the secret is very fresh cream, you know—"

"Frances," Hawk said "if you do not cease shooting your barbs into my father's hide, I will haul you upstairs and bind and gag you."

The two gentlemen, father and son, were standing together, Frances thought, perhaps for the first time in a good many months. She grinned at them and chewed on a bite of mutton.

"Belvis said that Lord Danvers' prize mare is here," the marquess said to his son after a few moments of peaceful silence. "Lady Margaret, a Barb?"

"Yes, indeed," said Hawk. "Gentleman Dan doubtless believes he's expired and gone to stallion heaven. Of course, one imagines that mare is in the same exhalted state," he added, sending Frances a leering look.

The marquess continued after digesting this ironic observation, "Frances wrote to me that Belvis has great hopes for Flying Davie in particular. Says he can take all comers at Newmarket, despite the fact he's only a four-year-old."

"Did she now?"

Retrench just a bit, the marquess decided. He helped himself to some dumplings.

"Belvis is letting me assist in Flying Davie's training," Frances said.

"I've never even seen you ride," Hawk said.

"I ride astride usually," Frances said, her chin going up. "It is much safer, as you well know."

"Yes, I believe I told you that."

Hawk pictured his wife in her trousers and felt his groin tighten. How, he wondered, would he seduce her this evening? Her passion of the night before did seem to have softened her toward him. It was perplexing. In his experience, when he gave a woman pleasure, she was his. He thought of her astride him and felt a dull flush mount his cheeks. He thought of covering her as a stallion would a mare, and his flush deepened.

"Where is your dear Marcus this evening, my dear?" Hawk asked.

Frances grinned. "I believe he is a bit taken with Cloris Melcher."

"The vicar's eldest daughter?" said the marquess. "Isn't she the chit with the yellow hair and the dimples?"

"That's her," said Frances.

"So you couldn't manage to keep him, Frances?" Hawk said.

Frances refused to be drawn. She gave a dramatic sigh and said very softly, "I am too old. Marcus told me so. He was ever so polite about it, of course, but—"

Hawk groaned. "I'm sorry I raised it. Forgive me, Father." He glanced at Frances' smug face and added, "After last night, I had hoped to find my wife gentled and weak with love for me."

Frances gasped, and Hawk wondered if she would hurl something at him.

The marquess smiled into his wineglass. How nice, he thought. They were coming together quite nicely. So proud, the both of them, but it appeared that his son had at last truly made love to his wife.

"We are both hopeful that Frances will have good news very soon," Hawk remarked.

Frances said, her voice cold as winter, "Yes, my lord. Then your *son* can return to London, where he doubtless belongs! I'll be amazed if he remains at Desborough until the end of the week."

"The end of the week is but two days away," Hawk said. He lounged back in his chair. "You wound me, Frances, you truly do."

"I should like to do more than that, my lord!"

" 'Hawk,' " he corrected mildly.

I am too old for this bickering, the marquess thought. "Ah, Otis, I believe I shall retire now. Do compliment Cook on the delicious dinner." His chair was gently pulled back, and the marquess rose. "I bid you good night, children."

Hawk rose politely and walked his father to the door.

"A game of piquet, Frances?" Hawk asked, coming back into the dining room to stand by his wife's chair.

"I suppose so," Frances said, craning her neck to look up at him.

"Or perhaps you would like to join me in bed?"

"I would not join you in heaven, my lord!"

"I wonder if I will have to resort to cream again," he said in a thoughtful voice. She felt his warm hand lightly touch her bare shoulder, and tried to pull away. His fingers tightened.

"Hawk," she said, her voice thin.

"Yes, my dear?" His fingertips drifted toward the inviting swell of her breasts.

To her utter consternation, Frances felt a deep spurt of something very warm and urgent between her thighs. She squirmed just a bit in her chair.

"Come along, Frances," he said very gently.

She shook her head. "I haven't tasted Cook's ginger cream!"

"If you are still hungry, I shall endeavor to satisfy you."

Frances' agile tongue wouldn't budge. "I don't want to," she said at last, digging in her heels.

"Actually, you have no choice in the matter," he said, and pulled back her chair. "Do you prefer that I carry you upstairs over my shoulder? Surely the servants have enough to gossip about without adding such a spectacle."

"I should like to play piquet."

"We can play anything you wish in bed."

"I want some brandy!"

"You can attack my body and tickle me without

brandy. There are other benefits as well to having a sober wife. Tomorrow morning I can frolic with you without worrying about your aching head."

Frances drew a deep breath. She rose with all the dignity she could muster, turned, and faced her husband. "I will come with you," she said. "But it will change nothing, my lord, nothing! I mean it!"

He smiled at her, a devilish, quite confident smile. "You won't be weak with love for me tomorrow?"

"I shall be strong with natural dislike for you!"

She sailed out of the dining room. He called softly after her, "I shall be right along, my dear. I have no desire to search out another hiding place in this house. Please contrive to remember that."

Frances was pacing her bedchamber, having dismissed an oddly smiling Agnes some minutes before. Her eyes kept to the adjoining door. He is a fiend, she said to herself. She was nearly incoherent with anxiety when the door finally opened and her husband strode confidently into her room.

"How lovely you are," he said, pausing to look her over.

Despite herself, Frances thought he looked extremely lovely himself. His dressing gown was a deep blue, and she knew he was quite naked beneath it. She managed to quell her unacceptable delight, shot him a deadly look, and said coldly, "I trust you didn't forget your cream?"

"So little faith you appear to have in me, Frances."

Hawk realized that despite her show of bravado, she was anxious and likely somewhat afraid, both of him and of herself and her response to him. He moved to the large wing chair and sat down. He gave her a long look and said, "Come here, Frances. Let's . . . talk."

He patted his thighs.

Frances took a step toward him, seemed to catch herself, and retreated two steps.

He patted his thighs again, his eyes never leaving her face.

"Oh, very well!"

She sat on his thighs, holding herself rigid as a board.

"My father is most fond of you," he said.

"I am most fond of your father, the wicked old man. To think that he would write you such a letter!"

Hawk clasped his arms about her waist and drew her back against his chest. Slowly she eased and began to relax.

"Hawk?"

"Yes, my dear?"

"Does a man wish to do this every night?"

"At the very least. Actually, you are so delicious I believe I could easily be induced to love you repeatedly until I collapsed into an exhausted heap."

"Oh."

"All I require is a modicum of encouragement, Frances."

"Before, you didn't require anything at all."

"True, and it was a duty, not a pleasure."

His voice was smooth as Flying Davie's silken neck. She felt him lifting her hair, felt his fingers lightly stroking the nape of her neck. He continued very quietly after a moment, "I am truly sorry for our first night together, and the other nights as well."

"You mean," she said, not wanting to give an inch, "that you got little pleasure when I was not . . . responding to you."

His hand raised from her waist and gently closed over her left breast. Frances gasped, and tried to pull away. "No, don't, Frances. Lay your head against my shoulder. That's right. Now, strive to have a bit of faith in your husband."

Hawk was relieved that she couldn't see his face. It was flushed with his nearly painful need. "You feel so exquisite," he whispered against her forehead. He opened the ribbons of her dressing gown and parted the material. When his hand closed over her bare flesh, both of them jumped.

"I don't like this," Frances whispered, more to herself than to him.

"Be patient," Hawk said. He eased her out of the dressing gown and her nightgown, baring her to the waist. He eased her back into the crook of his arm and simply gazed at her. "Just feel, Frances," he said. He cupped her breast, lifting it, then began lightly to stroke her.

Frances felt as though lightning was striking her. Shafts of intense feeling darted from her breasts to low in her belly. She remembered well enough the wild sensations of the previous night, and realized that she wanted to feel them again. She wanted to kiss him again, she wanted to touch him, she wanted to feel his mouth caressing her . . .

She arched against his arm, and Hawk thought he would expire with the pleasure of it.

He eased her further down, lowered his head, and kissed her breast. He felt her trembling, felt her breast heaving with her quickened breathing. He rested his cheek a moment between her breasts. He smiled a bit painfully when he felt her trying to move against him.

"Come," he said, his voice sounding raw to his own ears. He lifted her up from his lap and walked beside her to the bed.

"Frances," he said, gently drawing her to a halt in front of him. He slowly pulled off her nightclothes, then stepped back to look at her. Her thick hair was

flowing down her white back. His eyes followed the
lines of her, her narrow waist, her full hips. He swallowed. He reached out his hands and grasped her
hips, pulling her back against him. "Frances," he said
again, his warm breath against her ear.

His arms came around her body and he began to
knead her belly. Frances saw herself as she had been
the day of the mating, her back against him, his fingers low and caressing, her incredible need swamping
her, driving her . . . She felt his lips lightly kissing and
nipping her throat, her shoulder. It was like the stallion, she thought. When his fingers roved downward,
finding her, she couldn't help herself, she cried out.

Hawk knew well enough what he was doing, imagined
quite accurately the erotic image in her mind. He
closed his eyes, reveling in her warm, moist woman's
flesh, felt her swelling against his fingers. He brought
his other hand up and began to caress her breasts. He
felt the instant she was spiraling toward her climax. He
held her firmly, knowing she wouldn't be able to
support herself. He felt her head pressing back against
his shoulder, felt her beautiful legs stiffen, felt her
buttocks pressing against him.

He quickly turned her, not ceasing the play of his
fingers, and kissed her deeply, taking her cries into his
mouth. He felt himself fill, expand with something
hitherto unknown to him. He wanted to consume her
in that moment, fill himself with her, yet knew that his
manhood would do the filling.

He kissed her lips, her nose, her eyes, calming her,
stroked his hands up and down her back, and cupped
her buttocks, lifting her.

Frances looked up at him. Her eyes were dazed, her
lips slightly parted. She whispered his name, and in
the next moment he eased her onto her back, spread
and lifted her white legs, and came into her.

"Wrap your legs around me, Frances." She did, and he sucked in his breath as her thighs tightened about his flanks.

He stared down at her, saw her whisper his name yet again, felt her hands stroking over his buttocks, and was lost. He plunged deep, and moaned. He felt her legs rubbing against his hips. It kept going on, this intense pleasure, this deep need that threatened to engulf him. He closed his eyes, feeling himself exploding, shattering, and he didn't want it to stop.

"Frances," he said softly, and collapsed against her, his manhood still deep within her.

Frances accepted his weight. She was stunned. She felt his heart pounding against hers, felt his ragged breath against her cheek. She felt weak, and strangely sated, and doubted she could move even if the bed caught fire.

This lovemaking was odd, she thought vaguely. It trapped one. It trapped two into one, she added silently. She wondered, her hands gently rubbing his strong back, calming him, if he had been right, if now she would be gentled, would be weak with love for him—which had been his purpose all along.

He had seduced her most thoroughly. He had awakened feelings she'd scarcely ever thought about. Suddenly she grinned, laughing silently to herself. How long did it take a woman to become with child if this happened very night? Not long at all, she imagined. She sighed, hugged him tightly, and fell asleep.

Hawk returned to the world, blinking at his absolute loss of control, and more disconcerting, his loss of self. Frances slept and he knew he was too heavy for her. To his chagrin, when he shifted his weight, he felt himself grow hard inside her once more. This will never do, he told himself. She was his wife, that was all. Her purpose was to bear his children. A husband didn't rut his wife repeatedly as he did his mistress. But, he thought ruefully, he had changed all that himself. He had brought her passion, and her passion had changed him. He didn't like it. It was not what he was used to. She had a sharp tongue, and managing ways. She could easily enrage him, she mocked him without mercy, giving as good as she got . . . God, she was so lovely and so responsive.

He wanted her again, desperately. Furious with himself, he eased away from her, and rose. He stared down at her for a long moment, knowing if he stayed he would love her again. He forced himself to cover her, then quickly doused the candles and left.

His bed felt cold and empty and that made him wince. It never had before. Before he'd reveled in all the space, knowing deep down that he was free.

Frances awoke, aware of the bright sunlight flooding the room. There was a small smile on her lips, and she reached for Hawk. Her hand met nothing but pillow. She sat up quickly, her eyes searching her bedchamber. He was gone.

The bed was mussed, but not from the two of them sleeping together. He had left her after she'd fallen asleep. Why? She felt unaccountably disappointed, even hurt.

She remembered her thoughts in the aftermath of her pleasure, remembered thinking that this would perhaps gentle her, make her weak with love for him, wondering if he had been right about that.

"Damn you," she hissed toward the adjoining door. She ordered Agnes to fetch her a hot bath. She scrubbed herself furiously, only rising when the water was uncomfortably cold.

It was while Agnes was fastening the long row of

buttons up the back of her blue silk morning gown that she realized what she wanted to do.

There was a wide smile on her lips when she entered the breakfast room. To her chagrin, only the marquess was present.

"Good morning, my dear," her father-in-law said, studying her face.

She nodded, and asked without preamble, "Where is Hawk?"

"Up at dawn, so Grunyon told me, all togged out for riding."

Frances nodded toward Rosie and seated herself. Damn him, she thought, picking up her knife. *Oh, he'll not escape me. Let him ride until doomsday, he'll not escape me.*

"Has Hawk come around yet, Frances?" the marquess asked.

She cast him a startled glance, then understood his inquiry. "I don't know," she said. "He was most upset about the five thousand pounds. However, he has allowed the use of Gentleman Dan, and has said nothing about Flying Davie's training."

"You are a strong woman, Frances," the marquess remarked after a thoughtful moment. "I was gratified to hear that Hawk had come home. To tell the truth, I hesitated about that particular approach. Poor Marcus! I trust the young man knows nothing of his near-death at the hands of my son?"

"No, Marcus is quite innocently going about his affairs."

"I wonder why Hawk did return," the marquess continued. "I have given it much thought, Frances, and really don't understand his reasoning."

"Guilt," said Frances succinctly.

"I imagine that his guilt turned to something quite different when he saw you as you really are."

"Indeed," she said shortly. "He wanted to strangle me, when he'd stopped his yelling."

"Excellent. I knew my lad would come about."

This was said with such fond certainty that Frances dropped her fork and stared at her father-in-law. "Lad? Goodness, he is anything but a little lad," she said. "He is the most stubborn, conceited, arrogant—"

"Ah," the marquess said, interrupting her effusions. "I am glad to see that the lassie is coming about also."

"You, sir," Frances said between gritted teeth, "are the most abominable, ruthless, cunning—"

"It is so remarkably pleasant to be loved," said the marquess. He rose from his chair, walked to Frances, lightly kissed her cheek, and left the breakfast room.

"I am surely in Bedlam," Frances remarked to the silent room.

23

Every man to his trade.
—GREEK PROVERB

All I know how to do, Hawk told himself yet again as
he took Ebony over a fence, is wage war, love women,
and win at gambling. The stallion landed gracefully on
the other side and Hawk drew him up for a moment.
This was one of his favorite places—an oak-shaded
area by the River Ouse. He remembered it as a boy,
climbing out on a now-dead limb to dangle, then drop
into the water. Beatrice had been right behind him in
those days—shrieking as she jumped from the branch,
nearly drowning him when she landed. Where had
Nevil been? Odd, he couldn't clearly remember his
brother now. He sighed. That was because Nevil was
horse-mad and had spent all his time in the stables,
learning to train, learning to judge horseflesh, memorizing all the famous racers, their antecedents, their
times and distances. As was proper, he added to himself. He leaned down, selected a pebble, and skipped
it over the calm water.

A younger son is army-bound and he had gone and
had proved quite proficient at his metier. But he had
loved the horses, the smell of the stables, the excitement of watching a long-legged thoroughbred go
through his paces. But he had cut all that off, con-

sciously withdrawn, when he'd realized that Desborough wouldn't be his, that he couldn't involve himself. It was Nevil's birthright, Nevil's trade.

I could learn, he told himself. As Frances was now learning.

Frances—what was he going to do about her?

Lord, what a fool he'd been, not *seeing* Frances, not realizing that a dowdy little mouse was a most unlikely product of Alexander Kilbracken. *And she's a delight in bed*. He felt himself harden, just at the thought of her, and grunted at himself in disgust. He clenched his hands when his senses reminded him of her softness, the budding of her passion beneath his fingers.

"She is driving me mad," he said aloud to his horse. "I shall return to London. Very soon. Let my father amuse her. Let him deal with her sharp tongue and her managing ways."

And Desborough . . . what will you do about Desborough?

He dusted his hands on his pants, closed her and Desborough resolutely from his mind, and remounted Ebony.

"Where is his lordship, Belvis?" Frances asked, coming into the head trainer's office. She loved this small room with its smell of linseed and aged leather.

"I believe, Lady Frances, that he mentioned going to York on some matter," said Belvis. She said nothing more and Belvis added after a moment, "We have two more mares arriving this afternoon. Lord Burghley has requested Ebony to sire, and as his lordship is aware of this, I assume he won't be gone long."

Frances forced a bright smile to her lips and said, "I suppose that I have a good deal of work to do. Since we will be traveling to Newmarket in August, I must find the papers on Flying Davie and Clancy's Pride."

"Tamerlane will probably also be an excellent contender," Belvis said. "I believe his former lordship kept such things in the estate room. Mr. Carruthers should know."

Frances stopped at the eastern paddock and watched Tully take Flying Davie through his paces. The thoroughbred had beautiful strong shoulders, long legs, a deep, powerful chest. And he and the will to win. He was sleek now, even in a canter, his desire to break free apparent in the tossing of his head, his impatient snorts. She loved to stroke the vivid white star in the center of his forehead. His coloring was unique and she imagined that Davie knew it. He was a winner, and magnificent, and he was ready for the racing world to admire him. "You will get your chance," she said softly toward him.

Tully looked up and waved at her. She raised her hand, then turned and walked back to the house.

She spent the afternoon searching through boxed papers for the racers' pedigrees. She was dusty and tired by the time she had found them. Hawk hadn't yet returned and it was near to dinnertime, but she returned to the stables to show Belvis what she had found.

"You are reverted to your mouse facade, my dear Frances?" the marquess asked, observing his daughter-in-law's quiet, thoughtful face. He rather missed the ferocious badinage between his son and her. Marcus, as was his current wont, was dining again with the Melchers at the vicarage.

She smiled at that, and shook her head. "No, 'tis just that I have much on my mind. Would you care for some more braised ham, my lord?"

"No, I've quite stuffed myself on the calf's liver,"

said the marquess. "I wonder what the devil Hawk is doing in York. Gambling away his fortune, do you think?"

"Don't be silly," said Frances sharply, then flushed at her rudeness. "I apologize, sir. But you know as well as I that Hawk would never be so foolish. He . . ."

"He what, my dear?"

"He is a lot of things, but he isn't a wastrel."

"You know my son so well, Frances?"

She stared a moment at her brussels sprouts. Nasty things, she thought vaguely, resolving to speak to Cook. "No, sir," she said, "I don't know him well at all. I fancy that he will leave soon now, back to London I suspect."

"And the stud and racing stables?"

"I don't know. He doesn't confide in me."

"I know, he merely yells at you, and baits you until you want to pound his head."

She smiled but her face felt stiff. *Oh yes, that is true enough, my girl, but he also makes you wild, makes you forget yourself, makes you want to consume him.*

"Why do you believe he will leave soon, Frances?"

"He . . . he doesn't like me."

"I should say rather that he escaped today because he doesn't know his own mind. Men are rather easily confused creatures, Frances."

"Did you yell at your wife, my lord?"

"Rarely. She was much too restrained to do anything that might appear ill-bred. She was a duke's daughter, you know, and very aware of her own worth."

"I never wanted to marry," Frances said. "My experience with men was primarily with my father. I love him dearly, do not mistake me, 'tis just that he and he alone rules Kilbracken, and poor Sophia is forced to the most subtle underhanded measures to gain her way."

"I imagine that many women are in that position."

"Life is very short, sir, for such silly subterfuge."

"Is your stepmother unhappy, my dear?"

"No, certainly not. She and my father deal well together, actually. Indeed, I believe his rages are a source of pride to her, in an odd sort of way." She grinned at him suddenly. "Actually, Sophia is most successful in managing my father. He blusters and rants and carries on, and she just says, 'yes, dear, of course, dear,' 'it shall be just as you wish,' and does as she pleases."

"She sounds an intelligent woman."

"Yes, she is, unlike me."

"Ah," said the marquess. He saw Otis glide into the dining room, and said quickly, "Shall we adjourn to the drawing room, my dear? You seem quite off your feed this evening."

Frances smiled. "I am not a horse, sir."

"No," he agreed, returning her smile, "not even a filly."

The marquess strolled to the fireplace and leaned his shoulder against the mantelpiece. "So, Frances, you believe yourself unintelligent?"

"You have an exceedingly tenacious mind, sir! You listen too carefully. You don't forget a thing, you are just like your wretched son!"

"I understand that you enjoyed a mite too much to drink the other night, Frances."

Her eyes flew to his face and her cheeks flushed with color.

"My son is always on to take advantage of such a delightful occurrence, I imagine. Did he engineer, it, I wonder?"

"He . . . I hope he leaves soon, very soon!"

He was laughing at her, just like Hawk did, a knowing gleam in his green eyes.

"I am not used to spirits!"

"What troubles you this evening, my dear?" he asked, changing the topic so abruptly that Frances blinked at him.

She paused a moment, her fingers fretting with the fringe on her cashmere shawl. There was much on her mind but she wished to see Hawk first.

There were other things as well gnawing at her, and she carefully selected one of them. "I miss my family," she said.

"Your father and his rages?"

"Yes. I dealt with him well, but not like Sophia. I yelled back at him. He was a marvelous father to me."

"Ah, excellent training, it would appear."

"Hardly," Frances said in a very dry voice. Suddenly she grew very still at the sound of footsteps in the entrance hall. Hawk!

"Good evening, my boy," the marquess said as his son entered the room. He was still in riding clothes and his Hessians were dusty. He looked weary.

"Sir," Hawk said. He sent a flickering look toward Frances. "Forgive my dirt," he continued.

"Should you care for something to eat?" Frances asked him, her voice carefully neutral.

He shook his head. "I will bid you good night," he said, nodded again toward Frances, and left the room.

Frances felt sparks of anger surge through her. The miserable wretch! Had he visited a woman in York? She rose jerkily to her feet, forced a smile to her lips, and said to her father-in-law, "I am tired also, my lord. Tomorrow I shall be more myself."

The marquess watched her leave the room with her

shoulders squared, her chin high. Things were progressing quite nicely, he decided, and rang for some brandy. He decided that he wouldn't wish to be in his son's boots at this moment.

Frances soaked in a long, steamy bath, and sat quietly while Agnes brushed her hair its requisite hundred strokes. Then she dismissed her maid and climbed into her bed. Surely he would come to her tonight. An hour passed. *I should be pleased that he is leaving me alone. But what if something is wrong? What if something happened and he didn't wish to speak in front of his father? And I have much to tell him.*

She fretted, argued with herself, and finally, upon hearing the corridor clock chime midnight, eased out of bed, donned her dressing gown, and walked to the adjoining door. She raised her hand to knock, then lowered it. Perhaps he was asleep. Quietly she opened the door and slipped in. There was a sluggish fire in the fireplace and it provided the only light. Her eyes went to his bed, but he wasn't there. She frowned a moment, and moved toward the fireplace and the tall-backed chair that stood in front of it.

Her breath caught in her throat when she saw him. He was seated in the chair, completely naked, his chin balanced on his hand, his gaze fastened on the spiraling flames. She saw him clearly as he emerged from Lock Lomond, as naked as he was now. But now there were the shadows playing over his magnificent body, bronzing his flesh, and she wanted to touch him. She wondered briefly if he had lost weight. He appeared more lean to her studious eyes. She heard him sigh deeply and stretch his long legs in front of him. Her eyes fell from his chest to his belly, and further, to the bush of black hair at his groin. His manhood lay flaccid and she marveled that a man's body could change with such rapidity.

Frances felt a spurt of desire. She knew it for what it was now, for he had taught her. She reached out her hand, not meaning to, and it was at that moment that Hawk became aware of her presence.

He didn't move, merely said, "Hello, Frances."

He wasn't at all perturbed about his naked state. She swallowed a bit and replied, "Hello."

"What do you want?"

"I wanted to speak to you. I expected you to visit me, but you didn't."

"No," he said, sounding faintly abstracted, "no, I didn't."

He wouldn't look at her, dammit! Why the devil had she come in here? Why couldn't she leave well enough alone?

"What did you wish to speak to me about?" he asked maintaining his calm facade.

Frances moved toward the fireplace and gracefully sank down to her knees, her dressing gown flaring about her. His fingers itched to touch her, to caress her ... damn, he wanted to taste her ...

"Yes?" he said, and she heard the strange abstraction in his deep voice.

She drew a deep breath, but didn't look at him. "I found the horses' papers today. Belvis had told me we would need them for the racing at Newmarket."

"So," he said, sarcastic now, "you have decided that we will race now. You forget yourself, wife. I have not yet decided whether or not I will sell everything off."

"Please," she said, holding a tight rein on her temper, "please just listen for a moment. There is something most peculiar."

She had his attention now, and she met his gaze. "I took the papers to Belvis. He looked at them, then told me that there was a mistake. He read aloud the sire and dam for Flying Davie, and rubbed his jaw in that way of his. You remember of course that Belvis knows every racer from nearly the beginning of time."

"The point, Frances?"

"Flying Davie's dam is listed on his paper as being Pandora from the Belson stable. Belvis said that Pandora had had to be put down over a year before she was supposed to have foaled Flying Davie."

That got his attention. *"What?"*

"I said that Flying Davie's dam—"

He waved her to silence. " 'Tis naught but a simple entry mistake, that's all."

"Belvis also told me that when Flying Davie was delivered to Desborough Hall, he fully expected to see his papers so he could evaluate his sire and dam, for bloodline strengths and weaknesses. Nevil never showed him the papers, indeed, never showed him papers on several other foals as well."

"Odd," said Hawk, "most odd. Is it so important, I wonder."

"Belvis is quite perturbed about it." Frances suddenly realized that here they were speaking quite seriously, but her husband was naked. Most odd indeed, she thought, and turned to look at the orange embers.

"I shall discuss the matter with Belvis," Hawk said finally. He rose and stretched, and despite her best intentions, her eyes were on his body, following his every movement. "I am going to bed now," he said. His eyes suddenly rested upon her moist lips. "Would you like to join me, Frances?"

She froze at his drawling, quite confident tone. "Surely you are too tired, my lord!"

"Hardly," he said. "Even if I were, of course, I wish to breed an heir on you, and I must do my duty."

She felt a shaft of hurt so strong that she couldn't speak for a moment. "And once your duty is done, you will leave again?"

He arched a brow at her. "I wasn't aware that you particularly desired my presence here." Even as he uttered his bored, baiting words, he felt himself harden, and since he was naked, there was no way he could hide his interest from her. Damn her, why did she have to look so beautiful and alluring? "Didn't you come in here to seduce me, Frances?"

Frances lurched to her feet. "No! I . . . well, I wanted to talk to you, and now that I have, I will—"

"Too late, my dear," he said, and pulled her against him. "The little bird should have flown while she had the chance. Much too late now."

He began kissing her, holding her face between his palms. "For a time, at least," he said between kisses, "I shall not be burdened with your shrew's managing tongue."

"I am not a—"

His tongue glided gently into her mouth. She tasted him, and thought dizzily that he was more delicious than Cook's famous rolled jam pudding. She didn't realize until it was far too late that her arms were clutching about his back, that she had risen on her tiptoes to better fit herself against him. She felt his hands on her shoulders, loosening her dressing gown. When it fell, a pool of velvet at her feet, she didn't protest. His fingers slipped beneath the narrow straps of her nightgown, and the soft silk slithered down her body, joining the dressing gown. She felt him hard and urgent against her belly.

"Yes," she said, her words hoarse and deep in her throat, "I came in here to seduce you. You left me last night."

His hands cupped her buttocks and lifted her.

"Yes," he said, "yes, I did leave you. But I won't tonight, Frances." She thought she heard him curse softly, but the words blurred in her mind.

He lifted her completely off the floor. "Bring your legs around my waist. That's it. Now, relax, and let me . . ." He broke off, for he realized that his voice was trembling with need for her.

She obeyed him, not understanding—but only for a moment. She felt his fingers searching, probing, and in the next moment he was sliding slowly into her. She gasped, arching against his arms.

He grinned at her stunned expression and brought her hard down on him. Her eyes widened and glazed.

"Hawk," she whispered helplessly, her fingers gripping his shoulders.

"Yes, my dear? Do you like this?" His hands were caressing her buttocks, molding her tightly against him.

"I . . . don't . . . know."

"You will, but I must . . ." Suddenly his voice caught in his throat and he felt a roaring in his head, a tremendous tightening in his loins. He cursed viciously, then moaned, "Frances, don't move!"

She held herself against him, burying her face against his shoulder.

"I can't give you pleasure like this." He was panting, his heart pounding, as if he'd run from York back to Desborough Hall.

"Don't move!"

He walked quickly to the bed, saying tersely, "Hold on to me."

She wrapped her arms about his neck as he pulled back the counterpane and the blankets.

"Now," he said, expelling a deep breath. "Now."

He eased her down upon her back, at the edge of the bed, never parting from her. "You wanted to be seduced, Frances, and now you will get your wish."

There was something wrong with all this, Frances thought vaguely. He sounded almost angry with her, almost . . . She gasped when he suddenly pulled out of her and buried his head against her belly.

"Hawk!"

"Shut up," he said, and found her. "You wanted this, wife, and I shan't disappoint you."

But her small cries, her shuddering, drove him mad. And when she wove her fingers in his hair, and her body arched upward, he thought he would die with the pleasure of it. She moaned loudly, and that pleased him immensely. He felt her climax, reveled in it, but didn't come into her just yet. No, he thought, he wanted her to give herself and him more pleasure.

Frances felt dazed, felt limp as a dusting cloth. Then she felt the beginnings of that same frenzy and gasped, astonished at her response.

"Just feel," she heard him say, feeling his fingers on her and in her, and his mouth.

He brought her again to shuddering pleasure, and while she quivered with the final small convulsive shocks, he came into her, deeply, fully, and she pulled him down to her.

He closed his eyes, his teeth gritted, and was quickly beside himself. Her pleasure was a potent aphrodisiac, more potent that he could have imagined. He was nearly rough in his urgency, but she kept moving with him, stroking him, and his last thought was: *Damnation, I am well and truly lost.*

"I cannot move," Frances whispered.

"Nor can I," Hawk said, "but I must, or end up on the floor."

Frances was dazed and sated, and fatigue washed over her like a gentle wave. "Don't leave me, Hawk," she said, only vaguely aware that he was pulling her against him and molding the covers about them.

"Damn you, Frances," he said. He pulled her closer and felt her softness, felt her languid body flow against him, felt her trust.

Ah, Amalie, you have made me a fool with your damned bloody advice, he thought, kissed his wife's forehead, and felt himself fall into a deep, sated stupor.

❧ 24 ❧

*Quarrels would not last long if the fault
were only on one side.*
—LA ROCHEFOUCAULD

The marquess stared first at his glowering son, then at
his equally glowering daughter-in-law. There was so
much tension in the air he felt he could probably taste
it on his toast.

"Well," he said brightly, "it is a lovely day today."

Hawk grunted.

Frances speared a bite of egg. She was so furious,
she wanted to kill and maim—*him!* She had, she re-
called quite clearly, awakened some two hours before,
a silly, very female smile on her face, only to realize
that she was in her own bed, in her own nightgown, and
she was alone. Oh, curse him. She had felt gentled,
and soft.

Never again.

And he obviously had felt nothing, absolutely nothing, else why would he have carried her back to her
bed? And put her into her nightgown ... and looked
at her, and she hadn't known it. She'd probably been
dreaming silly women's dreams, fool that she was.

"When are you leaving?" she asked her husband in
so cold a voice that it could have iced the tea.

Hawk took another bite of toast.

"Leave!" the marquess demanded, looking startled.
"What the devil are you talking about, Frances?"

She said, seeing that Hawk was concentrating on the crock of creamy butter beside his plate, "Why shouldn't he return to London? After all, my lord, he cares not a farthing for Desborough Hall or the stud or our racers or ... or for anything!"

"Father," Hawk said, gently setting down his slice of toast, "I have sent a draft to your secretary, Conyon, for five thousand pounds. I trust that in the future you won't waste more of your money or mine."

It was too much. Frances eased back her chair and tossed her white napkin onto her still-filled plate. "A man's power," she said in rattling tones of sarcasm, "you don't care for anything save your own pleasure—"

"I shouldn't say that is precisely true," Hawk said mildly, and gave her a mocking, intimate look that made her flush, not with embarrassment, but with anger.

"You don't care! Sell the bloody stock! Go back to London! I'm sure I don't care either!"

"I believe first I shall check into this mystery with Belvis," he continued in that same mild tone.

"What mystery?" the marquess demanded.

"It would appear that Flying Davie's dam died before she could have possibly foaled him," said Hawk. "I think I shall have a look at the bill of sale." He shook his head. "So many responsibilities, so many duties, so many demands on my time and ... energy."

"You don't deserve to die in your bed, my lord! You deserve to be flogged—"

"By you, my dear wife?"

"I should flay you with inexhaustible enthusiasm."

"I do wish you two would cease your bickering for just a moment," the marquess said. "Ah, Rosie, more tea if you please."

Not another word was spoken until Rosie, her ears at attention, was forced with a very lagging step from the breakfast room.

"There has to be a simple explanation for this," the marquess continued. "What does Belvis say?"

"He doesn't understand it," Frances said, calming her ruffled feathers. "He is disturbed."

"It will doubtless all be explained when I see the bill of sale," Hawk said, dismissing the matter.

Several hours later, he realized that an explanation was not in the offing. No bill of sale could be found. He and Marcus searched every conceivable place. There were no bills of sale for Tamerlane or for Clancy's Pride either. Odd, Hawk thought, but shrugged it off. He had no idea what Nevil could have done with the papers, but doubtless they had to be somewhere.

He strolled out to the paddocks to observe Frances astride Flying Davie, taking him through a very controlled series of maneuvers. She was an excellent horsewoman, no doubt about that. And she'd been right about her natural ability with horses. Flying Davie followed her each instruction most willingly. She also enjoyed her riding habit, if that is what it could be called. She was wearing a brown wool skirt that was divided allowing the freedom of breeches.

When next he saw her, she was quite dirty, smelled of sweat and horses, and her hair hung in damp tendrils about her face. He wondered if she'd taken a toss and felt a brief spurt of alarm. But no, she came dashing into the drawing room waving a dirty envelope in one hand, a single sheet of paper in the other.

"From my father and Sophia," she announced, her eyes sparkling with enthusiasm. She had forgotten for the moment that she wished neither to see nor to speak to her wretched husband.

"Yes?" he drawled with great disinterest.

"They are all well, and Sophia asks to send my sisters here. Of course they will need new wardrobes and Sophia asks that I supply them. Perhaps within the month—"

Hawk stared at her, then roared, "I had to marry you, Frances, you have to be here of necessity, but I'll be damned in hell before I have your sisters underfoot, nipping at my heels! Nor have I any intention, madam, of allowing you to waste more of my money! Tell your bloody father that he can supply the blunt!"

Frances gaped at him, silent for an instant.

"And if Sophia thinks that I shall have the three of you in London with me, parading you all about to balls and such, she can just think again!"

She felt herself swelling with fury. "You bastard!" she yelled at him, unaware and uncaring in any case that Otis and Mrs. Jerkins were frozen in the hall outside the open door.

"You mean, petty, self-righteous prig! You are ridiculous and utterly horrible and I hate you!"

He watched her actually stomp her foot in rage, whirl about, and leave him alone. Only the horse scent remained.

I shall leave for London very shortly, he told himself. At last he had managed to make her despise him.

Frances fumed and paced in the estate room, cursing him in the most colorful language she could remember from her father's verbal rages.

"Ho, what's this?" asked the marquess. The whole point of loyalty, he knew, was to have a butler inform one of everything of interest that occurred. Otis, that pillar of loyalty, had filled his ears.

"Your damned son!" Frances yelled, turning on him.

"Yes?" he asked in an encouraging voice.

"He refuses to spend any of his precious money on my sisters! He even refuses to let them come here or to London or anything! I hope his toes rot off, I hope he smashes his hard head on the . . ." She ground to a halt, unable to find a suitable obstruction for his head.

"I should be delighted to provide money for your

sisters, Frances. And if it would please you, I have a somewhat improvident far-removed cousin who would be delighted to sponsor them. So you see, my dear, there is no reason for you to be so . . . concerned."

That drew her up. To her father-in-law's chagrin, Frances burst into tears.

"My dear!"

She turned her back to him, not wanting him to see her horrible loss of control. Finally she managed to get a hold on herself.

"Also," the marquess continued after a moment, "Hawksbury House in London belongs to me. Hawk merely avails himself of it when he is there. He has no say who may stay there, Frances."

"You are very kind, sir," she said, still sniffing a bit. Then she drew herself up, and her gray eyes, now nearly black, gleamed with purpose. "It is not your responsibility. It is *his,* and I shall force him to meet his obligations!"

"How?" the marquess asked.

"I . . . well, I'm not certain just yet. Perhaps I shall blackmail him when I find out his mistress's name in London."

"I shouldn't go quite that far," the marquess said quickly. "Really, my dear, I am a very rich man. There is no reason at all for you not to allow me—"

"No, sir," she said quite firmly. "No. I thank you, but it is not right and I could not accept your generosity. You have done too much for me as it is."

"Very well then," the marquess said, already determined upon his next move in any case. He patted his daughter-in-law's flushed cheek and took himself off.

He found his son butchering the billiard balls in the gentlemen's smoking room. He watched him strike a ball with such force it should have punched a hole in the black felt.

"Hello," the marquess said. "I should say, my boy, that your technique is lacking, just a bit."

Hawk shot him a narrow-eyed look.

"My boy," the marquess continued, his very gentle voice bringing his son to instant attention. "You will willingly provide funds for your wife's sisters. You will also apologize to Frances for your execrable behavior toward her."

Hawk very carefully laid the cue onto the billiard table. He said nothing.

"You know, dear boy, it seems to me that Frances, in all innocence, provided you with the perfect opportunity to dash her into the woodwork. I do wonder why you felt compelled to do it."

"So she went running to you, did she?"

"Actually, no. Otis, my boy, Otis."

Hawk muttered something about traitorous servants, and the marquess merely smiled.

"When I did track down your wife, she refused to allow me to assist her."

"She would," Hawk sighed.

"She is quite proud, you know."

"She is an accursed female!"

"Why, my dear boy? Why did you hurt her so?"

Curse the old man for his perception, Hawk thought. He heard himself say in a calm-enough voice, "I am leaving Desborough Hall soon and I don't want three females following me to London."

"I suggest that you take care what you're about, Hawk."

"Oh hell," Hawk said, smashing his fist onto a small tabletop that promptly collapsed. He stared blankly at the wreckage. "I will apologize to her. I will give her all the blunt she requires for her twit sisters, but I won't escort them all about London! If she wishes, she can cart them about York and even Harrowgate. Plenty of assemblies and nonsense there."

"May I suggest that you apologize to her quickly? She was muttering about blackmailing you."

"Blackmailing me! Why, that is ridiculous!"

"Your mistress, Hawk."

"She is a shrew."

"Your mistress, dear boy?"

"No, Frances," Hawk snapped.

"She is a handful, certainly, but a shrew, my boy? Surely you exaggerate, perhaps to protect yourself?"

Hawk cursed floridly and stomped out of the room.

The marquess slowly picked up the billiard cue and began a quite splendid, expert game.

Hawk forgot about returning to London, at least for the moment. That night Flying Davie became suddenly ill, and Frances, pale and drawn with worry, was in his stall until dawn. Hawk couldn't ignore the situation; he wasn't a complete bounder. He watched her care for the thoroughbred, saw that the horse trusted her, was quite calm when she touched him and ministered to him.

"The fellow will make it," Belvis said to him, stretching his back. "Lady Frances has such a way with her. I never would have believed that a woman . . . Well, that puts an end to my nonsensical notions. I wish I could understand why he got so ill. Lady Frances says it is something he ate, but his feeding is carefully supervised. Doesn't make sense, no it doesn't." Belvis shook his weary head, and added with a faint smile, "You are most lucky, my lord."

What to say to that? Hawk wondered, bone-weary himself.

Frances refused to leave Flying Davie until she was ready to fall asleep beside him in the stall.

"Come, Frances," Hawk said, took her arm, and pulled her to her feet. "Flying Davie is now in better shape than you. It's time you took yourself to bed."

Frances felt light-headed with fatigue, but also proud of herself. "He will live," she said with great satisfaction, and gave her husband a blinding smile.

There were smudges under her eyes, her hair was a ratty mess, her gown was wrinkled and filthy, and he felt something powerful move deep within him.

"You will eat your breakfast," he said in a stiff voice, "then you will go to bed. It's nearly nine o'clock in the morning."

"I am not hungry, just so tired."

He shortened his step to match hers. She weaved a bit as they walked toward the house, and he gently clasped her arm. He said abruptly, "I apologize for cutting up at you. I shall certainly be delighted for your sisters to visit you here. I shall pay for new gowns and the like for them." There, he'd said it. He waited hopefully to see that brilliant smile of hers again, but to his chagrin, she stiffened. "I think not, my lord," she said in a very even voice. "I intend to pay for their new gowns myself. Of course, I do thank you for allowing the two little waifs to stay in *your* house."

"You have no money, Frances, at least not enough to provide more than one outfit for each of them."

She waved her hand at him. "My ring is valuable," she said. "I intend to sell it. I shall go to York this afternoon."

It was a long time since dawn, but Hawk saw red.

"You will do no such thing!"

"Isn't the ring mine?"

"It is a family heirloom, it was worth far beyond the money it would bring. I forbid you to sell it, Frances!"

She came to a stop, pulled away from him, and said in a very clipped voice, "You may go to the devil, my lord. I assume the devil is in London. It appears a fine day for traveling. Why don't you take yourself off?"

"The only reason I don't shake you until your teeth

rattle is that you are too weary. Don't push me, Frances."

"Ah, your sense of fair play, my lord? Don't strike your opponent until he or she is able to fight back?"

" 'Hawk,' damn you! Fair play has nothing to do with anything. You will not sell the ring and that's an end to it."

She gave him a long look and tightly pursed her lips.

"Frances," he began, knowing her well enough now to recognize the signs of heels digging in.

She ignored him, walking more quickly. She came to an abrupt halt when two dusty carriages bowled up the drive to come to a halt in front of the house.

"Who the hell—" Hawk said.

Frances watched a nattily dressed gentleman climb out of the lead carriage, turn, and offer his hand to a lady.

"My God," Hawk said, "it is Edmund, Lord Chalmers, and my sister, Beatrice!"

He strode forward, his hand outstretched. "Good Lord, man, 'tis still an early hour. However did you manage to get Bea—"

He didn't finish, for his sister said in a very imperious voice, "Hello, Phillip. Everything looks the same, I see. Edmund and I have come to visit you. Oh dear, my father is here? And *who* is that, brother?"

Hawk turned to see her finger pointing at Frances, who stood like a filthy servant girl some feet away.

He drew a deep breath and said, "Frances, come here, my dear. She is my wife," he added.

"She sleeps in the stables? How very odd, to be sure, but given her looks, I am really not surprised. However—"

"She was caring for a sick horse," Hawk said briefly, cutting off his sister.

"How very odd," Beatrice repeated.

"You don't look terribly fit yourself, old boy," Edmund said. "The horse will survive?"

"He will. Frances has a talent for healing animals." He turned to see Frances at his side.

He performed the introductions, and Frances, smiling slightly, said, "I shan't allow either of you to come closer, I fear I am something of a disgrace at the moment."

"Nothing that a bath and rest won't cure," said Edmund kindly.

The marquess had reached them, and Frances was a bit taken aback to see Beatrice give her father a very cool kiss on the cheek.

Beatrice, Frances saw, was more beautiful than her portrait. She looked positively regal in her traveling gown of rich burgundy velvet, but her expression wasn't particularly warm. Edmund, on the other hand, appeared a most polished gentleman, and quite kind. His eyes sparkled with good humor and he greeted the marquess with charming deference.

"Shall we all adjourn to the breakfast room?" Hawk asked. "I was on the point of forcing Frances to eat a bit before she takes to her bed."

"I should like some tea," Beatrice announced, "after, of course, I freshen myself a bit. Gertrude, have a care with my jewel case!"

Frances looked from the older maid to Otis, who stood observing them all from the steps. "Otis," she called to him. "You will see to Gertrude and Lord Chalmers' valet, if you please."

"Certainly, my lady," Otis said.

"Officious sod," Beatrice said, her brows lowering a bit.

"Otis?" Frances asked in some astonishment.

Beatrice allowed another glance at her new sister-in-law, and couldn't suppress a shudder at her disgusting appearance. "Otis always was kind to strays," she said obliquely, took her fiancé's arm, and marched up the front steps into the house.

"That is my sister," Hawk said to Frances. "Ignore her. I've always believed she would mellow with age. Perhaps I was wrong."

"Edmund will keep her in line," the marquess said.

I certainly wouldn't want to try, Frances thought. She took herself to her room immediately and ordered a hot bath. It felt good to have Agnes twittering about her, clucking as if she were but a chick. She fell asleep in her bathtub.

"Frances."

She felt a hand shaking her shoulder and opened vague eyes. It wasn't Agnes' hand on her, it was her husband's. "You," she said, and tried to slither away.

"Certainly," Hawk said. "You will become as wrinkled as a discarded cravat." He held out a thick towel for her. Frances saw Agnes from the corner of her eye looking at once scandalized and excited. She rose from the tub and felt her husband enclose her in the towel. He picked up another one and began drying her hair.

"What of your sister and Lord Chalmers?" she asked, her voice a bit thin. She was frightfully embarrassed, she couldn't help it. It was broad daylight and her maid was standing nearby.

"Beatrice is resting and Edmund is looking at the horses." He was leading her toward her dressing table. She had no choice but to seat herself. "Agnes," Hawk called, "come and comb out her hair before she falls into another stupor." He patted her cheek and took himself off.

"Surprised as a toad without a lily pad, I was," said Agnes as she combed the tangles from her mistress's long hair. "His lordship entered quiet as could be, saw you in the tub, and . . . well—"

"Yes, I know." Frances said.

"I heard Mrs. Jerkins complaining to Mr. Otis about Lady Beatrice demanding this and that, as if she were mistress here."

Frances sighed. "It was her home for many years."

"Still, Mrs. Jerkins is none too pleased," Agnes said, the bit between her teeth. "And that sour-faced maid of hers—Gertrude, of all silly names—well, she was in the kitchen driving cook distracted, demanding a tisane immediately."

"Oh dear," said Frances. "You must dry my hair quickly, Agnes, I must see Mrs. Jerkins and calm Cook down, and—"

"Oh no, my lady. His lordship told me, he did, that you were to be in your bed as soon as may be."

Frances was too tired to argue with this most recent command from her husband. But sleep eluded her for some minutes. It was Edmund who wanted to buy all the Desborough stock. Was that the reason for his visit? What would Hawk do? She sighed, snuggling down beneath the covers. Obviously he wouldn't be journeying to London just yet.

Hawk entered her room a while later and smiled down at her sleeping face. He gently lifted a thick curl and rubbed it against his cheek. "What the devil am I going to do with you?" he said very softly.

When Frances awoke late in the afternoon, it was to see Mrs. Jerkins standing beside Agnes, her bosom heaving with indignation.

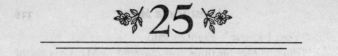

25

*I love nothing in the world so well as you:
is not that strange?*

—SHAKESPEARE

Hawk stared at his wife over a spoon filled with *soupe
à la Reine*. She looked beautiful, her glorious hair
piled atop her head with thick long curls caressing her
white shoulder. Her equally white breasts waited firm
and soft for his touch beneath the pale pink satin of
her gown.

He realized he'd given up his struggles with scarce a
whimper, surrendered unconditionally, and he continued to study her with fascinated new eyes. He'd realized it was all over for him when he'd stood beside her
tub staring down at her sleeping face. The longer he
studied her, the more he'd wanted to haul her over his
shoulder, throw her onto his bed, and love her until he
was insensate and she as well. Hell, he'd even decided
that he'd take her sisters under his wing, if necessary,
and to London.

The bachelor was a vague shadowy gentleman who
had expired, and in his place was a married man who
delighted in his state.

He hurriedly finished his soup. He was still caught
in his own startlingly new discoveries when Edmund's
voice pulled him back to the dinner table. "I say,
Hawk, you look as worried as a man who has just
wagered his fortune on the turn of a card."

Hawk smiled a bit painfully. "Not at all. Frances, my dear, cease fiddling with your bread. Have some of these delicious pork cutlets."

Frances dutifully nodded to the footman, James, to serve her a cutlet.

"Your cook sets an adequate table," Beatrice remarked to her brother.

You expected perhaps raw turnips and cold potatoes? Frances wanted to ask her sister-in-law. She said nothing, of course, and scarce attended the conversation about her. She still felt a shudder when she remembered Mrs. Jerkins' appalling upset.

"*She* questioned me as to the *cleanliness* of the sheets!"

Frances thought that Mrs. Jerkins' bosom would heave out of her black bombazine gown.

"And that *maid* of hers, that insufferable *Gertrude,* had the effrontery to claim that there was *dust* on the dressing table!"

Agnes didn't help matters. She gasped in outrage, stoking Mrs. Jerkins' already blazing fire.

"Giving orders to *our* staff as if she were mistress here! Carrying on that her *portrait* was in awful condition and needed cleaning. Restoration is more like it . . . and to her, not the painting!"

"I expect," Frances said calmly, after she finally managed to break into Mrs. Jerkins' diatribe, "that Lady Beatrice will leave soon enough. I don't believe that she cares much for the country. We will survive it, Mrs. Jerkins, and I"—she drew a deep breath "and I shall speak to her."

Mrs. Jerkins gave her a look that spoke volumes— Lady Beatrice would likely chew her up and spit her out with the leftovers.

"I should dress for dinner now," Frances had said, wishing she were back in Scotland, enjoying one of her father's fine rages.

Oh dear, Frances thought now, wondering if the inhabitants of the nether regions of Desborough Hall were arming themselves for insurrection. She heard Beatrice demand another serving of sweetbreads in ringing tones, and winced. She smiled toward James, and nodded. He looked impassive, but Frances suspected his ears were a bit red. She appreciated their loyalty, their protectiveness, and imagined that even if Lady Beatrice were of a saintly disposition, they would still refer every request to her.

"I say, Frances," Beatrice said after enjoying several bites of the sweetbreads, "I imagine you must feel dreadfully uncomfortable here—English gentlemen and ladies must be so vastly different from what you are used to in Scotland."

"Not at all," Frances said mildly.

"Not that there is much elevated company here in the wilds of Yorkshire, but still—"

"Lord and Lady Bourchier are most charming," said Frances..

"And most elevated," said Hawk.

"Ah, poor Alicia," Beatrice said, giving her brother a drawing look before continuing. "She had so hoped to ensnare Philip, you know, but he would have none of her. She is, of course, only a baronet's daughter."

"The Melchers are quite good-hearted."

"A vicar and his wife," Beatrice said, and shuddered delicately.

"You have become a snob, daughter," the marquess said.

"One must simply maintain one's standards, Father. It is such a pity that poor Philip had to travel to Scotland, for his—"

"I believe," Edmund Lacy interrupted his betrothed's overflowing spate of bad manners, "that you have sufficiently abused the topic, my dear."

And the servants will repeat what you have said to Mrs. Jerkins, Frances thought, *and then I shall have a rebellion on my hands.* She pictured Otis firing a cannon toward her sister-in-law, and grinned to herself.

"Well, I only wished to know why my poor brother felt it—"

"Bea, have some macaroni," Hawk said firmly. "Perhaps also some artichoke *bottoms.*"

Frances nearly choked on her wine. She sent her husband a warning look, and he smiled at her, an intimate, very mischievous smile that made her feel suddenly quite overheated. She blinked, wondering what the devil was wrong with her. And for that matter, what was he up to now?

The marquess said, "Belvis tells me that you saved Flying Davie's life, Frances. He is quite upset that the horse sickened from something he ate."

"He must have escaped the eye of his trainer and gotten a weed of some sort," said Edmund.

"Mushrooms," said Beatrice.

"Well, I fancy Belvis will watch him like a hawk now," Frances said.

"Two birds at Desborough?" Hawk asked.

"You and that ridiculous nickname of yours," Beatrice said with faint distaste, arching a perfect brow.

"Frances quite likes it," Hawk said blandly.

"How very odd of you," Beatrice said, staring at her sister-in-law as if she were a newly imported queer thing from an exotic land.

Enough, thought Frances. She smiled at her guests, nodded to James, and let him assist her to rise. "Beatrice, shall we leave the gentlemen to their port and conversation?"

"I didn't expect a sister-in-law," Beatrice said, once they were comfortably seated in the drawing room.

"I didn't either," said Frances.

"Philip has always been so very free, so opposed to matrimony."

"He still is—free, that is."

Beatrice started at that, but quickly forged onward. "I was most surprised to read of my brother's marriage to an unknown ... person from Scotland. I told Edmund that my father was behind it. The meddling old fool!"

So, Frances thought, even Beatrice knew nothing of the infamous oath. She wondered why Hawk hadn't told his sister the circumstances when he was in London. "Actually," Frances said, "I saw your brother bathing in Loch Lomond and quite decided that I wanted him."

"You saw him *naked*?"

"He wasn't bathing in his cravat."

Beatrice harrumphed.

Frances studied her sister-in-law for a long moment. "I should appreciate it, Beatrice, if you would refrain from directing the servants."

"I would say that someone needs to give them orders! Why, the dust, the filth ... !"

"Beatrice, you are my guest and my sister-in-law, but you are not the mistress of Desborough Hall."

"So," Beatrice said, her eyes glittering, "that is why my poor benighted brother married you."

Frances stared at her, at sea. "I beg your pardon?"

"You saw him unclothed and seduced him and got yourself with child."

Frances laughed, she couldn't help herself. "I never realized before that a female could get *herself* with child."

"My brother is a gentleman, of course, and you know quite well what I mean! Your levity is not at all becoming, Frances."

Frances wiped her eyes and said in a very thick

Scottish brogue, "I think I shall play the pianoforte.
Be ye fond of a particular tune?"

She didn't await an answer, but walked to the pianoforte and seated herself. She played until her arms
began to ache. She looked only once to see Beatrice
yawning. She launched into a Mozart sonata. When
she finally paused, she was startled to hear enthusiastic applause.

She turned on the stool and smiled. "Had I known
you had come in, gentlemen, I would have spared
your ears."

"Not at all, Lady Frances," said Edmund. "You
play most delightfully."

"She does many things most delightfully," said Hawk.

"Rather a surprise," said Beatrice. "Your technique
is most reasonable, for someone raised in Scotland."

Hawk wondered if he could muzzle his sister. She
was quite on her high horse, her lance targeted at
Frances. He no longer had to wonder about the purpose of this visit. Edmund hadn't said much, but Hawk
knew that he was here to encourage the sale of the
Desborough stock. It was just a matter of time before
he came right out with it. But not, Hawk realized,
when the marquess was present. Edmund wasn't at all
stupid; he would realize that the marquess would stick
his oar in.

He heard his father suggest that the young folk play
four-handed piquet.

"Well, Frances?" Hawk asked, sending her that new
intimate smile of his that made sweat break out on her
neck. "Shall we take on these two? They are both
quite proficient, I warn you."

"I should like very much to play," said Frances.

When the marquess kissed her cheek, he whispered,
"You are doing splendidly, my dear. I am quite proud
of you. Go for Bea's broadside, she is well-endowed in
that area."

With that very unfatherly observation, the marquess took himself to his bedchamber.

Serious players indeed, Frances thought some minutes later as she sorted her hand. She felt as if she were in a life-and-death match. Her husband was a demanding partner, but she didn't mind, for she had the suddenly overwhelming urge to win. She concentrated with all her faculties. She played with speed and finesse and when Edmund finally tossed down his last card, he exclaimed, "My dear Bea, I believe we have met our match! You two are killers. Pity you can't take Frances to White's, Hawk."

"And have her destroy all the collective manly pride? I thank you, no, Edmund. I shall keep her and all her talents right here, with me."

She frowned at him, wondering what was in his mind, what his motives were. Did he mean with those somewhat double-edged words that he wasn't returning to London?

Tea had come and gone long ago. It was time for bed, but Frances wasn't at all tired. She felt terribly excited, filled with anticipation. She looked to see her husband studying her intently, and she flushed, wishing she could kiss him and throw her cards in his smug face.

He grinned, a very masculine, satisfied grin, and she decided she would prefer to stuff the playing cards down his throat.

Hawk rose and stretched, yawning elaborately.

"Frances, my dear, are you ready too for your bed?"

"I believe so," she managed to say with just a slight tremor to her voice.

She wanted him to come to her—she wasn't about to deny it to herself. She waited patiently for the sound of his footsteps at the adjoining door. He entered some moments later, eyed her from across the room, and smiled.

"Hello," he said, stuffing his hands into the deep pockets of his dressing gown.

Time to beard the lion in his den, Frances thought. "Hawk," she said, "what are you doing?"

"Preparing to love my wife until she wraps herself around me and yells and becomes hot and—"

"I mean, what are you up to? You are not behaving as you should."

"That worries you, my dear?"

"You are so slippery," she said, frowning at him. "I wish you would stay exactly where you are until I understand."

"May I sit down at least?"

"I suppose so," she said grudgingly. She hadn't intended that he sit on her bed, but he did, of course. He sprawled on his back, his head resting on her thighs.

"Now, what worries you, Frances? You are handling Beatrice quite well. Otis has regained some of his color and informed me that Mrs. Jerkins won't poison my sister's tea."

"Your sister doesn't like me," Frances said, sidetracked for a moment.

"No, but she will come about. She cares about me, at least I think she does a bit, and when she observes that I can't keep my hands away from you, she will—"

"Enough of that! You are utterly impossible and I won't—"

"Won't what, my dear?"

"You are putting my legs asleep," she said acidly. "You are heavy."

"I certainly wouldn't want that," Hawk said, and in a graceful, swift motion, brought himself up beside her. His fingertips touched her nose, her chin, and finally stroked lightly over her lips.

"Hawk—"

"You are beautiful, Frances," he said, and there was no mockery in his voice now. Indeed, he sounded faintly worried.

He was leaning over her, his green eyes darker now, with desire, she knew, and she gulped. "So are you," she said, quite honestly.

He grinned, and the knowing, very warm intimate look was back. She felt his hand lightly touch her breast, and her eyes widened.

"I never knew that a simple touch could make me feel so very strange," she said.

"It makes me feel strange too." He closed his eyes a moment, and Frances had the feeling that he was memorizing her, learning about her.

He said abruptly, opening his eyes, "You will not sell your ring, Frances."

"I . . . I don't wish you to be forced into doing anything you don't wish to do. I don't wish to be beholden to you."

"I am your husband," he said, and she realized those words meant to him that any further arguments from her would be more than unwelcome. Likely the grounds for a shouting match, she thought, and gave it up, at least for the time being. There was not another thing in her mind, all her thoughts having vanished as the very pleasurable sensations were beginning to course through her body.

"Hawk," she said, her fingertips stroking his face, "I want you."

Those simple words, spoken so softly, with such longing, made him a wild man. He brought her with him, making her as wild as he. When he gently covered her mouth with his hand to feel the soft cries and raspy moans erupt, he lost what control he had left. His mouth replaced his hand and she felt his harsh, very warm breath fill her mouth as his manhood, thrusting deeply within her, filled her very being with him.

"Christ," he said on a long sigh, collapsing on top of her. "You will kill me, madam, before I have reached thirty."

"Well, I have nearly reached twenty, and am on the very brink myself."

He rubbed himself over her, felt himself growing hard within her again, and laughed at himself. "You make me a randy goat, Frances," he said, and began to fill her and move within her again.

"This is very nice," Frances said with great but inadequate sincerity.

She awoke during the night at the caressing kisses against her neck and a strong hand kneading her belly. Hawk was pressed against her back, his manhood hard and ready against her buttocks. She sighed and smiled in the darkness.

"Lift your leg, Frances," he said softly, and she did. She pressed her hips back when she felt him come into her. "Oh," she whispered, "all right, yes . . . oh!"

She felt him explode inside her, flooding her with his seed, even as his deft fingers sent her spinning into pleasurable oblivion.

He was still resting inside her when she fell asleep again.

Hawk awoke early the next morning, feeling as if he could conquer the world single-handed. Frances was cuddled next to him, so deeply asleep that he couldn't bring himself to awaken her. But he wanted to, oh yes, he did indeed. He sighed, rose, and went to his bedchamber.

He was feeling the happiest man alive when he entered the breakfast room sometime later. He was further pleased to find only Edmund at the table.

"Good morning, Hawk," Edmund said in his pleasant deep voice. "The ladies are still abed, I gather."

"I trust Frances is," Hawk said. "She had a most exhausting . . . day. She needs her rest." He wasn't aware that his face was a study of a contented man, but Edmund was.

"Marriage appears to agree with you," he observed.

"Yes, I concur. I found it most alarming, until I gave it up, so to speak. Have you and my sister set a date yet?"

"Yes, in September. I trust you and Frances will come to London?"

"Of course." Hawk allowed Rosie to serve him, then dismissed her. "I will tell you immediately, Edmund, that I have decided not to sell."

Edmund sucked in his breath at the stark, very final words. He was surprised. He supposed that he had assumed Hawk would allow him to convince and argue and cajole. But he hadn't, damn him!

"I see," he temporized.

"The stud, the thoroughbreds, they all mean a great deal to Frances." He took a bite of kippers, staring thoughtfully in front of him at nothing in particular. "I suppose," he said more to himself than to Edmund, "that I wanted to avoid taking over. It was Nevil's, after all. I felt, perhaps, that I would be stepping into his shoes and that it wasn't right."

"But you have changed your mind. Irrevocably?"

"Yes, I have."

"Well," Edmund said slowly, "I guess there is nothing more to say on the matter."

"No, I guess there isn't. You and Beatrice will stay with us awhile, won't you?"

"I would be delighted. However, it is possible that your wife may wish to pull out Bea's locks before too long."

This proved, unfortunately, to be quickly the case.

Hawk strolled to the paddock to see Beatrice instructing Frances on the training of Tamerlane. He groaned inwardly. Frances looked ready to spit in his sister's face. Belvis looked mildly amused, and poor Henry, an assistant trainer, stood gawking, his rather protruding blue eyes going from one lady to the other.

"Your method is all wrong," he heard Beatrice say in her ringing voice. "Must I keep reminding you that—"

"Good morning, ladies, Belvis." Hawk planted himself between the two women and began to stroke Tamerlane's nose. "He is quite a winner, don't you think, Bea? Frances, my dear, you aren't in your riding habit and I told you explicitly to be ready by eleven o'clock. Go along, now."

Frances escaped with alacrity. Although Beatrice put her back up, she had to admit, albeit grudgingly, that she certainly knew about racers.

When she returned to the stables but a half-hour later, dressed in a severely tailored dark blue riding habit, a jaunty hat over her hair, Hawk was waiting for her, quite alone. She skittered to a halt, suddenly very embarrassed.

He, however, was very matter-of-fact. He tossed her into the saddle, quickly mounted Ebony, and motioned for her to follow him.

"As the master instructs," she said to her mare, Violet, and sent her into a canter.

Hawk said nothing until they reached his special, private place by the River Ouse. He dismounted, tethered Ebony to a low branch of a yew bush, and lifted Frances from her mare's back.

"Hello," he said very softly as he eased her down the length of his body. Then he kissed her, most thoroughly.

He eased her back in the circle of his arms, delighted with her quickened breathing and her flushed face. "Now, how am I to get you out of all those ridiculous clothes? Not that you don't look charming, indeed you do. Perhaps I shall simply raise those skirts. Yes, that is what I shall do."

"Hawk!"

He grinned at her, lifted her gently, toppling her onto her back. She felt the soft grass beneath her, smelled the sweet scent of wildflowers.

"Lift your hips, sweetheart."

She did, her expression bemused.

She felt his hands on her body, felt him ease her skirts up about her chest. Then his hands were roving up her thighs to touch her.

"It's daylight," she said stupidly, watching him unfasten the buttons on his riding pants.

"Yes," he said, his voice deep and smooth as honey. "I can see you, all of you, at least from the waist down, most clearly."

She looked up at the shafts of sunlight filtering down through the overhanging branches and leaves. Then he was over her, and she saw only him.

He came into her and at the same moment slid his tongue into her mouth.

"Frances," he breathed, her name almost a blurred sigh.

And she responded, wildly.

❧ 26 ❧

An oyster may be crossed in love.
—*RICHARD SHERIDAN*

Frances' face was flushed, her heart pounding. She ran Hawk aground, thankfully alone, in the estate room.

He smiled upon seeing her, and quickly rose. "Hello, my dear. What do—?"

"Hawk," she gasped, quickly closing the door behind her. "I found them together!"

"I beg your pardon?"

"Beatrice and Edmund! I wished to speak to your sister, and entered her room, after I'd knocked, of course! They were in her bed, together!"

"Ah," said Hawk, grinning at her.

"They aren't wed! It was most mortifying. He was all over her, Hawk!"

"Did they observe your interest?"

"No, I slipped out before they saw me."

"They are to be married, Frances," her husband said mildly, sitting back to enjoy himself.

"Well," she said, puffing herself up to a bantam's stance, "you certainly weren't in my bedroom before we were married!"

That brought visions of the ghastly dowd. "God, no," he said, then grinned wickedly. "Actually, I was in a lovely widow's bed in Glasgow before we were married."

Frances stared at him, certain that she hadn't heard him aright. "What did you say?"

"Her name was Georgina, as I recall. Most lovely."

"You insensible block! You . . . you miserable . . ."

"Bastard? Bounder? Come, Frances, certainly you haven't lost your tongue? . . . So you have, huh? Well, silence in a woman is occasionally quite becoming. If you will take the trouble to remember the facts, Frances, you will recall that not only were we not married but also we both loathed each other."

"I still loathe you!"

"No you don't," he said, drawling out his words to a most improbable length. "You adore me, you desire me until the point of exhaustion, and as I recall last night—and that after lovemaking in the forest!—you rendered me limp as a—"

"I more than loathe you, I detest you!"

Hawk skirted his desk, his eyes darkening, even as the smile remained fixed on his lips. "Would you like me to prove your adoration, my dear?"

"No," she said, backing up against the closed door.

Hawk wondered vaguely if she would plant her fist into his belly. One could never tell with Frances, the unaccountable little witch. He very slowly, with great attention to her fisted hands, drew her against him. "You smell so nice, Frances."

"That isn't at all the point," she said against his shoulder.

He continued stroking his large hands up and down her back. "Why did you wish to speak to my sister?"

He felt her stiffen, and put her away from him so he could see her face. "Why, my dear wife, did you know that Edmund was with his betrothed? Did you enter her bedchamber on purpose?"

Her flush betrayed her. He was vastly amused at the thought of his wife wanting to see another man and woman in bed. "Did they look like us, Frances? Was your curiosity satisfied?"

"I don't know what we look like! I didn't mean . . . well, truly, it was horrible, I should never have listened to Gertrude—"

"What did grating Gertrude have to do with it?"

"She told me that she'd been looking for Edmund and when she couldn't find him she went to Bea's room and heard strange sounds and—"

"But you knew, didn't you, my dear? Indeed, you just made that up."

She looked as if she would protest a bit more, then hung her head. She nodded. "I suspected as much. All right, I did invent a bit of it."

"And then you come running to me with all this assumed ire! Most human of you, Frances. I find it delightful that there is a bit of wickedness in you."

"I am as dreadful as Gertrude, I suspect," Frances admitted, feeling like an absolute fool. Would he always see clearly through her? It was most disconcerting.

"Well, I shan't punish you. Indeed, I believe I should like to . . ." He broke off, casting a swift glance to the desktop. Unfortunately, it was covered with papers, books, and various odds and ends. He gave her a rueful smile. "I suppose I shall just have to reward you with some good news."

She gave him a suspicious look.

"I told Edmund that I will not sell out to him, or to anyone."

"Hawk!" She threw her arms about his back, alternately squeezing the breath out of him and exclaiming with delight.

He kissed her temple. "Such enthusiasm, love. It pleases me to please you."

Love. That made her suddenly very silent, very wary. Was it just another endearment gentlemen employed with little meaning?

"You are not returning to London, then?" she asked, holding her breath.

He arched a black brow upward, studying her face. "Do you wish me to leave, Frances?"

"I simply assumed that you would wish to. After all, your mis—"

"Ah, yes, my mistress. Most gentlemen have mistresses, you know. Do you mind, Frances?"

She didn't hear the grave seriousness in his voice, only the mocking drawl. "Why should I?" she snapped. "If you gave her up, then I should have to give up all my . . . lovers!"

"A dreadful prospect," he said, only the mocking drawl present now.

"You are remaining only because your sister and Edmund are here!"

"That could be partially true," he said.

"You are staying only because you are not yet bored with me!"

"Frances," he said very calmly, catching her chin in his palm and forcing her face upward, "you infuriate me, you make me want to throttle you, you prick huge holes in my man's pride, but you never bore me."

"You're remaining only until you have gentled me—your words, my lord!—and made me weak and silly."

"What an awesome memory you have, my dear. Are you feeling particularly gentled? Weak and silly yet?"

"No! Never! I shall—" She broke off suddenly at a shove against the door.

Hawk pulled her forward, and Marcus entered, saw the two of them together, and blushed furiously. "Oh, I didn't know . . . well, I can see to—"

"My dear Marcus," Hawk said pleasantly, releasing Frances, "her ladyship and I were just discussing the problem of the missing bills of sale. Have you discovered anything more?"

Marcus felt as though his collar were choking him. "No, my lord," he finally managed to say with but a ghost of his considerable aplomb. "I did, however, find bills of sale for others of the horses. But none for the three- and-four-year-olds."

Hawk actually didn't give a tinker's damn for the entire matter, but he managed to look suitably concerned. He smiled slightly toward his wife, who had regained a bit of her proper balance, and said, "Incidentally, Marcus, Lord Chalmers was regaling me earlier with stories of the racing world. He tells me there has recently been more than the expected amount of corruption, accidents, and the like. A prize thoroughbred of Lord Demerley's was poisoned before a race. The jockey was responsible and fled the country with quite a few guineas in his pocket."

"That is dreadful," said Frances. "I didn't realize that such things happened."

"Wherever money is involved," Hawk said dryly, "I suspect dishonesty is firmly entrenched."

"Speaking of jockeys," Frances said, her common sense firmly in place again, "I am used to riding, Hawk. And I don't weigh much. Do you suppose that I—"

"No," he said. "A lady doesn't do such things, Frances. I believe Belvis has a young nephew who is almost as small as you, my dear. He expects him to arrive by the end of the week. Since he is related to Belvis, I suppose we can trust him not to poison the horses."

Over luncheon that day, it appeared that Beatrice was ready to launch her own battleships. "You really don't know anything at all about racing, Philip. Bringing in mares for stud isn't difficult, of course, but racing! You must know that Edmund owns an excellent stable, the largest in Devonshire. And you have never cared anything at all about Desborough."

"Which comment should I respond to first, Bea?" Hawk asked mildly.

"I think you should sell. Edmund and I both are most excited about such a purchase."

Hawk arched an eyebrow, baiting her with his silence.

Beatrice frowned a bit, but forged ahead. "You know that everything would have come to me had I but been born a male. Unlike you, I have pride in Desborough, the tradition, the—"

The marquess spoke for the first time, smoothly interrupting his daughter. "You shall have Edmund's stables to muck about in, my dear. Hawk has obviously made up his mind. Leave off, I beg of you."

"It is *her* doing!" Beatrice said, glaring down the table at Frances.

"In part that is quite true," Hawk said honestly.

"She should go back to Scotland where she belongs! Why you should marry a nobody who—"

The marquess threw his spoon at his daughter. She gasped as it bounced off her bosom.

"Father!"

Edmund began to laugh. He leaned over and took Beatrice's hand and gently squeezed it. "You go too far, my dear. Perhaps Hawk will change his mind in the future. After all, the racing world is most demanding, quite costly, and there are all sorts of wicked people who must be dealt with. Finish your lunch and let us go riding."

An hour later, Frances was staring pensively around her bedchamber when Hawk entered through the adjoining door. She looked up and gave him a pained smile.

"How is my little nobody?" he said.

"I was surprised that you didn't tell your sister of the odd circumstances of our marriage."

"Had I fed her even a clue, it would have been raging through the *ton* within an hour. I had no desire to be pitied, laughed at, and otherwise mocked. Lord, I can just imagine how Brummell would have reacted."

"So, no one knows then, save us."

He flushed, and she pounced. "Who, my lord?"

" 'Hawk,' " he corrected automatically, buying himself some time.

But it was no use, she was tenacious. "Who, Hawk?"

"My mistress," he said baldly.

"You told your mistress about *us*?"

"You really should thank her, Frances," he said, trying to cover his chagrin with bravado. "It was Amalie who informed me quite clearly that I should make love to my wife as I made love to her."

Frances closed her eyes, but in her mind she saw her husband kissing and caressing a very beautiful woman whose face was blessedly blank. She turned slowly away from him, feeling a dreadful pain that she didn't understand, and walked blindly toward the door.

"Frances, you will not leave. If you don't come to a complete halt this very minute, I will ravish you right here on your Aubusson carpet. Your show of missishness is absurd."

"You can't ravish me," she said, and reached for the doorknob.

"Try me," he said, his voice grim.

She suddenly realized the import of her words, and blanched a bit. She looked at him very straightly and said, "I am not pregnant, as of this morning."

He groaned with heartfelt distress.

"It appears that you will have to visit a lady in York!"

"Were that my intent, she would not be a lady."

Frances lowered her eyes to the floor.

"Do you feel ill, Frances?"

"No, certainly not," she snapped, still not meeting his eyes.

"Then why are you acting like an embarrassed chit?"

"I don't like you," she said clearly. "I am not a chit, nor am I embarrassed. It is just from what you have said ... well ..."

"Frances, what is in that active mind of yours?"

"Ladies are not supposed to enjoy lovemaking."

He stared at her for a long moment, then threw back his head, laughing uproariously. He was laughing at himself, of course, but he was quickly brought to see his mistaken course when he felt a candlestick strike his chest.

"You intoxified brute!"

" 'Intoxified'? What the devil does that mean?"

"Well, perhaps I meant 'intoxicated,' but that doesn't really make much sense. Oh, you are still a wretch!"

"Frances, I lo—" He broke off, appalled at what he had nearly admitted to her. Now was not the time. Had he lost his mind?

"I am going riding," she said, and opened the door. "Would you please leave?"

"Yes," he said slowly, "yes, I shall leave."

He shook his head ruefully at himself, hearing her bedchamber door slam shut behind him.

The horse stall on wheels arrived that afternoon and caused a great deal of discussion. The smithy had managed to attach a driver's seat at the head of the stall and two horses would pull it.

"Very clever," Edmund said, inspecting it closely.

"It will make the racers lazy," said Beatrice.

"I hope Flying Davie won't object to it," Frances said, worried.

"Let's see," said the marquess.

Belvis brought Flying Davie to the stall. They placed straw inside the stall and ran a wooden plank on an incline to the narrow entrance.

"Now, my fine fellow, your carriage awaits," said Belvis.

Flying Davie regarded the small, enclosed space, and balked.

Hawk watched his wife regale the stallion with tales of how well-treated he was—like an emperor, indeed— and how he would be very well-rested when he arrived at Newmarket. He wasn't particularly surprised when Flying Davie, giving a final snort, dociley entered. His only sign of wariness was his twitching tail.

Frances beamed at the assembled company. "Flying Davie will win everything in sight," she said.

"There's a race near York next week," said Belvis. "We shall try Davie there."

Four days later, no one was more surprised than Edmund to see Lady Constance emerge from her traveling carriage in front of Desborough Hall.

"Connie!" Beatrice fairly shrieked, and darted down the front steps. "How delighted I am that you could come to visit! Such a bore, but you will add excellent *ton* to our group!"

The women embraced, Lady Constance looking a bit bewildered by this effusive greeting.

"What the devil!"

Edmund turned to see Hawk staring aghast at Lady Constance. "I am surprised myself, Hawk. I believe it is Bea's doing." He shrugged.

Constance was feeling altogether out of sorts. She

had received Beatrice's scribbled, urgent message and dutifully, hope in her breast, come to Yorkshire. She was beginning to think it was all a mistake, when she spotted Philip standing beside Edmund. She'd missed him dreadfully. She gave him a tentative wave, but was drawn up by Beatrice. "I am so pleased you came, Connie," Beatrice whispered meaningfully in her ear. "The little nobody he married is perfectly dreadful, you will see. He simply needs to be reminded that everyone important in London would laugh behind their hands at him were he to introduce her to society. Seeing you, my love, will certainly open his eyes."

Open his eyes to do what? Constance wondered, beginning to think her coming here was a vast and very stupid mistake.

Hawk greeted her kindly, seeing no other course of action. His father as well climbed onto his gallant charger and charmed the young lady. She was, after all, the daughter of one of his oldest enemies, old nibble-headed Lumley.

Beatrice fluttered about her friend, quitting her only when Edmund said with sincere threat, "I would speak to you, my love. Now. Constance will be just fine for the moment."

Beatrice shot him a look, but dutifully followed him into the gentlemen's smoking room.

"Why, Bea?" Edmund asked without preamble.

"You said it yourself, Edmund. Philip is refusing to sell to us—you—because of *her*. Once Connie charms him again, he will leave her here and return to London. He will quickly lose interest in all his newly discovered projects."

To her relief, Edmund looked very thoughtful. "I believe," he said finally, "that you are quite right, my dear. Your method is unsound, but your reasoning

. . . yes, your reasoning I applaud. At least I think I do. I shall give it further thought."

Edmund and Beatrice joined the company in the drawing room some minutes later. Constance had made the acquaintance of Frances Hawksbury and wanted to take to her heels. A pity that her horses were blown. She wanted to kill Beatrice.

She was saying to Hawk in a very clear voice, "I trust I have not disaccommodated you, my lord. I was journeying to Escrik to see my Uncle George and decided—quite a spur-of-the-moment decision actually—to stop by and say hello and offer my congratulations both to you and to your wife."

Beatrice looked at her with new respect. She'd firmly believed Connie to be something of a stupid block.

The marquess grinned behind his hand. Uncle George be damned! The fellow had been underground these many years, shot in a duel by his mistress's lover.

Hawk merely smiled, and Frances, not realizing anything, offered more tea and cakes to their unexpected guest.

Beatrice, loath to relinquish all her plans, turned her attention to Frances and said with great kindness, "You know, Frances, Philip and Connie have known each other—so very well—for the longest time now."

"Actually only about eight months," said Hawk.

"So *friendly* you have been!" Beatrice pursued.

"I as well," said Edmund unexpectedly. "Tell us the news from London, Connie."

"Well," Constance began, "you simply wouldn't believe the spectacle Lord Mallory is making of himself with Lady Lawton! 'Tis most disgraceful and Lady Mallory is creating quite a fuss!"

Hawk relaxed, for Constance, once started upon London gossip, could not be stopped until fatigue overtook her.

Frances merely blinked and let her mind wander. She knew none of the people Lady Constance was speaking about. She caught a wink from her father-in-law, and frowned a bit.

Bea had given up her drawing implications by dinnertime. Well, she had tried.

Frances was dressing for dinner when there came a knock on the adjoining door.

Hawk entered. "You are lovely, my dear," he said to his wife. "You may go now, Agnes."

"What have you there?" Frances asked, looking at him in her mirror. He opened a long velvet case and drew out a very green and sparkling emerald necklace.

"To match your eyes, my dear," he said.

"My eyes are gray!"

"Hummm," he said. "Hold still."

She felt his warm fingers against her neck, and felt those ridiculous very warm feelings begin to simmer deep within her, feelings that she had begun to discount during the past days. Odd aberrations, she'd thought.

"What do you think?" he said, backing up a bit.

She stared at the necklace nestled between her breasts. "It is beautiful. Why are you letting me wear it?"

"It is yours. It belonged to my mother and to her mother before her. If you should like the stones reset . . ." He shrugged.

"No, it is lovely. Thank you, Hawk." She rose from her dressing stool and frowned at him. "Why?"

"Why what?"

"Why are you giving it to me?"

His eyes were sparkling as brightly as the emeralds. "Green for jealousy," he said. "I hoped that my very generous gift would nip any ire you were nurturing in your lovely bosom."

"You mean calm my savage breast because Lady Constance is one of your . . . flirts?"

"Exactly. Of course Beatrice dragged her here and has made her most uncomfortable. Be kind to her, Frances, and we shall see her on her way—to her Uncle George—very soon, I don't doubt."

"Surely Beatrice can't think that you would divorce me!"

"Nothing so severe, I imagine. I believe she hoped I would see the light and follow Connie back to London like a panting pup."

"I wish Beatrice would leave," she said, and he smiled at her hopeful tone. "And I am not jealous, Hawk!"

"Not even a tiny bit?"

"You, my lord, can have your flirts and I shall have mine!"

"Poor Marcus," Hawk sighed. "The fellow is beset. You expect him to hold Miss Melcher with one arm and you with the other?"

She flushed, knowing she was so wide of the mark as to be in another county.

"Come, my dear, and give me a kiss before we go downstairs."

He pulled her gently to him, lifted her chin with his fingers, and lightly kissed her. "Ah, so very long. I suppose I must wait until tomorrow?"

He sounded so wistful that Frances was obliged to smile. "You have been keeping track?"

"Every single day," he said fervently.

"Marriage," Frances said thoughtfully, "makes one most aware of things one was never particularly aware of before."

"By that do you mean that you are counting days also?"

"No," she said honestly. "Indeed, I was beginning

to believe that all we . . . well, you know, the feelings
. . . were all in my head! That is all."

"In your head? How very repulsive a conclusion.
Shall I have to begin at the beginning again?"

She flushed slightly and shook her head against his
shoulder.

"You know, Frances, my bed has been very empty
without you." He sighed deeply. "Shall we go downstairs?" He patted her cheek and stood away from
her. "You look lovely."

He looked very lovely himself, she thought as she
walked downstairs beside him.

❧ 27 ❧

There is no pack of cards without a knave.
— SIXTEENTH-CENTURY PROVERB

Amalie looked thoughtfully at the careful arrangement of playing cards spread before her on her bed. *"Moi, je le savais"* she said to her empty bedchamber. "I knew this would happen, yes, I certainly did."

Amalie would be the first one to admit that philosophy and superstition weren't the most compatible of bedfellows, but she'd had this *feeling*. And the cards had proved her right, indeed they most certainly had.

She slowly reshuffled the cards and set them on the table beside her bed. *"Il faut penser, maintenant,"* she said quietly, and propped herself up on her bed pillows. Yes, I must think this through very carefully. After all, she really had no proof at all . . .

She had received the Earl of Rothermere's expected letter two weeks before. It appeared that he was now ready to be a faithful husband. He had sent her two hundred pounds and an assurance that the lease on her house would be extended to the end of the next quarter. Very generous was Hawk, and she missed him. Still, there was Robert, and she very nearly had enough for a substantial dowry. Never, she thought fiercely, and with French determination, would she go to her husband without a *dot*.

For that reason alone, she had let the very generous Lord Dempsey stroll into her life and into her bed. His name was Charles Lewiston and he was a very powerful man, particularly in the racing world. And he was a friend of Lord Chalmers, who was betrothed to Lady Beatrice, Hawk's sister. And he'd spoken when he was in his cups. Spoken of things that bothered Amalie. *Lord Dempsey hadn't seemed to know that she had been under Rothermere's protection* and after his bout with the brandy bottle, she wasn't about to tell him. "Indeed, soon we will have what we wish," he'd said, his voice slurred, his body thankfully, from Amalie's point of view, limp and sodden from the brandy. He was a rough lover and she had agreed to see him again only because of what he'd said.

"Ah, my lord, what is it you will soon have?" she'd inquired in a soft, rather awed voice.

"Desborough stock, all of it, and then it will be all over."

What would be over? Amalie wondered. She saw that he was on the brink of a drunken sleep, and said, "You are so brave, my lord, and so magnificent. Much more so than the former Lord Rothermere, Nevil. You knew him, I suppose?"

"Demned bounder," said Dempsey giving a satisfied snort, "selfish sod. We took care of him, oh yes, we did."

He was snoring loudly the next moment, and Amalie was transfixed by his words. She'd prayed devoutly that he would not remember what he'd said when he awoke.

She rose now from her bed and walked to her dressing table. She straightened a sheet of pressed paper and dipped the quill into the ink pot.

Frances shouted until she was hoarse, and when

Flying Davie flew across the finish line, she threw her arms about her husband's neck.

"We did it! We did it!"

Hawk, grinning proudly, kissed her.

She'd seen the other jockeys trying to knock Timothy from Flying Davie's back, seen the vicious swipes with riding crops. Thankfully, Flying Davie had managed to widen the lead and escape further harassment. Damned vicious brutes!

They'd won the meet at York, a grueling five-mile race that tested the mettle of all ten thoroughbreds entered.

"I'd say he's ready for Newmarket," said Belvis, rubbing his hands together. "As for Timothy, he needs a bit more instruction on how to keep his hide intact, but a fine job the boy did, yes, indeed, a fine job."

Frances had won two hundred pounds, for Flying Davie, an unknown, was at seventy-to-one odds.

"Most impressive," said Edmund, shaking Hawk's hand. "Tamerlane will run tomorrow?"

"Yes," said Frances, glowing with pride.

"And you, Frances, fully intend to repair all your fortunes?" Hawk asked, tweaking a curl beside her left ear.

"I believe I shall have another traveling stall made," she said.

"A very small, inconsenquential race," said Beatrice, smoothing out her gloves. "I shouldn't rely too much on the outcome."

"Then why ever should you wish to purchase our horses if you place no reliance on their abilities?" Frances asked.

Edmund shook his head fondly at his betrothed, took her arm, and followed Hawk and Frances to the winner's circle. Timothy was flushed and smiling, and so excited he could barely speak.

Hawk warmly congratulated his jockey on his victory, and also heard the grumbling from other racehorse owners. He saw money changing hands, a great deal of money. His ears picked up when he chanced to overhear one gentleman saying to another, "Flying Davie, huh, George! Where the devil did old Nevil pick up that magnificent piece of horseflesh? Odd coloring, reminds me of a thoroughbred I saw at Ascot last year."

George, wiping perspiration from his brow, grunted. "Nevil never said a word about it. You remember Nevil—always bragging about his finds. Why would he keep mum about this fellow?"

Hawk's interest was truly piqued when he returned to Desborough Hall to find Amalie's letter waiting for him. He saw Frances give him a rather penetrating look, and quickly excused himself and made for the gentlemen's smoking room. He read the letter once, and then again. His eyes went yet again to Lord Dempsey's words: *We took care of him, oh yes, we did ... Desborough stock ... it will be all over ...*

What the devil was going on here? Hawk knew himself to be a straightforward man, unused to machinations of this sort. In the army, he had lied, cheated, and otherwise employed every means known to soldier to provide Wellington with needed information, but in *this* world, the one he'd now joined, he was uncertain how to proceed. He decided in the end that the differences couldn't be so great after all. He had a problem and he must solve it.

He tracked down his father, who was enjoying a sprightly walk in the east rose garden. The warm summer air was redolent of their sweet scent. He shook his head at himself, for it made him think immediately of Frances.

"My boy," the marquess greeted him. "Frances isn't with me, more's the pity. I wager you can find her at the paddock."

"No," Hawk said, " 'tis not my wife I seek." He matched his stride to his father's slower one. "Was Lord Dempsey a close friend of Nevil's, sir?"

"Old Edward's boy, Charles, isn't that his name?"

"I believe so. Charles Lewiston."

"Lewiston was a blackguard," the marquess continued thoughtfully, dredging his memory. "I imagine that any son of his wouldn't be a particularly sterling specimen. I remember Nevil speaking of him, yes, he was a friend of Nevil's."

"And of course Edmund was also."

"Yes, certainly. Pity that Nevil couldn't have been more of a man, but . . ."

The marquess broke off, and Hawk frowned. "You told me once that you wouldn't force a Soho trollop on Nevil. I really don't understand, sir. Did he change so much?"

"You've forgotten his sneaky, mean ways, I see. He always was a petty, sniveling boy, and as a man, he got himself in with a scurvy sort of company. I saw little of him in the six months before he drowned, Hawk. He severed the connection, not I."

"I remember receiving your letter, sir. I recall wondering how the devil Nevil could be so careless as to get himself drowned. He was an excellent swimmer, I know."

"He was drunk, utterly castaway," the marquess said, distaste in his voice.

"Who told you that he was?"

The marquess blinked a bit and stared searchingly at

his son. "You know," he said finally, " 'twas Edmund, of course. Came to Chandos Chase immediately to tell me. (Most proper is our Edmund. I had to pry the details from him.) Edmund is a gentleman."

"Was Lord Dempsey one of the men aboard Nevil's yacht?"

"I don't know, Hawk. Why the interest now?"

Hawk was hesitant to speak further, and thus, hedged. "I'm not certain."

The marquess looked at his son's closed face and said, "I believe Edmund and Beatrice are to leave tomorrow. He, of course, must get his own cattle ready for Newmarket."

"Do you wonder, Father," Hawk said, "why Edmund is so very interested in buying all the Desborough stock? The price he offered me was beyond something grand."

"Ambition," said the marquess. "I believe Edmund has aspirations of equaling the records of Jersey and Derby. Can't fault a man for that."

"No, I suppose not," said Hawk. But why, he wondered, had Lord Dempsey spoken of the Desborough stock? What would be "all over"?

For some reason Hawk couldn't explain to himself, he made no mention of anything to Edmund. Their last evening together was amiable, and it seemed to Hawk that Edmund's wishes for racing success were sincere. Beatrice was not so amiable, of course, but Hawk didn't expect it from his sister.

Frances, sensitive to her husband's moods, a consequence that troubled her not a little, found herself yet again entering her husband's bedchamber late that night. This time he was in his dressing gown, not in his lovely natural state, sitting in front of the fireplace. A lone candle burned by his elbow.

She saw that he was holding a piece of paper in his left hand.

"What is this?" she asked, coming around his chair to face him, her finger pointing to the paper.

"Oh, Frances." He grinned at her. "I was on my way to you, my dear. Are you so very anxious for my company?"

She refused to be drawn. "Something has disturbed you, Hawk. What is it? What is that?"

"Surely a husband is entitled to keep some things to himself, Frances," he said. He carefully began folding the paper into a small square.

"Hawk ..." she began, straightening herself for battle.

"When are your sisters to arrive?" he asked, deflecting her charge.

"Oh, did I not tell you? I suppose I thought it *my* secret." Hawk merely smiled at her. "Very well, my lord, Sophia wishes to wait until the fall. She said something about a Little Season and my sisters gaining their polish before they're tossed into the marriage mart in the spring."

"We shall contrive to gain you a bit more polish before you squire them about," he said.

She watched him slip the small square of paper into the deep pocket of his dressing gown. He patted his thighs, and she decided a bit of guilt was in order. She gingerly set herself down, but made no move to cuddle against him.

"I sent the two hundred pounds I won at York to Sophia," she said, her voice a challenge. "She told me of a grand seamstress in Glasgow."

"Then the girls will likely be arriving in royal procession, for I sent another three hundred pounds to your father."

That was something of a shock, and Frances gave him a brilliant smile. He felt the familiar stirrings of lust and drew her against his chest.

"You are so very unexpected," she said, relaxing at the feel of his large hands roving up and down her back. He shifted his position and she felt his hardness against her bottom.

"Not really," he said, grinning at her. "Just a simple man who wants to bed his wife."

Frances could find no fault with this pronouncement. She could find no fault either with the following hour, and it wasn't until she awoke the following morning that she remembered the square of paper Hawk had placed in the pocket of his dressing gown. Even then it was but a vague memory.

She was in Hawk's bed, alone, and she was, she knew, smiling a very satisfied smile. *I adore you, Frances.* And then he'd come inside her, deeply and fully. She remembered vaguely telling him something, but she couldn't recall her words. Had she told him she loved him? That made her frown a bit. She forced her mind to her other concern.

What was written on that piece of paper? Why hadn't he wanted her to see it?

Two days later, Frances made her usual rounds in the stables. She'd gotten into the habit of working out Flying Davie over the five-mile track that wound over flatlands on the northern part of Desborough property, circling back to the paddock.

"You'll be working out Tamerlane today, Lady Frances," Belvis said. "Davie is to remain in the paddock this morning. I've got Timothy trying some of my special defense strategies."

"I think he should carry a pistol," Frances said,

remembering the slash on Timothy's thigh from another jockey's riding crop.

Belvis chuckled. "Not a bad idea. Lord, it might come to that. I hear that the Duke of Portland is trying his damnedest to improve racing standards, but it's slow going."

Belvis gave Frances a toss onto Tamerlane's back. "Remember to keep him close for the first mile." He added on a grin, "You might imagine jockeys beside you—mean devils, the lot of them. Kick at them, my lady. Try some of your more colorful Scottish curses on them."

She saluted him and click-clicked Tamerlane into the stableyard. She waved at her husband, then guided the stallion past the paddock to the flat field beyond. She laughed aloud with pleasure when Tamerlane snorted, jerking at the reins.

"You want to run, my boy," she said, patting his glossy neck. "All right, let us show everyone what you are made of."

Her riding hat was firmly fastened to her head, but when she loosed Tamerlane, she felt the wind tearing at it, and she smiled, feeling that mad exhilaration. Every so often, she turned her head to the side, growled at a vicious-looking jockey, and kicked out at him. Tamerlane held to his course.

There was but one jump on the entire course, a short three-foot fence that marked the end of Desborough property and the beginning of the Bourchiers'. They'd discussed with John pulling down the fence, but hadn't gotten to it just yet. Frances enjoyed the jump, and as they neared it, she pressed herself against Tamerlane's neck.

He soared over the fence and it was in that split second that Frances saw the raw-toothed thresher on the other side, its vicious iron spikes sticking upward. She didn't think, she reacted, trying desperately to stretch out Tamerlane's stride to clear the spikes.

He did, almost. Frances heard his agonized scream, felt his body twisting beneath her, and felt herself flying over his head.

She landed hard, and for many moments was insensible. She pulled herself upward and her eyes immediately fastened on the huge gash in Tamerlane's back left leg. The thoroughbred was standing very still, his chest heaving; she knew he must be in dreadful pain.

She jumped to her feet, tried her best to calm the stallion, then began running back toward the stables. The shortcut she took lessened the distance by some half-mile, but when she burst into the yard, the stitch in her side was so intense that she could scarce breathe.

Hawk saw her first. "Frances! What the devil!"

"Tamerlane . . . the jump, somebody placed a thresher up behind it. Hurt, he's very hurt."

"You're all right?" he asked.

"Fine, please, we must hurry!"

She heard Belvis shouting to bring the traveling horse stall as she gathered together ointments, bandages, and painkilling herbs she'd brought with her from Kilbracken.

Hawk took her up in front of him. He said nothing, merely dug his heels into Ebony's sides to quicken his pace.

Tamerlane was standing where Frances had left him, his proud head lowered. Hawk felt his throat close when he saw the gash.

"We will not put him down!" Frances said firmly. While she soothed the stallion and fed him the opiate, Hawk, along with Belvis, looked at the thresher. Tamerlane's blood showed like fresh rust on one of the spikes.

"Who would do such a thing?" Belvis said blankly, shaking his head. "Who, for God's sake?"

"Frances rides this way almost every day," Hawk said.

They both whirled about at the sound of Tamerlane's wild snort, but Frances had him in control. She looked filthy, her riding skirt ripped, her hair tangled and snarled, and she was focused entirely on Tamerlane.

She cleaned the gash very gently, applied the ointment, and bandaged the leg. "All right," she said, drawing a deep breath, "let's get him into the stall.

"He'll be all right," she said over and over again as she and Hawk watched Belvis close the stall door and leap into the driver's seat.

"Let's go back now, Frances," Hawk said.

Suddenly Frances felt the most searing, intense pain she'd ever experienced. Her face went white, and she staggered.

"Frances!"

"My shoulder," she gasped. "Oh God, Hawk, it hurts!"

He thought quickly, weighing his options, then said, "Let me help you sit down and I'll take a look."

He could feel her pain, feel her trying her best not to yell. When she was seated on the ground he said, "Now, let me get the riding jacket off." It was more easily said than done. The pain was excruciating, and Frances prayed for oblivion.

The jacket finally off, Hawk saw that the blouse was next. "I'll be as easy as I can," he said, and began unfastening the long row of satin-covered buttons.

Frances couldn't help the moan this time. It was deep and agonized and Hawk felt himself growing cold. He ripped the blouse off her to spare her more pain.

He saw the problem quickly enough. She'd dislocated her shoulder. He thought quickly, then said, "Frances, I can fix your shoulder now. It will hurt like the very devil, but then it will be over. Or I can take you back to the house and we can get the doctor to—"

"Do it," she said between gritted teeth.

Hawk swallowed. He'd done this several times during his army days, but the men were big and strong. She looked fragile, her flesh white and soft. He cursed, placed his hands on the shoulder, and forced the bone back into its socket. She didn't scream, she didn't make a sound.

"There," he said, so relieved that he was shaking. "It's over, Frances."

Her head fell back and he saw that she had fainted.

"I'm proud of you, love," he said as he gently laid her back on the ground, her riding jacket beneath her.

She regained consciousness very quickly and blinked up at her husband.

"It's over," he said, gently stroking her cheek. "You'll be all right now."

Her face lost its pallor and turned a light shade of green.

"You want to vomit?"

Frances swallowed convulsively. She shook her head.

"It's natural. Here, my dear, close your eyes and hold very still." He sat beside her, his back against an oak tree, and eased her head onto his thighs. He began to speak, softly, slowly, to distract her. "I remember the first time I did that, I was in Spain. One of my men had been thrown from a horse, just as you were. He had the very same reaction, but felt human again by the following day. It is curious that you felt no pain until it was all over. No one seems to understand how you can not even be aware of an injury until your mind is released from its urgency."

"I was terrified for Tamerlane," she managed in a thin voice.

"Yes, you were, and you kept your own injury at bay until you'd taken care of his. I remember after one particular battle, Grunyon got to me and demanded how I could have gotten so much blood on my boots. I had a thigh wound and wasn't even aware of it." He chuckled at the memory. "After he pointed it out, I of course felt the most awful pain imaginable." He paused. "Do you feel better?"

"Yes," she said, sounding a bit surprised. "I don't want to retch anymore."

"You will be bruised."

"Hawk, why?"

He didn't pretend to misunderstand her. "I don't know." The question had been swirling about in his brain, but with no answer. "Have you dismissed one of your lovers?" he asked, lightly ruffling her hair. "Did he not take it kindly?"

She wanted to laugh, but tried a brief chuckle, but it hurt too much. "What if I had been riding Davie?"

Riding Flying Davie indeed, he reflected, his thoughts striding down a new avenue.

"Are you ready to go home?" he asked, not yet wanting to answer her question.

"All right," she said.

Hawk stripped off his coat, lifted her in his arms, and placed the coat about her shoulders. "Now, don't try to do anything, Frances."

It wasn't easy to get her on Ebony's back without causing her a great deal of pain, but Hawk finally managed it. "Now, just lie back against me and try to relax. We'll take it very slowly, love."

Frances felt as though hot pokers were embedded in her shoulder, but she refused to give in to the pain. "I think," she said, "that I should prefer a beating."

He dropped a kiss on top of her head. "The next time you infuriate me, I'll consider it," he said, grinning over her head.

He realized after some moments that she'd fallen into a stupor, and felt relief. He urged Ebony into a gallop.

When they reached the stableyard, he saw Belvis' face go from relief to profound concern.

"She's all right," Hawk said quickly. "She dislocated her shoulder, but didn't realize it until all the excitement was over."

"I'll send one of the boys for a doctor," Belvis said.

"I fixed it already, but I do want Simons to take a look at her. Hold Ebony, will you, Belvis."

Hawk eased her down, keeping her tightly against his chest. Now that the crisis seemed to have passed, Hawk thought, striding toward the house, he was beginning to feel very shaky himself. He cursed quite fluently, but it didn't help ease the feeling of intense helplessness, the feeling of murderous rage. Why? And *who*?

The doctor, Mr. Simons, examined her, and pronounced Hawk a fine practitioner. "She'll be just the thing in a couple of days, my lord. Your quick action saved her interminable pain. You are lucky in your husband, Lady Frances."

Frances was drugged with laudanum and the doctor's face was spinning above her in the most disconcerting manner. "Yes," she said, the words coming out of her mouth without her mind's permission, "he is the very best of husbands."

Hawk smiled down at her. He gently patted her cheek and she turned her face against his open hand. He felt a surge of such deep caring that he couldn't have spoken had his very hide depended upon it. And then he felt the terror of losing her. He closed his eyes for a moment against his intense reaction.

When he opened his eyes, he saw that his father was regarding him most thoughtfully. He didn't fight his feelings, and merely nodded to his father.

"Sleep now, love," he said softly, and gently eased his hand away. He stood beside her bed, not moving until her breathing evened into sleep.

"Father," he said, turning, "I believe that you and I have some talking to do."

28

If I love you, what business is it of yours?
—GOETHE

"So, my boy, it's all over with you? Rolled up foot and guns? Tip over arse, eh?"

"Yes," said Hawk. "She is my wife, I love her, and I am supposed to protect her. A fine husband I am!"

"Have you told her of your feelings?"

"No." Hawk turned and poured himself a brandy. His father regarded him with some surprise. "Why ever not?"

"I suppose I am not so certain what she would say to me if I did tell her." He drank the brandy in one long pull, wiped his hand across his mouth, and gave his father a crooked grin. "We argue and she yells at me to go back to London to my mistress. I wonder if she cares at all. Our courtship wasn't particularly designed to engender the more tender feelings, and our initial relationship was . . . awful, in bed and out of it."

"She cares," the marquess said. "Frances' feelings are akin to an open book, if one knows how to read properly."

"I don't believe I have gotten beyond the preface," said Hawk, then immediately thought of her in his bed, her intense pleasure, her desire to please him as he pleased her. She *was* an open book to him at those precious times.

He heard his father say, "I had intended to take myself off, but now . . . this is a bloody mess, Hawk, and I don't mind telling you that I loathe mysteries."

"As I see it, Father, there is only one of two possible reasons. The first—somebody wants Frances removed. The second—she was supposed to be riding Flying Davie this morning, and he was the target."

"From what Belvis told me, had it not been for Frances' quick thinking, Tamerlane might have had to be put down. Now he believes that the leg will heal, not in time for the Newmarket races, though."

"I cannot imagine why anyone would wish to harm Frances," said Hawk, pursuing his own thoughts. "Now, Flying Davie is another matter. Who, though?"

"He made a fine appearance last week, Hawk. Many men weren't very pleased."

"Yes, a lot of money was lost, I doubt not."

"If Flying Davie was the target, then it had to involve someone here at Desborough. It required knowledge of Frances' habits with the horse."

"I know," Hawk said, and downed more brandy. "The goddamned bastard."

"Indeed. Of course this person is being paid by someone else. The question is, who?"

Hawk toyed with the idea awhile before blurting out, "It is possible, Father, that Nevil was murdered!"

The marquess simply stared at his son, but Hawk saw his hands fisting at his sides. He got a hold on himself and said tersely, "Tell me."

Hawk fetched Amalie's letter and gave it to his father.

"This Amalie," said the marquess a few minutes later, "is apparently an honorable woman—she certainly has your safety at heart. But perhaps she hasn't put herself in a terribly safe position, if what she says is true."

"No, she hasn't, and I was worried. I sent her five thousand pounds and told her to leave London."

"Nevil, as much as it grieves me to say it openly, was a greedy bastard. I knew it but chose to keep myself out of it. More fool I!"

"None of it was your fault, Father," Hawk said. "None of it. Every man chooses his own road, you know that. The question still remains, though, none of *what?*"

The marquess ruminated, saying finally, his voice meditative, "If Lord Dempsey was responsible for Nevil's death, then perforce it had to do with racing. And that, unfortunately, brings our Edmund to the fore."

Hawk cursed very explicitly.

"I know, my boy. There is Beatrice and all that."

"It occurred to me, Father, that it was Beatrice behind Edmund's push to buy me out. Perhaps it wasn't."

"Or worse, perhaps it was."

The two men stared at each other. Hawk very carefully set down his brandy snifter. "I am going to speak to Belvis. The horses, particularly Flying Davie, must be protected."

He didn't realize that his father still held Amalie's letter.

He didn't give it a thought, in fact, until he visited Frances that evening to share dinner with her.

"You look ready to slay dragons again, my dear," he said.

"I am thinking of one particular dragon, a very stupid dragon," she said, unsmiling.

"Ah," Hawk said, "here is our dinner." He took the bed tray from Mrs. Jerkins' hands and set it over his wife's legs. He raised the various lids and inhaled. "Delicious," he announced.

"All of her ladyship's favorites," said Mrs. Jerkins.

"Yes, I see," said Hawk. "Chicken with bechamel sauce, larded peahen, and her very favorite—tipsy cake."

He waited until Mrs. Jerkins had left the bedchamber, then said sharply, "Now, what is wrong with you, other than your shoulder?"

"This," Frances said, and thrust Amalie's letter at him.

"Damn," said Hawk. "I think I shall murder my father."

"How could you keep this from me! Do you believe I am some sort of weak-willed female whose delicate sensibilities would be grossly overset? You are an idiot, and I won't have it, Hawk!"

He sighed and seated himself beside her bed. "We're in deep trouble, Frances."

She was so surprised at his capitulation that she was without words for many moments. She saw the worry in his beautiful eyes and softened. But she didn't want to feel softened and gentled, damn him!

"You will try no more ploys to keep me in ignorance, Hawk."

"No, it is too late," he agreed. "Eat your dinner."

He uncovered his own dishes and took a thoughtful bite of the fluffy potatoes. "Too much salt," he said absently.

"The tipsy cake is delicious," said Frances.

"Are you in much pain now?"

"No," she said honestly. "Just very sore. You were right about the bruises. I look awful—all blue and purple and disgusting yellow-green."

"Sounds like those wretched caps you used to wear,"

he said, giving her a lopsided grin. "I shall see for myself after dinner."

"If you are thinking to seduce me, I suggest you forget it!"

He gave her a very *knowing* look. "I have the utmost respect for your body, my dear, though I must admit that my interest in some parts is more intense than in others."

"Well, I think that spot at the base of your spine is very endearing."

His smile faltered a bit. He could almost feel her soft mouth traveling down his back. "Touché," he said.

"I even like the hair on your legs. It feels all crinkly and soft and very . . . disturbing."

"I said 'Touché,' Frances."

"Not to mention those seductive muscles over your belly."

"Frances!"

She giggled and quickly regretted it. She sobered, recalling his perfidy. His sin of omission. "You are still a dragon, however."

"But you haven't said a word about how fascinating my dragon's tail is," he said, drawing her.

"Hawk—"

"Finish your dinner, love, and we shall speak of it. If you don't mind, my father should join us—that is, unless the two of you have already solved our mystery."

Frances sighed. "No, unfortunately."

She toyed a bit with her mashed turnips, then said quietly, "Why do you call me 'love'?"

"It is more appropriate than 'hate,' I think." Why did she have to ask? he thought, feeling irritated. She was pushing him, but he wasn't ready yet.

"Father told me you had sent Amalie money to leave London."

"Yes," he said.

"She is returning to France?"

"Yes, to marry. His name is Robert, and he is a farmer, and, I might add, a very lucky man."

"Do you believe that your sister is involved, Hawk?"

"I don't know, Frances. I pray she isn't."

"I like Edmund. Perhaps he knows nothing of this."

"Perhaps."

"Who on our staff could be disloyal to us?"

"Belvis is vastly interested in discovering the man's identity."

Frances took a bite of her peahen, then said, "I still wish to go to Newmarket."

His reaction was immediate and forceful. "No, Frances, it would be ridiculous. We shall take no more chances."

"Then you might as well sell the damned horses to Edmund!"

"You will not question me on this, Frances!"

"Ah," she said, giving him a creditable sneer, his own patented sneer, he realized. "So you are back to being my overbearing lord, my keeper, the arrogant master!"

"Don't push me on this, Frances, or I won't be tempted to compare you to a summer's day."

"You will not dictate to me, Hawk!"

"I will do just as I please with you, wife. Now, finish your dinner."

He saw she was sorely tempted to throw her tray at him, and said quickly, "Don't do it, Frances, you'll hurt your shoulder."

She sighed, giving up the fond desire. "You are right about that, I suppose. Hawk, I wish to discuss this entire matter with you, reasonably."

"All right," he said agreeably. "You never know, my dear, perhaps after you have done your wifely duty by me, I might be very amenable to your women's wiles."

"What about my shoulder?"

He merely grinned at her sarcastic tone. "I shall proceed with great care, you may be certain of that. Indeed, I might just begin with your beautiful belly and never travel higher. What do you think?"

"I think you are a goat!"

"You're blushing, Frances," he observed blandly. "If I were to touch you right now between those lovely thighs of yours, do you think that I should find you quite ready for me?"

She tried to heave her dinner tray at him, but the pain in her shoulder made her drop it. A chicken breast landed in her lap and she felt bechamel sauce begin to seep through her nightgown. She growled in frustration.

Hawk laughed. "I don't think I'll call in Agnes to assist you, my dear. Most embarrassing, I should say. Now, you will hold still, I don't wish you to hurt yourself anymore."

She lay stiffly as Hawk cleared the food away. She saw him grin widely at the stain of bechamel sauce low on her belly. "Go away," she said.

"I'll clean you up, my dear. I shan't tell a soul, I swear it to you."

He returned with a damp cloth, and before Frances could protest, he was lifting her nightgown, baring her to the waist.

She squeaked.

"It seems a pity to waste such exquisite-tasting sauce," he said, only to stop when she squeaked again.

"Hold still," he said again, and began to wipe away the sauce. When he finished, he tossed the cloth aside, leaned down, and kissed her stomach. Frances sucked in her breath, and then expelled it when his fingers caressed along her inner thighs, slowly upward, until he was touching her. "Very nice," he said, his breath warm against her belly. "More intriguing than the sauce, I think."

"I shouldn't like this, Hawk," she said in a very worried voice. "I am ill."

"Not here, you're not. Hold still, Frances, close your eyes, and relax. I'm going to make you forget all about your shoulder."

And he did. His mouth burned deep, making her shiver and groan, despite her best attempts to keep quiet. "That's it," he said softly, raising his head just a moment to look at her face. "Ah," he said, quite pleased with his progress, and returned to his task.

When she cried out her pleasure, he thought the world a very perfect place.

"A gentled woman, how very nice," he said, lightly stroking her limp body.

"I still don't like you," she whispered, wondering where her voice had fled to.

He ignored that, stripped off her nightgown, and tossed it to the floor. "I would get you another one, Frances, but it would only get in the way."

"Please cover me," she said. "I . . . I'm cold."

"You were right about that shoulder," he said, his smile turning into a frown. It looked awful. "God, Frances, you scared the hell out of me."

"It looks worse than it feels, I promise." She raised her hand and gently caressed his cheek. "I'm all right." He kissed her palm, and for a long moment they were silent.

"You're cold," he said finally. He gently pulled the covers over her. He gave her a cup of tea laced with laudanum. When he saw she was on the edge of sleep, he undressed and climbed into bed beside her.

She was beyond protesting, of course, and he very gently settled her against him.

"How can you love someone you don't like?"

His eyes widened in the dark room. Her voice was blurred, her words slow, but he understood, indeed he did. "It is a very common affliction," he said finally. "Go to sleep, Frances."

"You are always giving me orders," she grumbled. He thought she'd finally fallen asleep, but after some moments she whispered, "You gained no pleasure this time."

"You're wrong about that, love. Have you no idea how it makes me feel when you moan so sweetly while I'm caressing you? And when you flow over me, I want to shout."

"You make *me* shout," she said. "I forget everything."

"Me included?"

"No, you're part of me."

"I am never going to sleep without you again," he said softly. "Even when it is your monthly flow, I shan't leave you alone. Of course," he added thoughtfully, "I shall practice great nobility. Good training, I am certain my father would say. And when you are carrying my child, Frances, I will feel every move he makes inside you."

She was asleep, her breathing even and soft.

I could have lost her today, forever.

All his very pleasant thoughts faded. Damn, he said to himself. I must do something!

Everything changed the following afternoon. Belvis discovered one of his assistant trainers, Henry, mixing poison into Flying Davie's feed. He grabbed him, yelled at the top of his lungs, but Henry, scared for his life, managed to break away.

Hawk visited the magistrate, Lord Elliston, and the search was on.

Frances kept muttering, "We must find him, we must! Only he can tell us who paid him to kill Flying Davie!"

Hawk grunted. He was so weary he didn't want to move, much less speak.

His father jerked him out of his fatigue. "No reason not to go to Newmarket now," the marquess said.

"That's right," Frances said, adding her pence.

"No!" he shouted, coming up to his feet. "No!"

"My boy," the marquess said gently, "I don't hold any hope of tracking down Henry, more's the pity. The only way to bring out the parties responsible is to go to Newmarket."

"With Flying Davie," Frances said.

"We would be on our guard," said Marcus, edging into the ring. "Nothing could happen."

"All of you are about in the head!" Hawk shouted. "Frances could have been killed, dammit!"

"But I wasn't, and it wasn't me they were after."

"You could have been, and it is possible that it *was* you," Hawk retorted. "Remember, Frances, a disgruntled lover of yours?"

"You will cease riding that particular lame horse, Hawk," Frances said. "I will not be drawn or distracted."

"Infernal female! Men should be saved from your sort."

"*My sort!*" Frances squawked.

"Well, this man wasn't saved," said the marquess, his eyes twinkling at his son's flushed, very angry face. "You might as well give in, my boy. You do have a bit of grace left."

"This is not a democracy," Hawk said.

"Ah, I was forgetting," Frances drawled. "The lord and very superior master speaks."

"They are my horses, you are my wife, and, Marcus, I might add, you work for me! As for you, Father, why don't you take your opinions back to Chandos Chase?"

"Not a prayer of that happening, my boy," the marquess said jovially. "Damn, if I haven't enjoyed myself this much in an age—not that I wanted to see you harmed, my dear."

Frances waved this away. "It doesn't make sense, Hawk, to have the horses eating their heads off, paying trainers, and all for nothing. Besides, if you are truly worried for my safety, I promise not to let myself out of your sight."

"You are ill," Hawk said, digging in his heels at the edge of the cliff.

"I shall be just fine in a week," Frances said. "Flying Davie and Clancy's Pride are in prime condition. As for Tamerlane, we can leave him well-guarded here."

"I suppose you have already commissioned another traveling stall for Clancy's Pride?"

"Of course. Do you not recall my winnings from the York races? It will arrive before we wish to leave." Actually, she'd borrowed the money from her household accounts. She hoped Hawk wouldn't remember that she'd sent that two hundred pounds to her sisters.

He wanted to shake her until her smug teeth rattled, but it was to be denied him. He said something very uncomplimentary about the Earl of Ruthven's antecedents and stomped out of the room.

"The lad will come about," the marquess said, his voice complacent.

"The *lad*," Frances said in an acid voice, "needs to have a swift kick to his . . . shins."

"Just so, my dear. Just so."

Marcus blurted out, "I am going to marry Miss Melcher!"

"Oh dear," Frances said, feigning distress, "now my dear husband will taunt me with losing a prime flirt!"

Three days later, Henry's body was found in an alley in a seamy part of York. He'd been stabbed.

Hawk went on a rampage.

Frances offered Lord Elliston, the magistrate, another cup of tea. He was an older gentleman, and he looked very frail to Frances, until she saw his intense fanatical dark eyes.

Lord Elliston watched the earl pace the drawing room. It was most fatiguing to watch him. He set his teacup down and looked at Lady Frances, a most lovely young lady. Her lips, at the moment, were rather pursed as she followed her husband's progress.

"I don't imagine it was the result of a brawl, my lord," Lord Elliston said after a moment. "One wound, to the heart, clean it was, so to speak."

"I had no doubt of that at all," Hawk said.

"A cup of tea, my lord?" Frances said to her husband.

He shook his head impatiently. "Someone must have seen something," he said after a moment. "I think I shall bring in a Bow Street runner."

"You are quite right," Frances said. "I cannot imagine our villain hiring yet another man to do his dirty work."

"Have you any notion at all, my lord," Lord Elliston said, "of who could be behind this?"

"Yes," said Hawk, "but I have no proof."

"May I ask who?"

"Lord Dempsey," Hawk said.

Lord Elliston looked not at all surprised. "The man has quite an irregular reputation, I fear. Like you, my lord, I have my own racing stables, nothing grand of course, but still, I am aware of things. Egremont, the

Earl of Derby, was telling me some few months ago that the number of supposed gentlemen involved in the racing corruption is most disheartening." He rose to his feet. "I think your idea of hiring a Bow Street runner a good one, my lord. Perhaps you can speak of your concerns to the Duke of Portland. He will be at Newmarket. You know what he says, of course, about racing: 'Luck or skill or knavery decides the victory.' "

"Damn," said Hawk. "Frances, go rest now, you're looking somewhat peaked. Marcus, come with me. We shall send a message today to Bow Street."

29

What bloody man is that?
—SHAKESPEARE

"You fool! My God, man, do you know what you've done?"

Edmund Lacy, Lord Chalmers, shook with rage as he faced Lord Dempsey. "You tell me you didn't *know* that the woman was Rothermere's mistress! Idiot!"

Lord Dempsey tried to make light of it. "She's no longer under Rothermere's protection—why should she care, even if she did wonder what I was speaking of? In any case, who would believe some silly trollop?"

"Then why," Edmund said very softly, "did Amalie Corleau pack up her belongings and leave? Oh yes, she is gone, I checked, and Hawk had extended the lease on her house until the end of the quarter. Why would she leave if not out of fear of recriminations from you? There is little doubt in my mind that she has informed Hawk of what you said."

Edmund watched Lord Dempsey rise from his chair and pour himself a glass of port. Bloody fool! He'd never liked the man, had always feared what he would say in his cups. And he had spoken—to Hawk's mistress, of all people! Charles Lewiston, Lord Dempsey, and Nevil had always been good friends, until Nevil had become weak and frightened. Christ, what was he to do? Surely Hawk must have doubts about him now, grave doubts.

Henry, the stupid clod, was thankfully dead in York, with no traces to them. Dempsey had enjoyed killing him, had even bragged about it to Edmund, saying, "Pleaded with me, the little swine, so I made it quick."

"Kill them," said Lord Dempsey suddenly.

Edmund stared at him. He saw the bland viciousness in Dempsey's pale blue eyes, recognized that if pushed, the man would also kill him if he felt cornered. "Who?" Edmund asked, trying to keep himself calm. "Both Hawk and his lady?"

"Certainly. If the mistress is any sign of Rothermere's taste in women, I should like to spend a bit of time with his wife before sending her on to her reward."

"No," Edmund said. "All of England would be up in arms. Doubt not that the damned Marquess of Chandos knows all the facts. Even if he couldn't prove anything, we would be hounded out of England. The man has too many powerful friends, not to mention all the men Hawk knows in the War Ministry. I have no desire to flee the country, not with Napoleon spitting on every Englishman he can get his hands on."

"Then what is your plan?" Dempsey demanded, pouring himself another glass of port. "We've tried it your way, Chalmers, and it's been a damned failure."

"Flying Davie cannot go to Newmarket. If the horse can be destroyed, accidentally of course, then we are safe. Surely Rothermere will have his suspicions, but there would be no proof." Edmund suddenly smiled. "There is another thing, Dempsey. I have Lady Beatrice in the palm of my hand—"

"What part of her lovely anatomy?" Dempsey asked, his voice as leering as his look.

"Shut up, you fool, and listen! Any complications,

and I would most certainly use her for protection." He wondered if he could persuade her to marry him now. Surely then Hawk would have to back off. And the marquess, of course.

"What of the other racers?"

Edmund Lacy sat back in his chair and thoughtfully tapped his steepled fingers. "First we must plan to rid ourselves of Flying Davie. It shouldn't be too difficult . . . with a proper plan." His hands suddenly clenched into fists. "Damn Nevil anyway! If the stupid sod hadn't been such a weakling, none of this would be necessary!"

"I quite liked Nevil," said Lord Dempsey, and Edmund could only stare at him.

Hawk gently pushed Frances' damp hair from her forehead. Her breathing was still erratic and he fondly gazed down at her still-heaving breasts, and her beautiful dark pink nipples, still taut, lightly tantalizing the hair on his chest. Her shoulder still held faint bruises, but she had no more pain, just a bit of soreness.

"Hawk?"

"Yes, love?"

"You're still inside me." He moved convulsively at her words. "I love it when you're inside me." She arched up a bit to keep him deep.

He lowered his head and lightly caressed her lips, moist and sweet under his. "Do you think you will still want me inside you in fifty years?"

She gave him a heavy-lidded look. "Fifty years?" she asked. "Is that all?"

He laughed and rolled off her. She pouted, and he was startled at the innocent sensuousness of it. He balanced himself on his elbow, stretching along her side.

He touched his fingertips to her pouting lips. "Where did you learn how to do that?"

The sparkle of fun was back in her eyes. "I watched Viola perfect it in front of her mirror. It drove all the neighboring young men wild."

"May I request that you pout only for me?"

"Perhaps, if it is truly a request and not one of your lordly orders."

"I believe that orders should refer to the priesthood, don't you?"

She grinned up at him, saying wickedly, "You are almost as intriguing after you make love to me as during."

"Amalie told me quite clearly that a woman enjoys talk after she'd drowned with pleasure, not just snores."

She punched him in the chest.

"I have only seven years on you, my dear," he said in a marveling voice. "And you still can't keep up with me . . . verbally, that is. As for the rest of it . . ." He grinned down at her, and lay his palm on her belly, grinning more widely at her quiver. "Yes, the rest of it, well, I believe we can safely toss that damned jar of cream out the window."

That was certainly true, thought Frances. "You think, doubtless, that is because you are a man—your verbal greatness, that is."

"That and the greater natural intelligence that goes along with masculine endowments."

"You are tempting me to put some of that horrid horse-colic medicine in your tea!"

He had no retort to that, which surprised her. He said finally, "I should have seen you then. Perhaps not before we were married, but certainly afterward."

"You did see me! You blanched each time, and looked as if you were in acute pain."

"No, really *seen* you. Even on your hands and knees

kneeling over the chamber pot, your face a bit green. You weren't wearing those spectacles then, nor one of those prized caps of yours."

"I felt too awful to care," she said, grimacing in memory. "You were going to make love to me that night, weren't you?"

"I was going to try to," he said, and lightly moved his open hand up to caress her breast. He felt the slight quiver, and smiled.

"What if I had been truly ugly?"

"Then I would have had to concentrate on your beautiful body," he said promptly, his fingers now moving quickly downward. She was damp and sticky with him, and he wanted her again, desperately. He no longer questioned his intense need for her, he accepted it now, and reveled in it. A wife, he thought. *His* wife.

"Oh," she gasped, unconsciously raised her arm to bring him over her, and gasped again at the twinge of pain.

"Careful, love. Do you want me to drive you crazy with more pleasure?"

She nodded, knowing quite well that she wanted him, all of him.

"You are mine," she said, and lurched up at the incredible sensations created by his fingers.

"Yes, and I intend to be until I curl up my toes and pass to the hereafter. Now, where was I?"

He eased himself between her thighs, parting them widely. She blinked at him, feeling a moment of embarrassment at being so exposed to his eyes, but he merely shook his head, smiling at her. His eyes, darker now with building desire, studied her, following his caressing fingers. "So beautiful," he said.

Her muscles tightened, then slackened. "You know how much I want you, don't you, Hawk?"

"Yes," he said on a deep satisfied sigh, "yes, I do, love."

"Then why do you continue to tease me?"

"Tease you? Hmmm. Actually, I'm simply ensuring that you are truly gentled and weak and silly before I give you what you want."

"You bounder!" Then she gasped, and her eyes glazed. "Hawk!" she cried, and brought him into her.

Later, when Frances was asleep in his arms, his mind returned to the miserable problems they faced. They were to leave for Newmarket on the morrow. He was frightened; he admitted it to himself. And he felt helpless, no matter all the precautions he'd taken. He thought of Mr. Samuel Uckley, the Bow Street runner, and smiled into the darkness. A most unprepossessing little man was Mr. Uckley, like a ferret blessed with a hook nose.

"I don't like this, milord," Mr. Uckley had informed him as he tugged on his left ear. "I wants to bring my friend Mr. Horace Bammer in on this. Horace can stay here and poke about and I'll come with you to Newmarker."

And that was that, thought Hawk. He wouldn't have objected in any case. Mr. Bammer would provide more protection here at Desborough Hall.

He felt Frances' fingers tangle in the matt of hair on his chest. He felt her warm breath against his shoulder. He wondered if she would remember in the morning the words she'd shouted at her climax. "Do you truly love me, Frances?" he asked quietly. She murmured something in her sleep, and he was pleased. But worry continued to nag at him. How to keep her safe? His body grew taut the more he thought about the damnable situation. He had suddenly thought of the captain of the *Keymark,* Nevil's yacht, while he reviewed everything he knew with Mr. Uckley. He couldn't remember the captain's name. Nor had he ever seen Nevil's yacht, now his yacht, he'd realized with a start. But it was true, as Mr. Uckley had pointed out, that if there had been foul play, the captain had to know of it, and that meant, of course, that the "blinkin' cove" had been bribed to keep his mouth shut. Hawk decided then to send a message to Southampton to the *Keymark* and demand that the captain come to Newmarket. Then he would get answers by hook or by crook.

Hawk cursed softly and Frances said quite distinctly, "Alicia, did you feel ill when you were with child?"

Good God, thought Hawk. Unfortunately, the absent Alicia didn't answer Frances' question.

On the edge of sleep, Hawk had his own endless stream of questions, and none of them with answers. Why did they want the Desborough stock? Why did they want Flying Davie dead? Ah, Edmund, I think you are one of the villains in this, but dear God, I hope Beatrice isn't. He couldn't bear the thought that his sister could actually be involved.

Was Frances pregnant?

The Desborough procession pulled into the courtyard of the Lame Duck Inn the following evening at six o'clock. Situated on the outskirts of Doncaster, near the Doncaster racing tracks, the inn boasted a stable of requisite size, enough rooms for the fifteen members of their party, and a private dining room.

The day had been warm and Frances had hated every minute spent inside the stuffy carriage. Agnes wasn't the most stimulating of companions, her conversation consisting primarily of comments on each village they passed through, regardless of its claim to the unique or, more likely than not, the commonplace. This, of course, for her Scottish mistress, who had never seen England and required constant edification. Frances wanted to throttle Agnes by the time she alighted from the carriage. All her stubborn husband's fault, of course.

"You will not ride with your shoulder still sore," Hawk had said, and Frances cajoled, pleaded, shouted, and cursed, all to no effect, blast him!

"I will not take a single chance that your horse could become excited and you hurt your shoulder again."

"Damnable, overbearing, arrogant—"

"I beg your pardon, my lady?"

"Oh, nothing, Agnes! I am just bored sitting here doing nothing. The day is so very fine, not too hot, save in here, of course. That dratted man . . ."

Frances found no fault with either the Lame Duck Inn or its proprietor, Mr. Smith. Lord and Lady Rothermere were treated with great deference and provided a meal that tested Mrs. Smith's culinary abilities.

When their meal was over, Hawk rose, kissed Frances, and said, "Why don't you get some sleep now, my dear?"

"And you, Hawk?"

"I am your gallant knight. I will stand outside your door, lance in hand."

"I should rather have you inside my door. About that lance—"

"Frances! You shock me!"

"I but speak the way you do, husband," she said, gazing up at him through her thick lashes.

He felt that inevitable surge of lust for her, and it required all his strength of purpose to leave her. He contented himself with a kiss that left him breathing hard.

He slept near to the stable, Mr. Uckley's loud snores

dinning in his ears. They managed a fairly early start the following morning, their destination that day the King George Inn in Grantham.

Hawk slept in his saddle, a trick he'd learned in his army days on the Peninsula. Marcus, saddle-sore, rode with Frances in her carriage.

That evening, Hawk again left Frances and took himself to the stables to keep guard.

He was drowsy, his eyelids very heavy. Something was wrong, he knew it. He heard Belvis snoring. Something was very wrong. . . .

Shouts of "Fire! Fire!" jerked him awake. He stared blankly at the flaming roof of the stable, then shook his head vigorously to clear his dulled mind.

"Oh God," he said, and began to shake Belvis violently.

He heard the screams of the horses and bounded to his feet.

His movements were at first sluggish. Men were filling the courtyard, flinging buckets of water on the stable roof, and bravely trying to save the horses within.

Suddenly the heavens opened and it rained torrents. Within moments, the fire was out, leaving only dismal trails of smoke weaving upward.

Hawk, his face blackened with smoke, looked at Belvis. "We were fools," he said. "Complete fools."

"Drugged?" said Marcus.

"I'm the one to blame," said Mr. Uckley, looking so abashed that Hawk hurried to reassure him. It was Marcus who was holding Flying Davie's halter, the horse quivering with fear, his eyes rolling wildly, but otherwise unhurt.

"Frances!" Hawk suddenly sent frantic eyes toward the inn. "See to Clancy's Pride!" he shouted over his shoulder, his long legs eating up the distance.

She was sleeping soundly, a drugged sleep, and he
shook her until she finally opened groggy eyes.

"You weren't the target, Frances," he said slowly,
stroking her hair. "Someone drugged our food and set
the stables on fire. We've been saved by an act of
nature. It's raining so hard the roads will probably be
flooded."

"The horses?"

"Safe, thank God. Belvis is seeing to them. It was
Marcus who brought Flying Davie out unharmed."

Inquiries made of the owner led nowhere. He knew
nothing, indeed was indignant at such a suggestion
that the food was drugged. No, no strangers had slipped
into *his* kitchen. Of course he would make further
inquiries, but Hawk placed little reliance upon his
doing anything.

The roads were very muddy the next morning, but
not impassable. Hawk elected to continue to Newmarket. They arrived, bone-weary, at nearly ten o'clock
the following night at the Queen's Inn. The marquess
was waiting for them, his face alight with pleasure.

"I'd hoped you'd push on," he said, embracing his
son, then Frances.

Hawk told him what had happened, and the marquess looked ready to explode with fury. "It's too
much, dammit!" he yelled. Frances, afraid that he
would expire with apoplexy, offered him a glass of
Madeira. "Incidentally, Hawk," he said after a moment, "I've sent a message to Captain Anders of the
Keymark, asking the fellow to join us here."

Hawk smiled. "I did also," he said, "only I didn't
know the fellow's name."

"I should have thought of it sooner," the marquess
continued, upset with himself. "Damn, I've been a
blind fool!"

"Don't distress yourself further, Father. Now, would you like to join us for a late dinner?"

Newmarket was a town unlike the others they'd passed through, Frances saw the following morning. It boasted many inns and shops and stables, since for many years its livelihood had been dependent on the races.

" 'Tis the Duke of Portland who owns much of Newmarket Heath," the marquess told her as they strolled along the main street. "He has plans, I hear, to clear off acres of the furze and scrub and lay down grass for training grounds. Costly, though, probably will take him years to get it done, if ever."

When they reached the stables Hawk had rented for the horses and their trainers, Frances grinned to see many gentlemen clustered about the horses' traveling stalls.

"Fascinating idea, my lord," one gentleman was saying to Hawk. "You are to be congratulated."

"Actually, it was my wife's doing. She was the one who found the smithy in York." He looked to see her, and beckoned. "Here she is, gentlemen."

Frances was quite aware that the gentlemen found no favor with *her* contribution.

"I say, my lord," Sir Johnathon Luddle said, "this one stall has been damaged. Fire?"

"Yes, there was an unfortunate . . . accident on our way here."

"Your cattle all right?" asked another gentleman.

"Yes," Hawk said.

The man snorted. "Damned nonsense, if you ask me, and I'll wager it was anything but an accident! We're all paying fortunes to protect our cattle from villains. Did you hear about Ashland's problems?"

There were many ladies in Newmarket and Frances

quickly discovered they were all as interested in gambling as the gentlemen. Gambling, flirting, and gossip as well, in equal portions, she quickly amended to herself. As for herself, she had fifty pounds. It would all go on Flying Davie. Only her husband would be the recipient of her flirting.

There was a party that evening at the Golden Goose, the entire inn having been hired by Lord Delacort, a very elderly gentleman with gout who held court from a mammoth chair in the center of the large parlor, his leg propped up on several pillows. A nervous-looking man, reed-thin, stood by his shoulder, ready, Frances thought, to spring into action when Lord Delacort so much as whispered a command.

"I should own the damned inn," Lord Delacort was complaining in a loud, quite carrying voice. "Ridiculous to make old Neddy, the proprietor, rich as Croesus. Timmons, you will see to it tomorrow."

"Yes, my lord," said Timmons quickly.

Lord Delacort appeared to ruminate on this for a while, then beckoned imperiously at Frances. "Come here, girl!"

"Don't worry, Frances," the marquess said in her ear, "the old codger doesn't bite—at least I don't think he's taken *that* up yet. When he was twenty years younger, though, I wouldn't have put anything past him."

Frances merely grinned, saw that Hawk was caught in close conversation with a good half-dozen gentlemen, and started toward the imperious old man.

"Oh dear," said the marquess suddenly. "Beatrice!"

"And Edmund?" Frances asked in a low voice.

"I don't see him. Oh dear, what the devil shall I do?"

"I think, sir, you should greet her naturally. I shall see what Lord Delacort wishes."

"Who are you, girl?" Lord Delacort asked instantly the moment Frances curtsied before him.

"Why, I am Frances Hawksbury, Countess of Rothermere."

"Ah, so you're the chit responsible for those traveling horse stalls. Can't imagine how ye'd do that. A chit and a woman, after all."

"That is certainly true, my lord, and for the other, why, what does it matter?"

"Quite a quick tongue you've got, young lady," Lord Delacort said, bushy brows raised at her.

Frances smiled back limpidly.

"Bring me a glass of port, Timmons," he commanded in the next breath.

"But, my lord!"

"Shut your stupid trap, Timmons, that fool crackbones hasn't a brain in his rattling head!"

"I think I shall have some punch," Frances said. "Would you care to join me?"

Lord Delacort glared up at her, the bushy gray brows now a straight line above his eyes. "Think to wrap me around your finger, do you, girl? Just like that husband of yours?"

Frances laughed at that. The thought of Hawk succumbing to any blandishments from her was vastly amusing. Well, perhaps not all that amusing, she added, smiling wistfully to herself.

"I have heard he is a good man," Lord Delacort said, pointing a gnarled finger toward Hawk. "No one believed he would take to racing after he took his brother's title and estates. Ah, Nevil. He was a one!"

One what? Frances wondered. She accepted a cup of punch from Mr. Timmons, thanked him, and offered it to Lord Delacort. He snorted, cursed poor Mr. Timmons with great fluency, and took the cup.

Frances thoughtfully drank a bit of the rack punch.

It was very sweet and she didn't particularly care for it. She said after a moment, her voice carefully neutral, "Did you know the former Earl of Rothermere, my lord? Nevil Hawksbury?"

"Certainly," Lord Delacort said on another snort. "Shouldn't speak ill of the dead and all that, but I didn't like the fellow! Always prancing about, pretending he knew more about training and racing than the best men in England. Nonsense, of course."

"Yes," said Frances, somewhat disappointed. She didn't care a bit about Nevil prancing. "You are racing tomorrow, my lord?"

Lord Delacort grunted. "Don't think you'll take the prize on the five-mile race, girl! My Persian is a stout fellow, strong as the devil. What's your thoroughbred's name?"

"Flying Davie, sir," said Frances. "He's but a four-year-old, but I fancy he will make an excellent showing. He is also quite strong and his will to win most remarkable. His first race was in York, and he won."

"Stupid name," said Lord Delacort, and drank the remainder of his punch. "Awful stuff, fit only for females."

"I believe, my lord," Frances said with grave honesty, "that it is even too awful for me."

"Just what does your father-in-law have to say about you, Miss Impertinence?"

"He adores me," said Frances blandly.

"Harrumph," said Lord Delacort. Frances thought that escape was a possibility, for Lord Delacort appeared to be focused on something else. Before she could make her escape, however, his lordship said in a ruminative voice, "You know, girl, I lost a very valuable foal—and he'd be four years old now. His name was Starfire. My grandson named him that, cute lad."

"He died, sir?" Frances asked without much interest.

was so formidable that she found she shuddered, and
not from the cool evening air.

They reached the left wing of the stables. It looked
an armed fortress. Belvis, three grooms, two trainers,
and Mr. Uckley surrounded the two stalls.

"You take no chances, I see," Lord Delacort said,
blinking as they came into the well-lit stables.

"No, sir, not a one," said Hawk.

Frances placed a gentle hand on Lord Delacort's
arm. "Sir, this is most important. You must see Flying
Davie. Belvis, would you please?"

Belvis opened the stall and brought Flying Davie
out of his stall.

There was absolute silence, all eyes trained on the
horse and the gouty old man.

Flying Davie stood docilely, regarding the intruders
with baleful patience.

Frances stared at Lord Delacort. She saw his eyes
widen, heard him whisper, "Starfire."

She felt a strange sort of relief, and her eyes met her
husband's. She saw pain there, and felt immense sor-
row that it had ended this way.

Beatrice said sharply, "I don't understand any of
this! Why is his lordship calling him Starfire? Really,
Philip—"

Hawk turned very slowly to face his sister. "Bea,"
he said very gently, "I fear that our brother was involved in stealing horses—foals bred from racers."

"That is absurd, ridiculous! Has *she* been filling
your ears with that . . . drivel?"

"I fear it isn't drivel, Bea. We should probably have
figured it out much sooner, what with no bills of sale
and Belvis' memory that Flying Davie's supposed dam
had died a year before he was foaled. I'm sorry, Bea,
but Edmund had perforce to be involved with Nevil in

this. Lord Dempsey as well. As to the others, we do not know."

The marquess said, "It was clever of them, very clever. Who would ever suspect such a respected stable as Desborough of being involved in such a scheme?"

He added after a moment, his voice trembling just a bit, "It also appears, my dear, that your brother was likely murdered by his accomplices."

Beatrice's anger turned to panic. "No! Not Edmund! No!"

Frances thought Beatrice would faint. Her face was perfectly white, her hand clutching her father's sleeve.

"The accidents started after Hawk refused to sell to Edmund," Frances said, feeling very sorry for her sister-in-law. "Don't you see, Bea? If Hawk had sold all the Desborough stock to Edmund, no one would have ever discovered the truth. Because Flying Davie's markings are so distinctive, he would probably have been shipped to America and sold for a princely sum. As for the others, and we don't know how many are involved, Edmund probably could have raced them without fear of their being recognized by their real owners."

"Your logic is inescapable, Frances," said a soft voice from behind them.

"Edmund!" Beatrice shrieked, whirling about. "Tell them it isn't true, tell them—"

"I cannot, my dear. It is true, you see." Edmund's pistol was trained on Beatrice's breast. None of the men moved. He continued to Hawk, his voice emotionless, "You have the luck of the devil, Hawk. I was most distraught when I learned Frances rode Tamerlane and not Flying Davie that morning. Then, of course, the damned horse should have been killed in the fire at Grantham."

"It is no use, Edmund," Hawk said.

"Unfortunately I must agree with you. However, I have no intention of fleeing the country without some ... security. You have too many fighting friends, Hawk, and I know they would search me out. I intend to ensure that they don't. Come here, my dear Beatrice. Now."

"You damned bastard!" the marquess shouted. "Don't you dare—"

"Shut up, old man!"

"Edmund," Hawk said very quietly, "why did you kill Nevil?"

"I will tell you, Hawk," Edmund Lacy said, his eyes narrowing. "Your brother was greedy, then a weak fool. We were making plans that week on his yacht, great plans, but Nevil was frightened. He wanted out. He was in his cups, incidentally, and Dempsey, well ... he—"

"Nevil was a fool," said Lord Dempsey, coming into the stable, a deadly pistol in his hand. "I merely helped him over the railing. He was too drunk to save himself.

"You filthy bastard!" the marquess thundered, and stepped toward Dempsey. "You murdered my son!"

"Don't, Father," Hawk said, putting a restraining hand on his father's shoulder.

"Now, as I was saying," Edmund continued, "I have need of you, Beatrice."

"You bloody coves!" Mr. Uckley exclaimed in frustrated fury. He forced himself to be calm. "You'll never escape with the lady. Best give it up now."

"I was right about Hawk's women," said Lord Dempsey, his eyes traveling from Frances' face to the tips of her slippers. "I'll bring her also."

"You touch her," Hawk said very softly, "and I'll kill you myself, very slowly and with great enjoyment."

Lord Dempsey laughed. "You won't do a damned

thing, my lord! And if you're stupid enough to try, I'll kill her."

Frances edged closer to her husband.

"I don't suppose we can do away with all of them, eh?" Lord Dempsey said to Edmund, disappointment in his voice.

"Don't be a fool," Edmund snapped. "Leave Frances be. We require only Beatrice."

"I won't go with you," Beatrice said very clearly. Her eyes were steady upon Edmund Lacy's face. She repeated, more forcefully, "I won't go with you. I cannot believe I was so deceived in your character, my lord."

"A pity about my character, but I fear you have no choice, my dear," Edmund said. He indicated the pistol in his hand. "Come here, Bea, now."

"You betrayed me, you used me," Beatrice said. "You killed my brother." She drew a deep breath. "You will have to kill me, for I will not come."

Edmund Lacy looked startled for a moment. "Such fire from you, my dear. Dempsey, keep that pistol of yours trained on the marquess. Any of you try anything, and the old man will die."

Edmund grabbed Beatrice and pulled her roughly against him, trying to still her flailing arms.

Beatrice struggled, her nails raking his face. Edmund raised his hand to strike her, then froze. In that instant, there was an unearthly shriek—a woman's shriek.

Amalie jumped on Lord Dempsey's back, her hands clamped about his jaw, jerking back his head.

Then there was pandemonium.

Frances blinked at the sight of Beatrice smashing Edmund's jaw with her right fist with incredible strength and venom. He reeled and was caught by Mr. Uckley.

Dempsey, a wild woman on his back, struggled,

cursed, tried to aim the pistol, but Hawk was on him, forcing the pistol upward. The pistol fired and hit the unfortunate Mr. Timmons in the arm.

Beatrice, Marcus, and Mr. Uckley were pounding Edmund to his knees.

Hawk drove his fist into Lord Dempsey's jaw. The man groaned and slipped to the straw-covered floor, unconscious.

Hawk pulled Amalie to her feet and brushed her off. He was grinning widely into her flushed, triumphant face, until he heard his wife say, "Thank you, ma'am, you saved us. Who are you? How are you here?"

He cursed softly, the full import of Amalie's rescue bursting into his now-uncluttered mind.

He cleared his throat. "Frances, my dear, this is a very good friend of mine. Let Mr. Uckley fetch the magistrate, then the three of us will enjoy a comfortable talk."

It was another hour before Hawk, Frances, and Amalie were ensconced in the parlor. The marquess had escorted Beatrice to her bedchamber. Lord Delacort had most solicitously looked after poor Mr. Timmons, yelling at the hapless doctor each time Mr. Timmons happened to make a sound.

"This is Amalie," Hawk said simply.

Frances knew, of course. She gazed at the beautiful Frenchwoman, and without a word, walked to her and embraced her. "You are very brave and we thank you. For everything."

Hawk breathed a sigh of relief and proceeded with manly stupidity to blunder. He grinned, and drawled with woeful cockiness, "*Everything*, Frances?"

Both women turned on him.

"You will not act the bastard, Hawk," said Amalie, "or I shall regret saving your English hide."

She shot a look at Frances, caught her nod, and Hawk felt his arm suddenly jerk behind his back by Amalie. He shot her an incredulous look, then yelped, doubling over, pushed to his knees by Amalie as Frances' right fist connected with his belly.

Frances was dusting her hands together, a smile of smug enjoyment on her face. "I was almost as good as Beatrice, I think," she said.

"He perhaps deserves more," said Amalie, releasing his arm. She stood over him, her hands on her hips.

"I rather like a man on his knees," said Frances.

Hawk didn't move. He wasn't that stupid. They were killers, he knew it. He looked from one to the other, and threw up his hands. "Ladies, I surrender!"

"A bit of groveling might save you further mortification and pain, my lord," said Frances, enjoying herself immensely.

This was too much. Hawk roared to his feet, grabbed his wife against him, only to feel Amalie's very strong fingers in his hair, pulling with all her might.

He gritted his teeth and felt his eyes water. Escape, he thought. Only a complete fool would stay. He quickly released Frances, fought free of Amalie's very strong fingers, and fled from the parlor.

He came to an abrupt halt in the outside corridor, frowning ferociously as he heard the gales of laughter from the two women.

"What is this, my boy?"

Hawk turned a chagrined face to his father.

"What the devil is going on in there? Don't tell me you were idiot enough to introduce your mistress to your wife?"

"They nearly killed me," said Hawk, rubbing his hand over his belly.

The marquess gaped at him. "They?"

"Attacked by two furies. Brought to my knees. Made to grovel. Unmanned."

"I think that about covers it," said Frances, giggling in the open doorway, Amalie beside her.

"Oh my God," said the marquess. "Excuse me, my boy, but I am not fool enough to get involved in this!"

"Coward!" Hawk shouted after his departing sire.

"Well, my lord," Frances said, "Amalie and I are now ready to discuss matters. If you swear to keep your mouth shut, unless spoken to, we will allow you to join us."

Brutality and then a tea party, Hawk thought in some disgust some minutes later when the three of them were seated in a most civilized manner, teacups in their laps.

Amalie said, "I couldn't just leave for France, not knowing what that awful man would do."

"You are very brave, Amalie," Frances said. She tried desperately not to picture Hawk making love to this exquisite piece of womanhood.

Amalie merely shrugged. "All is well now," she said. She beamed at Hawk and Frances. "As our magnificent French playwright Corneille said, 'And the combat ceased for want of combatants.' You are now satisfied with this man, my lady?"

Frances gave her husband a very drawing look. "I shall keep him in good form, Amalie, I promise."

"A brute for a wife," Hawk remarked.

"The logic of the heart is absurd," Amalie said, and raised her teacup in a toast.

And good-bye to my bluestocking mistress, Hawk thought.

"Julie de Lespinasse said that, didn't she?" Frances asked, her eyes sparkling.

"Yes," Amalie said, bestowing another pleased smile on her.

"My governess, Adelaide, was much taken with her," said Frances.

The rest of my life with a bluestocking wife, Hawk thought, and lowered his head, rumbling laughter erupting from his throat.

The two women looked at the Earl of Rothermere, then at each other. Amalie shook her head. "I wonder if the strain has been too much for him."

"If it is strain he suffers," said Frances, "it is most certainly a very lordly strain."

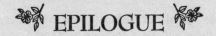

❧ EPILOGUE ❧

A loose end is never tidy.
—*EIGHTEENTH-CENTURY
PROVERB*

"Finally, my boy, finally! I knew you could do it if you truly set your mind to it!" The marquess beamed at his strutting son and vigorously shook his hand.

"What?" Frances protested loudly. "Your *boy* did little enough, my lord. I did everything!"

"Well, not quite everything," Hawk said, leaning down to ruffle his wife's hair. "And he does look like me, Frances. That in itself tells the tale—men and husbands are much stronger, their will is the more—"

"I suggest," said Lord Ruthven, grinning at his son-in-law, "that you retreat just a bit. Women, you know, Hawk, get strange notions."

At that point, Charles Philip Desborough Hawksbury, Viscount Linley, let out a furious howl.

"Men begin very early," Sophia observed, "to get their way."

"And they never stop howling, Sophia," Frances said. She saw that her husband was on the point of saying something in all likelihood very improper, and added quickly, "I shall feed this little man, then join you downstairs."

Hawk kissed his wife, then joined his father and father-in-law.

Frances heard her father-in-law say, "Yes, indeed, my grandson will be a famous horseman and racer. I can see it in his eyes already."

Hawk said, "He has Frances' eyes, Father."

"Just so, my boy," said the marquess, "just so."

Frances shook her head, imagining the look on her husband's face.

She smiled up at Sophia as she unfastened her gown and put Charles to her breast.

"He is a beautiful child, Frances."

"Yes, he is."

"I thought that Hawk was going to box the doctor's ears. He was in a state, my dear."

"He always is," said Frances, grinning. "What do you hear from Clare?"

"She is studying with Mr. Turner, a most unexpected honor for her. What is even more of a surprise, her husband most heartily approves."

"I always believed Daniel to be a prize catch, and a most reasonable man," said Frances.

Sophia's eyes twinkled. "He is also beginning to believe himself much beleaguered, my dear. Viola is driving him wild with all her beaux. He complains that he is forever stumbling over her lapdogs, as he calls the young gentlemen. Of course, Adelaide merely smiles in that unconcerned way of hers."

"You must tell Daniel that Adelaide will see that Viola's lapdogs do nothing improper." Frances stroked the black fuzz on top of her small son's head. "Daniel will survive all Viola's machinations," she added.

Sophia shook her head. "When I think that Hawk could have possibly chosen Viola! Dear heavens, what a mismatch that would have been. Even more appalling is the thought of Hawk marrying Clare!"

"The marquess firmly believes in fate, Sophia. It is his august opinion that no matter my disguise or lack of one, I would have ended up with my husband. I wonder if that is true."

Sophia chuckled. "All I can remember is wanting to throttle you, Frances!"

"Then you can imagine how Hawk feels upon occasion. It infuriates him when Otis and Mrs. Jerkins always side with me."

"You are happy, are you not, Frances?"

"More than I could ever have imagined," Frances said fervently, shifting her small son to her other breast. "And you, my little darling, will indeed be a great horseman. You do have my eyes, don't you?" Frances raised her own sparkling eyes to her stepmother's face. "I forgot to tell you, Sophia, but we are going to Ascot in two weeks." She continued, her eyes lighting with anticipation. "Flying Davie is running, of course, as is Tamerlane."

"I was most surprised to hear that Lord Delacort gave you the racer as a sort of belated wedding present."

"I wasn't," said Frances in a droll voice. "I believe if the marquess would allow it, Lord Delacort would adopt Hawk. He visits often now. With poor Mr. Timmons in tow, of course."

Sophia chuckled. "I understand from Hawk that you correspond with Amalie."

"Yes indeed. She and her Robert are doing quite well with the farm." Frances paused, sighing a bit. "It is odd, but I normally don't remember all that awfulness. —Edmund killing himself, and Lord Dempsey shot whilst trying to escape from Mr. Uckley. I feel so sorry for Beatrice."

"You wouldn't, not any longer, my love, if you had seen her in London two weeks ago. Quite the belle, you know. Scandals are forgotten, particularly when the Countess of Rutherford runs off with her head groom! Now, that was most titillating!"

"Frances, come along, will you?"

She looked up to see her husband standing in the doorway, his eyes fastened on her suckling son. She gave him her special smile, and Sophia quickly rose.

"Why do you not keep her company, Hawk, and I shall entertain the gentlemen downstairs."

"Well, Frances? How much are you going to feed that hungry little beggar?" He sat down beside her on the sofa.

"He is as you are, my lord," she said primly. "As Sophia said, a male, no matter his size, doesn't change. He simply becomes more so."

"Well, perhaps a bit more so, but his, er, preferences do shift," Hawk said. "Incidentally, Lyonel is here to pay his respects to the heir. His Great-Aunt Lucia is with him."

"No wonder you escaped up here!"

"You are right about that," he said fervently. "She was readying to turn her cannon on me, and Lyonel—blast him—was egging her on."

Charles sent a blurry look toward his father and burped.

"That is one thing he excels in," Frances said, lifting him over her shoulder.

"The major thing I excel in is denied me," Hawk said on a mournful sigh.

"You are a randy goat, my lord!"

"Frances," her husband said in a wounded voice, "your mind travels most improper roads. I was thinking about riding with you, of course."

"Riding?" she asked, a brow arched.

"That too," Hawk said, and kissed her laughing mouth.

ABOUT THE AUTHOR

Catherine Coulter, best-selling author of both Regency romances and historical romances, faithfully watches *Perry Mason* reruns, scrounges in used bookstores for unheard-of goodies, and has an incredible crush on Mr. July—1987.

All sixteen of her novels are available, including such Regencies as *Rebel Bride, An Honorable Offer, An Intimate Deception, Lord Harry's Folly,* and historicals, *Devil's Embrace, Devil's Daughter, Sweet Surrender, Chandra, Fire Song,* and the Star Trilogy. *Midsummer Magic* introduces the Magic Trilogy.

Catherine enjoys hearing from her readers and answers every letter. Please write her in care of New American Library.